MOSTLY DEAD MELVIN

FOINAH JAMESON

Vampire teeth prosthesis art by
© 2010 PicturePartners
licensed by iStock
Bio photograph by Foinah Jameson

Published by
Smoking Simian Scribbles
Foinah Jameson
PO BOX 80682
Portland, Oregon 97280

Printed in the USA

This book is dedicated to three very special people ~

Derek, Solas, and Luna.

You are my heart.

TABLE OF CONTENTS

CHAPTER 1

POOR PITIFUL PEARL GETS THE LEAD IN THE PLAY

Poke. Poke, poke-poke.

"Hey, dude! You can't sleep here."

I cracked open an eyelid and blinked against the daylight. A man was standing over me, his finger aimed and ready for another prod at my chest as I lay sprawled half on the sidewalk and steps in front of my apartment building.

He tsk-tsked me. "You're going to get in trouble."

I tried to sit up but my head felt dizzy, and I slumped back down on to the steps with a groan. I felt weird. Really weird.

"What happened?" I slurred.

"I dunno. You been here all morning. What happened to your neck?" He pointed. "That doesn't look good."

I reached up and felt two crusty holes a few inches below my ear. Uh-oh. I licked my lips and tasted copper, then ran my tongue over my retainer (yes, I was wearing a retainer), gagging at the taste. Something disgusting had taken over my tongue.

What happened last night?

The man was just standing there, staring at me. "I saw the lady drop you off." It sounded like a question rather than a statement, and I squinted my eyes against the sun trying to fry my retinas.

"What?" Oh boy was I dizzy, my memory distinctly patchy in places.

"She was strong! She carried you all the way here from her car and then dropped you on the steps. Who was she?" he asked.

Images came back to me in a sickening rush, and cold sweat popped up on my upper lip as I finally remembered part of my night.

I was at a dingy downtown bar drowning my sorrows in cheap happy-hour liquor when I saw a girl sitting two stools down from me. She was alone and I noticed she was watching me. I figured, what the hell, and sat down beside her. No one else was going to chat her up and maybe I'd get lucky. She was pale and smelled a little off, but she had a nice smile.

Beggars can't be choosers.

But she had the last laugh after all.

She got me good. Lured me to her car, let me believe that it was something special. We talked, we laughed....

She leaned in and kissed my neck. I felt the brief sting of her teeth and a moment of pain, and I actually swooned. I thought it was a hickey. What did I know? After a few minutes she pulled away and told me that I tasted awful, like fast food and Crisco, and I should have been insulted, but I wasn't. I was too dizzy, caught up in the moment and probably woozy from the blood loss. Instead I just smiled and tried to kiss her again. I was clumsy and stupid, still wearing my retainer, and I clunked against her face and cut her lip as I mashed my lips against hers. It was just one drop of her blood, lapped up in my befuddled attempt at passion. She shoved me away and wiped a kiss-smeared crimson bead from her lip, but it was too late. The deed was done. She looked horrified.

"Ahhh, crap!" was all she said.

Indeed. That's when I passed out and then woke up here on my front steps.

I was going to be sick!

I managed to stand up and stumble into the building.

"Hey, Mister! You dropped something." The man caught up and handed me a note.

I took it with shaking fingers, unfolding and reading it slowly as I climbed into the elevator.

Melvin, sorry about all this. It wasn't supposed to happen. Hopefully you don't have the dark gift - you'll know in a day or two. If not, consider this your free pass...you tasted awful anyway. You should clean up your diet.

If so, well, good luck with everything. Thanks for the evening. - Maddy

ᛦ

I barely made it to my apartment before the nausea hit. My bowels felt like they were filled with jagged little pieces of glass, twisting and shredding as they rode the roller coaster ride down from my stomach. I was panting and moaning as I fumbled the key in the lock, desperate not to foul the hallway, mortified at the thought of my neighbors catching me in this state; most of them already thought I was weird enough. Another cramp hit as I finally got my door open, tumbled into my apartment then kicked the door closed with my foot.

I moaned again as I crawled on all fours into the bathroom. Definitely not one of my finer moments. This was awful. Actually, awful doesn't even begin to cover it -- I was ass warmed over and then re-served to me in a shot glass. The previous night's adventure was still fuzzy in places, playing hide-and-seek-peek-a-boo. Every time I'd start again to remember what had happened, the rational part of my mind would slam down a wall and the memories would fuzz over again. Uh-oh.

Dizzy and weak from blood loss, and thirsty...so very thirsty, I drank at least twenty glasses of water but couldn't quench myself; this had to be the worst hangover I'd ever had. I didn't think it was possible to be burning up and freezing to death at the same time. If I was dying, I was surprisingly okay with that. Death would be a mercy right now. Ugh.

Oh, God, what the hell did I eat?

An image of Maddy's blood-smeared lips popped into my head briefly and I almost passed out.

Stop it!

I called in to work and told my boss that I was coming down with something awful and most likely contagious.

You were bitten by a vampire, dumbass.

I shuddered and ignored my inner voice. "There's no such thing," I mumbled, even as I started shivering again. "It's just food poisoning. Yeah, that's it."

More like blood poisoning.

I bundled up in a quilt and curled up on my bed with Maddy's note clenched in my fist. Boy, she was a real nut job. I was glad it hadn't gone any further with her; what kind of relationship would that be with a girl who was so obviously delusional? Huh? I didn't want to think about the bite on my neck, couldn't equate the dizziness with loss of blood. I ignored that last memory of my blood glistening on Maddy's fangs...yes, fangs. I knew I saw fangs, but I buried that memory. Yup. Oh yeah.

Maddy was a vampire...yeah, right. But maybe she really was, and that's the only reason she gave me the time of day. Ouch. I'd been used. How sad. That's me, though; sad, completely lonely, and let's not leave out scared.

Deep down I knew I was lying to myself on so many levels. Sure I was disappointed that Maddy was gone, a girl who had liked me enough to take me to her car and swap spit, but I also knew something was happening to me; something bad. Maybe the Dark Gift after all. The thing I had coveted for so long in my make believe La-La Land just might be the real deal.

Yay? Nope!

My body was tingling, but my limbs felt heavy and dead. *Dead.* As the sun rose higher in the sky exhaustion swept over me, and I slipped into a surreal coma dream that was the beginning of my end.

I was floating above my bed. The room was dark but I realized that I wasn't alone.... Someone was here with me. I focused through the balloony feeling in my brain, and stared down in shock at what I saw: myself lying there, my body beneath me pale and sweat-soaked, huddled and shivering in the quilt. The feeling of disconnect was so profound that I found myself floating higher towards the ceiling, unnoticed by my comatose self below. I flailed my arms in a swimming motion and got control enough that I was able to descend to the floor next to the bed.

"Hi, Melvin."

I spun around, losing control and floating again, and saw a dark shadow standing next to me. It had no features, and its voice echoed as if coming through a tinny cell phone speaker. The shadow reached out and grabbed my arm, pulling me back down next to it.

I said, "Who are you?" It was all I could come up with at the moment.

"Is that what you really want to know?" it asked mockingly. "You can do better than that." The shadow pointed at my body on the bed and crossed its arms (I think it had arms). My abandoned body convulsed on the bed, puffing out the quilt grotesquely from the spasms and twitches, and my floating self was nauseous; nauseous and terrified. The room was filling with a dull mist that was pushing in from the corners. That couldn't be good.

"Come on, lad. We're on the clock here."

"What's happening?" I stammered. A shadow with a posh English accent, this was the strangest dream I'd ever had.

"All right," the shadow sighed. "Einstein you're not, but that question will do." It leaned over my comatose form and tucked the quilt under my chin, and then sighed heavily as it turned to face me.

"Let's go in the other room, this part tends to creep out an initiate even though I also enjoy the moment. But it would be better for you in the other room."

It pulled my arm and we were suddenly in my sparse living room. The shadow opened up its jacket, a detail I missed originally, and pulled out a stone too large to have been hidden in there. The shadow handed it to me, and the weight anchored me to the floor.

"Whoa...." I said.

The shadow shrugged its shoulders. "Yes, whoa." It cackled briefly and then sat down on my couch. "You might want to sit down for this, Melvin."

I obeyed. What else was I going to do?

"Am I dreaming?"

"No, Melvin. You aren't dreaming, you're dying."

I gasped and dropped the stone, which made me start floating again. Very patiently the shadow pulled my leg and reeled me in to the couch.

"Maddy, my dear, you messed up with this one," it muttered to the encroaching mist. "Melvin, hold on to the stone and listen to me. Just try and stay focused, all right?

"I'm Mr. Happy. Yes, I know. A dreadful moniker but meant to be uplifting. While the job description lacks certain details, I'm a self-appointed overseer of these types of things. A cataloguer if you will. More of a morbid spectator actually, but I like to check in with the anointed and offer some tips for the transition." The shadow tented his hands on his lap.

"Did I hit my head?" I blinked a few times.

"Silence for now, Melvin. I am speaking. While you are a rather banal and uncouth evolved monkey, you must show me some respect. Dredge some up from that rather corpuscular form, now, or I shall grow very, very cross. Trust me, you don't want to see me cross."

I recoiled at the venom in Mr. Happy's dictionary-based slap, and slumped into the couch. Possibly dying or simply dreaming, I invented snooty phantoms to torment me. Living ones weren't enough. The shadow sighed heavily and shook his head.

"You have an opportunity here, although I must say I don't have much faith in you. You're rather pathetic, you do know that don't you, Melvin?"

I feebly nodded and clutched the stone tightly to my chest. This was unreal. I stared at the stone in my hand, wide-eyed and dazed.

Mr. Happy patted me on the shoulder, his touch cold and inhuman. "Hmmm, yes. Life hasn't been kind to you, but it's what you make of it that counts. I'd say you don't have a lot to count at this juncture." The shadow cackled again and then leaned forward, his face inches from mine. I saw a swirling depth in those vacant features, like looking into the abyss; I think I may have even heard screaming.

"Focus, my boy. You, Melvin Morton, are ascending to the dark realm."

"Crap," I wheezed.

"Indeed. Others who have a vested interest in these sorts of matters will be most displeased with darling Maddy's indiscretion. However, there's no going back now. I personally think you'll make a dreadful vampire, but time will tell. Hopefully you'll just die. That would be wonderful, don't you think?"

"No! I don't want to die." I sat up and glared at the shadow. "Wait a minute! This isn't really happening. Vampire? No way."

"Oh way, Melvin. Very way as a matter of fact."

"I bet I got food poisoning from that cheap happy hour buffet." I nodded to myself. Yeah, that was it. I was dreaming or hallucinating.

"My God, but you are dense. You really don't want to die? It would be so much easier in the long run. Just choose that instead."

I looked around the room at the encroaching mist filled with the outlines of writing forms, at the stone I clutched against my chest, and then shook my head. "Yup, it's the toxins. Wow, you even sound real. Vampires? Yeah, right." I grinned. This was the most bizarre dream!

"You think those green tinged snacks are to blame for your plight? Think again, my boy. I didn't see a buffalo wing bite you on the neck! You think that was Cajun sauce on Maddy's lip?"

"Maybe this is alcohol poisoning. I'll wake up covered in puke, and then I'll be fine."

"Are you that stupid? I'm becoming cross, Melvin."

"Maybe a virus--"

"Focus, Melvin!"

"Maybe Maddy put a Roofi in my drink."

"I should just let you founder and figure all this out on your own!" The shadow stood up and snatched the stone away from me. I started floating towards the ceiling, but it didn't matter; it was all a vivid, toxin-laced, fever induced, hallucination dream combo.

Maybe I was dying after all.

"You're on your own, Melvin. Such a waste of precious gifted blood. I hope for your sake you just die." The shadow shouted up at me, but I just ignored it, deciding instead to go with the weightless sensation of my usually over gravity-bound slab of a body. I felt a lurch inside and then I was back in my room, floating over my bed again. The shadow was standing in the doorway watching me.

I said, "Okay, shadow thing or whatever you are, here we are...back in my room again with the spooky mist. What now, Mr. Happy?" I giggled.

The shadow tensed, and then morphed into my second grade teacher, Mrs. Nance, the one who used to call me "Melvin Moron" and belittle me at recess. She grinned wickedly and then ripped off her face to reveal a nasty clown head beneath the flesh. That hit a nerve (clowns are just icky...who likes clowns?), and I cowered against the ceiling.

I think I made Mr. Happy cross. Yes, I definitely made it cross. She, it, evil clown head rose up off of the floor and came sailing at me, shrieking like a banshee.

It screamed, "Now you die," as the mist merged with the shadow being and swarmed over my body on the bed.

DIE?

And I did. Mostly.

I woke up tangled in the sweaty quilt, fiery pain lancing through my chest. It felt like I had a steel band around my heart, squeezing tighter and tighter with each slowing heartbeat. I looked around frantically for the shadow-Mrs. Nance-clown thing, but I was alone in my bedroom. That should have given me some solace, but then I saw the mist coiling over my body.

The pink tinge of the sunrise through a gap in the curtain filled me with dread. I tried to sit up but was paralyzed, immobile, with bright flashes at the edge of my vision as more pain rocketed through my unresponsive limbs. Exhaustion sucked at me as I gasped for breath, and then my heart stopped.

I died. Alone.

I was sucked into a black and empty abyss...no white tunnel of light, no fond faces of loving family members to welcome me to paradise.... Not even Mr. Happy to mock me some more. Just one solitary image: Maddy's smirking face as she deposited me on my front steps.

I don't want to die!, I shrieked at her.

Then I suggest you don't, was her reply as everything around me faded to black.

⋏

I sat up in bed just as the last rays of sun ducked down behind the horizon for the day; I'd been out cold for eighteen hours, a fact I learned by looking at my digital watch that displayed the date and four different time zones if I so desired.

Eighteen hours? Uh-oh. I blinked a few times and found that I could see just fine in the darkness, everything had a faint glow like I was looking through night vision goggles. I stretched, expecting to feel a wave of nausea or cramped muscles from my sickness during the last few days, but I was fine. More than fine, actually. Energy coursed through my body in waves of electric tingles. My only discomfort was that I was hungry; ravenous. Starving.

I jumped up and ran into my kitchen, and flung open my refrigerator door. Before I knew what I was doing I had a package of raw hamburger and was stuffing the bloody clumps into my mouth, slurping and chewing. Then it hit me: raw meat?! I dropped the package and spun around to the sink where I retched and gagged, the chunks coming up in coppery bursts. Through the bile, the blood still tasted like ambrosia.

I sank to the floor and started crying. I calmed to just muted sobs and realized something was missing -- my heartbeat. I couldn't feel my heartbeat! I grabbed at my wrist and dug for a pulse, and finding none repeated the search on my neck. Nothing. I jumped up and ran into the bathroom. I skidded to a halt at the sink and stared at my reflection in the cracked and dirty mirror; I was blue. My skin was blue. And my overbite was worse...it had to be a trick, an illusion. I turned on the light and it was worse illuminated.

"Holy crap! I'm dead!"

That's when my heartbeat decided to start up, just a couple of times, and go still again. Then the hunger resurfaced; I wanted blood, and lots of it.

"I'm a vampire." My gums tingled and my overbite extended further...no fangs just clumpy, crooked incisors and timid canines trying to poke through my retainer. "I think."

And then, pathetically, I passed out. I wasn't out long, though, maybe five minutes, but when I came to I repeated the whole process: checking for a pulse, eating raw meat and puking it up, staring at my reflection; I thought vampires couldn't see themselves in a mirror? Oh, I had so many surprises in store for me.

Over the next few days I slowly accepted my fate and decided to put all of the vampire myths to the test. I grabbed a crucifix -- nothing. I took my picture and it came out fine -- I looked even bluer on film. I went down the street to a Catholic church, walked right in, and dipped my hand in holy water. Nothing happened. I tried to turn into a bat or a wolf, and just felt stupid after an hour of trying. I jumped off the roof of my building and fell three stories while trying to fly. I got banged up when I hit the ground, but it didn't really hurt, though. And nobody saw it happen so I was in the clear. I bench pressed my couch without any effort at all. I even tried sunlight... muted Portland rainy sunlight. It wasn't comfortable, but I didn't die. Well, die more.

The only thing I couldn't do was drink someone's blood. No way. Un-uh. That gave me a case of the queasies like nothing else. So what did I do? Why I went to the Internet of course. I checked my symptoms with the vampire site I frequented, haunted, obsessed over, and confirmed that I was definitely, most completely screwed.

My world turned upside down with a routine of sleeping by day and waking at dusk (in my own bed and not a casket!), a schedule that mostly worked out fine since my security job at the mall was at night. But could I go back to work? I had to. I didn't have any money, and I couldn't afford to get evicted. And my sick leave was coming to an end.

So I went back to work. My boss freaked when he saw me, but I assured him I was fine -- what else was I going to say? Could I use the Americans with Disabilities clause if he tried to fire me? Does being a vampire even qualify? I had to forge a doctor's note to come back to work -- thank God for the Internet and all the handy templates available! The boss commented that I didn't smell too nice and suggested, in the nicest way possible, that I start using a stronger deodorant. Ha! I've started hiding car air fresheners in my pockets so now I smell like pine, strawberry and decomposing, mostly dead vampire.

What else can I do? I'm a vampire. It sucks.

I regret that pun.

⋏

MASTERSOFTHENITE
BLOGLINE ∞ JUNE 28, 2014 ∞ MOOD: Blue

My name is Melvin Morton -- not Vlad or Fang or anything else exotic or sexy -- just Melvin, and I'm a vampire. Life dies and then you suck. Kind of.

That got your attention, didn't it? Your late-night surfing on the web has brought you to my story and I can just picture you now. Yes, you are probably draped in something black and depressing, holed up in your dank little room and hunched over your computer, devouring tales of dark fantasy like candy. Or better yet, you are the weird fat kid, lonely and desperate like I used to be, searching for something else to be, something to numb the pain of your daily existence; something different than what you are.

Well guess what? It doesn't get any better than this and being a vampire isn't what it's cracked up to be. My story isn't fantasy; it's real life. Almost. Halfway. More of a parody, really.

When I was a real boy, not this blood-craving sham Pinocchio I've become, I was fascinated by the all the thought and drama of the Masters of the Night. I saw every film, read every book, studied myths and legends, and haunted the Internet with every moment of my spare time. It was my hobby, my escape, my fantasy and it wasn't supposed to be real; just make-believe. But I still wanted it.

Hero worship is a real let down when you learn the truth.

I was the fat kid growing up. I didn't even have the sense of humor that we chubby folk are supposed to be hardwired with as a defense mechanism. Laugh with me, not at me, right? Nope. Just a big-boned, slightly pimpled and greasy-haired outcast that grew up into an overweight and still pimply dullard who worked security at a mall. I'm not a stupid man, far from it, but I lack even the basic social graces to blend in with society -- high school was a nightmare. Can you imagine even being shunned by nerds? College was a poor man's dream... Nothing ever went right for me. I even still wore a retainer for a terrible overbite.

Take my name for instance: Melvin. Why would a parent do that to a child? Did my mother view the ultrasound, see my blobby form floating in her womb and think to herself, *Bummer. I'll name him Melvin?*

Have you ever met anyone named Melvin that wasn't lonely and just plain weird in one way or another? I didn't think so. I'm named after a juvenile bully right-of-passage, for God's sake. I'm underwear wedged into a butt crack, personified. My parents doomed me to life a mediocrity and hardship from the start. I would have changed my name, but it was like an oily stain that seeped into who I am, who I was and into what I became. I'm just Melvin.

Now I'm undead, actually just mostly dead. That didn't even go right. My ascension to the dark realm was an accident. Yes, an accident.

Everything you've ever heard about vampires being beautiful, dark, sultry and exuding lusty sex appeal is a lie. Vampires have power, but it's not the romanticized Hollywood version. You don't become an enchanting beast when you turn, you just become an undead version of yourself. If you were beautiful when you became a vampire, you stay that way in un-death. If you were ugly...you stay that way forever: warts, pimples, retainer and all.

One drop of cursed blood from a pale, strange girl named Maddy was enough to change me, but not enough to make me whole. Dark Gift, I don't think so; more like a turd with a shiny bow on it. Looks intriguing from a distance, but up close you see it for what it really is.

My body shut down and restarted with a stutter. My heart still beats occasionally, I can tolerate the sun on overcast days and I've turned the palest shade of blue -- like I've held my breath for far too long. I got the unending craving for blood, but the thought of actually drinking it makes me queasy. Besides, I didn't get the sharp pointed teeth, only a more enhanced and exaggerated overbite. I have keen senses: I can hear the roaches crawling through the walls of my cheap apartment, and I can see in the dark. I smell terrible -- worse than when I was alive. My body can't seem to decide whether it should decompose or make the transition to the fully undead. I guess I have forever for it to decide.

Other than the being mostly dead thing, my life hasn't changed. I still work security at the mall and I still have bills to pay. And taxes. And I'm still an outcast. I've looked for Maddy and other vampires, but I'm alone here in this city. Humans go out of their way to avoid me now, even more so than before. They think I'm diseased. I guess I am, and with no real cure in sight.

Suicide? That makes me almost as queasy as the thought of drinking blood. Besides, could I even die properly? I don't want to risk it and make things worse than they already are.

I watch my old vampire shows on television and rent DVDs to pass the time. I just watch and laugh. I have to. If I don't I'll cry. Their version of the Masters of the Night is, after all, just fantasy. Oh, and that shtick about holy water and crosses...all Hollywood.

Even my favorite novelist, who wrote about vampires with such pain and beauty, has abandoned me. She's become a born-again Christian so my hero, the beautiful blond Frenchman who becomes such a demon immortal, is lost. There will be no more tales in which to escape. All I have now is reality, but reality can be stranger than fiction...

Being a vampire isn't what I thought it would be and I realize now that being human wasn't as bad as I thought it was. I guess the grass is always greener, right? Looking back, I could have been a better person, but probably not. I'd be a better vampire, but I can't. I was never particularly evil in life, just human, and now I don't know how to be really much of anything at all. I realize that I'll have to eat someone eventually; the craving is so intense and fast food just doesn't touch it.

So where does this leave me? Muddling along and late for work. Take this tale to heart and be careful what you wish for.... Get a life while you still can. Remember: Life dies and then you suck...kind of.

- Melvin

ADD A COMMENT ∞ REPLY TO POSTER ∞ BLOCK USER

CHAPTER 2

CH-CH-CHANGES

I sat back and stared at the screen, my skin crawling with those invisible little clammy hands that pinched and poked resulting in gooseflesh. Fright bumps. Nerve lumps. Ugh.

Why did I post this?

Well, the damage was done. Masters of the Nite dot com had a new blog entry. Alert the media, Melvin had something to say! Right. Who cares? Just me so far, and it was safe enough, I hoped, to share with other fangophiles (and maybe a real vampire or two). Welcome to the twenty-first century, Mr. Dracula. Snerk. However, this wasn't going anywhere near my friendless Facebook profile.

But I was getting tired of sitting around feeling sorry for myself. Feeling so alone. Well, again alone with all of the other Internet losers who surfed the vampire site. Maddy had destroyed my pitiful life two months ago and I thought I'd go mad from the experience, but I didn't. Or maybe I was crazy right now and just didn't know it.

Something had to change. I couldn't go on unliving like this. Time to go do something vampy. Vampiric. Vampirish. Whatever it is that we're supposed to do.

▲

I made a checklist of all the things I knew about vampire legends, and then ended up crossing a bunch of it out that I knew from first hand experience was bunk. Really only four things were left: I was undead, I craved blood, I was scary strong, and I had keen senses. Woohoo. Did I have other undiscovered powers? I went though my DVD library and picked some of my favorite vampire stuff for tips. Maybe I needed to embrace the stereotype. I smiled. Hell, why not?

I slicked my hair back with some Vaseline (it's all I had), practiced my scary face and sexy face in the mirror, and doused myself in cologne to mask my particular ripeness until my eyes stung from the fumes.

Should I put on body glitter?

No, too cheesy.

I bumped my retainer, discarded and forgotten on the edge of the sink, and a feeling of nostalgia for the days of nerdly innocence washed over me.

Oh well, enough of that!

I did one pit smell check, gave my reflection a thumbs-up in the mirror, and headed out into the night. I was wearing a long black trench coat that felt like a cape; I was cool. Hip. Invincible.

My God was I delusional.

But I was a vampire with a plan.

⅄

I kept to the shadows as I walked through the streets towards a nightclub called Dante's. I skulked and flitted, trying to blend in with the darkness. I ignored the curious looks from people I passed; nothing would sour my mood. I had nervous little jitters in my stomach as I paid the cover charge and entered the club.

You can do this.

A metal cover band was playing on stage, and the club was vibrating and pulsing with energy as I eyed the room from a darkened corner and saw three mini skirt clad girls standing at the bar. They were stunning, way out of my league, but I was a vampire! I had super powers!

I took a deep breath, put on a brooding expression, and casually strolled towards the bar. I caught my foot on a table leg and stumbled a bit, looking around to see if anyone had noticed, and then ran a hand through my greased hair to smooth it down. I grimaced then wiped my palm on my pant leg, but there was still Vaseline between my fingers. Gross.

"Dude, you're blocking my view," a guy said from the table next to me.

"Oh, sorry," I said quickly and then bumped into another chair as I tried to get out of the way. This wasn't going well. Not well at all. I pushed my way through the crowd and got to the bar. I tried to catch the bartender's eye, but he ignored me.

Maybe this isn't a good idea...No! Stop it! You can do this.

I stood behind the three women, psyching myself up for what I was about to do.

"Hello," I said, deepening my voice. They ignored me, too.

Okay...Frank Langella sexy vampire, Angel brooding vampire, Spike cocky vampire, or Edward sullen vampire? No... He's not a real vampire, but he does have the moves.

I cleared my throat and winged it with a combination of all four.

"'Allo, loves," I said with a ridiculous sounding English accent while I licked my lips then pouted them out slightly. I winked, but I think it was lost in the glare of the stage lights on my glasses. One of the girls, a bleach blond with spiky hair, looked over her shoulder at me and smirked. Uh-oh. I stared intently at her, widening my eyes slightly while I concentrated on a vampire glamour.

Feel my power...you are mine...blah, blah, blah.

I think I was doing it right.

"You want to come with me," I said.

"What did you say?" she squinted at me and leaned forward. It was working! I raised my hand and beckoned to her. "You want to come with me. Now."

The girl elbowed her friend who turned around with crossed arms. Again with the uh-oh. Should I try it on all three?

"I am Melvin." I reached out and took the first girl's hand, forgetting that I had Vaseline all over my fingers, and tried to kiss her fingertips. My overbite tingled with the contact of lips upon warm skin.

Oh yeah, work it!

She snatched her hand away quickly, squealing, "Eeeew. Yuck!" as she grabbed a napkin and swiped at the mixture of hair slime and spit that I'd left behind.

"You are mine," I said, my voice cracking a bit at the end because of my overbite and nerves.

"Um, no I'm not, creepy guy. Go away already."

I waved my hand in front of her face, wiggling my fingers in a desperate attempt to be hypnotic. Why couldn't I glamour her, damn it? The third girl turned around, took one look at me and started laughing.

"Seriously?" She wrinkled up her nose, smirked at her friend, and then said, "Are you for real? Oh, honey, that's just sad. At least the accent was interesting. Should have kept it up."

I took a step back. The second girl, obviously the meanest one of the bunch, took a step towards me. "Knock-knock," she said.

I gulped. "Um, who's there?"

She shook her head in amusement. "Smell mop."

"Smell mop who?" I grimaced as I said it; the punch line was the final kick in the gut. I should have just walked away right then.

"I already do, you stink." She burst out laughing.

The spiky blond smirked. "Sorry, but she's drunk, and you are creepy. What are you supposed to be? A ninja Smurf?"

I held my head up and made eye contact. "I'm a vampire," I said.

I pouted my lips again, widened my eyes, and tried to look broody. Why? Why? Why? I think I looked like a chicken having a seizure, but I was determined.

"You are very beautiful. Don't be afraid, embrace your dark desires and come with me."

"Yeah...no, not gonna happen. Thanks for the compliment, but you should go now. Go on, buh-bye." She made a shooing motion with her hands.

I sighed, mortified beyond belief, and stumbled through the crowd towards the door without looking back. The cool night air felt good against my skin and the darkness called to me in a way that was only for the undead.

Right. Whatever. I laughed self-consciously at the thought that I could do anything vampiric. Glamour? Another Hollywood myth struck off the list. I should have started with something easier.

Oh well. At least I tried.

I took off my coat and handed it to a man panhandling on the corner.

"This night never happened," I said to myself.

This story is going with me to the grave if I ever get one.

I went home, dialed up my blog, and ordered a pizza.

⋏

There are some weird people out there. Yes indeed. Sad, pathetic, bizarre, lonely, bitter, denizens of the Internet who latched onto my blog like crack. Even though the negative out weighed the positive in the comment spectrum, I couldn't help but read what was posted. My life's routine consisted of craving blood, working a job I hated, craving blood and being too cowardly to do something about it, and surfing the Internet. The World Wide Web has plenty to say about vampires, most of it absurdly wrong, but I had to look anyway. While it was utterly stupid to post my story on a blog, I felt a perverse pleasure out of walking the edge. Pushing that envelope, being an exhibitionist.

Look at me! Look at me!

Maybe someone would figure me out. Maybe an angry mob with torches and pitchforks would storm my castle. Maybe someone would help. Maybe.

BLOGLINE COMMENT: FROM ANONYMOUS

HEY, YOU SUCK!

REPLY TO POSTER ∞ BLOCK USER ∞ REPORT POST

Wow, good one. Except I don't, anonymous. That's the problem.

BLOGLINE COMMENT: FROM BLOODCRAVER666

Excellent blog! Tone down the pity party and I'll keep reading. Bite someone already.

REPLY TO POSTER ∞ BLOCK USER ∞ REPORT POST

I'll get right on that.

BLOGLINE COMMENT: FROM SEXYGOTHCHICK18

CHECK OUT MY PROFILE -- PLENTY OF HOT GIRLS ARE WAITING FOR YOU. VISA, MASTERCARD, PAYPAL ACCEPTED

REPLY TO POSTER ∞ BLOCK USER ∞ REPORT POST

Whoa.

BLOGLINE COMMENT: FROM MICKEYMOUSER

Cool concept! I love fanfic, what movie or RPG is this from?

REPLY TO POSTER ∞ BLOCK USER ∞ REPORT POST

Um, my life.

BLOGLINE COMMENT: FROM Madmother

Who do you think you are? Stop spreading this nonsense! Kids are on the Internet -- you should be ashamed of yourself. Vampires...all that blood and sex and gore. SHAME ON YOU!

REPLY TO POSTER ∞ BLOCK USER ∞ REPORT POST

Oh give me a break, lady. There's worse stuff on cable.

BLOGLINE COMMENT: FROM BORIS_THE_SPITE_HER

Mr. Vampire, please bite me so that I can be a vampire, too. I'd do a much better job than you.

PS - Girls are mean. Fat girls are mean. You should have known better. Bite me.

REPLY TO POSTER ∞ BLOCK USER ∞ REPORT POST

How do I even answer this one? Uh, no. Clever username despite the ick factor.

This next one takes the cake!

I feel loved, no really, warm fuzzy love like a cactus hug. People like this make it worth living. Sigh.

BLOGLINE COMMENT: FROM ANONYMOUS

LOOSER!

REPLY TO POSTER ∞ BLOCK USER ∞ REPORT POST

Genius.

Fifty more comments waited, but if they all were in the same vein I might cry. I really am a looser. Ha.

⚔

MASTERSOFTHENITE
Blogline ∞ August 18, 2014 ∞ MOOD: Blue

First off I'd like to thank the readers for all of the warm and fuzzy comments on my last post. "Looser." Oh boy, I haven't heard that one before. By the way, it's spelled LOSER. This blog is my lifeline, so back off.

Now on to what's going on: Most of you think this is a fiction I've created for attention. You just keep thinking that, kids. Vampires can't be real.

The hunger is maddening. I can barely stand it. But as with everything else in my pathetic excuse for a non-life, I can't do anything about it. I tried, though. I suppose it's a funny story, especially since the joke's on me.

It's been four months since I had my chance encounter with Maddy. Bitch. Why didn't she just finish me off? Either kill me or turn me all the way. It's not fair, but life isn't fair. Neither is mostly death for that matter. Still no sign of her. Maddy has left the building, the stupid cow. She could have at least stuck around to see if I'd changed. Oh well, no use crying over spilled blood, right?

Work is the same. People are afraid of me, which works well for my job description: Night Security! Someone taped a hazmat sticker to my locker as a joke. Yeah, that was good one. I'm laughing my stinky blue butt off. But I can't quit, and my boss won't fire me. Life goes on...ha.

I finally psyched myself up to eat someone. Well, it was more of an impulse thing. And yes, it ended badly. The universe truly hates me.

I've been ordering pizza almost every night since the change, and it's always the same guy who brings it. He's grown used to me; I won't say that he's nice or even polite. Actually he's a jerk, but he's the only one on duty at 3:00 AM when I order, and I tip well for the trouble. I get the meat lovers' special and then load a bunch of raw hamburger on top of it here at my apartment. Yeah, it's disgusting, but it had worked until last night.

Lately Pizza Bob (that's what I call him) had been acting kind of funny around me, always peering over my shoulder to get a look into my living room, taking my money with his finger tips and holding it away from his body like it's toxic. He even asked me if I had some kind of disease? I just laughed at him. Then he asked me if I was a tweaker, and quickly decided, out loud, that I was too fat to be one. Now that was just rude. I growled at him and slammed the door, sans tip.

Last night I was starving so I ordered another pizza, dreading the encounter with Pizza Bob. Maybe I'm psychic or something. Ha, again.

He showed up all cocky -- you know the type: handsome, athletic, a cross between surfer chic and preppy bum, and totally dumb as a post. Something snapped inside of me. I could hear his heart beat, his blood rushing in his veins so warm and inviting! I don't know what came over me.

I yanked him into my apartment and put my hand over his mouth to keep him from screaming (I saw that in a movie once) while I grabbed him around the throat with my other hand and lifted him off of the floor. He struggled, and almost got away as I kicked the door shut with my foot, but I held fast to his throat. This was my chance. Maybe if I drank some blood I'd turn fully. My gums tingled, my overbite extended out further over my lips -- still no fangs -- and I snarled. I leaned in to bite him, and I smelled his fear. It was revolting. His eyes were bugging in their sockets as he mouthed, *What are you?*

"I'm supposed to be a vampire," I whispered as I dropped him and stumbled back.

I couldn't do it. I just couldn't.

He turned to run and got tangled up in the pizza bag at his feet. Before I knew it he was falling, headed right for my coffee table, and his skull made the most disgusting noise when it connected with the corner. He twitched a few times, and then went still. Deathly still. I realized I couldn't hear his heartbeat anymore...he was dead. He hadn't even screamed, but his blood was still warm... dribbling out the crack in his temple. I reached out with shaking fingers and touched it, a tingle rushing up my arm as I brought my hand to my lips. One flick of the tongue is all it would take and I'd be on my way.

Pizza Bob convulsed, a last electron firing in his shattered brain, and I squealed like a little girl. I jumped back and cowered in the corner until I was sure, absolutely sure that he was deader than dead. The smell of his blood in the room made me dizzy, and I let out a little moan as I wiped my fingertips on my pant leg.

Sometimes I wonder if I'm on a vampire version of Candid Camera, the stuff that happens to me.

I knew his car would be like a beacon for trouble so I took his keys and drove it out by the airport. No one saw me as I parked in a field under a stand of ragged trees and blackberry brambles. The thorns pricked and pulled at my flesh, but there was no pain. I wished there had been; something to make me feel less of a monster. I managed to get the stupid tack on delivery sign disconnected and stuffed into the trunk without much trouble, and I didn't even bother with wiping away my fingerprints; maybe deep down I wanted to get caught, end this nightmare of an existence.

Maybe by putting these words here in cyber space I've already doomed my-self. Ha! But maybe this is just a fantasy, right? It's just a story, so I'll finish it.

It was a long walk home, but I needed the time to figure out what I was go-ing to do. This was something that was going to come back and haunt me if I wasn't careful. When I got back to my apartment the delivery guy was still very dead, so I shoved his body into the corner. I know, I know. Not very nice of me, but come on. He was just lying there, and it was creepy.

No one had come looking for him, no cops banging on my door, so I calmed down a bit. Maybe it might work out after all.

I took out the cold pizza, grease and slimy cheese congealed on the top, and sat down on my couch. I didn't even add the raw hamburger; I just sucked on the pepperoni until I felt the sun coming up. This was the last pizza I'd have for a while, at least until I found another place that delivers so late, so I had better enjoy it. I royally screwed the pooch on this midnight snack. I even felt bad for Pizza Bob, well, only a little. He was a jerk after all.

Maybe the next one will go better....

Melvin

REPLY TO POSTER ∞ BLOCK USER ∞ REPORT POST

⋏

"You better do something about that soon."

I jerked my head up and saw Pizza Bob pointing, with a disgusted look on his face, at the bloated and fleshy pile of clothes in the corner. He crossed his arms and glared at me.

"Crap. You're still here?" I asked, wiping a puddle of foul tasting sleep drool from my chin. I must have dozed off; it was close to dawn.

Pizza Bob scowled at me and drifted closer.

"Uh, duh. Where else am I gonna go?"

Flies were buzzing around the pile, the drone of their wings sounding like 747's in my sensitive ears, and I pushed myself up from the couch with a grunt. I should have lost some weight before I mostly died.

Add that to the pity list why don't I? I took off my glasses and cleaned them with a less greasy edge of my shirt; I didn't need them anymore, my eyesight was perfect, but the glasses were an anchor to my past life. I wanted them. I put the glasses back on and turned slowly to look at my visitor who had shown up the next night after he died, hovering next to the decomposing body, bewildered and angry.

I said, "Just go away, okay?"

"And I repeat, where else am I gonna go? Huh?"

"Into the light?" I shrugged.

"Oh yeah, that's real funny, mister. We've been over this already, dickhead. You killed me so now I'm stuck." Pizza Bob went hazy for a moment and then reappeared right next to his corpse that was covered in hundreds of tree shaped car air fresheners to mask the smell of rot. He kicked at the body, his phantasmal foot just passing through, but it was enough of a disturbance, a chilling vibration in the aether, that a blanket of flies erupted into the air. They swarmed and buzzed around me while I waved my hands frantically around my head. Pizza Bob laughed humorlessly and then went back to his sullen glare.

I should have seen it coming; he'd done the same thing every day for the last week. The flies settled back onto the corpse, their routine reestablished, and I flopped back onto the couch again with a weary sigh. I stared at him.

"You're awfully sarcastic for a dead guy, ya know that? And for the umpteenth time I did not kill you." I glanced over at his body, and my stomach rumbled loudly enough that Pizza Bob heard it and scowled. It was humiliating.

He gave me a thumbs down. "Uh yeah, yeah ya did."

"No, I was going to kill you, but I chickened out. You were the one who freaked out when you realized I was a vampire--"

"Yeah, right. Some vampire," Pizza Bob muttered. "Toothless creep."

I ignored his sarcasm, it was all he really had left and who could blame him? "You freaked out, tripped over your own feet and the pizza bag, and fell. You split your head open, cracked your skull like an egg on my coffee table, twitched a few times, and then unceremoniously crapped your pants and died on my floor.

"Ergo," I pointed at the body, "I did not kill you.

"A technicality. But you better get used to it. I have the distinct feeling that every time you have a snack they'll stick around. Call it a ghostly case of the repeaters." Pizza Bob snickered and then belched loudly. The ensuing smell was ghastly, worse than the sickly, sweet aroma of fresh alpine meadow and rotting meat that permeated the room. Maybe I should have used strawberry.

Ah, but he was right. I was going to have to dispose of that sloppy pile soon. Undoubtedly someone was starting to notice the smell. Hopefully the neighbors would think it was just me; I had a distinct odor of my own.

Wow, this really sucked. Everything, all of it. My life (HA!) was a sad joke. I still hadn't managed to eat anyone yet, and I was starving. You wouldn't know it by looking at me, though. Still fat, pimply and greasy. Oh God how I craved human blood, but the thought of drinking it still made me want to retch. I looked up at Pizza Bob miserably and shook my head. Four months of undeath and I was trying to live on junk food.

And now this.

"Please, I'm begging you. Just go away."

"No can do, dude. Trust me, if I could, I'd be outta here on the next shaft of golden light." He floated over and plonked down on the couch next me, as much as a ghost could plonk.

He grinned wickedly. "I think you're screwed. There's not something right about you. It's like you're not a vampire but you ain't alive, either. Maybe that's why you'll keep seeing us; one foot on either side of the barrier. You are so screwed." He was delighted that I was suffering.

"This sucks," I said. "Nothing I ever read about vampires said anything about this. Of course a lot of what I read wasn't true, either."

"How long you been a vamp?" Pizza Bob snickered. "A wussy vamp?"

"What do you care?"

"Call it morbid curiosity. Well, you can't be that old; I'm surprised you've lasted as long as you have. God, you really are pathetic, and ugly as the back end of a scabby cat."

"And you're dead." Ha! I'd scored a hit with that one. But he was right, so score one for the dead guy. Damn.

"You're right," I muttered. "It's been four months. Nothing ever goes right for me."

"That's all?" Pizza Bob snorted.

"It was a girl. I met her at a bar."

"Way to be a player. I bet she was fat and ugly. She'd have to be to go for a guy like you," he said with a sneer. But he'd hit the nail on the head, kind of, whatever.

"Look...do you want to hear my story or not?"

"What else have I got going? I want to hear how you got suckered." He gave me a thumbs-up. "See what I did there?"

"Good one." I rolled my eyes.

"Was it scary? I bet you cried."

"No...and yes, she was a big girl," I admitted.

"I knew it. Big girls need love, too."

"Just shut up and listen. I saw her sitting there and figured I might have a chance. She said her name was Maddy and I thought to myself, *Maddy Fatty*, without much guilt, I might add."

"Wow, you are a dick. Looked in the mirror lately?"

I ignored him and kept talking. It felt good to tell someone my story.

"I did feel sorry for what her childhood must have been like, though. Another victim of the parental naming game. She laughed when I told her my name was Melvin, but it wasn't a cruel laugh, more a sympathetic chuckle at my lot in life. Something clicked. Maybe it was just the fact that she was actually talking to me, laughing at my jokes, even flirting a bit, but I liked her. I actually really liked her and better yet, she seemed to like me. Why was I such an idiot?"

"That's an easy one--"

I held up my hand to silence Pizza Bob, and he smirked. I sighed.

I said, "One thing led to another and soon we were out in the parking lot making out in her car like a couple of teenagers, something I had never done before, by the way. It was magical. We laughed at the world and talked and kissed some more. I should have known that the universe would throw a monkey wrench into the works. I did mention that nothing ever goes right for me."

"Get to the good part already. The part where she scared the crap out of you and made you cry!"

"I didn't cry. I didn't even realize I'd been bitten." I nervously fingered the place on my throat where Maddy had left her mark. "I cut her lip with my retainer and got one drop of her blood. Just one frickin' drop. That's the last thing I remember."

"That's it? Really? I sat through this whiny, petulant, Lifetime movie summary for that? And now you're a vampire? Oooh, lucky you."

"Hey. I'm not a full vampire...I don't know what I am except mostly dead." The sad confession sounded desperate in my ears, but did nothing to temper bitter Pizza Bob.

"Pretty soon someone's gonna notice that smell...." He pointed at his body. "Guess what happens then? They'll know what you mostly are and then it's stake through the heart time."

"Maybe that would be for the best."

"Naw, that'd be too easy an out for you. I wanna see you suffer.

Daylight was coming and the weariness of my dead, mostly dead body was pulling me down. I leaned back and closed my eyes while Pizza Bob cackled next to me, the sound following me into my darkness. I wondered if I would ever dream again?

⚑

I awoke to an uncomfortable tingling on my skin. I cracked open an eyelid and saw sunlight streaming through my dirty window onto my body, the curtain lying in a musty heap on the floor. It was late afternoon, probably another hour or two before sunset, and the sky was hazy with clouds. The air stirred next to me and I turned my head to see Pizza Bob crouched on the arm of the couch, hovering over me like a buzzard. He noticed I was awake, and scowled.

"Damn!" he shouted. "I thought that would do more!"

I couldn't help the smirk on my face as I got up and walked over to the window. With my back turned away from him I inspected my arm for blisters. The blue tint to my skin had taken on a nasty dark tinge where the sun had baked it, but I had already experimented with sun exposure and knew it would just be minutes before my skin faded back to its melancholy hue. If I stayed in direct, unclouded sun for too long (about five hours), my skin would indeed bubble and blister. But because I was just mostly dead I could tolerate overcast days, and I doubted I would go up in a cloud of Hollywood ash anyway. My internal clock still put me to bed at dawn, but I'd started awakening earlier and earlier each day while the sun was still high in the sky. Maybe this was my version of vampire insomnia...I'd be a day owl. Or maybe it was just another way for the universe to torment me.

Chuckling mirthlessly to myself I rehung the curtain and headed for the kitchen; I was starving and had a carton of pig livers waiting. On one of the vampire shows I used to watch the lead character drank pig blood because it supposedly tasted close to human. I was willing to give it a try; I hoped it wasn't more Hollywood hype or that I would throw up because I was eating raw pig livers. Bleh. Desperate times call for desperate measures.

"Do you know how long it took me to get enough energy to do that?" Pizza Bob screamed near my ear.

I'd also gotten used to his tirades over the last week, but this was the first time he'd managed to physically move something. I suppose it was an impressive feat.

"No," I said with a tired sigh. "And I don't really care, either." Maybe he'd finally get tired of tormenting me and shove off into the great unknown. "Maybe you could try vacuuming next time."

"I'll get you."

"And my little dog, too?" I asked sarcastically. The confused look on Pizza Bob's face was priceless.

"You don't have a dog."

I rolled my eyes and walked right through him, scattering his form briefly. He hated that.

"I said you don't have a dog," he hissed as he sailed past me and sat down on the couch where I was going to sit. Instead I bypassed him and sat down at my desk, pig livers in hand, and fired up my computer. While my blog loaded I fished out a liver and tentatively took a bite. It was disgusting, more of a texture thing, and I shuddered. Underneath my revulsion though, I felt something stir; the blood was pretty tasty after all. Maybe it was just a mental block I had about human blood -- I didn't seem to mind raw hamburger. Oh well, it was a start and

I managed to swallow the bite without retching, then noticed Pizza Bob staring at me with revulsion.

That did it. I took another liver and popped it into my mouth, slurping and chewing noisily because it bothered him so much; that was the only thing that kept me from puking. Maybe having Pizza Bob around would push me towards more desperate and depraved acts. I picked up a piece and mashed it around so that the liver was pulpy and clinging in bright purple chunks on my tongue.

"Do I have something in my teeth?" I asked innocently, and then chuckled when the ghost paled even further.

Pizza Bob's eyes darted towards his corpse, and I felt something give inside me; I was being a monster. I wasn't ready for that yet. Defeated, I put down the carton and focused on my blog. I felt him standing behind me, and braced myself for the ensuing script.

He said, "You killed me."

"No I didn't."

"Yeah, ya did."

"Get over it."

"You're a dickhead."

"And you're dead." I looked over my shoulder and saw him just floating there, all anger gone from his face. He looked pathetic.

He's just like me now.

Part of me still felt a little bad for him, but I knew if I let that show he'd start in again.

"Finished?" I asked quietly.

"For now." He was staring at my blog, concentrating on reading what I had written. "Not that whiny crap again! Why don't you do something nice for the guy you killed and dial up some porn?"

"If you leave me alone for just a little while, maybe I will." I was letting my guilt do the talking.

"Deal," he said continuing to hover over my shoulder. "Hee-hee!" He pointed at one of the comments. "That guy DarkPrince1509 ripped you a new one! Creepy much? But I kind of like his style."

BLOGLINE COMMENT: FROM DARKPRINCE1509

You fraud. You worm. You petulant and whining little pussy. How dare you claim the Dark Gift and then flaunt it and waste it by hiding behind this web site. WHY WON'T YOU ANSWER ME?! I hate you, hate you, hate you!!!! I'm going to find you and drain you by cutting your head off. If you won't share then I'll take what should be mine. I love you enough to do that. How can you do this to me? I thought we understood each other. I hate you. I'll get you. I wrote you another poem...did you see it yet? Comment back on my page when you get a chance.

REPLY TO POSTER ∞ BLOCK USER ∞ REPORT POST

I scanned the rest of the blog comments, ignoring Pizza Bob's glee, then hit the block user button next to DarkPrince's name. He had to go...that guy was a real psychopath. He'd first begged me turn him, extolling the virtues of being a creature of the night, and when I ignored him he began his "court-ship." Um, nude photos and close ups of his wand of evil were just a bit off sides. Totally offsides. Yech. When I sent him a polite note asking him to stop, well, that's when the name-calling and threats started. I wasn't too worried about him, though. His blog user profile listed him as living in Akron, Ohio -- that alone was enough to garner him some pity, but I made sure to keep my location here in Portland private. I figured he wouldn't wander too far from his mother's basement and the frozen burritos he undoubtedly lived on. They probably weren't real pictures of his winky either; the Photoshop job was pretty obvious.

It would be too hard to find me anyway unless Darkprince1509 was a hacker. I shuddered as I pictured him showing up on my doorstep in a long, dark cape, pale make up and the requisite fake fangs. I made a weak promise to myself that if he indeed showed up I would definitely eat him, or at least make the effort.

However, his crazy posts set the tone for the other readers and I found myself with a 'fan base' of what seemed to be teenaged to early twenty-year-old men. I still couldn't get a girl...a live one at least. Or one that didn't take PayPal.

"I can't believe you keep a diary like this," Pizza Bob said scornfully. "Don't you worry that someone is gonna investigate? Plus these people seem crazy."

Without thinking about it I chuckled and looked at him with a stupid, moon-eyed grin. "Yeah, I know. No one knows where I live, though. But I'm just so freaked out I need to talk about everything. I can at least pretend I've got someone who cares listening to me. I can pretend at least." I couldn't believe I was having a friendly moment here.

"Wow, bummer dude." Pizza Bob genuinely sounded consoling, and then he stiffened up, scowling at me.

I said, "Look, I'm really sorry about what happened to you. If I could take it back I would."

"You really are a pussy." He sneered at me, and then pushed the container of livers off the desk and onto my lap. He was definitely getting stronger, and I have to admit I was a little afraid of what he'd eventually be able to do to me. Pizza Bob took one withering look at his moldering corpse in the corner, and then faded away, leaving behind the smell of ozone. That must be the scent of the energy he'd used up for the little parlor trick now soaking through my pants. And the smell *was* better than his rotting corpse in the corner.

But I knew he wouldn't stay gone; he couldn't. He was trapped here with me, stuck in a situation he had no control over. Just like I was stuck being mostly dead. Ironic.

So I sat back and enjoyed the silence of my room while I could. Except for the flies buzzing I was alone, and after an uncomfortable span of listening to the fly orgy in the background I realized that I didn't like it. My whole life I've been alone, even in a crowded room I stand ignored purposefully. Pizza Bob was annoying but he talked to me, talked at me actually, but it was directed at me, to me, and I missed him. My own captive audience.

I glanced over at his corpse and winced. I'd find a way to make up for what I had done to him. I knew that under other circumstances we would never be friends, but now we were stuck with each other; maybe forever.

I'd only ever had one friend in my life, when I was ten years old, but her family moved away and I lost her. She was a hunched and chubby thing, homely to the core, but I never forgot her wicked sense of humor and brains. She was too smart for her own good, and such a mouth she had on her! Kids only picked on her once, and then went away in tears from her scathing and cutting comebacks. I used to sit in awe of her. When she left, a hole opened up in my heart that never got filled again...it still ached now. I hoped she remembered me as fondly through the years. What would she think of me now? She'd probably forgotten me. Yeah, what was there to remember anyway?

Stop whining.

What about Maddy? I wondered where she was. If I could find her then maybe I'd get some answers, a little help, and a shoulder to cry on. Or a neck to throttle. No, I'd probably cry and embarrass myself like usual.

It was just so unfair to leave me floundering like this. Why didn't she kill me when she'd had the chance? I thought about her note and got angry all over again: Hopefully you don't have the dark gift....

Thanks for checking up on me, Maddy. What a pal. *I'd like to exchange this Dark Gift. Do I have the receipt? Of course not.*

In my spare time I scouted all the dive, happy hour, booze caves I thought she might frequent; dark little bars where her pallor and odor would be over-looked by bar flies (but that hadn't mattered to me at the time, had it?) eager for a one-night stand. But no one remembered her.

I scanned the papers for reports of mysterious deaths, followed postings about unusual symptom outbreaks on the health department web site, but there was zip, nada, nothing. I wondered why I didn't see any other vampires here in Portland. Shouldn't I be able to sense them now? One of the perks of joining the club? Maddy couldn't be the only one. Who made her? There had to be others here. This town was perfect for the solar challenged; Oregon was famous for it's cloudy, miserable weather. We webfoots reveled in the jokes of getting "rust burns", and forsaking umbrellas, but in all truth some summers could be hot without a drop of rain for a month at a time. A secret we kept to ward off inter-lopers; something that now could possibly kill me. Great. But this summer had been fine and dreary, and I'd deal with the sun issue when I had to. If I survived until then, that is.

But still Portland was on par with San Francisco in the gloomy weather department. Besides the weather, the City of Roses had a dark underbelly that locals knew of, but spoke little about. Human trafficking...missing persons, the whole KEEP PORTLAND WEIRD mindset. There should be more vampires here.

Either Maddy was clever or she was really gone. But I'd find her...oh yes, yes I would. If not her, then at least another vampire. Wouldn't that be just swell.

I shrugged and stared at the computer screen. Should I write more about Pizza Bob? No, not yet. I tapped my finger on the desk and then shifted the mouse. I dialed up a porn site for the ghost, hoping he'd notice and come back.

"Thanks."

I jumped at his voice right next to my ear. I hated when he did that!

"Here," I said as I got up to give him my chair. I didn't want to hang out with a ghost and watch porn. That just set off the creepy alarm a little too much. "Knock yourself out, buddy."

"Bite me, jerk wad," he said with a smirk. "Oh, wait...you tried that." He laughed and then tuned me out, focusing on the flickering images on the screen.

I had to hand it to him, Pizza Bob had a sarcastic grasp of the obvious.

CHAPTER 3

A Series Of Unfortunate Events

I awoke to the sound of thunder. Joy. Another day of muddling through my un-life routine. I rolled over and looked at the curtain covering my open window, and watched it puff and sway with the wind coming through. I smelled the ozone in the air, and stuck my tongue out to taste the crispness of it. The tang, almost coppery in essence, suddenly reminded me of blood. My stomach rumbled, and just like that I was depressed.

I used to love the rain. Late afternoon summer rain that cooled everything down and made everything new.

Now it just meant that I could walk freely in the daytime, no worries of turning the color of an over ripe plum, or heaven forbid possibly bursting into flame. And now it smelled like blood.

The one thing I needed most, but was too weak to take.

Perhaps Maddy was dead. Well, hopefully really dead instead of undead. I let a little evil smile linger on my lips as I imagined some horrible Hollywood ending for the vampire, and then frowned. Regardless, she was gone and it was just me now; Official Sort Of Vampire in Residence. Well, me and a pissed off ghost.

Speaking of Pizza Bob, I looked up and saw him glowering at me from the corner of the room. I gave a tired wave, which he ignored. Whatever.

My stomach rumbled again, and I sighed heavily. Time to get up and quit my daily wallowing. I sat up and did a sniff check on my pits; still vile with a hint of potpourri. Lovely. I just sighed again and rolled out of bed. I grabbed my clothes and got dressed without taking a shower first; I was already depressed so I figured, screw it. It was still five hours until my shift started at the mall, but I was restless. And hungry. And still me. And I didn't even want to go to work.

I could already sense that today was going to be one of those days.

Pizza Bob trailed behind me, mimicking my walk and making farting noises as I headed into my bathroom. I glared at him and slammed the door in his face. Thankfully, he stayed put and didn't follow me in.

"You need to fire your decorator," he said through the door. "Seriously. It's like Comic-Con threw up in your place."

"Well no one asked you." I silently berated myself for even acknowledging him. Now he'd never shut up. I came out of the bathroom and saw him holding one of my Buffy collectibles.

Pizza Bob smirked at me. "You have dolls. Little boy vampire dolls everywhere." He waved an Angel action figure and dropped it on the floor. "It's creepy."

"Hey!" I snapped as I picked it up reverently. "They're action figures and collectibles. Buffy the Vampire Slayer, Dracula, Angel, I have them all."

"Dude, they're toys."

I walked into my living room and froze. All of my movie posters and framed magazine covers were now sporting mustaches and glasses drawn with a rainbow of sharpie colors.

"Damn it!" I yelled "Really?" I just shook my head at him.

"Oooh, you don't like it?" Pizza Bob crossed his arms and gloated.

I stood there with my hand over my mouth for a minute, and then forced myself to ignore him. There was nothing I could do about it now. Besides, for some reason Nosferatu now looked like Gandhi with the new little round glasses drawn on. I stifled a smirk and tried to appear angry.

"You're a child." I looked around at my apartment in disgust and then scowled at the ghost.

"You're a child," Pizza Bob sassed back.

I grabbed a cushion off of the couch and threw it through Pizza Bob's form, dissipating him completely. "Take that, ass hat."

He didn't instantly re-materialize; he'd used up too much juice for the ghost graffiti. Hooray for me! A break. But as soon as he was gone I realized I kind of missed the banter. Wow. I was starting to like the jerk.

I picked up as much of the mess as I could, carefully putting my vampire figurines back on the shelves where they belonged.

"They're action figures, damn it," I said to the empty room.

I stared at Gandhi Nosferatu and started laughing. It was pretty funny after all. Oh well. My stomach rumbled, and with a defeated sigh I headed into my kitchen for some breakfast. I felt a tingle in the air and knew the ghost was on his way back.

"Melvin, we need to talk." Pizza Bob materialized right next to me. "It's important."

"Well, aren't you the Chatty Cathy tonight?" I smirked. "Rather cheery, too. Vandalizing my apartment make you feel all warm and fuzzy?" I wasn't angry anymore, nope, not at all. Just hungry.

"Yeah. Actually it did." Pizza Bob smiled.

"You going to apologize?"

"Whatever. Dude, it's time."

I was warming up a combination of raw hamburger and pig livers in the microwave, and squinted at the timer. I flared my nostrils and caught the intoxicating scent of the blood, not quite at body temperature yet, and shook my head.

"No...it needs a few more seconds."

Pizza Bob reached past me and turned off the microwave. "Seriously? You have to stop eating this crap."

"Hey! It was almost perfect." Now I'd have to start the process again to get the timing right.

"Not the timer time, you moro--" Pizza Bob caught himself. I could see him trying to stay calm; that made me nervous. "It's time to sack up and go bite someone."

"Say what?" My mouth hung open for a moment. *What are you up to?*

Pizza Bob rolled his eyes. "I can't keep watching you do this night after night. You sit in your living room, staring at the television until it's time to go to work, or you just sit on the couch and play with your creepy vamp dolls on your days off."

"They're action figures," I mumbled defensively.

"No. GI Joe is an action figure. Those are creepy little dolls. You've had enough wallowing. You need to go get your vampire on."

I crossed my arms over my chest and took a step back. "What are you up to? I'm not going to go out and make you playmate."

"That's not why I'm doing this," he said with a smirk. "You couldn't get a Playmate; you're probably scared of bunnies."

"Wha? Oh...yeah...funny." I rolled my eyes. "Why the sudden good cop/bad cop shtick?"

"You're boring the crap outta me so I've decided to help you." The ghost shrugged. "You're a vampire, it's time to go act like one."

"Oh, gee...thanks. Tried that," I pointed at him, "don't need another one of you around here." I reached through his arm and opened the microwave to retrieve my breakfast. It was tepid. Damn it.

I headed out into the living room, sat down on the couch, and began stuffing the livers into my mouth; I was starving tonight. Pizza Bob again materialized next to me with a smirk on his face.

"See? You're doing it again. You had a lifetime in Loserville. Now's your chance to move up to Coolsville."

I snorted and sent a blob of liver into my sinuses. Bleh! "You did not just say that to me. What is this? 1950?" I made a series of disgusting noises until the chunk cleared and I swallowed it, choking down the bland, rubbery wad with a grimace.

He was right. This had to stop. Even I was getting sick and tired of my petulant whiny monologues. And worse yet the hamburger and livers just weren't doing it for me much anymore.

I'm a vampire. Get over it.

"Just copy what one of your little vampire dolls would do, except, well, you know, if they were a real vampire and not a toy." Pizza Bob grinned at me and I flinched.

Did he know about my other attempt at the bar? How embarrassing!

"You need a motivation." He held up my Spike/William-the-Bloody figurine and waved its hand at me. "I wanna kill the slayer! Oooh! Ahhh...look at me! I'm a scary vampire who actually eats people!"

"Shut up."

I snatched the doll (damn it! I mean action figure!!!) from his hand, stood up and headed over to my computer desk, stuffing wads of my unsatisfying meal into my mouth as I sat down, and then stood up again, chewing and swallowing on auto pilot while consuming raw meat at ease. Disgusting. I needed something new, a distraction.

Maybe a walk. What could go wrong? I'd been hiding in the apartment, hiding at my job, so maybe I'd try hiding in plain sight for a while. And I had to get away from Pizza Bob. I didn't trust him and this new supportive, buddy-buddy thing he was trying even though I knew he was right. Damn it. I flipped him the bird and grabbed my keys.

"Hey! Where are you going? You need to listen to me. I can help you, dude. You just need some confidence." He blocked the door.

Ha! Like that will stop me.

"I'd move if I were you." I impressed myself with the menacing tone.

"Bite someone while you're out. You can do it. Just Nike it, man. I wanna see blood on that overbite when you get home, mister." He looked over at his corpse in the corner and grimaced. "Oh...and bring back some more fly strips."

"Screw you." With a grin on my face, I walked through his form and scattered him to vapors.

I opened my front door and saw my neighbor, a twenty something hipster carrying his bike down the hall. He started to say something, a mumbled "wassup?", but saw who I was and ignored me instead.

Right back at ya, buddy.

I let it roll off of me, intent on salvaging my mood, and headed down the stairs to the street. I saw a variety of people -- the locals, a few winos, some punks, the downtown apartment crowd, and realized why I loved living here. Portland is weird. Just weird enough for me to still fit in.

A kid with a mohawk spare changed me, and then gave me a high-five when I flipped him a dollar.

"Dude...is that a full tat? Awesome tint, man." I realized he was talking about my blue skin. Snerk.

"Making a statement about the suffocation by societal pressure even as you wear the rags of the man," he said as he pointed at my security guard jacket. With a conspiratorial wink, he headed off on his skateboard towards another mark before I could answer.

Mad props from a street kid. It buoyed me, though. I people watched as I passed the library, deciding that maybe life wasn't so bad. So I was undead, or mostly dead. There were worse things to be. Possibly.

A schizophrenic transvestite wrapped in newspaper pants and a halter-top jumped in front of me with his hand up. He had blue eye shadow in great smudges under his bushy eyebrows, and he lewdly waggled his tongue at me.

"Looky, looky, looky...another marimba player. Needs a bath and a breath mint!" He cackled and then twirled away.

Ah, Portland. I'm up one minute then brought down the next. But I had to laugh. Crazy is as crazy does.

Takes one to know one, pal.

I wanted to shout after him that his eye shadow didn't match his halter-top, but that would be petty. Instead I just laughed. The day wasn't starting too badly after all. But I was still restless. I lived downtown, but my job was way out in East Portland -- a long bus ride through suburban hell. I didn't feel like spending any time out in the boonies with nothing but used car lots and tweakers. I wanted to stay local, ease into a better frame of mind.

Maybe I could go to dinner at Jake's Famous Crawfish, hit a happy hour in a dark bar...mingle. I couldn't afford Jake's and I didn't feel like mingling. I felt caged in.

I smiled to myself and decided to follow my melancholy. I'd go to the zoo. What could go wrong?

⋏

From now on when I say to myself, "What could go wrong?" I'll realize that everything can. And will. If I'm involved, that is. The second I walked through the front gate of the zoo it was like some subliminal alarm went off in the aether.

A tremor in the force. The first animal I tried to see, a mountain goat that made the oddest high pitched keening sound when he saw me or just smelled me, leapt from his perch, committed a death defying ninja-like flip (much to the delight of the crowd), and dove into his cave. I should have just turned around and left right then.

Instead I went to see the bats. Bram Stoker would be so proud. I nudged my way past a group of kids and stood inches from my nocturnal cousins of myth, hoping to sense some kinship, simply glory in the humor of it all. I was hoping for vampire bats, but I got regular bats. Gentle, timid fruit bats; not so timid apparently. Something about me set them off and they all began bouncing around in their enclosure; smacking into the glass, just generally freaking out, all right in front of me. Perhaps they were collectively enraged at my existence -- the mongrel half-breed that shamed their mythos and symbolism. I could attempt to analyze and anthropomorphize their reaction till I was blue in the face (ha!), but it seemed silly. The fact that I was rationalizing struck me as silly as they thrashed and flopped, antagonized to the point of frenzy, and I laughed so hard that I had tears in my eyes. The bats became so agitated that one of the zoo officials cleared everyone out of the exhibit quickly.

I was mortified.

Two-for-two so far.

It only got worse. The tiger tried to jump the moat to get at me, and the wolves began howling when I neared their enclosure. In fact the alpha male bared his teeth and bristled. The elephants went berserk, and again a zoo employee shut down the pachyderm hall and shunted all of us visitors out quickly. The same thing happened in the chimpanzee display, but instead of a stampede they all threw copious amounts of poop at the glass where I was standing. Their screeches and hollers echoed out after me when I left. I noticed that security was starting to follow me as I made my way to the polar bears.

The polar bears were the only animals that didn't freak out. What they did was much worse. One of them stood up, sniffed the air, and then looked at me curiously. It then popped into the water and swam up to the window, hanging there while eyeing me oddly. It started pawing at the glass, casually but insistent, the whole time looking me right in the eye. One predator to another. It made my gums tingle.

A woman watching the scene unfold came quietly up behind me. She said, "They aren't afraid of anything, you know. Nature's perfect predator. They would be at the top of the food chain if they could drive a car."

Drive a car? I turned to look at her with a bewildered expression on my face. "What?"

But my overbite had extended, I was blue, and I smelled decidedly unpleasant. But.... No one was around at the moment; I could take her and bite her, drink her dry and be done with the fear. So what if she haunted me? She was a nutso. It would drive Pizza Bob crazy.

I heard her heartbeat racing and my overbite extended further as I took a hesitant step towards her.

She gasped, took a quick step back, then mumbled something under her breath as she bolted from the room. That's when security showed up.

"Sir...."

I dropped my head and lisped through my unleashed overbite, "I'll go now." I sneaked a peek at the polar bear, and he looked like he was smirking at me. Oh man.

As the guards escorted me from the zoo, the cacophony of animal cries drowned out the announcements coming over the loud speakers: The zoo is closing. Please make your way to the exit in a timely manner. We apologize for any inconvenience.

Security asked that I not return.

So much for making the most of my day. And there was no way I was going to work now. I got on the bus and rode towards downtown in silence, shunned on the bus as usual. It made me miss Pizza Bob a little bit. Just a little.

Maybe everything might get easier if I just kept at it. And monkeys might fly out of my butt.

Probably just bats.

Angry fruit bats.

I got off the bus in Old Town, hoping some of the melancholy of the area and the homeless people who hung out here would buoy me. Nothing like looking down on the less fortunate to make you feel better, eh? How sad is that? I figured at least I had a roof over my head and a job. So what if I was mostly dead.

These people had it far worse than me. But the more folks I encountered, the darker my mood grew. It didn't matter how drunk, stoned, or crazy they were, the homeless at least had an identity, a community. I was still searching for mine. I saw the nightclub, Dante's, up the road, the shrine to my vampiric fumbling, and that clinched it for me. No more waffling. Tonight I was going to eat someone!

I wandered through the darkened streets until I hit the industrial area, nice and abandoned, perfect for the hunt. My super hearing picked up the sound of someone coughing, and I followed the hacks and gasps to a darkened alleyway where a man was hunched over, his back to me. He was too busy yorfing up a lung and hadn't noticed me yet.

Perfect!

I raised my hands up over my head like claws and started creeping forward slowly, channeling my inner Nosferatu, hoping I looked properly vampiric. I hesitated when the man turned his head and spat a gross looking glob of yuck onto the pavement. Was he contagious? Could I catch something nasty if I ate him?

Stop stalling! You can do this.

I started creeping forward again, enjoying the predator feeling coursing through my body.

I can do this...I can do this....

I readied for the lunge as my overbite extended.

The man sensed movement behind him and turned to stare at me with rheumy eyes, and I faltered mid-step, my hands still stretched and comically splayed like talons. I looked ridiculous.

I put my hand up in front of my mouth to hide my teeth and lisped, "Um, you okay?"

I just can't do it!

The man coughed once and spit at my feet. "Sound like it?" He wheezed. "What the hell are you doing, son?"

I turned and ran away, and kept running for blocks until I tripped over a furry lump on the road and went down hard, rolling to a stop against the curb. I looked up and saw two beady eyes glaring at me. It was an animal. A mangled, angry, suffering opossum that had been hit by a car and left for dead, but it wasn't yet. *Hey! Kind of like me.* I smelled the blood, so warm and inviting, and my overbite extended again. As I stood up the thing hissed at me.

"I know how you feel," I said. "It's been that kind of day. A series of unfortunate events." The scent of blood was intoxicating. It was driving me nuts and I was so hungry.

It can't get away...you could end its suffering!

Before I could talk myself out of it, I pounced. Less than graceful, I snatched the animal up by its tail, wincing at the sound of crackling vertebrae, and bit the damned thing on the neck. He was a fighter, though; he got in one good bite on my face before he went limp. I drank my fill and then burst into tears at what I had done.

"I killed it!" I sat on the curb crying, holding the dead opossum in my lap until the first hints of sunrise graced the morning sky. I laid the body on the pavement and wiped my snotty nose on my sleeve, then dabbed at the blood on my hands and face with my shirttail -- the wound was healing and I hoped it wouldn't scar. I couldn't go home looking like this. I knew Pizza Bob was going to give me grief if he knew I'd chickened out twice and then settled for roadkill. How humiliating!

But the sun was coming up and I had to go. I ran home bathed in the rays of early dawn, and then came face-to-face with Pizza Bob as I opened my door.

"Crap," I muttered.

He saw the blood all over me, cheered, and gave me a fist bump. "Sweet! You did it! Rock on, stinky! Tell me all about it!" He looked around the apartment for the ghost of my victim. "I can't wait to meet him! I know you didn't bite a girl!"

I thought about the opossum and sure enough I started to sniffle a bit. Oh man.

"Yes, yes I did." He didn't have to know it was an animal. "I fed."

The ghost floated up closer to me, stared at the healing bite on my face, then squinted his eyes at me. "Wait a minute...."

I just stood there with my lip quivering. He reached up and pulled a wad of blood soaked fur from my collar. "Are you kidding me? What did you do?"

"It was suffering," I said with a quaver in my voice. "I couldn't help it; I just ate it...I'm a bad person!" I started to cry. "Poor thing left on the side of the road--"

"Oh. My. God. You are hopeless, dude. I give up." Pizza Bob glared at me and threw the fur in my face. "You ate roadkill!"

"Do you think it's going to haunt me?"

"I hope so. That'd be priceless." He looked over at his body still decomposing in the corner. "You forgot the fly strips."

I winced. "Leave me alone," I said as I flopped onto my couch. "The more you tease, the worse I feel. But at least I tried!"

Pizza Bob floated in front of me, glaring and shaking his head in disgust.

My eyes drooped as the sun rose higher in the morning sky. "Poor little opossum...so tasty...so sorry...." I mumbled.

He started laughing. "A frickin' opossum? You are the worst vampire ever."

"I know. I don't suck."

"Ha! I see what you did there. Good one, stinky." And then Pizza Bob disappeared in blast of icy cold air.

I curled up on the couch, hugging the piece of fur like a Teddy bear; a Teddy bear that smelled of garbage, blood, failure, and death. Cheery, right?

Yeah...not so much.

⚔

MASTERSOFTHENITE
Blogline ∞ September 18, 2014 ∞ MOOD: Blue

No new adventures to speak of, at least none that I want to admit to, just a lot of wallowing and self-pity. I know, I know...it's getting old. Okay, I need help. I'm terrible at this undead thing. I thank those few of you who have sent me encouraging private messages. It means more than you know. To the others I say, "GET A LIFE." Born again Christian vampires? Are you kidding me? I'm not (nor was) a religious person, but that whole zombie Jesus thing is a bit off sides. There's a line, folks. Every time you guys try and post a comment or a link I'll keep deleting it. Forever. And yes, I have that much time.

And now to the Satanists. You guys are seriously twisted. Just because I'm a vampire.... Wow. Seriously, wow. I'm really hoping those barnyard scenes were Photoshopped. The same deleting standard applies to you whack jobs as well.

It's been a while since I posted, I know, but things have gotten out of control. I won't go into much detail, but suffice it to say there is indeed an afterlife. You thought the whole vampire thing was hard to swallow (no pun intended)? Well, how about ghosts? Time for a little Haley Joel: I see dead people.

Woo, shiver. I don't see people in the plural...just one former person. My midnight snack; attempted midnight snack I should say.

Pizza Bob won't go away. It's like being in high school all over again -- bullied daily with the only respite my time at work, and I hate my job! The ghost can't leave my apartment -- yeah, the body is still there (I'm too icked out to move it), so his spirit must be linked somehow. If I have to live forever with his constant nagging I'll go insane. I thought I'd get used to his company, but no. I have an idea about getting rid of him, but believe it or not he reads this blog! If it works out I'll post about it. The whole experience has put me off trying to bite someone else; the price is just too high.

I received a notice from my landlord today. My neighbors are starting to complain. Any suggestions on odor eradication (besides the obvious removal of the body!) would be greatly appreciated. I've got one week to make it go away or I'm out on my stinky blue butt. On my salary this is the cheapest place I can afford.

I've discovered pig livers. They aren't too bad. I don't think I'll ever be able to bite someone so keep your fingers crossed that the local butcher keeps up his supply for me. I've tried some other blood; won't go into detail, but I'm content with cow and pig for now.

Please be on the look out for a fat girl named Maddy. Yeah, that Maddy. I'm looking for her! PM me if you spot her. She likes happy hour.

- Melvin

ADD A COMMENT ∞ REPLY TO POSTER ∞ BLOCK THIS USER

CHAPTER 4

SECOND VERSE, SAME AS THE FIRST

"**D**on't be mad." I snapped open a garbage bag and stood staring down at Pizza Bob's corpse, which was looking a little worse for the wear. The Indian summer month and my lack of air conditioning had not been kind to him; the body was bloated in places with a waxy, oily sheen. Luckily I'd already put down a shower curtain underneath the remains a couple of weeks before. I should have thought of it the night he died, but I was a bit rattled.

Because the body had been making disturbing gurgling and popping noises, I was afraid it would explode soon. As it stood, my damage deposit was in serious jeopardy because of the seepage stain on the hardwood floor. I didn't want to think about what would happen to the walls and ceiling if he popped. Gah!

"I deserve better than this," Pizza Bob said.

"What am I supposed do? Huh?" My hands were shaking at the thought of touching the goopy mess, even through dish gloves. "I've got to get rid of the body!"

"Yeah, well, I deserve better than a Hefty Cinch Sack."

"It's not like I'm going to throw you in the garbage, I'm going to *bury* you. Any place in particular you'd like to go?" *Like into the light maybe?*

"Screw you. How about going back to living again? Huh? Can you do that?"

"I wish."

"I can't watch this," he said, and disappeared with an angry glare.

My plan was to bury him in hallowed ground, get rid of his body -- the anchor here in my apartment, but I hadn't really thought it through. Pizza Bob had been a fairly big guy in life and wouldn't fit into just one bag. And then how was I going to transport him? I didn't own a car, and the bus was out of the question.

Maybe a taxi?

One thing at a time.

I crouched down and grabbed his foot; it came right off the leg with a sickening slurp. I hate to admit this but I screamed -- it wasn't a quality scream, but it certainly was humbling. Some creature of the night I'd turned out to be.

I dropped the foot into the bag and tentatively tried the other foot. It came off, too; the flies and their offspring had done a pretty good job on the connective tissue. Nature's little helpers; a vampire's best friend. How sick am I?

Enough stalling, just get it over with!

I took a deep breath, adjusted my rubber gloves and pretended it was just a project, a game of slimy Jenga. Pretty soon I had Pizza Bob broken down like a carved turkey at thanksgiving, and portioned out into two garbage bags. Gross and disgusting, but now easily moveable.

Pizza Bob reappeared as I was tying closed the last bag.

"I'm leaking," he said, and I saw a puddle forming under the first bag. Gross!

With a shudder I triple bagged his remains and then scrubbed the entire floor with straight bleach. The majority of the stains came up and it looked like I might get out of this all right. I was running late for work so I left Pizza Bob hovering over the bags while I went to take a shower.

He was waiting for me outside the stall when I got out, and handed me a towel; he was getting stronger with the moving things and it made me nervous. That's all I needed. A full-blown poltergeist making my life even more miserable. Living with Pizza Bob was like having a creepy, nosy roommate who didn't pay any rent. Hopefully he'd be gone soon; the glorious hallowed ground theory.

"Privacy?" I demanded, but he ignored me.

He said, "I know where I want to go. It's gonna be awesome!"

Uh-oh. I didn't like the sound of that.

"I want a Viking funeral."

"What?"

Pizza Bob grinned. "A Viking funeral, man. The helmet with the horns, the boat, the fire, the whole works." He crossed his arms. "You owe me."

"How the hell am I going to do that?"

"Not my problem, dude."

I got dressed in my uniform and walked out into the living room; I was pleased that the stench was almost gone. When the bags left I'd just have to contend with my own particular ripeness. A throw rug over the little stain in the corner, a new set of air fresheners, maybe some incense, some bug spray and fly strips, and the landlord would have nothing to complain about. The smell would be no worse than the exotic cooking smells coming from my diverse set of neighbors. In fact I'd take my smell over kimchi, nasty pickled cabbage, any day. That brought a little smile to my face as I sat down to put on my shoes.

Ugh. Speaking of kimchi....

Pizza Bob settled on the couch next to me. "I want a Viking funeral," he said firmly. "It's so Thirteenth Warrior."

Yeah, that was an awesome movie; Beowulf done Crichton style. I thought Antonio Banderas was pretty cool, in a manly way of course, and had done a good job of being a Viking warrior. So Pizza Bob wanted a Viking funeral, just like the dead Viking king; of course he did...who wouldn't? It screwed with my hallowed ground theory, but I had to admit the thought was pretty cool. With the body gone maybe Pizza Bob would leave, too. And I did kind of owe him.

"I'll do my best," I said, and I meant it.

I got to work and started walking the mall. Where was I going to get a boat? I stopped at a toy store and found a plastic Viking helmet, and then had an epiphany. A blow up raft! The sporting goods store was closing in fifteen minutes so I hustled over and found a small one. But it was $300, way out of my budget. Then I saw something that would be perfect -- necessity is the mother of invention! I bought two big inner tubes for river floating, and figured I could tie the two together and wedge the garbage sacks into the middle.

Ha! I was good at this.

I bought four bottles of camp stove propane and some outdoor torch oil for the flame requirement. I thought it was funny. Citronella-scented oil to ward off pesky little bloodsuckers.

Good one.

Now all I had to do was figure out how I was going to get to the river with two garbage bags full of dead Pizza Bob, light him on fire without anyone seeing, and escape before I got caught.

I'd figure something out.

As an afterthought I stopped by the video store and bought a copy of the Thirteenth Warrior as a going away present.

⚔

I woke up to Pizza Bob sitting on the bed next to me. He just didn't get the boundary thing!

"Dude, I thought you'd never wake up!" He was unusually chipper this afternoon.

I checked my hand for shaving cream, felt to make sure my eyebrows were still attached and unshaved, and then felt my head to make sure there was hair. Everything was where it should be, but it wouldn't have been a shocker to wake up to something like that. Last week he'd drawn a handle bar mustache on my face, and devil horns on my forehead with a sharpie pen. Pizza Bob loved the petty little torments since he couldn't kill me out right. It was like living with Kato from the Pink Panther movies.

"This is cool, dude." He had the dvd in his hand. "Sets the mood for my send off. Thanks!"

"You're welcome." I sat up and stretched. "But we might have to wait a few days for the Viking thing. I can't figure out how to get to the river. I'd walk, but twenty miles with two garbage bags filled with body parts, river tires, and a shopping bag filled with propane and a Viking helmet might look a bit weird.

"I don't want to get stopped. That might be awkward." I yawned, and my stomach rumbled.

"What about my car?" he asked.

"Um, no. It's gone."

"Well go get it, jerk. That was a good car."

"I'm sure you've been reported missing," I said diplomatically.

"I doubt it. My boss probably thinks I just bailed with the pizza money." Pizza Bob shrugged.

"That's sad." Wow, he might just be as pathetic as me.

"Whatever, dude. So go get the car."

"Again, I don't want to get stopped. And if I drive your car, the way my luck is, I'd get stopped with your body in the trunk."

"That would be funny," Pizza Bob said with a snort.

"Yeah, a laugh riot. But then you wouldn't get your Viking funeral."

Pizza Bob held out both of his hands, palms up like he was weighing something. "Hmmm, on the one hand seeing you arrested for my murder, interrogated, investigated, possibly dissected when they find out you're a vampire; getting myself a little justice." He lifted one hand higher than the other. "On the other hand, getting a wicked awesome Viking funeral!"

Pizza Bob grinned at me.

"Just rent a car," he said matter-of-fact.

"I don't have that kind of money. I used most of what I had for the funeral stuff."

"Always focusing on the negative, dude. I've got money."

"Ghost MasterCard?" I said, and instantly regretted it. Pizza Bob glowered at me.

"In my wallet, ass-hat." He shook his head. "You did grab my wallet before you stuffed me in those bags?"

I pursed my lips and looked at him sheepishly. He had a way of making me feel so stupid sometimes even though I knew my IQ was way above his; but he had bully logic. How can you argue with bully logic? My stomach growled again and I finally got up, Pizza Bob following me into the kitchen where I grabbed a carton of pig livers.

He said, "You really are a moron, you know that? I've got at least three hundred bucks in there. I was gonna buy some weed after my shift."

"Shocker," I said sarcastically.

"Whatever, pig sucker."

"Touché." At least he didn't mention the opossum.

"Plus there's about sixty in pizza money. I can't believe you just left it there. You're either lazy or stupid. I vote for both."

"You should have said something sooner. Maybe I was just respecting your privacy."

"Yeah, right. A polite murderer. You'll kill me, but you won't rob me." He winced as I chewed on a liver. "God that's disgusting."

"Don't start, okay? You need to cut me some slack." I hated how whiney I sounded.

"Whatever, princess. I'm telling you about the money now so go get it."

The last thing I wanted to do was dig through the sloppy contents for his wallet, but I did need the money. And I didn't want to look like more of a wuss than I already was. I gave a little shudder at the thought of dipping my hand into that bag, feeling the slippery flesh, stirring up the stink again. I was doing another mental shudder when Pizza Bob shook his head again in irritation, and floated over to his jumbled remains. He crouched down and plunged his hand through the second bag, his ghostly arm just passing through the plastic like air, rooting and digging until he found the wallet.

"It's in this one, but I used up my juice finding it. Man up, dude."

I retrieved the wallet and carried it pinched between my thumb and index finger into the kitchen to rinse in the sink. The money was in good condition, not too stained or stinky. I saw Pizza Bob's driver's license but avoided looking at the picture. I didn't want to know his real name, as it was he kind of reminded me of that actor Owen Wilson, but the fact he was an organ donor made me chuckle. He'd donated his organs all right. Millions of flies and their off spring worshipped his corpse like a shrine.

"What's so funny?" Pizza Bob demanded.

"Gallows humor."

"I don't watch foreign films."

That made me laugh harder. "No, gallows humor."

"That comedian who smashed fruit with a sledge hammer?"

"No," I was laughing so hard I was crying. "That's Gallagher." I wiped at my eyes with my sleeve.

"Gallo like the wine?" he asked, starting to get mad. "I don't get it."

I stopped laughing for a second, saw the confused look on his face, and then lost it completely. I hadn't laughed this hard in forever. He just floated there glaring at me.

"I'm sorry, really. Wooooo." I took a few deep breaths and got myself under control. "They used to hang criminals from platforms called gallows."

"I still don't get it. What's funny about hanging people? That's twisted."

"Oh, please. I'm going to rupture something if you keep this up." I started laughing again. "Go Google gallows humor."

"Google this," he said, and flipped me off. "You're a real asshole sometimes."

"So you keep telling me." I couldn't stop giggling as I fanned the money out on the counter to dry. "I'm sorry. You're right." When I was sure that I was done laughing I turned around and looked at him.

"Thanks for the money, but I can't use cash to rent a car. We'll have to think of some other way for me to get to the river."

"I saw your credit card statement and you've got plenty of room for a car rental." Pizza Bob looked smug.

"That's not cool," I muttered. I should have guessed that he was a snoop. But what did it matter? He'd be gone soon, so I forced a cheery smile as I put the dvd I brought home for him in the player.

"Get over it, I was bored," Pizza Bob said with snide grin. "So get on the phone and call CheapWheels; they'll deliver the car here by the time the movie's over."

He was right. The car showed up just as the ending credits rolled. I loaded the bags and the rest of the gear into the trunk with Pizza Bob watching from the window. I felt a little bad that he wouldn't be able to see his own funeral; but really, who gets to anyway. I waved, he scowled, and I set off for Sauvie Island where it would be deserted near the river.

I was just pulling onto Highway 30 when Pizza Bob appeared in the passenger seat. He startled me so badly that I veered into the wrong lane and gave a trucker his dose of adrenaline for the evening.

"It worked!" the ghost shouted over the semi's blaring horn while pumping his fist in the air.

"What the hell are you doing here?" I was watching the rear view mirror nervously, positive that a cop had seen my erratic driving and would pull me over any second; or that the trucker would turn around to come kick my butt. The latter was more unlikely, but it still added to my stress level. Could vampires have a stroke?

Pizza Bob was babbling at me. "I couldn't miss this, it's gonna be so cool. I just concentrated real hard on my body, and whoosh...here I am."

At least I was right about the body connection. Woohoo, score one for the vampire. And thankfully no cop materialized behind me. Woohoo times two.

Just ten miles to go; focus on the positive.

"Are we there yet?" Pizza Bob asked with a grin.

"No."

"Are we there yet?"

"No."

"Are we there--"

"No! If you keep asking me I'm going to dump your body on the side of the road."

"Geez, lighten up already."

He was silent the rest of the trip until we turned off onto a dirt road and parked by the riverbank.

He started to say something but I held my hand up. "Yes, we're here."

We sat staring at the city lights of Portland up river. The night was cool and clear, the stars twinkling merrily overhead, and it just felt right.

"This is a cool spot, Melvin. Well done."

"Are you ready?" I asked.

"This is gonna be epic."

I unloaded the trunk and piled everything on the sand.

"Um, Melvin. How are you gonna blow those up?" He was pointing at the deflated inner tubes.

"Oh."

"Holy crap, dude!"

"I'll think of something," I said quickly. I picked up an inner tube and stared at the air valve. I put it to my lips and blew. It was difficult at first, but then I just used a combination of brute strength and patience on the stem; it worked. Vampire lungs like Superman. It was actually really cool. This vampire thing had its perks.

"Did you see that?" I sounded all giddy.

"Woohoo." Pizza Bob twirled his finger in the air. Did he get that from me, or I from him? Damn!

"Well, I thought it was cool," I muttered to myself. "Let's see you do it."

"Just hurry up, stinky."

I got both tires blown up and duct taped together, and then I settled Pizza Bob's bags of body in the center with the propane bottles shoved inside.

"Dude, which bag has my head in it?" Pizza Bob asked.

"I don't remember."

He just shook his head in disappointment, and then stuck his hand into the bags. After a minute he said, "This one."

I duct taped the helmet on that bag and doused everything in lamp oil.

"Tiki Oil? Are you serious?"

I shrugged. "I thought it was apropos...you know, the human torch."

"That's funny."

"Thanks."

"Is that gallows humor?"

"Yes."

"Okay." He gave me a thumbs-up.

"Okay," I said, and then froze.

"What?"

"I, um, I forgot a lighter," I said, afraid to look at him.

"Are you doing this on purpose or are you really this stupid?"

This was horrible. I felt like an idiot as I stood dumbly staring at him.

"Maybe the car has a cigarette lighter," I offered meekly. I started to go look, but Pizza Bob shook his head.

"It's a nonsmoking car, Sherlock. There's a lighter in my back pocket, in that bag." He pointed and I grimaced. Reluctantly I opened up the garbage bag and dug around, pulling out various body parts until I found the lighter.

"You know what? I'm doing the best I can here," I snapped. The parts wouldn't go back in the bag right so I had to settle for an arm sticking out, the hand flopping at the end.

"Stellar work, dude. Stellar. Be proud of the way you've bumbled through the body disposal of your first murder victim." Pizza Bob was floating over the river, smirking at me.

"I didn't have to do all this. You killed yourself and blame me. Now I'm trying to be nice."

"Whatever." But he was smiling now. He adjusted the fingers so that he was giving the world the bird. "That about sums up the situation."

I might just miss him after all.

I pushed the tires out into the river and looked at Pizza Bob. "Ready?"

"Say something," he said.

"Something."

"Good enough."

I smiled and lit the bags. I pushed the burning pyre further out into the water and watched until the propane tanks exploded. It was spectacular. When I turned around Pizza Bob was gone.

"Oh, thank god!" I did a little dance on the sand. Things were finally looking up for old Mostly Dead Melvin, yes indeed.

I was still smiling when I opened my apartment door at home.

"Did ya miss me?" Pizza Bob shouted, and I thought I was going to throw up. "You didn't think that would get rid of me, did you?"

I slumped onto the couch.

"Nope, no siree. I can go anywhere I want to now. Awesome!" he gloated.

I lay down on the couch and covered my ears.

"My life sucks," I moaned.

"Thanks for the funeral, that rocked when the bags exploded."

"You're still here. Why? Why is this happening to me?" I couldn't believe how much the universe had screwed me.

"Dude, my body is gone. I'm free wheeling now!"

"Just go away, please. I'm begging you."

"Where else am I gonna go?" Pizza Bob flopped onto the couch next to me with the dvd remote in his hand. "We should have video taped the funeral. It was awesome, man."

I actually prayed for death as he started the Thirteenth Warrior over again.

"Hey." Pizza Bob nudged me. "Go make some popcorn so I can smell it while we watch the movie."

I curled up tighter on the couch and buried my face in the cushions. Life wasn't fair. Undeath wasn't fair.

"Seriously, hop to it. I put on the director's cut with commentary. We can compare my send off with the movie version. I need popcorn, dude."

I bit the pillow and sobbed. Yeah, it was pathetic.

"Are you crying?" Pizza Bob yelled. "Oh my god, you are. What a total pussy." He cranked the volume on the television, and I lay there, face down in the cushions until the sun came up and I finally passed out.

⅄

MASTERS OF THE NITE
Blogline ∞ October 5, 2014 ∞ MOOD: Blue
Two words: Viking Funeral. It didn't work. Should have stuck with hallowed ground. What a total pisser.
- Melvin

REPLY TO POSTER ∞ BLOCK USER ∞ REPORT POST

⅄

"Why are you being such a dick?"

I sighed as Pizza Bob ranted next to me in the food court at the mall. Yes, my life had become even more miserable; everywhere I went, Pizza Bob was sure to follow. Thankfully no one else could see him, or better yet hear him, either. I had no peace, no respite from his running commentary about the failings of my non-life.

And here we were, at the mall, just me and my shadow. Joy.

"I mean it, dude. They're just having fun." Pizza Bob floated over to a table with four teenagers sitting haphazardly in the chairs, some rocking back on two chair legs, the others slumped like lizards sunbathing across the table. The ghost stared at their basket of fries longingly. "Oh, man! I miss curly fries."

I ignored him and addressed the oldest and meanest looking boy; his body language screamed LEADER!!!!

"You guys have been here for three hours, there's a huge mess on this table, you're being loud and lewd to the staff and other patrons. It's time to go."

"Check it out," the boy mocked to his friends. "Rent-a-cop here is flexing. What's with the blue skin? Halloween's weeks away!" He laughed and waved his hand in front of his nose. "You ever hear of deodorant?"

Pizza Bob snorted and gave him a thumbs-up, frowning when the kid didn't acknowledge him. Of course the boy wouldn't, I was the only one who had the joy of seeing the ghost.

Pizza Bob nodded at me. "That was a good one, Melvin. You do stink."

"Wow, good one," I said in a perfect imitation of him.

"Whatever, Rent. A. Cop," the boy sassed back, the other boys laughing loudly.

My god how I wished I could just eat the little smart ass, or have real fangs to scare the crap out of him at least. Instead I took a deep breath and leaned over menacingly. With one hand I gripped the leg of his chair and lifted the boy a foot off the floor. Sass boy's eyes bugged out, and he gripped the edge of the table.

Not looking so cool now, are ya? I let him dangle for a minute.

"Now look here," I whispered. "I hate my job, I don't get paid enough to babysit pimply-faced, moron bullies like you, and I'm having a bad day. A bad life, in fact." I gave the chair a little shake. "Yes, I know I stink, but that's my problem that can't change. Your problem can.

"You don't have to be such an ass, you know. If you really want me to I can embarrass the hell out of you in front of your little glee club, make you cry like a little girl," I said leaning in closer so he could smell my breath. "It's all up to you, pimple face."

"Uh, no sir," he squeaked.

"What was that?"

The boy cleared his throat and cast a furtive glance at his buddies who were watching all this with their mouths hanging open. Even Pizza Bob was silent, just staring at me like I'd grown a third eye or something.

"I said no, sir," the boy mumbled.

I set the chair down, and held his shoulder in a vice grip that would leave a nice set of bruises. I waved over one of the busgirls. "Conchita, this young man has something to say to you."

"I do?" he asked as the small woman shuffled over to the table with a nervous smile. I squeezed the boy's shoulder a little harder, and he whimpered.

"Yes, you do." I said. "You want to apologize for making such a mess here, and yelling profanities at the cleaning staff. You understand their job is very tiring, and you didn't mean to add to their workload or be such an ignorant fool."

Okay, I decided to embarrass him just a little. If I couldn't bring myself to be a vampire and bite the jerk, at least I could get a little pay back for the underdogs of the world.

"I'm sorry we made a mess and said things to you." The boy was staring at the table, afraid to look up at his friends.

"And?" I prompted.

"The ignorant fool thing he said," the boy mumbled. It was close enough.

I let go of his shoulder and stepped back. "See? That wasn't so hard, was it? Manners will take you far in life, and respect given is respect earned." *Wow. Did I just say that?*

The other boys pushed back from the table and stood up quickly. They gathered the garbage on the table, wiped up the obscene words written in ketchup with extra napkins provided by Conchita, and high tailed it out of the food court. Sass boy was frozen in his seat, afraid to move in case I grabbed his shoulder again.

"Why are you still here?" I asked, and he jumped up and ran out of the food court without a look back.

Conchita finished wiping off the table and smiled at me. "Thank you for that."

She started to take my hand, but instead put her hand in an apron pocket, her aversion beating out her gratitude. I smiled back and moved out of the way so she wouldn't have to pass by too close to me; She was holding her breath and fingering her crucifix as she watched me out the corner of her eye.

I'd like to say it didn't, but that hurt my feelings. I sighed as Conchita moved off to clean other tables across the food court.

"Dude." Pizza Bob was standing right next to me and I jumped at the sound of his voice. He snuck up on me all the time, and I'd never get used to it.

"Seriously, I take back the dick thing." He playfully punched me in the shoulder. "Sticking up for the working class."

"Whatever."

"Speaking of working class, that Conchita is hot! Maybe you should try and bite her, you know.... Kill her so I won't be alone."

"You're an idiot," I snapped. "A hormonal specter that's more of a monster than I am! She's a mother of four, and one haunting is more than enough."

"You are so selfish, Melvin. You suck. I hate you!"

"Get over it, I didn't mean for this to happen to you, and I've apologized enough for your death. You killed yourself, damn it!"

"You owe me."

"I gave you a Viking funeral."

"So?"

"Blah, blah, blah! I don't owe you anything."

Pizza Bob looked down at his clothes, forever the same loud Hawaiian shirt and stained khakis, and gave a weary sigh. "You know, this used to be my favorite shirt...now I hate it." He looked at me glumly. "At least you get to change your clothes."

"Big deal. A security guard uniform. At least you look the same, but I turned blue!"

"Oooh, check her out!" Pizza Bob nudged my arm.

A young mother pushing a stroller heard my one-sided conversation and looked to see who I was talking to. I waved, but the damage was done -- just the crazy night security guard having a deranged argument with himself. The woman stared at my blue face, caught a whiff of my eau de rot with strawberries, pulled a U-turn with the stroller, and quick walked in the other direction.

"Have a nice evening, ma'am," I called to her, but she ignored me. I sighed (I was doing that a lot lately) and sat down in a chair.

"I so would do her," Pizza Bob cackled and sat in the chair next to me. "When I was delivering pizzas up in the West Hills, there were a few desperate housewives, if you know what I mean. I miss it. I really, really do. All those Milfs and Cougars wanting the salami on the side, if you know what I mean."

"Just shut up. Please." Yes, I know what he meant. That mental picture would stick with me for a while. Time to poke out my mind's eye with a stick. I put my head in my hands and sighed heavily for emphasis.

This was hell. I was in hell, that's what this was. I wasn't really a vampire, I had in fact died that night months ago from food poisoning. Now I was in hell, being haunted and tortured everyday for the sins of my wasted life.

"I won't shut up and you can't make me, dickhead," Pizza Bob sing-songed next to me.

How long would my penance be? Eternity?

"Hey, I'm talking to you."

Maybe I was just in a coma somewhere, or locked away in a mental institution in the midst of a psychotic break. Pizza Bob was just an hallucination. Yeah. That sounded reasonable and more realistic than hell.

"You can't pretend I'm not here."

If I just ignored him, Pizza Bob would go away.

A sharp nudge to my rib cage dashed that hope immediately.

"Holy crap! Look at those fun bags!"

With another weary sigh I took my head out of my hands and looked where Pizza Bob was pointing. He was a pig, but he did have a good eye for fun bags. Come on! I'm just mostly dead, and a breast man. Go figure.

My breath caught in my throat, and I had to blink a few times.

She was a goddess. Beautiful. Radiant. And she was staring right at me. My heart chose that moment to start up and thud in my chest for a few beats; I thought I might faint.

"Melvin, you go and bite that girl right now. Do it. She is so friggin' hot and you owe me one. You so owe me one. Just grab her and do what you do!"

I couldn't move. She was beautiful; her eyes, her lips. She was perfection. That honey-colored hair offset her alabaster skin and her lavender/blue eyes seemed to stare right into my soul! I don't care how cheesy that sounds, I wanted to melt. And that body!

Oh dear God!

"Bite her!" Pizza Bob shrieked, and I jerked in my chair. The woman was still staring at me and I blushed -- something I didn't think I could do anymore because I had no heartbeat thus no blood pressure. Mark that one down in the curio book. My mind was spinning; I couldn't believe I was thinking about something like that while the most gorgeous woman I had ever seen in my entire pathetic life sat staring at me.

I'm sure I looked like a blueberry, a stinking, rotting blueberry in a cheap polyester uniform, and I was mortified. The woman wouldn't look away which induced the sensation of being a bug under a magnifying glass; something to be handled with tweezers and rubber gloves, something to be horrified by and mocked. That was me, Mostly Dead Melvin the freak of nature, the sideshow freak. The freak. The rotting blueberry-colored-bug-on-a-stick.

Then the woman smiled and stood up. She was headed towards me. I'm sure she would berate me, embarrass me for daring to even glance in her direction, yet I couldn't move.

"Jesus, look at those tits!" Pizza Bob moaned. "Holy crap! She's coming over here! Do something!" He shoved me and I fell off the chair. I decided to stay under the table, as good a plan as any because I wanted to just dissolve into the floor rather than hear a harsh word out of that angel's mouth. I watched her feet stop at the table, and I held my breath.

"Melvin?"

I gasped.

"Melvin Morton, is that you?" Her voice was soft and sweet. I couldn't believe she knew my name.

"Are you all right?" she asked as she crouched down and peeked under the table. "It is you!"

"For Christ's sakes, just do it!" Pizza Bob shouted as he hovered over her.

I glared at him standing right behind her, and said, "Go away!"

The woman looked at me in shock, and then grinned. "Did you hit your head, Melvin? What's wrong? Don't you recognize me?"

Recognize her?! I gulped as she reached out for my hand.

Pizza Bob was jumping up and down. "You know her? Holy crap!" He started making rude gestures while grinding his body against hers with an obscene grin on his face. "Oh yeah, baby, yeah! Daddy likey!"

"I said go away, you bastard!" I shouted at him.

The goddess pursed her lips and scowled, but she was still so beautiful. "You're not still mad that I moved away are you? Come on! I was ten!"

WHAT?! It can't be!

"Abby?" I hit my head on the underside of the table as I rushed to stand up. "Abby Abbisnson?"

"Wow, I haven't heard that name in a while." She laughed.

"It's you...it's really you!"

My best friend in the world...the girl of my dreams...but she was so different! But it was her all right. I couldn't believe it; she'd come back to me.

And then I passed out.

How embarrassing.

CHAPTER 5

Guess who's coming to dinner

"He's got no pupil response. I can't get a blood pressure--"

"Look at how blue he is! Get an airway started!"

"Prep the portable defibrillator! He's got no pulse!"

"Melvin...dude. You better wake up." Pizza Bob's voice floated into my subconscious as I lay on the floor surrounded by the mall's first aid team, my supervisor included.

I remembered Abby, and mentally cringed. How much more humiliation was I supposed to suffer? And then I felt my shirt being ripped open.

"Wait, don't move yet." My ghost was laughing at me. "They're gonna shock you, and it will be awesome!"

My eyes flew open and I grabbed the cardiac paddle out of my supervisor's hand before he could jolt my heart. He gave a little cry of surprise, and fell back on his butt.

"Oh my god! Melvin!" Abby was crouched over me, hugging me tightly. "We almost lost you!"

I laughed despite being so embarrassed as I sat up. "I'm fine. I'm fine." I pulled my shirt closed over my bulging, blue belly, totally humiliated that my chest acne and fat was on display.

"What happened?" my supervisor demanded.

I stammered for a minute and then blurted out, "Low blood sugar."

I looked around at the crowd of gawkers and frowned. I found my glasses, and of course one of the lenses was shattered so I just stuffed the ruined pair in my shirt pocket. My supervisor was still hovering near me with the portable heart shocker in case I passed out again. He looked a little disappointed that he wouldn't get to use the thing after all.

"Sir," one of the aid station guys said as he tried to put the blood pressure cuff on me again, "the ambulance is on its way so just lie still. You gave us all a scare with no pulse. Your blood pressure is too low and your core body temp is dangerously low. In fact I don't know how you are even conscious right now."

I slapped his hand away, ripped off the cuff, and handed it back roughly.

Pizza Bob was hovering behind Abby again, and was laughing hysterically. I was glad no one else could hear him.

"Cancel the ambulance," I said as calmly as I could. "I'm fine, really."

"Melvin--"

"I said I'm fine," I snapped at my supervisor. "I'm sorry I scared everyone, but I know I'm okay."

"You don't look so good, Melvin," Abby said carefully.

"He always looks that way," someone muttered behind her thinking I wouldn't hear it. Fat chance. Vampire eardrums!

"It's part of my condition," I said self-consciously. "I have a slow metabolism...and stuff."

And stuff? How lame am I?

I was, however, completely freaked that I had passed out. In front of Abby. She saw my fat. Someone kill me please.

Abby stood up and made little shooing motions with her hands. "You heard the man!" she said crisply. "Cancel the ambulance and let him be." She reached down and hoisted me up while staring at my supervisor. "He'll be going home now."

He said, "Um, there's paperwork, the incident report--"

"I'm sure you're quite capable of filling that out on your own. You are the supervisor, correct?" Her tone was sweetly firm, and I couldn't help smiling. Yes, this was my Abby.

"I guess," he said with hesitation.

Abby opened her purse and retrieved a business card. She handed it to him, and my supervisor's eyes bugged out when he read her name.

Abby said, "I see you recognize me, so there shouldn't be any problems for Mister Morton. He and I are dear old friends."

"No, no of course not, Mrs. Brokerman," my supervisor said quickly. "Melvin, take as much time as you need."

Mrs. Brokerman? She was married? Of course she was.

And then my face blanched as I recognized her name. Brokerman Associates owned the mall, the corporation wrote my paycheck. What were the odds? Huh? While I was elated at seeing Abby, I was mortified that it had to be now. But of course it did. The universe hates me.

"Very good. Now, Melvin, we'll take my limo and I'll see you home." Abby patted my arm and I could feel the jealous eyes of the mall staff burning holes in my back as we walked away. Even Pizza Bob was stunned into silence; it didn't last long, though.

"Is this that friend you talk about sometimes?"

"I've never told you about her," I muttered.

"What was that?" Abby asked.

"Nothing. I was talking to myself," I said a little too quickly.

Pizza Bob nodded at me. "Yes you do. Every time you fall asleep--"

"I do not!"

"What?" Abby asked.

"I wasn't talking to you." I smiled nervously.

"Are you sure you didn't hit your head?" she asked me with a concerned look on her face.

"No, I mean yes. No I didn't hit my head."

Pizza Bob was walking backwards in front of me with an amused smile. "You do talk about her."

"I don't even dream so how could I talk about her?"

"You talk in your sleep. And you snore, too. You talk about her constantly." He fluttered his eyelids and faked a swoon. In a high pitched, girlie voice he said, "Ooooh, Abby. I love you. Aaaaabbbbyyy."

"You're an ass. I do not."

"Do too. Wow, she's rich, dude. But I thought she'd be as ugly as you."

"She was," I said with an eye roll.

Abby looked at me sideways.

"Hi," I said to her like an idiot.

"Um, hello," she said back nervously.

"I'm just talking to myself."

"I see that."

Great. Not only was she married, she saw my fat and thought I was also crazy as well. Yup, this was hell.

The limo was double parked in front of the mall doors, and the chauffeur hesitated when he saw me. Abby cleared her throat and he snapped to attention.

"Giles, this is my dear friend Melvin Morton. We'll be taking him home."

"Very good, ma'am." He opened the door and helped Abby into the yacht on wheels.

"I live downtown off of SW Jefferson and Ninth," I said awkwardly.

"I'm sure," the chauffeur answered smartly. He looked at me with disdain, wrinkling his nose when he caught a whiff of my charming scent, and then practically closed the door on me before I was all the way in the car.

Abby poured herself a cocktail, offered me one, which I declined, and then stared at me over the rim of her glass.

"Melvin, I'm worried about you. Please don't be offended, but you look awful. I wasn't quite sure it was even you when I first saw you, but I'd recognize those eyes on anyone. Such adoring eyes."

"Um, thanks," I squeaked self-consciously. She'd noticed the way I was staring at her in the mall. Great. Add creepy stalker guy to the list of things wrong with me. I wondered if she knew how much I had loved her when we were kids?

Abby was smiling at me coyly. Maybe she did, but she had too much class to say anything. Besides, if she was freaked out then she would never have come over in the first place. Right? She interrupted my mental fencing.

"Your 'condition', what is it? What's with the blue skin, the terrible smell, and the talking to yourself?"

"She's blunt. I like that in a woman," Pizza Bob said with a laugh. I glared at him and then looked out the window.

"Abby, I thought I'd never see you again."

"Oh, well, here I am," she said with a laugh. "I almost didn't recognize you back there. But how could I forget my best friend in the world? And those adoring eyes." She pursed her lips and then looked out the window to avoid my gaze. "I thought about you over the years, but I suppose I was a bad friend because I didn't try to find you.

"I had no idea you worked at my mall," she said with another embarrassed laugh.

"Surprise," I said. "I tried to find you, but it's like you disappeared."

She laughed again (I loved the sound). "In a way I did. Abby Abbinson became Abigail Priscilla Barrington, and then I got married and became Priss Brokerman. Tahdah!"

"You look good. I didn't recognize you." I groaned. "That didn't sound the way I meant it. I, you, I--"

"Mommy married a plastic surgeon after we moved to California."

"Oh, okay."

Pizza Bob laughed. "I knew those boobs were fake!"

"Shut up!" I hissed in his direction. He stuck his tongue out at me.

Abby took my hand. "Melvin, who are you talking to? What's happened to you?"

"You wouldn't believe it."

"Is it a brain tumor? My maid's cousin, or something like that, had a brain tumor. Or maybe it was sinus infection. I don't keep track really."

"It's not a brain tumor," I said quietly.

"Yeah, you need a brain to have a brain tumor," Pizza Bob said with a snort. He was sitting next to Abby with his arm draped over her shoulder, his hand hovering near her breast.

"I mean it, just shut up." I leaned forward with my fists clenched. "And get your hands off of her."

Abby looked at the seat next to her briefly and then back at me. "Oh, Melvin. You're breaking my heart."

"I'm sorry," I mumbled.

Pizza Bob leered at me. "Boo-hoo, dickhead. Just bite her and get it over with, you big pussy."

I ignored my disgusting ghost and focused on Abby.

"Is it drugs? Are you a crack head?" She gave me a little smirk, and I knew she was teasing just like when we were kids. "Internet porn?"

"Worse." I smirked back.

"Jolt cola and Pop Rocks?" She arched her eyebrows.

"Ha."

"Lead poisoning from licking your D&D figurines?"

"You got me. Who can resist licking an orc?" I gave a little eyebrow wiggle.

"God, I've missed you, Melvin." The ice clinked in her empty glass as she raised it in a mock toast.

"Me too, Abby. Me too."

Pizza Bob made a gagging sound. "You guys are making me sick. On second thought don't bite her. I don't care how hot she is; if I had to listen to this crap for an eternity I'd go insane."

"Now you know how I feel," I said smugly to him.

"Oh, Melvin, I wish I did," Abby said with feeling.

"I wasn't talking to you," I said with a weary sigh. I couldn't keep doing this, seeing Abby just made me hate my life even more because she was so perfect and I was, well, I was me.

"It was nice seeing you again." I hoped she believed me. "But I'm too messed up. It's complicated, and I wish I could tell you, but I'm embarrassed enough as it is."

"Don't be ridiculous, Melvin," she snapped. "You can tell me everything. You always could."

"Yeah, Melvin. Don't be ridiculous. I'd love to hear you try and explain it all, especially the part about me!" Pizza Bob was now sitting on Abby's lap and licking her cheek. There wasn't a damn thing I could do about it, either.

I closed my eyes and gritted my teeth. This was by far the worst night of my life, hands down. Definitely hell. Nothing ever went right for me.

"Melvin?" Abby sounded worried. "Melvin, don't shut me out."

The car stopped at a huge wrought iron gate that rolled slowly open, and then we pulled up a winding driveway towards a house that looked like a palace.

"Where are we?" I asked. "I live downtown. Where are we, Abby?"

"Home." Abby smiled sweetly at me. "Let me help you, Melvin."

"I'm beyond help," I said sadly.

"Dude, suck it up." Pizza Bob yelled. "This place is awesome. Don't ruin it for me."

"I thought you changed your mind," I said to him in the most caustic tone I could muster.

"Of course not, Melvin." Abby shook her head.

"I wasn't talking to you."

"Oh, of course."

"Abby, I'm beyond help," I said again.

"We'll see about that," she replied as the chauffeur opened the door.

"I'm uncomfortable with this, Abby. Please just take me home."

"Nope. I found you tonight for a reason, and I'm not losing you again. Suck it up, Morton. I'm going to help you."

⅄

Abby settled me in a guest room bigger than my whole apartment. In fact the bed was bigger than my kitchen. The room had its own bathroom with a sunken tub and three showerheads mounted in the wall. Intimidating.

"Melvin, you know that I adore you so don't be offended." Abby was standing in the doorway with her arms crossed. "You stink. You smell like road kill and potpourri. I think you've almost put me off strawberries and vanilla."

"Okay."

"My god, you must be sick. Not even a decent come-back." She crossed the room and opened a wardrobe filled with thick, plush robes. She handed me one.

"Take a nice soak and a shower."

"Ask her to wash your back," Pizza Bob said. I ignored him, but my fists were clenched again. "I need to see her naked, naked and soapy."

I clenched my teeth and shook my head.

"Don't be insulted, Melvin." Abby looked hurt.

"It's not you," I managed to say.

"Oh, right. Someone's talking to you again."

"Boy, no flies on that one." Pizza Bob patted her on the butt, but without substance.

"Stop it," I hissed.

Abby shrugged. "You certainly have gotten odd. We've got a lot of catching up to do. Are you hungry?"

My stomach rumbled on cue, and she smiled. "I'll have the chef prepare something. Does steak sound okay?"

"Uh, yeah. That would be great. Rare, please." All of this was too unreal; I felt like I was in some Dickens story. "Hey, Abby...uh, where's Mr. Brokerman? Are you sure it's okay to just kidnap me? Won't he mind?"

"He's in Dubai. He travels most of the year so I get to do whatever I want," she said with a faraway look on her face.

"And whoever she wants, eh?" Pizza Bob nudged me, and I dropped the robe.

"Shut up," I sounded like a broken record.

Abby smirked at me. "Right. See you in an hour. I can't wait to hear what you've been up to." She gave a little wave, and then closed the door.

"I wish you'd stop making me look crazy in front of her," I said as I picked up the robe and wandered into the bathroom.

"You don't need my help for that, nutbag. I'm gonna check out this place, it might be haunted!" Pizza Bob cackled.

"It is now," I muttered as he disappeared.

I couldn't figure out how to work the shower. Showers. There were buttons and knobs everywhere so I gave up and just soaked in the tub, using five different bars of soap because they were there -- they all smelled wonderful, fruity but in a masculine way I hoped -- then rinsed off under the faucet. It still was awesome. My personal odor was masked by the different scents, but I still smelled the rot underneath. I hoped that Abby wouldn't.

"You smell like a homo," Pizza Bob sniped.

He was back. Too bad. I was hoping that another ghost would eat him.

"That's so pleasant," I said through a grimace. "How do you know what a "homo" smells like?"

"By smelling you."

"Wow, ooh, good one. You should take your act on the road. I hear the skin-heads and klan have an open mike night."

"What's that got to do with smelling like a homo?"

I rolled my eyes. "Sarcasm. Do you need to Google that, too? And that word is not a nice word at all the way you are using it. It's hateful the way you say it, use it as a slur, try and demean gay people. I realize you're an angry ghost, but you don't have to be hateful."

"Whatever. I was just trying to be funny and you got all personal."

"Of course I had to be haunted by a prejudiced, homophobic, womaniz-ing gas bag who's smart as a doorknob. Why not? My life just wasn't miserable enough."

Pizza Bob floated there with a hurt look on his face. "I don't hate anybody but you, dickhead. You don't know anything about me. I went to college, you know." He shimmered for a moment and then disappeared.

Actually I didn't know. He went to college; I didn't. Go figure. At least I had some peace and quiet now that he left in a quite a huff. I think I actually hurt his feelings! Oh well.

Maybe he was gone for good; I should be so lucky. He was probably just pouting and planning something humiliating for me as revenge.

My clothes were gone when I came out of the bathroom. At first I thought Pizza Bob took them, but there was a note from the maid. I had an instant panic attack at the thought of someone going through the pockets and finding all of the car air fresheners, but there was nothing I could do about it now. The note said I would have fresh clothes in the morning. I wrapped up in the robe and made my way down the long hallway until I found the stairs. This place was huge, and I wondered if Pizza Bob had found any other ghosts. That's just what I needed. As it was, this house, mansion, villa was huge and strangely devoid of warmth. I was surprised that Abby could be comfortable here, but people can change over the years. Outwardly she certainly had! I passed by portraits and framed photographs of an older man in various locations around the globe; he looked important. I paused in front of one photograph where he was shaking the hand of George Bush Sr. Wow. A bigwig. There was another photo of the man with some sort of sheik.

Was this the mysterious Mr. Brokerman? Abby said he was in Dubai. She also didn't seem too disappointed that he wasn't around.

Don't go there, Morton.

I looked around at the opulence of this place and my stomach rumbled from a mixture of raw nerves and plain old hunger.

I smelled the blood from the steak, the scent making my mouth water and gums tingle, and followed my nose into a small dining room. Abby was there waiting for me with a smile.

"Hooray! You win the prize," she said with a grin. "You've navigated the maze."

"This place is impressive."

"You should see my house in Italy. But I like this one better. I'm here more."

"Is it haunted?"

"No," Pizza Bob and Abby answered in unison.

"I wouldn't be too sure about that." I glared at Pizza Bob who had decided to reappear next to the table.

"You've gotten even weirder over the years, Melvin." Abby pointed to a chair at the table, and I sat down.

"You look all nice and comfy in the robe," she said. "Your clothes were vile so I had the maid throw them out."

"What am I supposed to wear? That was my only uniform, Abby."

"I'll find you a better position than security guard. No more uniforms for you. And you're the same size as my husband, he's got clothes you can wear."

Wow, she liked fat guys. Rich fat guys that were alive and didn't smell like road kill.

Again, don't go there, Melvin. She just feels sorry for you.

"Abby, I don't need your charity. I have clothes at home, which is where I should be." I actually didn't want to go back to my roach-infested squalor, but it was the principle of the thing. "I like my job, I like the hours."

It was a half-truth.

"Oh, don't be like that. I haven't seen you in forever so just let me spoil you for a bit."

I looked at her, all beautiful and rich, happy to see me, and I decided to get over myself. It wasn't charity. And I did hate my job.

"Friends?" she asked.

"Forever, Abby. Forever."

The smell of the steak was driving me crazy, but I didn't want to be rude and just attack my plate. Oh, but it looked and smelled so good! Steak isn't an accurate description of what had been prepared: cow, a side of beef fit better. The slab of meat on my plate was huge and dripping blood. Abby saw me practically drooling and laughed. I loved the sound.

"Dig in, Melvin!"

I noticed she had a place set as well with a steak as big as mine for herself. Impressive. I finished in record time, ignoring the side dishes that could feed a small army in of themselves, then tipped the plate to drink the pooled juices; all that delicious blood. I didn't realize that Abby was watching with complete fascination.

"That's classy," Pizza Bob said in my ear and I jumped, the plate clanging on the table like a gong. "You look like a dog, Melvin. Way to impress the girl."

"Wow, you were hungry. No one can accuse you of being a vegetarian," Abby said with a laugh.

"I'm sorry. I must look like some barbarian." I wiped at my mouth with embarrassed stabs of the linen napkin. Pizza Bob was sitting next to me with a sour look on his face; I must have really hurt his feelings earlier. He flipped me the bird and I laughed. Abby laughed too, and I was amazed that most of her steak was now gone, too.

"Don't be ridiculous, barbarians rule," said Abby as she picked up her steak bone and gnawed on the end.

"Do you eat like this all the time?" I asked, staring at her trim figure.

"Sure. That's what liposuction is for!" We both laughed, but I hoped she was kidding about the fat sucking part.

"Melvin, I meant what I said earlier."

"Yes, I have gotten weirder, Abby."

"Not that, silly. I have missed you."

"Ah, so cute and squishy. I'm tearing up here," Pizza Bob said with a girlie squeal. It was difficult, but I ignored him.

"You've done well for yourself, Abby. Or should I call you Priss?" I asked.

"No, Abby is good."

"Do you have any kids?"

"Are you kidding? You know what I really look like under all of the plastic surgery. You think I want to pass that on?"

"You weren't that bad!" I laughed. "I think you'd make a great mom."

"I'm far too selfish, and I like being spoiled and rich. Besides, this body cost too much money to be defiled by stretch marks."

Abby pulled a beat up photo album off of one of the chairs and came over to my side of the table. She opened it, and I was shocked to see that it was actually a scrapbook. She'd saved all of our notes, cards, drawings and photographs from when we were kids together.

Abby had an adorable, crooked grin on her face. "See? I told you I'd never forget you. You were, are, the best friend I ever had." She reached out and held my hand.

Pizza Bob leaned in and then gasped at a photo of Abby at age ten. "Gah! Holy crap, she's a circus freak!" He looked at Abby, then down at her photo, then back again at the transformed woman standing beside me. "That's it, she's ruined for me."

"I always thought you were beautiful, Abby," I whispered.

"Thank you, Melvin," she said with a little hand squeeze. "But you were the only one. When mommy married the surgeon, he couldn't wait to get me under the knife. No one else has ever seen this scrap book; not even my husband." She snorted.

"I like to pull it out and sneak a peek every once in a while so I stay grounded. I went from Quasimodo to a beauty queen, but kept the inner snark alive.

"Really, I was a beauty queen: Miss Teen California." She smiled radiantly and I could just picture her walking down the runway while mentally mocking the other contestants.

"Anyway," she said with a dismissive wave. "I sailed through college on step-daddy's money, got a masters in business, met the persistent Mr. Brokerman, and then settled into a life of luxury. I suppose I'm happy enough. I get to do what I want, when I want. Daniel, my husband, is rarely around anymore because of his work duties, but that's all right. That's fine. Quite fine indeed."

Okay, the husband was hardly around. Yay for me, right? Yeah, right.

"I still think you'd make a great mom," I said quietly.

"That's what charity work is for," she said, snapping the book closed.

Was I charity work? I looked down at our entwined hands and rode a wave of self-pity.

"Enough about me," she said as she gave my hand a little reassuring squeeze. "What about you? Are you married? Girlfriend?"

"You're joking, right? Look at me, I'm no prize," I said, hoping she'd negate that and say I was perfect. But no.

"You can say that again," Pizza Bob mumbled.

Abby let go of my hand. "What happened to you?"

I wanted to tell her, I really, really did. But how would she react? I put my elbow on the table and cradled my chin in the palm of my hand. I caught a whiff of my armpit, a little gamey with a side of putrid, and sighed.

As if reading my mind Pizza Bob said, "Just tell her, dork. What's the worst that could happen?"

Sometimes he acted like he cared. That made me uncomfortable. Rude and derisive I could handle, a nice Pizza Bob usually meant he was up to something. But in this case he was probably on the mark. What was the worst that could happen? Hysterical screaming and a stake through the heart?

"You're right," I mumbled.

"What was that?" Abby asked.

"I said all right."

"All right what?"

"All right I'll tell you my pathetic story." Here went nothing. "Well, after you left I never made any friends -- that's not a guilt trip at all. Everyone else was just so stupid and boring after you. I muddled my way through high school, had great grades but no money for college. My parents died in a car wreck when

I was a senior, so I was left on my own. No money, nothing. Not even any close relatives to help me out."

"Oh, Melvin. I'm so sorry."

"It was a long time ago, Abby. My parents were older, weren't very touchy-feely or affectionate, but it was sad when they died. I tried to get myself together, though. I tried scholarships and grants for college, but something always went wrong. I worked a bunch of different jobs, and then settled in at the mall as a night security guard.

"My life was nice and boring until about six months ago," I said with a sad smile.

"Is that when you got sick?"

"You could say that," I muttered.

"Melvin, my money is at your disposal. We'll find the best doctors and get you all better. The finest care that money can buy."

"I don't think what I have has a cure--"

Abby grabbed my hand again. "What have the doctors said? Is it cancer? Tumors? A rare disease? My stable hand's mother had some form of cancer, I don't know what kind, but she seemed to recover all right. I bought her a nice wig to replace all the hair that fell out from her treatment.

"And then one of the women on the library committee got bitten by a bug of some kind, nasty little thing, both her and the bug." She laughed. "Anyway, she saw a specialist up at OHSU and they fixed her up right as rain. Of course the swelling in her face never really went down so I suggested a variety of low brimmed hats."

"Is she for real?" Pizza Bob looked at her while twirling his finger by his temple.

"Hush," I whispered at him, but of course Abby thought I meant her.

"Oh, god, I'm sorry Melvin. I just prattle on sometimes. What did the doctors tell you?"

"Uh, well..."

"You haven't seen a doctor? Why not! That's absurd and irresponsible of you. I'll just make a few calls in the morning and we'll get you right in with an internist."

"Abby, I really don't think this is something for doctors. I've made my peace with it, mostly, and I'll be fine with whatever happens."

She looked stricken. "Is it AIDS?"

"I told you that you smelled like a homo," Pizza Bob said.

"You just don't get how much of a prejudiced sounding ass you are? Do you? Stop being mean!" I shouted at him, but again Abby thought I was talking to her.

"No, Melvin, no. I didn't mean--"

"Abby," I said while trying to calm myself down, "I wasn't talking to...oh, never mind."

"You're a little touchy about that, aren't ya, Princess," Pizza Bob said dramatically.

"You just don't get it. Apparently death does not bring enlightenment." To Abby I said, "It's not AIDS."

Tears welled up in Abby's eyes. "Oh, Melvin. It's cancer then, isn't it."

"No. I kind of got bitten by something, too."

"Really? Well I'll ring the specialist at OHSU and get you in immediately."

"Abby, it wasn't a bug."

"Well...what was it? I'll take care of you, so don't worry. Just tell me what it was so I can get you in to see the right person. They have cures for lots of things now."

I leaned back in my chair and stared at her. Maybe she wouldn't freak out.

"I don't think there's a cure for what bit me, Abby."

"Quit being so cryptic, Melvin. Just tell me what bit you."

"Ooh, this is gonna be good." Pizza Bob was sitting on top of the table next to her with a lopsided grin on his face. He did a drum roll on the tabletop with his fingers, and then pointed at me.

I said, "It was a vampire."

She laughed and slapped me on the arm. I just sat staring at her, and then she stepped back with a slight grin on her face that faded into a frown.

"Oh, you're serious."

"Yes, Abby. It's the truth." I watched her watching me for a moment, and then I couldn't take it anymore. "I guess I'll be going now."

She put her hand up, index finger raised, and I froze.

"Well...hmmm. You didn't have a heart beat...you smell weird." She chewed her lip and I braced myself for whatever she was going to say next.

Pizza Bob had his hand cupped over his ear and said, "Survey says?"

Then Abby made me love her even more.

"I suppose that's easier than cancer. How's it working out?"

Pizza Bob's mouth fell open and he shook his head. I smiled.

Yup, that's my Abby.

"Not so well." I laughed and told her my sad tale of woe.

"You poor, poor, dear sweet Melvin!" Abby hugged me despite my odor, which was rising again. "How scared you must have been."

"I managed."

"So you really haven't bitten anyone yet?" she asked.

"Well, I tried, but it didn't go so well. Not ever. The last time I tried, he freaked out and hit his head on my coffee table; he died on his own."

"Hey!" Pizza Bob hit me on the head.

"You did!" I yelled.

"You didn't have to tell her that," he said angrily.

"It's the truth, moron. I don't know why you're sticking around and bothering me. It was your own damn fault!"

Abby tapped me on the shoulder. "Melvin, is that who you keep talking to?"

"Yes." I crossed my arms. "It's a pizza delivery guy. I've tried to get rid of him, but he's intent on making my life hell."

"He's here now?" Abby looked around the room.

"Of course. He's standing right beside you."

She gave a startled yelp and jumped sideways. "Sorry. Sorry. That caught me off guard."

Pizza Bob laughed and looked at her like she was crazy. "She doesn't flip out that you're a vampire, but goes ass crackers at the thought of a ghost."

"Leave her alone." I stood up and took a step towards him.

"You're not the boss of me. I'll do what I want." The smell of ozone crackled in the air, and Pizza Bob pinched Abby on the butt.

"Ow!" she yelled and then spun around angrily. "Now you listen here! That was crass and vulgar; no one touches a lady like that. You must be a horrible person. Or were a terrible person in life, or however this ghost thing works to make you be here!"

Pizza Bob floated back behind a chair. He looked startled.

"I'm sorry, Abby. He can be a pig. Did he hurt you?" I was mortified.

"Of course not," she snapped. "And he'd best not do that again."

"Dude. She's got spunk," Pizza Bob gave a thumbs-up.

"Shut up!" I yelled at him. Pizza Bob put his hands up and smiled.

"What's he look like?" she asked.

"He's kind of tall, preppy-like," my ghost scowled and I glared back, "he's stuck in khaki shorts and a loud Hawaiian shirt. I think he looks a bit like Owen Wilson."

"Oh, hey...thanks, dude," Pizza Bob said with a grin.

"He even sounds like him sometimes." I looked at the ghost. "Did you ever see the movie Bottle Rocket?" I asked him.

"I liked that one," he offered with a grin. "But I have a better nose."

"Yeah, I guess you do." It was so easy for me to slip back into that comfortable chatter even when I was angry with him.

Abby squinted her eyes, looking for the ghost, and then turned towards me with a knowing smirk. "Whatever. Melvin, my neighbor's housekeeper is from Jamaica."

"Okay."

"Jamaica...voodoo...spirit work?" she said in exasperation. "We'll go see her tomorrow and get her to do something about your ghost problem."

"Oh, hey, wait a minute," Pizza Bob stammered. "Let's not do anything rash. Tell her I'm sorry. I'll be good."

"You think she can do something?" I whispered.

Abby smiled confidently. "Well, she is from Jamaica."

Pizza Bob was hovering in front of me. "Tell her I'm sorry, dude. Seriously. That hocus-pocus-voodoo-crap scares the hell out me!"

I ignored him.

"I'll be good, Melvin. Tell her I'm sorry." My ghost was shimmering in and out of focus. I felt sorry for him; his particular situation was kind of my fault. I did try to eat him, after all.

"He says he's sorry," I mumbled.

Abby arched her eyebrows. "He should be."

"Well, he seems to be."

"Oh, I am." Pizza Bob gave a thumbs-up that lacked sincerity.

If Abby knew someone that could help him pass on, then I was all for it. Definitely. Boy, she was taking this all too well; no doubts or screams. Maybe she was just in shock.

"Abby, are you sure you're okay with all of this? Aren't you afraid of me, afraid I'll bite you or something?"

"Of course you won't, Melvin. I said I was going to help you and I will. You're my best friend, and you're going to be the best vampire that ever was."

Now I was shocked. She really was taking this too well.

"So," she blurted out in an excited rush of breath. "Do I need to get you a coffin or something? How can I make you more comfortable? Do I need to cover the crucifix in the main room? I have so many questions!"

I laughed. "Abby, I sleep in a real bed. Crosses and holy water are all Hollywood."

"Oh." She sounded a little disappointed. "Show me your fangs."

Pizza Bob snorted and I glared at him. "I'm being good," he said.

"Abby...." I hesitated. "I, uh, I don't have fangs."

"Oh."

"I'm not a very good vampire so far. But I do crave blood," I offered.

"Well, that's something at least." She patted my arm. "We'll get you all fixed up. This is going to be fun. I'm going to help make you into a great vampire; delightfully evil."

"This is going to end badly, Melvin," Pizza Bob said with a smile.

Oh boy.

"What about sunlight? Is that why you work nights? Why are you blue? Can you turn into a bat? Did the garlic on the steak hurt you?" She peppered me with questions until the sun came up and I simply fell asleep.

CHAPTER 6:

I Love That Hoodoo That You Do So Well

"Just let me do the talking, Melvin." Abby knocked on her neighbor's door. "Is the ghost with you?"

"No, he's hiding somewhere," I said quietly just as the door opened and an older black woman wearing a cream-colored business suit greeted us.

"Good day, Mrs. Brokerman. I'm afraid Miss Kelso is not in residence," she said while eyeing me. I was fidgeting uncomfortably, wearing one of Mr. Brokerman's expensive suits, and self-conscious about my odor. No air fresheners in my pockets.

"That's all right, Antoinette. I'm actually here to see you," Abby said as she brushed by the woman, pulling me into the foyer behind her.

"I see," said Antoinette. She didn't have an accent, and she wasn't dressed like a maid. Curious. She didn't even seem that scary for a voodoo priestess.

"Would you care for some tea?" she asked.

"Oh, that would be lovely. Thank you." Abby beamed at her.

Antoinette settled us in a parlor, and then brought in a tray filled with cookies and a pot of tea. She poured us our tea and sat down.

"How can I be of service, Mrs. Brokerman?"

"This is Melvin Morton, a dear old friend of mine, and he's having some problems that I believe are in your area of expertise."

"I see." The woman appraised me, wrinkling her nose ever so slightly at my aroma, and then took a sip of tea. It made me nervous. I wondered if she knew what I was?

Antoinette set her cup down on the saucer, and cleared her throat delicately. "Do you need help with your house-keeping staff, Mr. Morton. I could supply you with some wonderful references if you'd like. I'm afraid I'm quite busy here as head of Miss Kelso's domestics to take up another position."

"Uh, no, uh...." I looked at Abby for help.

"Antoinette, I suppose you could say he needs to clean house." Abby laughed. "Is this some kind of code? I've never talked to someone like you before about this sort of thing."

Antoinette folded her hands and said through pursed lips, "Someone like me? I'm afraid I don't understand what you mean."

Little alarm bells were going off in my head.

"You don't? Oh. Well let's try again," Abby said. "Melvin is having problems with a rather nasty ghost. I'd like to retain your services to remove the problem."

"Pardon me?"

"Voodoo, of course."

"Is this some kind of joke, Mrs. Brokerman?"

"No, of course not. You are from Jamaica, and I thought everyone from Jamaica knows voodoo."

Antoinette put her hand over her mouth and stifled a laugh. After a pregnant pause she said, "I'm from Jamaica Plain."

"And?" Abby asked.

"Massachusetts," Antoinette said with a full laugh.

"Go Red Sox," I offered as I grabbed Abby's hand and pulled her up from the couch. "Thank you for the tea, Antoinette, and I'm sorry we bothered you."

Abby smoothed the wrinkles in her skirt and looked around the room in embarrassment. "Well, that was awkward. I was so sure you could help us. I'd appreciate it if you kept this conversation just between us; no need for Miss Kelso to know."

"Of course, Mrs. Brokerman." Antoinette hesitated, looking at me briefly. "I may not be able to help you, but I might know someone who can."

"Really?" Abby said a little too eagerly.

"Try the Peterson's cook, she is from Haiti. I overheard Miss Kelso and Mrs. Peterson discussing it."

"Thank you, Antoinette. We appreciate this," Abby shook her hand, there was an awkward moment of silence, and then we left.

As soon as we were out the door, Abby burst out laughing. "Did you see the look on her face? My god that was embarrassing."

"She's watching us through the curtain," I said with a chuckle.

"At least she wasn't offended once I told her what I wanted."

"And she pointed us in the right direction. Let's just hope the cook isn't from Haiti, Pennsylvania." Both of us started laughing harder. I looked over my shoulder and saw Antoinette wrinkling her nose. "She's still watching."

Abby gave a little wave at the window where Antoinette was discreetly observing us, and the curtain closed quickly.

"I hope she doesn't tell anyone, Abby."

"So what if she does? Everyone in this town, everyone with more money than they can count has some eccentricity. I could tell you stories that would make your head spin."

"What did I miss?" Pizza Bob asked from behind a porch column.

"Wrong Jamaica." I said, laughing again.

"Good."

"Don't get comfortable." I smirked as we walked down the sidewalk.

"I take it he's back," Abby said with a scowl. But I felt bad for the stupid ghost. I did.

"Yes, but cut him some slack, Abby. He's had a rough time of it." I took Abby's hand and led her towards her front gate. Pizza Bob floated beside me.

"Thanks, dude."

"Shut up."

"Okay."

Abby pointed at the Peterson home. "It's almost dinner time, so we'll pop in later and see the cook."

"Why are you going to see the cook?" Pizza Bob asked.

"You don't want to know," I said quickly.

"Aw, crap." He looked over at the Peterson house and shivered.

"Can't you just ignore him, Melvin?" Abby was squinting her eyes and trying to see Pizza Bob again. After a few seconds she just gave up.

I said, "He won't let me, Abby."

"Hmpf." Abby started walking away and I couldn't tell if she was annoyed with me or with Pizza Bob. I glared at him.

"Thanks a lot, you jerk. I've been trying to make everything up to you, I've humored you, and I gave you that cool Viking funeral. All you do is make me miserable in return."

"You started it by killing me."

I gave a little frustrated growl. "Don't start that again. Take a little responsibility! I admit that I tried to eat you, but you are the one with the clumsy feet and a thin skull." I was angry and my gums were tingling. No longer feeling any pity, at that moment I think I could have bitten him, and done it right this time. "Sometimes you make me wish I had killed you."

"You did."

"I did not!" I clenched my fists. "You did, you floating bag of retard."

"A technicality," he said dismissively. "And that's not a nice word to use."

"Really? You're coaching me on what's politically correct now? I know it's not a nice word, that's why I said it! GAH! I finally catch a break and find my friend, and all you can do is be an asshole. Why can't you be nice to her? Huh?" I stuck my hands in my pockets and started shuffling down the road.

"Hey, I like the suit," Pizza Bob said trying to be chummy.

"Really?"

"No." He laughed and floated behind Abby making pinching gestures at her butt as she walked up the driveway.

I looked back at the Peterson house and grinned, an evil smile that made my face feel tight. I hoped that whatever the cook was going to do to Pizza Bob would hurt. He'd earned it. Maybe this was the first step in me becoming a monster.

Abby was on the phone when I found her in the parlor.

"Thank you, Margaret. I appreciate it." She hung up the phone and gave me a happy little nod. "That was Margaret Peterson. I told her I needed to borrow her cook for a special Caribbean dinner I was planning. Clever of me, eh?"

"When do we meet her?" I looked at Pizza Bob with a cold smile on my face, and he could tell I was planning something awful.

"She'll be here in an hour." Abby said smugly, following my gaze to the corner where Pizza Bob was hovering behind a potted fern. "I wish I could see him, damn it."

"He's hiding behind the fern."

"He's like a cockroach," she muttered angrily.

"He's like a cockroach," Pizza Bob mimicked.

Abby glared at the plant and then shrugged. I was glad that she couldn't hear him.

She patted my arm. "Melvin, I had Giles swing by the butcher and get you some pig livers. You said that's what you like. However, I don't think I can watch you eat them so I'll be in the library; I've got some research to do. Your meal is plated and waiting for you in the small dining room. Bon appetite."

Just like that, Abby's focus was elsewhere and she left the room without even looking back at me.

"Melvin?" Pizza Bob peeked from behind the plant. "Dude, don't do anything rash."

"I'm ignoring you," I said as I walked to the dining room and sat down. There was a feast waiting for me. I felt regal as I took a bite of a pig liver with a silver fork off of a china plate.

"Melvin, I'm scared. Okay?"

I kept chewing and tried to ignore him.

"I've seen too many movies about this voodoo stuff. I don't want to be blasted into nothingness, man. Seriously."

I wiped my mouth on a napkin and looked at him. "You've brought this on yourself, you know."

"No I didn't! I'm the victim here."

"Enough! Why did you stick around? Why didn't you just move on through the light or whatever happens when people die?"

Pizza Bob sat in a chair and nervously picked at a loose thread on his ghost pants. He shrugged his shoulders and mumbled something.

"What?" I asked.

"I said there wasn't any light. There wasn't anything. I just woke up next to my body."

"Oh."

"I tried to leave, I really did. But I was just so mad at you that is was easier to stay, you know?"

"I guess." I was losing my appetite from Pizza Bob's apparent misery. That monster feeling was slipping away, too. I'd never be any good at the evil stuff.

Pizza Bob began picking at his shoe. "I'm still pissed that I'm dead, but I don't have anywhere else to go. I've kind of gotten used to you." He offered a smile that I didn't reciprocate. "You're just so pathetic, dude. I kinda feel sorry for you."

"You have a funny way of showing it, jerk." I pushed the plate away and stood up.

"Yeah, well, I'm sorry." He floated over to me. "Please don't send me away. I'll be good."

My vampire ears picked out the sound of the front door opening and Abby greeting someone warmly; the cook was here.

"It's out of my hands, sorry."

A gasp from behind me made me whirl around quickly. Abby was standing there with the Peterson's cook, a young girl about twenty years old with skin the most beautiful shade of coffee brown, and her hand covering her mouth; the source of the gasp. I was instantly embarrassed, mortified, completely sure that my blue skin and rotting odor had given me away, but her eyes were wide and alert as she stared at Pizza Bob, who was trying to hide behind another potted plant; a big Ficus. He was too freaked out to even disappear.

Holy crap. She could see him. It wasn't me after all.

"Marcella, this is my friend Melvin Morton." Abby walked over and took my hand. "I'm afraid I told a bit of a fib to Mrs. Peterson."

"Yes, ma'am," Marcella whispered.

"I'm not really throwing a Caribbean flavored dinner party. I need your particular expertise on a dire matter for Melvin."

Marcella hadn't even looked at me yet; she was staring intently at Pizza Bob who was now looking at me with pure terror on his face.

"Dude, she can see me," he shouted. Marcella just nodded at him and, well, so did I.

"And just what is my particular area of expertise you are wanting, Miss Priss?" The girl was fixated on Pizza Bob. I was fixated on her, relieved not to be the focus for once, lulled by the accent, so musical and lilting; I could listen to her talk all night. Plus Marcella was beautiful. Pizza Bob just looked terrified. Abby was blissfully ignorant of the whole exchange.

"Well, um, without trying to stereotype I assume you know voodoo?" Abby patted Marcella's arm, but the woman seemed annoyed.

"And?" Marcella demanded. "Miss Priss?"

Miss Priss? Then I remembered Abby's other name. It sounded so out of place, but still kind of sexy coming out of the Haitian woman's mouth.

Abby paused for a second, and then just plunged right in. "And, Melvin has a problem with a ghost that won't go away. I'll pay you whatever this sort of thing is worth."

"I can't take your money, Miss Priss." Marcella finally turned and looked at me. "I can't help that one, ugly he-she brought this on hisself."

Pizza Bob pointed at me. "See! Even she says it's your fault."

"Hey, that's not right," I pouted. "He-she?"

"Why won't you help him?" Abby asked, her voice childlike and hurt.

"I don't traffic with Loogaroo." Marcella wrinkled her nose and spit on the floor at my feet. "Loogaroo always an old woman...how you got dis ting inside you...I don' want to know, but you a bad ting!"

I was stunned. Pizza Bob was laughing. Of course he was. The "he-she" pushed all of his snark buttons.

"Hey! I'm a guy," I snapped.

"You nothing."

Again I was stunned into silence.

But Abby got angry.

"What the hell does that mean?" she demanded.

Marcella pointed at me. "Loogaroo, Miss Priss. You got to put him out, he drink you dry!" She sneered at me. "Vampire."

Now that was just rude.

Abby bristled. "No he will not! Melvin is a dear friend and he's having trouble right now. How dare you insult him like that!"

"I call it like I see it, ma'am. There's some ting wrong with him, all right. Walking dead, half-living Loogaroo." Marcella spit on the floor again. "The stink of him."

"You got that right!" Pizza Bob said gleefully from beside me. He wasn't afraid anymore. Yay for him.

Abby crossed her arms. "That's enough spitting, Marcella. If you won't help Melvin, then do it for me. That ghost pinched me."

"The dead are jealous of the living, Miss Priss. As long as your pet Loogaroo stays in dis here world, the spirit man will go nowhere."

"That's just great," I moaned. "Hey! Wait a minute, I'm not a pet."

"Righteous!" Pizza Bob said with a fist pump.

Marcella just shook her head sadly. "Nothing to be joyous about, spirit man."

"She called me a pet." I whined. Another crack in that old fragile self esteem.

Abby asked Marcella, "You can see him? You see the ghost?"

"Of course I can, Miss Priss."

"I'm not a pet. Do I act like a pet? I could be dangerous, eventually, when I work myself up to it." Everyone was ignoring me, focused instead on Marcella and her righteousness.

"Isn't there anything you can do?" Abby sounded desperate.

"Of course there is, but like I said...I don' traffic with Loogaroo." Marcella started to spit again but Abby poked her in the arm.

"No more spitting, Marcella."

The woman took an envelope out of her purse and spilled some powder onto her palm. Marcella turned to me and blew the powder in my face. I coughed and sputtered; it was like pepper spray and lemon juice in my eyes and nose.

"You forget you smelled me, vampire. Miss Priss want to make herself a meal, that her choice. You'll not come after me."

"I'd. Never. Do. That," I sputtered as I frantically wiped at my watering eyes and runny nose.

"Your spirit man shows me otherwise."

"Ha! She's on my side," Pizza Bob gloated.

"I'm not on your side at all. You're a nasty, hungry spirit. Petty and vindictive. Your death was your own doing, by your own hand even," said the beautiful girl that was a little scary now.

"Ha on you, dickhead," I snapped at Pizza Bob, who was now glowering at Marcella.

"But it is tainted by him." She pointed at me. Damn! "Best for everyone if you could move on, spirit, but you won't, can't."

"I like it fine right where I am." Pizza Bob nudged my arm.

"You want dat ghost gone, only one ting to do, Loogaroo."

"What can he do?" Abby was excited again.

"I don't care for that word," I said hotly. "It sounds nasty. My name is Melvin."

And I don't like your accent anymore, so there.

Marcella laughed at me. "Your name is as dead as you should be." Ouch. "Leave this world."

She meant die. Expire. Melvin has left the building.

"I don't think I can, it just might make this worse," I said with a little too much bitterness.

"Oh you can, and should. The sooner the better."

Maybe she was right.

Abby grabbed Marcella's arm and marched her to the front door, Pizza Bob and I trailing behind. "That's not going to happen. So, off you go, Marcella. Thanks for stopping by. I'd appreciate if you didn't mention this to anyone."

"Everyone who comes near you is in danger, Miss Priss. I can't stay quiet."

My shoulders sagged a bit as I said, "Maybe I should--"

"Shut up, Melvin," Pizza Bob and Abby said in unison.

Abby put on her scary, business, just scary Abby face. "Let me put it this way, Marcella. One word about any of this and I call immigration."

Marcella laughed at her. "I'm a citizen, Miss Priss."

"Very well. Then I'll get you fired and blackballed in this town, this state, this country...anywhere you try and work. No one will hire you when I'm through."

Marcella's eyes widened. "You are threatening me?"

"Well of course I am, dear. I'm rich and well connected. I doubt just voodoo pays well, and you need to eat. Everyone needs to eat." She grinned wickedly at me, and it was scary.

Abby was fuming and I was afraid she was going to have a stroke; I heard her heart beating too fast, the blood rushing in her ears.

Marcella glared at Abby. "You be a brave but stupid woman. I don't take threats idly, Miss Priss."

"Neither do I, Marcella. Melvin is my friend, my best friend in the world. I just found him again and there's no way in hell I'll abandon him now. Melvin didn't ask for this to happen, to become a vampire, and he's a good man. I'd do anything to keep him safe and happy."

"You say dat now, Miss Priss. But he'll turn on you."

"No I won't!" I shouted.

"No he won't!" Pizza Bob said at the same time. I looked over at him kind of shocked.

"Look," he said, "you're and absolute douche sometimes, but you're not a bad guy." Pizza Bob held out his fist for a bump. I went with it.

"I guess, ditto. When you behave, that is." I smiled.

Marcella watched this with a wary eye. "I'll pray for you, Miss Priss. Loyalty to a friend is admirable, but in dis case dangerous." She eyed me again. "You remember what I told you, don't you come for me or I'll do something bad, worse than what you are, Loogaroo."

"I wouldn't bite you if you were the last person on earth," I said rather contemptuously. This garnered another withering stare that made me flinch. Damn she was scary!

Marcella looked away to Abby. "You truly don't know how bad it is dis ting you do, Miss Priss. You're secret is safe for now, but don't come to me for help later when tings goes bad. You've made your choice." She walked out the door without looking back.

"What a horrible woman," said Abby as she slammed the door. "Melvin, you should go and eat her tonight."

"Un-uh, no way. She scares the crap out of me. Imagine being haunted by that."

We all stood there in silence for a beat and then burst out laughing.

Abby sobered and then patted my hand. "I'm sorry she couldn't help us, Melvin."

"That's okay. I think Pizza Bob and I have come to an understanding."

Abby arched her eyebrows at me, and Pizza Bob floated over to her side.

"Tell her I'm sorry," he said.

"He says he's sorry."

"I don't believe him." She crossed her arms defiantly and glared at an empty space thinking he was floating there. I almost laughed but decided that wouldn't be a good idea. Abby really looked angry.

"We need some ground rules," I said to Pizza Bob. "No more pinching."

"Deal." He nodded.

Abby said, "And stop pestering Melvin."

I made eye contact with Pizza Bob who just looked blankly back at me. And then we both started laughing again. Yeah right, that was like telling a herring to go bowling. Wasn't going to happen.

Abby was less than amused.

CHAPTER 7

MONKEY SEE MONKEY DO

I awoke to rain pattering against my window, the sound delicate and muffled by the heavy velvet curtains Abby had put up for me. I looked over at the clock and saw it was 3:30, two hours until sunset. I let the drip-drop of the rain soothe me for a while until my stomach rumbled uncomfortably. I sighed and forced myself to get up from the bed that cradled and cushioned my body like a cloud. This was the good life. Abby's life. Mine by proxy.

I was wearing silk pajamas. Yes, I said silk pajamas. Heaven. I smiled as I pulled on one of the cushy robes from the wardrobe then made my way down to the kitchen.

The house was unusually quiet today; no staff hovering, or even my ghost to greet me. Pizza Bob had been distracted of late. He'd been fascinated by one of the maids, Emily, following her everywhere, occasionally flipping up her skirt Marilyn Monroe style when he had the energy. I warned him that she was getting terrified and was bound to quit soon. The poor woman was afraid to tell Abby about the incidents for fear of looking crazy, but everyone had a limit. What's worse the girl was terrified of me also, scared to be alone in the same room.

Yesterday I'd had enough and smiled at her, maybe a bit too aggressively. I said, "Don't worry...I don't bite."

Her eyes were as big as saucers as she backed out of the dining room quickly. I just don't know what came over me. I was going to have to apologize I guess. I was trying to be nice; kind of.

The rest of the staff are keeping their distance, all except for cunning Giles who glares at me at every chance. What's his deal? Even Abby is a little distant, distracted. She spends most of her time locked up in the library, studying and reading about vampires I suppose.

I got to the kitchen and startled the cook; the woman let out a little scream when I tapped her on the shoulder that made me yelp back at her in response.

"Mr. Morton, I, I, I apologize," she said while trying to catch her breath.

I smiled, closed lipped, and nodded at her. It's not like I'd done anything to warrant this treatment. Abby told the workers that I was recovering from a rare illness that had almost killed me. I don't think they bought it. Everyone put their hands reflexively on their throats when I was near, and I noticed an increase in religious-themed jewelry on the staff: crucifixes were the most popular.

I had been nothing but nice, polite, effusive in my gratitude. I wasn't sleeping in a coffin, and I hadn't bitten anyone. So I was mostly dead; it's not like I advertised that fact. I knew the cook suspected something about me, though. There'd been some "extra" garlic in all of Abby's food lately. Some has even found its way into my stash of pig livers. All garlic does is give me smelly burps. That's all -- no howling agony of vampire myth, just vile indigestion and aromatic discharge. That combined with my already gamey aroma just made me more self-conscious.

Abby was at risk of a mutiny in her house staff. All because of me. I hoped this wouldn't turn into a bad horror movie with an angry mob bearing torches, pitchforks or kitchen implements, and wooden stakes, the intent to kill the vampire and save brave Mrs. Brokerman from my despicable hold. I worried that they might turn on her, too.

Of course I was just being melodramatic; I hoped that's what it was.

"I came down for a snack," I said without realizing how it sounded. Of course the cook gasped. I just shook my head and opened the refrigerator.

"Thanks." I held up a carton of pig livers and hoped the cook was embarrassed.

"Mr. Morton...." She was pointing at the refrigerator. "Mrs. Brokerman prepared a health shake for you."

I arched my eyebrows and peeked back in the fridge. There was a thermos with my name stenciled on it. Abby had been going on lately about me needing more iron and b-12 in my diet, and this was her solution.

A health shake for a vampire. Ha!

"Mrs. Brokerman left instructions to heat the contents in a mug in the microwave for exactly fifteen seconds." The cook took the thermos from the shelf, flinching when she brushed my arm accidentally.

The second she unscrewed the thermos cap the aroma of something wonderful filled my nose. My gums started tingling and I had to put my hand over my mouth to hide my overbite, which was extending. When the microwave dinged, nervously the cook handed me the mug.

"My god! This smells so good!" I took a big gulp and almost fainted in delight. It was ambrosia. Whatever it was, it was just what I needed.

"Would you like your breakfast plated and served in the dining room, sir?" The cook was staring at the livers with revulsion, which she covered quickly with just a slight grimace when I looked at her.

"No, no. I'll eat these in my room," I said, waving the carton of pig livers in the air. But I didn't actually want them anymore. I wanted more of Abby's health shake.

"Is there any more of this?" I asked hungrily, shoving the mug into the cook's hands.

"Of course, sir." The cook prepared three more mugs and set them on a tray, my cue to leave. I mumbled my thanks and went back up to my room.

I drank one mug while I walked. Whatever Abby had made was perfect. There was blood in the mix, definitely blood, and I had to find out what kind of animal it was; certainly delicious and better than pig!

Thank you, Abby.

I wondered where she was? I stood still and focused my vampire eardrums -- I still got a kick out of this super power stuff. Abby wasn't in the house, I couldn't hear her at all. I knew the sound of her heartbeat, her breathing, and I could find her anywhere if I focused; but she wasn't home. I giggled because I was better than any watchdog. Whatever was in the health drinks had given my senses a boost, though. I felt great; still a bit peckish, but all in all much better than usual.

I quickly slurped down the pig livers, they tasted less than appealing now, finished the other two mugs, and then felt antsy. Briefly I thought about finding Pizza Bob, but I didn't want to know what he was up to.

That poor maid.

I sat down at the computer desk, started to dial up my blog, but I had too much energy to just sit still. I felt claustrophobic in this grand room, my self-imposed exile of luxury. Oh, poor pitiful me. Five days ago I was living in squalor, well, not exactly squalor but less than awesome. I had a job I hated, and despite Pizza Bob's chronic company, I was desperately lonely.

I was afraid the Universe would notice my happiness here with Abby and snatch the rug right out from underneath me. I wasn't used to being happy. Part of me was delirious with joy, but that darker part of my brain that usually ruled kept whispering that I was still a loser, a user, a walking bag of rotting fat. It was only a matter of time until Abby saw that, too.

I paced back and forth in the room a few times, and then went to the window. I parted the heavy curtain and saw a beautiful, wet, cloudy day outside. Perfect. Suddenly, I wanted, needed to be outside as the sun set. The pull of the night was so intense that I just put on shoes, took off my robe, and wearing only my silly silk pajamas, I jumped out of the window.

I should mention that my room was on the third floor -- oops. I landed with a heavy thud on the back lawn, and lay there quite still, hoping no one had seen it happen.

"What a friggin' dork," Pizza Bob said as he hovered next to me. "What are you doing?"

"I don't know," I said with a grin. "Going for a walk."

"I just don't get you sometimes, dude." Pizza Bob stared up at the sky. "It will be dark soon. What do you want to do?"

I have no idea why I said it, but I did. "Let's go see what Marcella is up to."

"Let's not. How about a peeler bar?" Pizza Bob certainly loved the nudie bars! He noticed my pajamas and smirked. "What's up with that?"

"They feel nice." Boy, whatever was in that drink was making me feel giddy. "I don't feel like going to a strip club...Abby doesn't like them. I just want to lay here for a bit," I slurred.

"You seem different. What's up?" Pizza Bob was squinting at me. "Are you high? Dude!"

I laughed and lifted my face to feel the rain on my skin. It was amazing.

"Did you take something? 'Shrooms? What?" he demanded, but with a laugh. "You're trippin', dude! I'm jealous."

"Abby made me a health drink. It was awesome! I had four of them."

Pizza Bob stopped laughing and looked at me. "Oh. She did it."

"Did what?" I asked.

"Did you like them?" He was kind of shimmering in and out of focus, something that happened when he was angry or nervous; Pizza Bob didn't look angry. Uh-oh.

"What did she do?" I sat up, suddenly feeling queasy. "WHAT DID SHE DO?"

"Don't be mad. I saw her this morning with a cooler that had a bio waste sticker on the side."

Oh, I didn't like where this was going. "And?"

"And it had packets of blood packed on ice inside. Abby sent the cook away because she didn't want anyone to see what she was doing. I watched her mix up the blood and something else in the blender, but then that maid, Emily, arrived for work and I started following her."

I groaned. *Oh, Abby, what did you do?*

"How do you feel?" he asked.

"I felt great until I knew. Do...do you think it was human--"

"I don't know, dude. Abby's a strange one."

"Why didn't you warn me?"

Pizza Bob shrugged his shoulders. "Emily, man. She's hot."

I heard a car pulling up the drive and I stood up. My pajamas were soaked through and clinging uncomfortably to my belly fat. My euphoria of earlier was gone; I was back to being Mostly Dead Melvin, half-dead loser extraordinaire; blood drinker. What had Abby done?

Speaking of Abby, it was she in the car; I heard her heartbeat and recognized it immediately. It was faster than usual.

"Abby, what have you done?" I moaned as I slopped through the grass to the front of the house. I saw her go in through the front door with another cooler in hand. Giles saw me and glared.

The feeling's mutual, pal.

"I hate that guy," said Pizza Bob. "He's a creepy little prick."

"I couldn't agree more." I smiled at Giles who just closed the front door with a hard thud. I heard the lock engage, and I laughed.

I'd discovered a new trick in my arsenal of undead gifts. I could pick locks with my mind. Cool, eh? Any lock. I just pictured the bolt sliding back and voila, open door. It was born out of necessity actually. The day before my fated reunion with Abby at the mall (the most embarrassing day of my life, and the best day of my life), Pizza Bob had locked me out of my apartment when I went to take some garbage to the chute in the hall. Needless to say I was angry. I could have broken down the door with my freakish vampire strength, but that would draw too much attention. So, one thing led to another and I discovered my new power.

I smirked as I paused at the front door. I heard Giles breathing heavily on the other side, anticipating my having to knock.

Surprise! I put my hand on the knob, concentrated for a second, and the lock disengaged. Without giving Giles a chance to move, I opened the door quickly and the hard oak made a satisfying thud against his face.

"Oops, sorry about that," I purred as he clamped a hand over his broken nose to staunch the flow of blood. My gums were throbbing, and my over bite extended before I knew what was happening. His blood smelled like salvation, and I almost leapt at him, but Abby's voice behind me stopped me dead in my tracks.

"Oh, Melvin. You're up!"

I was frozen, staring at Giles who was staring back with a look of pure terror on his face. It was Pizza Bob all over again, but this time I didn't care about the fear. Giles knew how close he'd come to dying there, and I liked it.

Oh, maybe not. Suddenly I felt sick. I couldn't believe what I'd almost done, but at the same time I realized the balance had shifted. Giles knew not to mess with me now. I put my finger to my lips in a silent "shhh", and smiled. Giles gulped, but nodded.

"Dude!" Pizza Bob looked smug. "That was wickedly ninja, man." He was holding up his middle finger, inches from Giles face but the man couldn't see it. I still appreciated Pizza Bob's gesture, though.

"Hello, Abby," I said with false cheer in my voice. I was mad at her. Very, very mad. Her health shake was making me a monster, a monster I might not control next time.

"I was hoping to be back before you got up. I have a surprise for you." She ignored Giles completely, which made me smile, and took my hand. She led me into the kitchen; the cook was gone.

"Why are you all wet? And why are you in your pajamas?" she asked as she handed me a paper towel.

I just stared at the cooler on the counter. Sure enough this one had a bio waste sticker on it.

"Abby," I said with a remarkably calm voice. "What is that?"

"Oh, it's part of the surprise. I know you are having a hard time with the blood drinking thing--"

"Oh, oh, Abby, what did you do?"

She looked taken aback. "I've been doing a lot of research and I'm worried about your health."

"I don't have health, Abby. I'm dead. Mostly dead or whatever." My hands were shaking.

"Yes you do too, Melvin." She patted me on the hand affectionately. "Anyway, you're having a problem with the blood drinking thing so I thought we'd start out slow and work our way up. I brought some special blood this morning and made you a health shake."

"I had it," I whispered. Abby missed the undertone of horror in my voice, and smiled brightly at me.

"Did you like it?"

I felt dizzy. "A little too much, Abby."

She opened the cooler and removed a packet of blood. "That's great! Let me make you some more."

Instantly my gums started tingling and I was worried about that damned overbite. I made choked, gasping sounds and Abby was at my side immediately, the blood packet abandoned on the counter.

"Melvin, what's wrong?"

"Abby, what did you do?" I moaned.

Pizza Bob drifted over to the counter and read the sticker on the packet of blood. Suddenly he burst out laughing.

"Dude, it's monkey blood."

My jaw dropped. Monkey blood? I looked at Abby in shock.

"Where did you get monkey blood, Abby?"

She seemed stunned and then she pursed her lips. "So you could taste the difference. Damn. But was it good?"

I laughed. "It was divine. But monkey blood? Why?"

"We're primates, Melvin. I figured starting out with chimp blood would get you over that mental block you've got going."

"She's clever," Pizza Bob said appreciatively.

"Where in the hell did you get chimp blood?" I asked.

"Don't be silly. I have lots of money and people owe me favors."

I had a sad vision of some smiling chimp being drained for my breakfast, Abby standing there with a bowl to catch the blood. I shuddered.

"This was someone's pet? Oh, Abby...."

"No, of course not. I pulled some strings at the primate research center. I can get as much as I need, no questions asked. Money has its privileges."

I eyed the packet of blood and drooled. I wanted more. But I had a sudden fear of that craving. Maybe just a taste here and there and I'd be fine.

"Thank you, Abby. You're a good friend for helping me. I, I, I don't know how to thank you," I said with a quavering voice.

"Just get better and then I'll think of something," she said with a smile. A dark smile that made my stomach quiver.

Oh boy.

CHAPTER 8

HAPPY AS A PIG IN....

MASTERSOFTHENITE
Blogline ∞ October 25, 2014 ∞ MOOD: Blue

You will not believe what has happened to me! I ran into an old friend, my best friend, from when I was a kid. Unfortunately it was at the mall where I work. I couldn't believe it, and it turns out she's rich. Not just, 'Okay, I can eat this month and have cable TV', rich...she's like own the cable company rich. In fact, she owns the friggin' mall. How's that for a small world. There was the embarrassing part where I fainted right in front of her, and the mall paramedics thought I was dead (no pulse...GO FIGURE!). When I woke up I wished I were dead, though. My shirt was ripped open, my fat hanging out, a defibrillator charged and ready, and of course there she was watching the whole pathetic, mortifying scene unfurl. I had to do some fast talking to get the paramedics to leave me alone.

I couldn't believe she was there and she wasn't even that repulsed by my blue skin and vile odor. She was just happy I wasn't dead -- ha! And you know the best part? She cares about me. Corny, huh? She's married (sigh, but it's not like I have a chance!), but she's trying to help me with my undead problem.

I told her everything and she took it well -- didn't freak out or try and stake me...HOW COOL IS THAT?

I've been staying in her mansion (yeah, I said mansion), and it's been interesting. I still have my ghost with me. She tried to help with that, too, but it went badly. Yeah, yeah, of course it did.

Do you know how awkward it is to be insulted by a voodoo priestess? The woman spit on me. That story is worthy of a post all it's own. Maybe later when I have time to tell it right -- it's a doozy! But out of all of this I've come to a detente with Pizza Bob. He's not that bad, really. My friend can't see him, but she hates him none-the-less.

I haven't tried to bite anyone else yet. I'm not even tempted. Well, maybe a little. I hate the chauffeur. You would too. I have supplemented my diet of pig livers with chimpanzee blood. We're all primates, right? I'm working my way up the DNA ladder until I get the stones to go for human blood. I'm wary, though. The chimp blood makes me a little reckless, but I think I've got it under control. Hopefully. If not, the chauffeur is first on my list.

Anyway, Halloween is coming! I've got my costume all picked out for the big day: a zombie Smurf. Kidding. It should be a fun night. I'll post about it later.

Hooray for me! Life is working out pretty well for old Mostly Dead Melvin. I hope I just didn't jinx myself...

Remember, if you see Maddy message me immediately. She'll probably be out on the spooky night.

-Melvin

REPLY TO POSTER ∞ BLOCK USER ∞ REPORT POST

BLOGLINE COMMENT: FROM BLOODCRAVER666

You sound like a girl. Snap out of it already! Monkey blood? ARE YOU KIDDING ME? Eat the husband, get the girl, her money, her mansion...

Why am I even reading your blog? It's like a train wreck.

REPLY TO POSTER ∞ BLOCK USER ∞ REPORT POST

I don't sound like a girl, I'm just giddy. And chimp blood is good -- don't knock it.

BLOGLINE COMMENT: FROM MICKEYMOUSER

Dude! Sweet!

REPLY TO POSTER ∞ BLOCK USER ∞ REPORT POST

My sentiments exactly.

BLOGLINE COMMENT: FROM BORIS_THE_SPITE_HER

I bet she's fat.

REPLY TO POSTER ∞ BLOCK USER ∞ REPORT POST

You must be related to Pizza Bob.

BLOGLINE COMMENT: FROM ANONYMOUS

I SAW MADDY. SHE SAYS SUCK IT! LOOSER!

REPLY TO POSTER ∞ BLOCK USER ∞ REPORT POST

⅄

Whoa. That was my first reaction to that last comment, then I realized that ANONYMOUS was probably lying. Just someone with too much time on his or her hands taking a jab at the Internet freak. I doubted I'd ever really find Maddy.

Still, I hated the fact that there'd been a little adrenaline spike when I saw her name on the computer screen. And maybe my blog was starting to sound less than my usual self. But was that such a bad thing? I was happy. Sheesh.

I heard commotion downstairs; someone was here at the house. Abby had a busy social calendar with all of the charity work she did, business advisors for the corporation showing up randomly to go over reports, but no real friends that I noticed. That was sad.

There were women who showed up and made the appropriate social kiss on the cheek, babbled about fashion, gossiped about other women around town, but I could see there was no sincerity in their chatter. And I hid out of view rather than be subjected to their insincerity. It seemed like social climbers and hangers-on surrounded Abby. Ooh, hangers on. That hit a little too close to home.

I've been here ten days now in the guest room. The house staff is used to me by now, well, as much as they can be. They are forcibly polite but distant. The only openly hostile person around is Giles the chauffeur, but that has mellowed since his unfortunate collision with the front door. Apparently he's also some sort of bodyguard for Abby, and insists on accompanying us on any social outing in public; when I accompany her to shop for clothes for me. I think Giles is spying for Mr. Brokerman, who is due home in a little over a week. I'm worried about that. I don't want to think about him too much. I see his photographs everyday, those accusing eyes glaring at me from the celluloid frontier, and I shudder. He looks mean. Really.

My dear friend doesn't seem to miss her husband much, she never speaks of him and I certainly don't bring him up. Why would I? As long as I'm here and he's not I can pretend this is all mine. How pathetic is that? Denial. What a beautiful thing for a delusional, mostly dead mooch carrying a torch for a woman who is turning out to be a little odd in her own right.

Some of Abby's statements and attitudes about me killing someone for a meal make me nervous. But maybe I'm reading too much into it. She's just trying to help, right? She's also just a little too into the vampire thing; like she's star struck with the idea.

And even though Abby keeps insisting that I could have a better job at the mall, she still hasn't done anything about it. My supervisor at work put me on sick leave with pay and benefits, under Abby's instructions, but I feel like time is running out. My apartment rent is due in six days and I feel like a bum, a user, just hanging out here at the mansion, being pampered and taken care of. I'm used to it. I have a new wardrobe courtesy of Abby, she has good taste, but there's no way I could ever afford these kinds of clothes on my own. I felt weird letting her buy me this stuff, but I let her anyway.

Pizza Bob has held true to his word and been good. Mostly. He still makes obscene comments about Abby every day, spies on her in the shower, but she can't hear him or see him. He's also still fixated on poor Emily. And he mimics and mocks Giles at every chance for me. It's so hard to keep a straight face when that happens, and the chauffeur watches me like a hawk. I can feel his dislike for me, and his fear, but he never lets Abby see it. Oh no. Giles is Mr. Helpful when she's looking.

"Checking up on your blog?" Pizza Bob asked as he floated into the room. I hoped he hadn't been spying on Abby again. I also hoped Emily wasn't fully insane yet.

I sighed heavily. "Yup."

"Anything good?"

"Nope."

"Well, aren't we chatty today?" He hovered by my chair and peeked at the computer screen. "Someone saw Maddy, that bitch that bit you?"

"No, it's that jerk, Anonymous. He's lying." I pushed back from the desk and stretched.

"How do you know that?"

"Just a feeling. Maddy doesn't want to be found, and I doubt she'd send me a message like that."

Pizza Bob gave a snort. "Yeah, cause she's such a classy gal."

"I'll find her. It was awful what she did to me, and I've been thinking about all that lately. I never told you about the night I turned."

"Do I care?" Pizza Bob shrugged

"Don't be pissy. There was something weird that happened, more than me just becoming what I am."

I needed to talk about that dream that I had had. The more I obsessed over it the more I was convinced that the shadow man, Mr. Happy, had been there. That it was real. And if he was indeed there then that meant that Maddy might be in trouble with the others of our kind like he had intimated. I hoped she'd gotten her butt chewed royally. But then how come no one else had come looking for me. In a way I was glad; what if they were like Mr. Happy?

I smiled nervously. "It was freaky."

Pizza Bob perked up. "Was she kinky?"

"You're a pig. Never mind."

"Fine. I read your blog. It sounded lame anyway."

I felt defensive. "It wasn't Maddy. There was someone else there when I woke up."

"You dog!" Pizza Bob punched me on the shoulder. "And here I was thinking you died a virgin."

I ignored that last part; why give Pizza Bob more ammunition for the future. "It was creepy as hell. He said his name was Mr. Happy."

Pizza Bob fidgeted uncomfortably in front of me. "I don't wanna know your nickname for your junk, dude. And I'm going to pretend that's what you were referring to because otherwise I'll get creeped out thinking about you with a dude."

I laughed at him. "It was a shadow that called itself Mr. Happy. He said he oversaw the ascension to the dark realm, whatever that means."

"Oh, okay." Pizza Bob nodded, but I could tell he didn't believe me. Actually he seemed a bit too nonchalant about it.

"I'm not telling you a story, he was there and scary as hell."

"I said okay. Okay?" Pizza Bob wouldn't make eye contact.

"I've been thinking about him lately--"

"Dude, TMI. Way too much information," Pizza Bob said loudly.

"I think he was a demon or something. I've been waiting for him to show up again."

I started to Google "Mr. Happy" and got nothing but porn sites. Oops. Pizza Bob floated away from the desk and across the room.

"That's not it," I said with a nervous chuckle.

"You are a freak."

"You like Porn."

"Not that kind...."

I Googled "Ascension to the dark realm" and got 2,214,985 hits. That would take forever to pick through. I looked over my shoulder at Pizza Bob.

"Hey, you said there wasn't any light or tunnel or anything when you died, right?"

"Rub it in, jerk," Pizza Bob sniped.

"I'm just asking. But did you see anything? Was there a mist? Was anybody with you?"

"No, dude," he said a little too quickly. "I don't want to talk about it."

"Okay, all right. I just am getting a little nervous about things. About Mr. Hap--"

"Dude! Enough. You're serious about this?"

"Yeah, yeah I am. It was just too real to have been a dream. I'm freaked he's going to show up again. Add that to my sense of mooching here at the mansion, and I feel all twitchy." I shuddered.

"If he hasn't shown up by now I wouldn't worry about it," Pizza Bob said, again without making eye contact; almost like he was hiding something. But did I care? Not really. Petty as it seemed I felt my problems were more important.

I shrugged. "I feel like we should get out of here."

"Don't be ridiculous, Melvin."

"I'm not used to all of this attention, and I feel like a bum."

"You are," Pizza Bob said with a snicker.

I shook my head and sighed. "I'm serious. This all feels wrong, like I'm taking advantage. I've worked all my life, never had friends, I'm used to being alone."

"You're always focusing on the negative, man. Abby's your friend, she likes doing this for you."

"Maybe," I said.

"Look, this whole situation has been a big drag for you. Poor, poor Melvin." Pizza Bob fluttered his eyelashes dramatically. "I'm a terrible vampire, I'm such a loser, nobody likes me, I can't do anything right...."

"Hey!"

"I'm not done," he snarled at me. "I lived in a pig sty and I smell bad. I'm fat and nobody loves me. I'm secretly gay. Blah, blah, blah." Pizza Bob glared at me.

I just rolled my eyes. "You've got issues about the gay thing. I'm not gay that that matters. There's nothing wrong with being gay."

"I think it's you that's got issues. Everybody's a little gay, but I read that vampires are *all* gay or bi. It's in the movies, you know."

"That is the stupidest thing I've ever heard."

"What about Lestat?" Pizza Bob smirked at me.

"That's just the way Anne Rice wrote his character. That's make-believe. Besides, Angel wasn't gay...he did it with Buffy."

"That was just on screen. Who knows what else went on?"

I couldn't believe we were arguing the merits of fictional vampires and their sex lives. "You don't know what you're talking about."

"Dude, I'm just repeating what's in pop culture." Pizza Bob shuddered. "All that sex and violence and sex. You need to get your vampire on."

"Well, Hollywood has it all wrong. I'm living proof of that."

"Living, ha!" Pizza Bob snorted. "You call what you're doing living? Moldering is more like it."

I just shook my head at him. "Are you done?" I asked.

"No, not even close. Things are finally going okay for you and what do you do? Piss and moan like some teenage girl. Snap out of it, dude."

"You don't understand. I'm not moldering, well, maybe a little because my body can't decide to die or what. And here I feel like a user, a full-on, full throttle moocher. The primate blood is making me feel funny, and Abby's been a bit distant in the last few days. Her husband is coming home."

Pizza Bob laughed at me. "Melvin, you are an idiot."

"Why?"

"Because. I think I liked it better when I was mean to you. At least you had a little spine. Now, bleh."

"I just don't like feeling like a charity case, or a project." I was sounding pathetic. "Or a pet."

Pizza Bob burst out laughing. "Are you serious? Dude, I've seen the way you look at Abby. You've got it bad for her, but she's off limits you think. She's married. But she's like you, moron -- slightly, actually mostly off kilter, and she doesn't think of you like a pet."

"Abby is my friend," I said defensively.

"Yeah, yeah. But you'd be on her like white on rice if you could." He leered at me.

I was mortified again. Maybe that's why she was so distant.

"Oh, crap. Does she know?"

"I don't know. That girl has got some issues of her own; she's out there sometimes. Totally off in her own world." He twirled his finger by his temple again. "But you need to grow a pair. You're a vampire, dude. You're supposed to be a bad ass, not this simpering weenie. It's getting old."

"I guess." But Pizza Bob was right. It was time to start being a vampire, a bad ass. How? By drinking more than monkey blood.

Um, not yet.

"Thanks," I said to him. "You've turned out to be an all right guy."

"Oh, gee, I feel so special. Hold me, Melvin." Pizza Bob smirked as he floated towards me. "It's so Oprah."

I flipped him off and Pizza Bob burst out laughing. "That's better, more like it."

There was a faint knock on my door. "Mr. Morton, Miss Priss would like you to come downstairs please," the maid said quietly. This was weird.

I looked at Pizza Bob who just stared at me blankly, and then he shrugged. If Abby wanted to talk to me she usually came and got me herself.

"Mr. Morton?" the maid, Emily, asked again through the door.

I got up and opened the door a little too quickly, and the maid jumped back startled. Her hand flew to her neck and she looked at me wildly. Yup, she knew what I was.

I smiled reassuringly, I hoped, and said, "Thank you. Tell her I'll be right down."

"Y-yes, sir." The maid backed away and then rushed down the stairs.

"See, she's scared of you," Pizza Bob said reassuringly. "Become the bad ass, Melvin."

I looked at him kind of sideways. "Why are you helping me?"

"Okay, here's the truth. It makes this haunting a little more fun when you bumble your way through things. This kinder, gentler vampire crap you've got going is getting wicked boring. Again. More so than before; back then you were just clueless, now it's like a conscious choice to be this way."

"Oh. I see." I frowned.

"I meant what I said a while ago, you aren't a bad guy. But come on! You're boring the crap out of me. This time I'm really trying to help you. You should listen to me or I either have to go back to tormenting you, or I have to find someone else to haunt because you're such a pussy."

He could leave? That would be great! But then I'd be all alone. Alone with Abby. And her husband. Alone. Damn. Go back to tormenting me? Double damn!

"I better go see what Abby wants," I said.

I found Abby in the grand room, a formal sitting area off the small parlor. There was a woman with her, a very odd woman. I hesitated in the doorway and stared at the visitor.

She was old, gray hair done up in a swirling bun on top of her head, her face a web of wrinkles, but her eyes were the most shocking feature. They were a piercing blue, and were focused on me intently. There was a strange smell in the air, tangy and musty all at once. I dug through my scent memory, and it finally registered: formaldehyde, embalming fluid. She smelled like a pickled frog in a science class.

"Whoa, she's creepy," Pizza Bob said from behind me. "Looks like that librarian ghost from Ghostbusters."

The old woman smirked. "I'm rather fond of that movie actually."

Abby looked at her curiously but the old woman just patted her hand and said, "Never mind there, dear."

My jaw dropped. Pizza Bob pushed me out of the way and floated up to her. "You can see me?"

The old woman rolled her eyes and beckoned me forward. "Hello, Mr. Morton," she said as I approached the couch.

Abby stood up, gave me a hug and then said, "Melvin, this is Vernonia Ruttle. She's here to help you."

"Dude, I've been good. She can see me! Is Abby sending me away?" Pizza Bob was talking so fast that the words all seemed to run together.

I looked at Abby and then at the Vernonia. "I don't know."

"Of course you don't," Vernonia cackled. She looked at Pizza Bob and winked.

"You don't know what, Melvin?" Abby asked.

Vernonia smiled at her. "Never mind, dear. He's just a bit bowled over." To me she said, "I'm going to help you blend in, Mr. Morton."

I noticed that she had two small valises on the floor at her feet. Keeping her eye on Pizza Bob she slowly lifted one of the cases onto her lap, and opened it.

Was she a witch? Was Pizza Bob going to get sucked into that case and be trapped? In terror, he was clutching at my arm, unable to move, and Vernonia seemed to be enjoying the drama of the moment.

With a flourish she rotated the case and said, "Tah dah!"

I started laughing. Pizza Bob hesitated and then looked inside the case, finally letting go of my arm with a sigh. The case was filled with makeup; bottles and bottles of makeup.

Abby saw the look on my face and said quickly, "Vernonia is a specialist. She's the premier makeup artist for the Portland Center for the Performing Arts, and she is also the cosmetic artist preferred by clients' families at the finest funeral homes here in town." Abby was pleased with herself, unaware of the fright she'd given Pizza Bob. "I thought your skin type might benefit from her expertise."

"But she can see me," Pizza Bob whispered in my ear.

"Now that's our little secret," Vernonia said, letting the words have a double meaning. Obviously Abby didn't know that Vernonia could see and hear Pizza Bob.

"You're too modest, Vernonia," Abby said.

"Um, Abby," I said with a little too much worry in my voice. What had she told this woman about me?

Abby smiled indulgently. "I told Vernonia that you've been very sick. Practically at death's door but are much better now. However, you feel self-conscious out in public."

"Don't worry, Mr. Morton. Discretion is my middle name." Vernonia opened the other case and pulled a color pallet out, setting it on the coffee table with a pleasant smile. She turned to Abby. "Dear, would you mind letting Mr. Morton and I have a few moments alone to get started. This is a big step for him."

"Oh, of course. Melvin, I'll be in the library if you need me."

The second Abby was out of the room Vernonia laughed. "Your ghost looks like he's seen a ghost, Melvin."

"Who are you?" Pizza Bob demanded.

"Why, I'm Vernonia Ruttle, just like Mrs. Brokerman said. The question is, who are you?"

"I'm with him." Pizza Bob flicked his thumb at me. He was definitely uncomfortable with the whole situation.

"Hmmm. So you are. And who are you?" she asked me.

"I'm Melvin."

"Cryptic. I like a good puzzle. I'd say you've been more than a little ill, maybe a little dead, eh?" She wrinkled her nose slightly at my odor, and then laughed. "Don't be uptight about it. Come sit down."

"You're really just a makeup artist?" Pizza Bob asked.

"Just a makeup artist? Ha! But in this case, yes." She turned her focus on me. "By the smell of you it's been what, nine months since you died?"

I was stunned into silence. Pizza Bob answered for me. "It's been about six months, I think. I've been with him for two."

The woman winked at me. "So what are you, dear? Zombie? Thrall? Ghoul?" Vernonia sounded so sincere, so unfrightened.

"I'm...I'm a vampire." I said.

She wrinkled her eyebrows and frowned. "Really? Are you sure?" I just nodded feebly. "I don't mean to sound rude, but with the blue skin and all I figured you to be more of a zombie really. Hmmm, curious. You aren't going to try and bite me are you?" She laughed.

"Dude, you have the weirdest crap happen to you." Pizza Bob was laughing, too.

"I don't do that. It hasn't worked out so well." I looked at Pizza Bob with a guilty grin.

"I see. That explains things a bit better." Vernonia eyed Pizza Bob for a moment and then started pulling out her bottles of makeup.

"Do you know many zombies?" I asked. This was unreal.

"Oh, no, not personally."

"How come you know so much about this stuff?"

Vernonia smiled coyly. "I do work at a funeral home, dear. I've seen all sorts of odd things."

"Are you a witch?" Pizza Bob asked her.

"No, not really. I just see dead people and have a knack for all things super-natural." She reached over and patted my arm. "I'm sorry if this whole situation is upsetting. I figured it must be something odd from Mrs. Brokerman's inquiry. She's such a dear, dear girl."

"Does Abby know about you?" I asked.

"Abby? Hmmm, that's sweet," she said with a little wink. "Does she know about me? Hmmm. I certainly hope not. I'm a very private person about this sort of thing."

"Do you know any other vampires?" I let a little hope into my voice.

"No, sorry." Vernonia was holding up different shades on her color pallet next to my cheek. "Has that dreadful shadow been to see you yet? This is his bailiwick."

I gasped and looked at Pizza Bob. He wouldn't look at me.

"Hmmm, I'll take that as a yes. Dreadful thing isn't he."

"Are we talking about Mr. Happy?" I couldn't believe how much stranger this day could get.

"Is that what he called himself? Horrible little shadow beast with an English accent?" she asked.

"Yup, that's him."

"Did he help you?"

"No, I made him cross."

"Oh dear, he does hate that. Is that why you're blue?"

"I don't know exactly. I just think I didn't get enough of Maddy's blood to turn me all the way." Wow!

"Maddy, is that the one who made you? Why didn't she just give you more?" Vernonia looked confused.

"I was an accident. Maddy dumped me on my building steps with a note stuffed in my pocket. That's the last I heard of her; she left me to do all this alone."

Vernonia sighed in disgust. "Young people these days...no follow through. What a horrible thing to do to you, Melvin. You seem like such a nice boy, too." She cast a furtive glance at Pizza Bob, and I pretended not to notice.

"Lady, you're ruining my bad ass, sorry for the swearing ma'am, pep talk I gave him earlier." The ghost looked at Vernonia sheepishly and she waved him off with a smile. "He's gotta stop being nice and start being a vampire." Pizza Bob was sitting on the coffee table, looking uncomfortable in his new role as my mentor. It was pretty strange.

"Well, I suppose that will be inevitable," Vernonia said with a sigh. "But he seems like such a sweet young man for a vile creature of the night."

"Thank you." I just wanted to crawl into her lap and get a big hug. "But how do you know Mr. Happy?"

She grimaced. "He's popped into the funeral home when I'm working." She frowned and added, "He thinks I'm quaint," while making quote marks with her fingers.

"Do you think he'll be back to see me?" I asked, suddenly nervous.

"I don't know," said Vernonia.

"Don't tell him you met Melvin. I don't want anything to do with Mr. Happy. He sounds like a freak." Pizza Bob was pawing through the bottles in the case and making a huge mess.

"You're quite the manifester, aren't you?" Vernonia said in amazement. "It's rare to be around a ghost with so much gumption. Usually when someone dies they don't remember who they were or much of anything really. The angry ones are the worst."

"Oh, he's angry." I smiled.

Pizza Bob flipped me off and then apologized to Vernonia.

"Well, aren't you two the pair." Vernonia chuckled as she straightened out the makeup bottles. "If that dreadful shadow shows up I won't mention you at all, Melvin. Now, let's get started, shall we?"

She held up the color palette one more time and then reached for a bottle. "Let's try some desert sand...warm tones should off set that blue I think. We must be careful not to tint you green!"

"You're the expert." I grinned.

"I suggest going for one of those all over spray tans that are so popular."

"I didn't think of that."

"Why would you, dear?"

"Right. That's why you're the expert." I smiled.

Vernonia worked on me for an hour, asking questions about my life before I was bitten, how I knew Abby, what I thought the future held for me. I saw Abby peek in on us a few times and then sneak away so I wouldn't feel self-conscious. I told Vernonia my sad tale, even the part about Pizza Bob and his death. She just shrugged and kept working. Surprisingly the ghost didn't interrupt with his usual bravado. Vernonia then asked me about Abby again.

"She was my best friend when we were kids, my only friend ever actually," I said quietly.

"Hey, what am I?" Pizza Bob asked hotly.

"Sorry," I said in surprise. "I thought I was just convenient."

"Ouch. I guess I earned that."

Okay, so I had two friends. I smiled and continued my story.

"It's just a wonderful turn of events that Abby and I found each other again." I had a stupid grin on my face.

Vernonia smiled sadly. "Melvin, far be it from me to pry or make judgments, but she is married. And you are a vampire."

"I know," I said meekly. Thankfully Pizza Bob was keeping quiet. "But I've missed her."

"She's quite fond of you, too. But...."

"He knows, Vernonia. Let him be happy for a while."

I looked over at Pizza Bob and smiled gratefully. He really did surprise me sometimes.

"You're quite right. It's none of my business anyway. I just hate to see fragile people do fragile things. I have a soft spot for orphans and abandoned souls." She patted me on the cheek softly.

"We're done." Vernonia held up a mirror. "Oh, you can see yourself, can't you?"

"Yes, that's just a myth. Lots of things about vampires are myths." I looked in the mirror and smiled at the new man looking back.

Pizza Bob started laughing at me. "Dude, you look like Michael Jackson!"

"No I don't!" I looked in the mirror again. "Do I?"

"Of course not, dear. You'd need the glove." Vernonia started laughing. "I'm kidding. Kidding. I think I did a wonderful job. You like lively."

"You look fine, Melvin." Pizza Bob hiccupped, and then smothered another bout of giggles.

"You're just used to seeing him blue," she said tartly to the ghost. "Melvin, I'll leave a few bottles of this color for you. It's waterproof so you'll need to remove it with cold cream. Don't forget to use the sponge when you apply the concealer or else it will look smudgy. Can you remember how to use the eyeliner and lip liner?"

I sat staring into the mirror with a smile on my face. I looked normal, better than normal. The makeup covered my old acne scars and balanced out my skin tone. In fact, I looked quite handsome. Well, not as homely as before. At least I looked human.

"I can't believe it," I whispered. "I'm a real boy!"

No more Pinocchio for this guy. Now if only I could drink human blood I'd be perfect.

"You're a drag queen," Pizza Bob said with another round of giggles.

"Be nice," Vernonia reprimanded. I was still staring into the mirror with a shocked smile on my face. "Melvin, using this makeup will help you to blend in and feel normal around people. They won't stare. Just don't over do the eyeliner." Vernonia put my supplies in a small zippered bag and handed it to me.

"Carry this with you at all times for touch ups. Can you do this preparation on your own?"

"Yes, Vernonia. I can't thank you enough."

"Such a dear, dear boy," she said with a touch of sadness in her voice. "If you decide to go with a spray on tan, we can adjust the makeup accordingly."

"Melvin, can I see?" Abby was standing in the doorway, she'd crept up so quietly, and I turned around slowly, nervous about her reaction.

She gasped and then broke out into a huge smile. "Oh, Vernonia, he's perfect! Thank you so much!"

"See, Melvin. She likes you," Pizza Bob said with a little elbow nudge.

Vernonia nodded at him sadly and then whispered, "Melvin, take care of yourself and remember what I said. Try and stay nice for as long as you can, dear boy."

CHAPTER 9

IF WISHES AND BUTS WERE CANDY AND NUTS....

I escorted Vernonia to the front door like a gentleman should. And that's how I felt; normal looking skin, nice clothes, and a nice house. Gentlemanly. Okay, the nice house didn't belong to me but I was here, so I pretended it was mine. Lord of the manor. Abby was thanking Vernonia profusely, while at the same time practically shoving her out the front door. Abby kept grinning at me and I felt my heart start up briefly; that smile could raise the dead.

Before Abby got the door closed Vernonia put her business card in my hand.

"Melvin, if you need anything please don't hesitate to call. I'll keep you in my thoughts so let me know how things work out for you," she said with a hand squeeze. Pizza Bob was hovering near her with a puppy dog grin on his face.

"What about me?" he asked.

"Of course, of course. Pop in and say hello anytime." To Abby she said, "Melvin is a very nice young man, it was lovely meeting him, and I'm glad I could help."

"Thank you, thank you so much," Abby said and shut the door. It seemed kind of rude, but Abby was bouncing with excitement.

"Melvin, come with me. I have another surprise for you."

Pizza Bob wiggled his eyebrows at me and made a lewd gesture.

"No...." I shook my head in confusion. "You think?"

He just grinned.

Abby was too excited to notice my exchange with the ghost, and tugged on my hand impatiently. "Come on! I can't wait for this."

Uh-oh. This surprise felt different than the others -- there was a charge in the air, a little tingle that ran up my arm when Abby touched me. She looked flushed and eager. Could it be? After all of my wishing and dreaming the moment was here, and now that it was here I was too freaked out about it. But I let myself be led down the hallway towards the back of the mansion. Abby stopped at a pair of heavy doors that led down to the wine cellar.

"Abby," I squeaked, and then cleared my throat to sound more manly. "Abby, what are we doing?"

"It's a surprise! I have everything all set up down there."

"Ummm, ummm." I was floundering.

"But wait, I have something for you first."

Abby reached into her pocket and pulled out a blue box with a bow on it, which she handed to me with a flourish. "I got you something! Something that will help with your little problem."

Pizza Bob said, "A little blue pill in a little blue box for a little blue man with little blue balls?"

My eyes bugged out, and I made a little choking sound. "Oh, god!" I gurgled, which made Pizza Bob grin wickedly. I really, really hated him for seeing this.

"Don't open it here, wait till we get downstairs," Abby said with an impish grin. "I'm so excited! Quit stalling and just open the door. Oh, this is going to be fun!" She squealed.

Pizza Bob slapped me on the back. "Don't worry, dude. I'll be there to give you pointers. You'll look like a pro!"

Oh double god. This is horrible. I don't want to do this. Not this way. Not yet!

"Melvin, sweetie, what's wrong? Aren't you curious?" Abby looked hurt. "I wanted this to be special, something you and I would remember forever."

I opened the door. "Okay, should I go first?" My voice was shaky.

"I want to see the look on your face, but you should go ahead of me," she said, and gave me a little push towards the stairs. "Be sure and take off your jacket first, you don't want to get it stained."

My knees buckled, and Pizza Bob hoisted me up so I didn't fall. "Dude, I can't keep this up...man up. Man up!"

I took a deep breath and started down the stairs on my own two feet. Pizza Bob was at the bottom waiting for me. "Whoa," he said with an eyebrow wiggle, "this chick is kinky with a capital K. You won't believe this."

My heart was thudding again in my chest. None of this felt right, nope, not at all. Abby was married. I was just a friend. And a virgin. This had to be a dream. Maybe I misunderstood her, but she wanted me to take off my jacket. What about my pants? Maybe she didn't want to see my fat? Maybe she liked the idea of me, but was really repulsed by my body.... I was repulsed by my body!

Oh god, what am I going to do? I'm a vampire. She's a human; a perfect human. Does she love me? Is this charity?

Oh bleh, I'm gonna throw up. Don't throw up. I'm dizzy.

I got to the bottom of the stairs and froze.

"Do you like him?" Abby asked. She stepped down onto the concrete floor and approached the unconscious man laid out by one of the wine racks.

Oh crap. It's worse than I thought.

"He's a magazine salesman," Abby said eagerly. "He looked a bit on the homeless side so I drugged him and brought him down here for you."

"For me?" I looked horrified. Did Abby think I was gay? "What am I supposed to do with him?"

Pizza Bob was laughing hysterically, doubled over in fact. I was so embarrassed.

"Oh, don't you like him?" Abby looked disappointed. "I thought for sure you'd like him."

"Oh, Abby, um...." I was backing away slowly. I just wanted to die, more, all of the way.

"Open your present!"

I had the box locked in a white-knuckled grip, but didn't dare move. She watched me for a moment, and then pried my fingers open and took the box.

With a sigh she popped it open and held up the present; the capper of it all. Literally.

A pair of vampire teeth, two sharp fangs that would fit over my canines thus completing my persona, sparkled from the satin lining; taunting me. At that moment I would have preferred the little blue pill.

"I thought they would help with your little problem, give you a confidence boost." Abby looked so pleased with herself, and utterly clueless. "Do you like them? I had them made special, just for you."

"Oh, damn."

"Dude," Pizza Bob said through a smirk, "Try them on!"

"No!" I snapped, staring at the man on the floor in horror. Was this some sort of sick foreplay?

"Dude, ramp it down." Pizza Bob waggled his finger at me like I was a toddler in a tantrum.

"Piss off," I hissed. The ghost just stuck his tongue out.

"You don't like them?" Abby pouted, pointedly ignoring to the exchange with my ghost to pretend he wasn't there.

"Um, yeah, sure, thanks," I managed.

Abby followed my gaze to the unconscious man, and then smiled. "You should try them on, make this a full experience."

"No...no...I don't think...um, yeah but no." I was starting to get a bit nauseous, and feared I was on my way to another mortifying black out. I took a little step back.

"Well you should at least try him. Just one bite, Melvin. For me?" Abby crouched down and lifted the man's head, exposing his neck. "You've done so well with the other blood."

"Oh!" That was a relief. "You want me to eat him!"

"Of course, what did you think?"

"Never mind." I looked at Pizza Bob who was hiccupping because he was laughing so hard.

Pizza Bob stopped laughing when he saw how angry I was. "Dude, the look on your face was priceless! Oh, I wish I had a camera!"

"Did you know she was doing this?" I asked him.

"Yeah! I saw the whole thing happen," he said through a snort.

Abby glared at me. "Melvin, that nasty ghost is here, I know it. This is private and I want him to leave."

I ignored her and kept at Pizza Bob.

"You knew and let me think it was "That"?" I was angry now. "Are you that evil? How could you!"

"Come on, dude! I couldn't help it...you looked so excited, and terrified, and nauseous...dude, it was too much to pass up."

"I'll get you for this." And then I looked at Abby who stood there with a mixture of confusion and annoyance muddling up her usually lovely face.

She said, "Focus on me, Melvin!"

"That's all you do, Melvin. Tell her I said to shut up." Pizza Bob rolled his eyes.

"Both of you, knock it off. All I can focus on is the guy on the floor. What the hell?"

Abby said, "I thought he'd be perfect, Melvin. I've been doing a lot of research and it turns out you really need to feed soon. It will make you feel better."

I sighed heavily. "Oh, wow. I, uh, don't know what to say, but --"

"He's perfect and won't fight back. You might even get a buzz from the drugs in his blood," she offered with a wink.

"Abby, you have to let him go. I can't, won't do this."

"Melvin," Pizza Bob warned. "You're being a pussy. She went to a lot of trouble for you here. You're gonna hurt her feelings."

"But, Melvin...." Abby looked upset all right. "Why?"

I looked at Pizza Bob, then down at the drugged man, and then at Pizza Bob again. "I just can't, Abby."

She put her hands on her hips. "Well, I don't even know why I bother if you aren't going to try. You can't go on like this." She stuffed the fangs into my pocket, turned away brusquely, and stomped up the stairs.

"She's right, Melvin." Pizza Bob was looking at the man on the floor. "Maybe I was just a fluke. You know, because my death was sort of an accident."

"So you finally admit it?" I said with an angry sneer. I was so furious with him right now. He set me up for one hell of an embarrassment here; he'd gone too far this time.

"Dude, quit being melodramatic. I admit my death has extenuating circumstances, but it's still your fault I died. If you hadn't tried to bite me in the first place I wouldn't be here now." He shook his finger at me. "But this time it might be different."

"You're okay with this? I can't believe you two. Has Abby gone nuts?" I started backing away towards the stairs. "I'm not going to kill someone, okay?"

"I think you'll regret this later."

"I already regret it now."

"Don't be like that, Melvin. I'm sorry. I should have warned you, but, come on, dude. Be the bad ass, it's time."

No, it was time for me to leave the mansion before Abby did something stupid; something that would damn her, something that she thought would help me. No, I couldn't let that happen.

I checked my pocket for my wallet, brushed the sharp fangs with my fingers, got a case of the queasies, and then ran up the stairs and out the front door into the night. Pizza Bob didn't follow me.

I got to my apartment building just after ten o'clock. I didn't have my keys, but I knew the super would still be up watching the news. I rang the buzzer and waited patiently by the speaker box until I heard a static-laced voice boom at me.

"Yeah?"

"I'm sorry it's late, Mr. Kovali, but I lost my keys. Can you let me in?"

"Who is this?" the voice demanded.

"It's Melvin Morton, sir. Apartment 310."

Silence greeted me. "Um, hello?" I said, but Mr. Kovali had disconnected.

I stood by the door waiting for him to buzz me in, but nothing happened. I buzzed his apartment again, but no one answered this time. That was weird. And frustrating. I was getting ready to buzz him again when Mr. Kovali appeared at the front door in his bathrobe and slippers. He stared at me for a few seconds and finally opened the heavy door, but stood blocking the entrance.

"I was told you weren't coming back," he said with mild curiosity.

"What?" I sputtered. "Who said that?"

He squinted his eyes at me. "You look better. All dressed up in that fancy suit. Not sick anymore?"

"Yes, I'm much better. But who said I wasn't coming back?"

"That lady who's taking care of you. She paid your rent for not giving me thirty days notice, brought in a cleaning crew, and that was that." He shifted uncomfortably in the doorway. "She said you were too sick to take care of things yourself so I took her at her word."

I couldn't believe it. Abby evicted me from my apartment.

"When did this happen?" I demanded. I'd just left the house an hour ago. I guess when she was mad she moved fast.

"Oh, seven days ago," he said quickly.

I was stunned. I leaned against the building and closed my eyes against the rage building inside of me.

"Hey, are you okay?" Mr. Kovali asked.

"Do I look okay?" I snapped back.

"Well, you look better than you did."

"He's right, Melvin," Pizza Bob said.

"Aw, crap. Not you again." I opened my eyes and glared at him, but Mr. Kovali took a step back in fear. "Why won't you just piss off?"

Mr. Kovali puffed out his chest. "Don't be angry at me. You need me to call someone for you? That lady left me her number." The man was inching his way back inside of the apartment building entrance.

"She's the last person I want to talk to. Where's my stuff?" I was clenching and unclenching my fists, and felt my over bite trying to extend. Damn that chimp blood! It just made me want the real thing!

"Melvin, take it down a notch," Pizza Bob said with a grin.

"What? Now you don't want me to bite someone? Go to hell," I muttered.

Mr. Kovali was fully inside the building now and trying to close the door. "There's no reason for that kind of language. That lady seemed official, proper, she had a lawyer document with her."

I glared at him. "Where is my stuff?"

"She had a moving company come and pack up your place." I smelled the fear coming off of the old man in waves. And it didn't bother me, in fact it made me hungry.

"Where's my stuff?" I asked Pizza Bob, but it appeared that I was talking to empty air to poor Mr. Kovali, who was starting to really get scared.

The man said, "I told you, that lady moved you out. Ask her where your stuff is."

I took a deep breath and glared at my ghost. Pizza Bob just shrugged.

I said, "Let me into my apartment, Mr. Kovali."

The door was almost closed and he said through the crack, "It's been rented," and slammed the door. He stood for just a second staring at me, and then bolted up the stairs to his apartment.

"What are you doing here?" I asked Pizza Bob.

"I was worried about you. Abby was real upset when you left."

"How could she do this to me? Huh? What am I supposed to do now?" I sank down and sat on the step.

Pizza Bob sat down next to me. "Go home."

"This is my home, dumb ass." I stared at the empty street with my anger simmering deep inside. "How dare she do this."

"She was trying to take care of you, that's all. She didn't think it would be a problem...she was going to surprise you I think. There have been workers renovating her carriage house. I think it was meant to be a place for you." Pizza Bob picked at his shoe.

"She should have asked me what I wanted. I told you I was starting to feel like one of her projects."

"Melvin, it's not like that." Pizza Bob stared over my shoulder at the building entrance. "That guy is probably going to call the cops. We should boogie."

"I'm not going anywhere with you. I hate you."

Pizza Bob frowned. "I said I was sorry, dude."

"Go to hell."

A homeless man shuffled by pushing a shopping cart loaded with plastic bags and empty bottles. He was hunched over and babbling to himself, but he noticed me sitting there and ambled in my direction.

"Hey, buddy. Got some spare change?" He held out a grubby hand.

"No, I'm homeless," I said.

"Nice suit for a homeless guy." He pulled out a paper bag with a bottle of something nasty inside, and took a long swallow.

"Oh yeah? It's all I have." God I was pathetic; a two thousand dollar suit on my back and not a penny in my pocket except for my ATM card. At least I had my rent money and sick pay in the bank. Joy. But no place to go. And the police were probably on their way. And I was hungry, damn it.

The homeless man gave me the once over. "Should get yourself a cart." He looked at Pizza Bob. "What about you?"

Pizza Bob gasped. "You can see me?"

"Why shouldn't I see you? Got any change?"

"Um, no. I'm a ghost." Pizza Bob looked at me, and then incredulously back at the man with the cart.

"Yeah, yeah. You're a ghost and he's a vampire. This town is going to crap, and people say I'm a crazy bum." He shook his head and started to wheel his cart away.

"Wait!" I jumped up. "How do you know I'm a vampire?"

"You stink," he yelled over his shoulder.

"Come on," I said to my ghost, my anger forgotten, and jogged to catch up with the homeless man.

The man looked over his shoulder and grimaced. "Great. Whadda ya want now?"

"Have you seen other vampires around here?"

"Naw. I don't hang with the undead." He pushed his cart faster. We were blocks away from my apartment now.

Pizza Bob floated in front of him. "How come you can see me?"

"Because I'm dead, too." The man paused in his cart pushing, and stared at us. Pizza Bob and I exchanged a look, and then the man started cackling maniacally.

"Gotcha!" He pulled out his paper bag bottle and offered me some. I declined. He offered Pizza Bob a sip. "Go on, it won't kill ya!" This made him chuckle even more.

"Melvin, we should go." Pizza Bob tugged at my sleeve. "Bag man here isn't playing with a full deck."

"Of course I'm not, sonny boy. I'm crazy." The man did a little dance in the street. I was fascinated. It was like watching a car crash; I couldn't look away. Finally there was someone weirder than me in the world.

"Are you for real?" I asked.

"Sometimes," he said indignantly. "Look, fun and games aside, I'm a troll, okay? I got bumped from my spot under the 405 underpass by a bunch of goblins out on a tear. Turf war or some kerfuffle in the ranks. It's been a bad day and I don't have time to waste on a clueless newbie. You're much too stupid to be out here on your own, so take my advice and go back to where ever it is you came from."

"A troll?" I smirked. "Seriously?"

The man leaned in and sniffed me. "You haven't bitten anyone yet. Am I right?" He looked over at Pizza Bob and laughed. "I don't smell it on him, just cow, pig...and monkey? Oh, that's rich." The troll burst out laughing.

"He's working up to it," Pizza Bob said in my defense.

"Well, the makeup helps him blend in, but any other night folk will spot him for what he is. He's a babe in the woods out here. Take him home or back to the zoo for a monkey snack."

"I don't do zoos," I snapped, remembering that fateful day and the chimps with their poop flinging.

"Mmmmm, monkey snacks. You don't do zoos. Well boo-hoo." He cackled and did a little hopping dance.

I was staring at him like he was crazy; I was too weirded out to be offended about the monkey crack. He had to be pulling my leg.

"A troll? Goblins? You're kidding."

The man sighed in disgust and took off his hat. Two horns poked out of the side of his head through matted hair, and his ears were pointed and furry like a German shepherd's; on the whole his head was less than human. I just gaped at him.

"Boy, he is a slow one." The troll put back on his hat and pointed a finger at me. "You seem like a nice guy for an undead, so I'm trying to be pleasant. This town is real territorial for the night folk. You'd be a piece of candy for the nastier groups out here.

"Be best if you got a few bites on your resume before you started slumming, Mr. Nice Suit Makeup Guy." The troll adjusted his hat and then took another sip from the bottle.

"My name is Melvin," I mumbled.

"Yeah? Whatever. They call me Bertram." The troll picked at a mat of hair sticking out of his hat and came away with a wriggling bug, which disappeared in a flash into his mouth.

I cringed and said, "Eew." It just popped out, and Pizza Bob elbowed me.

"Friggin' newbie," Bertram said with a sulfurous smelling belch. "Yay for me. I get to be your first troll. Just be glad I'm not one of those greedy, little back stabbing and conniving goblin creeps." He turned in the direction of the 405 and shook his fist.

I sank down into a crouch and went blank. My mind was having a bit of a vacation; I couldn't believe what I was hearing.

Okay. Recap time. In the last six months I'd discovered the hard way that vampires were real. That ghosts were real. That Voodoo was real. Okay maybe real; Marcella hadn't actually done anything except see Pizza Bob and threaten me. I had my experience with Mr. Happy validated by a strange, but kind, woman who could see dead people. And now I was talking to a troll. And there were goblins. And other scary things that went bump in the night.

The troll said to Pizza Bob, "That kid ain't quite right, is he?"

"No, no he isn't," my ghost answered.

"He's a piss poor vampire, not scary at all."

"Yeah, it's been disappointing so far. I got stuck with a boring one. Wanna hear about it? Melvin tells it better than me."

The troll squinted at Pizza Bob and smirked. "Not really. Where's his maker?"

"She dumped him."

The troll was bending over and looking at me, scrutinizing my clothes, my odor, my face. I tried to ignore him and keep wallowing in my temporary insanity.

"Harsh. Where are his fangs?" he asked.

"In his pocket, but check out the over bite. Melvin, show him the fangs Abby gave you!" Pizza Bob laughed and pointed at me. He was getting awfully friendly with the troll at my expense.

"Wow. No wonder he hasn't bitten anyone yet," the troll said with a sneer. "Fake fangs?"

"No, that's not his problem. He's just squeamish."

"You're joking! What a laugh!"

I stood up and wiped my face. "Hey, standing right here," I snapped.

The troll just stared at me. "So?"

"You're a jerk." I glared at him. Jerk? That was the best I could come up with?

The troll grinned wickedly at me. "No, no, sonny boy. I'm a troll. While I like my meat a little fresher and not so dead, I haven't eaten in a week. I wouldn't mind doing the world a favor and snacking on you. I bet you might just taste like goat." He pulled his lips back and exposed a row of nasty, sharp teeth. "Maybe monkey."

Uh-oh. I was strong, freakishly vampire strong, but he was a troll, and a mean looking one at that. Would it even be a fair fight?

"Oh yeah?" I tried to sound intimidating, but the troll's laugh let me know what he thought of that.

"Ya got spunk. Go home, vamp. I'm one of the nicer ones you'll meet at night." He winked at me, pulled fifty cents out of his pocket and tossed it to me. "Go call someone to pick you up, newbie."

The troll laughed and started pushing his cart again. I stood very still and watched him go.

"Let's go back to Abby's," Pizza Bob said when the troll disappeared around the corner.

My anger was back, and I glared at my ghost. "No. She's done enough, and so have you. Abby's the last person I want to see."

"You don't have anywhere else to go, dude."

"I could go to a hotel," I snapped.

"Don't be an idiot, Melvin. No one else cares about you, and this has turned out to be a big scary world with scary things in it. You don't have anyone but Abby and me."

And then I remembered Vernonia's card in my pocket.

CHAPTER 10

LET'S DO THE TIME WARP AGAIN

Vernonia Ruttle drove an old Mercedes wagon with tinted windows, and I knew it was her before the car rolled to a stop next to the phone booth. The car had an old world class, just like Vernonia. She got out and stood with her hands on her hips, eyeing the dark street warily before she looked at me.

"Melvin, what on earth is going on?" she asked as she came around and opened the passenger door for me.

"Thank you for coming, Vernonia. I'm sorry I was so short with you on the phone, but I needed you to get here as quickly as possible."

"You made that quite clear, dear. I'm in the middle of a job so we need to get back." She hustled me into the car and looked for Pizza Bob. "Where's your ghost?"

"He took off."

Pizza Bob was annoyed with me, thought I was being an idiot for running away, and had undoubtedly gone back to Abby's. That was fine with me.

"What's happened? Is Mrs. Brokerman all right?" Vernonia asked quietly. I tried to not let the hurt creep into my voice from her subtle accusation, but the anger edged in instead.

"Abby's fine," I snapped, and then winced at Vernonia's reaction. "I'm sorry, Vernonia, but it's been a really bad, weird, icky night. Thanks for rescuing me here."

She started the car and headed onto the freeway. "Melvin, I was a bit surprised to hear from you so soon. You sounded so broken and fragile on the phone, of course I'd come for you." She reached out and patted my hand absently.

"I'm sorry to pull you off a job. Is it a big show?" I asked.

"Oh, no, not at all. I'm working at Morrison's tonight."

Damn it!

I sank lower into my seat. We weren't headed to the warmth and safety of a theater, but to her other job instead. Vernonia didn't notice, and went into detail.

"An elderly gent left a pan of cocoa cooking on the stove, and he and his wife died of smoke inhalation. The fire fighters put out the small blaze before he and the missus became toasted. Sad really. But that's life."

I bit my lip to stop it from quivering.

"Toasty deaths don't call on my makeup expertise," she said a little too casually. "Nothing I can do for those, but this case will be a piece of cake. The family wants dear old mother and father looking regal for the funeral."

I shuddered. Morrison's was a funeral home, the last place I wanted to be even though Pizza Bob's moldering corpse had kept me company for so long. Bodies didn't scare me, but ghosts made me uncomfortable, and somehow I knew I'd see some with Vernonia. It had been that kind of night. And with my luck even Mr. Happy would show up, too. Vernonia took my hand, startling me out of my morbid revelry.

"Melvin, something has happened, hasn't it?"

"Vernonia--" I didn't know where to begin. "Abby went too far."

I told her about the man in the wine cellar. I even showed her the fangs. She just rolled her eyes.

"Oh dear." Vernonia navigated the Portland streets with ease and let me ride in silence. We finally pulled into the employee parking area at the back of Morrison's Funeral Home, and she parked by the door. I dreaded going into this place.

"You know, Melvin, in her own strange way your friend was trying to help. Not that I am condoning what she did." Vernonia sighed and got out. "I do hope she let that man go."

"Me too," I said from the car; I didn't want to get out.

Vernonia was unlocking the funeral home when she noticed that I was still sitting in the Mercedes. Understanding dawned on her face, and she crossed back over to the car quickly.

"I'm sorry, Melvin. I didn't even think that this place might make you uncomfortable." She worried her key ring. "Would you feel better waiting for me out here? I shouldn't be more than another hour or two."

Two hours? Sitting in this creepy parking lot alone for two hours? Ugh.

"I don't want to get you in trouble," I said trying to sound, well, not sound like a simpering, scaredy-cat, blue, half-dead excuse for a vampire. "If you could call me a cab I'll find a hotel--"

"Don't be ridiculous. You need someone to talk to right now." She took my hand and led me out of the car and to the door. "It's not any trouble for me at all. The only people here are you, me, and the Andersons in the prep room. I don't think they'll mind."

"Okay." What else could I say?

"I just hope they're not rude to you," she said flippantly.

Rude? I hope she didn't mean that literally.

We went down a long, dark hallway that ended with a door marked employees only. Vernonia used her key and I saw the recently deceased Mr. and Mrs. Anderson each laid out on their own table; the woman in a lovely blue evening gown and the man in a tuxedo. But I also saw Mr. and Mrs. Anderson hovering in the corner in their pajamas, staring at me anxiously. Oh, great. More ghosts. Literally.

"Where have you been?" the old man demanded as Vernonia approached the table where his body lay in a state of artful cosmetic restoration. "My face is only half done. Shoddy, shoddy work."

I groaned, and the ghost fixed his steely gaze on me.

"Who's this?" he asked while Mrs. Anderson trailed behind him.

"Hello, um, sir. My name is Melvin Morton."

What was the etiquette here? Sorry for your loss? Sorry you died? You look good, considering.

"Are you here to do my hair?" Mrs. Anderson asked me.

Vernonia rolled her eyes. "Mrs. Anderson, I've already done your hair in the nice style from your anniversary photo. You said you liked it."

"I suppose," the ghost said with a dismissive wave.

"Speak now or forever hold your peace," Vernonia said with a smile. "I just want you to be happy."

"Yes, I'm sorry. I don't mean to be rude, but all this has come as a bit of a shock you know," Mrs. Anderson said while peering at her corpse. "You've done a lovely job, but when you do my makeup I'd like to have a bit of color; we were supposed to go on Bahaman cruise next week."

"Would you like to look tan?" Vernonia held up a bottle of darker makeup.

"Would it be too much trouble?"

"Of course not, Mrs. Anderson. Your family just wants you to look nice in the coffin."

"Not too tarty, all right?" Mrs. Anderson looked at her anniversary picture with a sad smile. "I'm too old for tarty."

"Why Mrs. Anderson, you will be the belle of the after life when I'm through with you."

"Let her finish with me first," Mr. Anderson snapped. "I don't want to miss my own funeral waiting for you to get ready. The story of my life, fifty six years of waiting on you and your make up."

"You never complained before," Mrs. Anderson retorted with a smirk, and her husband smiled.

"You're already beautiful, sweet heart."

I just stood there watching the exchange with a stunned expression on my face.

"What's your deal?" Mr. Anderson asked me gruffly. "You don't seem right. Are you dead, too?"

"Mostly," I answered with a chuckle that was threatening to turn into hysterical laughter any second now, but Vernonia saved me.

"Mr. and Mrs. Anderson, this is my friend Melvin Morton. He's a vampire who's having a very rough time of it tonight. I know you've had a trying time as well, but let's make Melvin feel a bit at ease under the circumstances. He's new to the supernatural."

"Poor dear," Mrs. Anderson said with a sympathetic pat on my arm that passed through my flesh like vapor.

"Hmmmpf, vampire, hmmpf," the ghost man said as he looked down at his corpse. "We all have bad days. Stupid hot chocolate."

"Now, Henry, don't blame the cocoa for this. You forgot to turn off the stove," Mrs. Anderson chided softly.

"Don't you start that again!" he sniped at her. "If you would have made me the damn cup in the first place then this wouldn't have happened."

"You wanted the cocoa, not me. I've waited on you hand and foot for those fifty-six years. It was about time you did something for yourself! And what a fine job you made of it, too!" his wife roared back.

As the ghosts argued Vernonia ignored them and began working on Henry's face again. I had to admit Henry's corpse looked better than his ghost did. Could my night get any stranger?

"Vernonia," I whispered. "Does this happen a lot? Ghosts?"

"With unexpected deaths, yes. But I suppose most deaths are unexpected in their own way. This is that anger I was telling you about earlier; makes the spirit linger longer." Vernonia shrugged her shoulders.

"Most times it makes it easier when a spirit sticks around long enough to tell me what they want to look like. Takes the pressure off, and I feel better knowing they'll move on happy." She chuckled and looked at Mr. and Mrs. Anderson still bickering. "I bet they were quite the couple in life."

"They're quite the pair now," I said with an eye roll.

"I'm surprised, although I don't know why I should be," Vernonia said quietly for only me to hear, "that you can see them."

"I don't know what to expect anymore," I muttered. "It's not like there's a handbook for all of this."

"I suppose." Vernonia just kept applying makeup, and slowly Henry's face took on a healthy glow on the table; she really was good at this. Henry and his wife had taken their bickering to the corner, and I was left standing in the middle of the room listening.

"So much for till death do us part!" Henry yelled. "Am I going to be stuck with your nagging and harping forever?"

"What a horrible thing to say!" his wife declared. "It's not like you listened to me when we were alive... why should death be any different?"

I had a vision of Pizza Bob and I arguing like this in fifty-six years, and cringed. Dear god, no. I tried to tune the ghosts out, and went to stand beside Vernonia.

"Are there any other, uh, um, ghosts here?" I asked.

"There were, but I think they've moved on," Vernonia said over her shoulder.

"Will those two move on?"

"I certainly hope so, but each case is different. Take your ghost for example."

I winced. "He decided to stick around. I thought that once I got rid of his body he'd leave."

"Oh, that sounds like quite the story! Got rid of his body?" Vernonia didn't sound horrified, but nothing seemed to rattle her.

I said, "I thought that if I put him in hallowed ground, like a cemetery, Pizza Bob wouldn't have ties to this world anymore."

"That was clever of you."

"Yeah, I saw it on a show about ghosts. But Pizza Bob had another idea. He decided he wanted a Viking funeral instead."

Vernonia laughed. "Tell me that's not the business I read about in the papers."

I shrugged. "I didn't really think it through."

The story had been in the news. A badly burned and dismembered corpse had washed up in the industrial area down river from Sauvie Island. Some of the remains were adhered to a half-melted inner tube and the body had yet to be identified. It was speculated to be the work of a serial killer. Lucky me.

Vernonia laughed again.

"A Viking funeral? I bet that was interesting."

"Yeah, it was pretty cool, but Pizza Bob ended up being free to follow me everywhere after that."

"Yes, that's what happens with determined spirits. He doesn't seem that bad of a fellow," Vernonia said.

"He shocks me sometimes, makes me want to kill him most times, but I'm sort of used to him now. I can't believe he's so up for me becoming more of a vampire. It's crazy, Vernonia. I'm freaked out by the last six months, by finding Abby and seeing what she's capable of--"

"Melvin, you have to talk to Mrs. Brokerman and make sure she let that man in the wine cellar go." Vernonia was standing with her arms crossed.

"I don't want her to know where I am," I mumbled.

"What man?" Mrs. Anderson asked, distracted from her domestic squabble. Even Henry had floated over.

"It's a long story," I said.

"We aren't going anywhere." Henry pointed at the bodies.

"Don't be morbid, dear," his wife said.

"Hmmmpf," was his answer, but Henry reached out and took his wife's hand. How sweet.

"Well?" Mrs. Anderson prompted.

What did I have to lose? I told them about Abby's impromptu snack. Mrs. Anderson shocked me completely.

"What a nice thing to do," she said.

"Are you kidding me?" I shouted. "It was a terrible thing to do, especially to the man concerned. What is up with everyone around me? Huh? Suddenly murder is okay?"

Henry Anderson raised an eyebrow. "You sure don't act like a vampire."

"So everyone keeps saying," I said with a curt nod.

"Are you sure you're a vampire?" Mrs. Anderson asked me while trying to get a peek at my nonexistent fangs.

"Of course I'm sure. I'm just not a very good one."

"Mr. and Mrs. Anderson, please leave Melvin alone." Vernonia brought out a folding chair and set it next to her table so that I could sit down, which I did with another one of my trademark sighs. Vernonia handed me her cell phone.

"Call Mrs. Brokerman."

Vernonia's phone started ringing in my hand, and I nearly dropped it as I handed it back to her. She looked at the caller ID and smirked.

"Speak of the devil," she said, and then answered the call.

"Hello, Mrs. Brokerman. I was just about to call you." Vernonia listened to Abby on the other end of the line with a frown on her face. My vampiric hearing could hear both sides of the conversation, and Abby sounded upset.

I flinched in my seat as I felt Mrs. Anderson's ghostly hand rest on my shoulder. "Mrs.?" she asked me with an arched eyebrow. "You cheeky little devil."

"It's not like that!" I retorted, and focused on the phone call again. Abby was asking if Vernonia had seen me, and Vernonia was nodding her head at me.

"Mrs. Brokerman, Melvin called me from a pay phone and I picked him up downtown. What made you think to call me?" Hesitation and then, "I see, just a hunch. Of course you can talk to him."

Vernonia tried to hand me the phone, but I wouldn't take it. Vernonia covered the speaker with her hand and scolded me.

"Stop being such a child, Melvin. You need to know if that man is still in the wine cellar, and you have to stand on your own two feet." She put the phone in my hand and stepped back.

"Melvin, are you there? Melvin?" Abby sounded desperate. "Please talk to me."

I sighed into the phone and said, "Hello, Abby."

"You scared me to death when you left! Why would you do such a bad thing?"

"Because of the *bad* thing you did, Abby." I was speaking in code because Abby wasn't supposed to know that Vernonia knew about me or about the man in the cellar, and Abby couldn't know about Vernonia and her gift. Secrets, secrets everywhere! I was dizzy from it.

"How did you know where to find me?" I asked her.

"That nasty ghost of yours left me a note. He told me you were with Vernonia," she said. "I guess he was trying to help."

"Oh." Another curve ball from Pizza Bob.

"Melvin, please don't be angry with me. I'm just trying to help you."

I gritted my teeth. "Abby, you should have asked me first. Asked me what I wanted."

"I guess...."

"No, Abby, no! I thought we were friends."

Abby gasped. "Of course we're friends! Why else would I kidnap someone for you to eat? Why else would I be doing all of the things I've done for you! I've gone to a lot of trouble you know, and you don't seem to give a damn one way or the other."

Mr. and Mrs. Anderson were hovering right next to me trying to eavesdrop. "Go away," I hissed.

"What was that?" Abby asked.

"Abby," I said trying to sound calm as Mr. Anderson gave me a haughty look and drifted back into the corner with his wife in tow. "You know I've been grateful, but you're doing things without thinking about my feelings now. You know I don't want another incident like the pizza guy." I let that sink in.

"I didn't think of that," Abby said quietly. "I thought that was just an accident."

"Well, I don't want to find out! And my apartment was my apartment. You didn't even ask me first!"

"That was supposed to be a surprise. I thought you'd be happy," she said sadly.

Vernonia tapped me on he shoulder and whispered, "What about the man?"

"It was a surprise all right. What about the surprise in the wine cellar?" I arched my eyebrows at Vernonia in an are-you-happy-now? look. "Is that taken care of and sent away?"

"Yes, Melvin." Abby said petulantly.

I gave Vernonia a thumbs-up and she pumped her fist in the air happily.

Abby said, "Melvin, I'm sorry about all of this. You're right. I've been so caught up that I didn't think to ask you about any of it. I'm sorry."

I felt my anger ebbing away. "Abby, I'm sorry too. I like you and have been just letting you take care of me. I should apologize for taking advantage."

"What a little gentleman!" Mrs. Anderson exclaimed from the corner, and I smiled at her. I couldn't help it; she thought I was a gentleman; if only she knew.

"Don't be silly. Melvin, can I come get you...please?" Abby asked.

I looked at Vernonia, at the ghost couple, and decided I'd had enough excitement for one evening. Abby and I had unfinished business and we needed to talk. After that I'd figure out what to do with my half-dead life.

"Yes, Abby. I'd like that." I told her where I was and she said she'd be here in twenty minutes. I handed the cell phone back to Vernonia, and then gave the woman a big hug.

"Thank you, Vernonia. Thank you for being my friend."

"Such a dear, sweet boy," she whispered in my ear. "Things are going to be all right, Melvin. You'll see."

Vernonia gave me a fierce squeeze and then pushed away.

She said, "It's time for you to be strong." That sounded like a brush off. Who could blame her? She had her hands full already with the undead, why should I continue to add to her drama.

Vernonia turned her back and said over her shoulder, "You should go wait in the parking lot, no need for Mrs. Brokerman to feel more out of sorts about all of this tonight. Besides, I need to finish up Mrs. Anderson."

"I guess so."

"You'll be fine, Melvin. You're a vampire. You need to remember that."

"Okay." I looked at the pair of ghosts standing next to me. "Well, it was nice meeting you. Good luck in the after life."

Mr. Anderson extended his hand for a shake, and it was like grasping at air, but I returned the gesture.

"Good luck to you, Mr. Morton. You'll get your sea legs on this vampire thing I'm sure."

His wife kissed me on the cheek. "Be brave!" she said, and I tried to give her a brave smile in return. She just patted my arm and floated away with an amused look on her face.

"Thank you, Vernonia. I'll never forget your kindness." I shifted awkwardly from foot to foot and then realized I was just stalling. "Okay then, I'll be going now." Vernonia had already said her goodbyes, so she just waved over her shoulder.

Yup, I was dismissed. But that was okay. I had that effect on some people. I should count my blessings; at least she'd come to rescue me from downtown. There was that at least.

I went outside and stood under one of the streetlights at the edge of the parking lot to wait for Abby. Every little sound made me jump -- the rustling of branches in the breeze, dried leaves skittering across the black top, and raccoons or opossums foraging next to the dumpster. I had visions of the goblins that the troll had mentioned showing up and mugging me, so of course I let out a high pitched squeal when someone tapped me on the shoulder from behind.

"Damn, Melvin! Jumpy much?" Pizza Bob was hovering behind me with a smirk on his face.

"You! You rat fink, tattle tale dickhead!" I lunged for him, but he disappeared and then reappeared a few feet away.

"Whoa, I didn't think you'd be this mad."

"Oh, you haven't seen how mad I can get!" I shouted. "My life doesn't suck enough for the universe so you make up for it. Why would you tell Abby where I was? What part of I don't want to see her did you not understand?"

"Dude, you need to chill."

"Chill? Really? She's on her way here, but I'm still not happy. Why in the hell did you meddle?" I was secretly glad that Abby was coming for me, but I was equally angry with the ghost. No sense in letting him think he'd won!

"Melvin, you've got no street smarts and you're safer with her than anyone. That troll got me thinking."

"I hate you."

"Oh boo-hoo."

"Screw you."

"Come on, buddy."

"Don't buddy me; we're not buddies or pals or anything. You're just some pathetic jerk who wasted his life like I did, and then had the misfortune to show up at my door. I wish I'd never tried to bite you!"

"Ditto, ass hat! I'm not that fond of you either."

And then Pizza Bob slugged me, right in the stomach. I doubled over, and then dropped to my knees; it felt like I'd been hit with a sledgehammer.

Now I'm not a tough guy, had never been in a fight before, but I'd grown cocky about my vampire strength and super powers. The fact that I was getting my butt kicked by a ghost was the last straw in my fragile self-esteem, so I just kneeled on the asphalt, wallowing in my misery.

Ozone crackled in the air, its smell metallic and sharp, and I knew Pizza Bob was readying for another blow. It was bad enough the first time so I jumped up quickly waving my hands, and this scattered the ghost's form into vapors as he was about to kick me in the head.

He didn't reappear for a minute, but when he did Pizza Bob was shimmering in and out of focus. He'd used up too much energy with his attack to do anything but hover and glare at me. He was too weak to even speak. Finally!

I massaged my stomach and sat down on the ground, glaring back at him and a little embarrassed about the whole episode. Someone started clapping behind me, and I jumped to my feet quickly and spun around; not before I caught Pizza Bob's terrified expression, though.

"Oh Fudge!" I shouted. Actually I said something worse, I think, I hope. A true Little Ralphie moment.

Staring back at me with his swirling, shadowed face, Mr. Happy gave me a theatrical bow.

"Fisticuffs at a mortuary, how splendid!" He pointed at Pizza Bob and said, "A duel between the dead and the mostly dead. Interesting. Come here."

It was like something took hold of my ghost and yanked; Pizza Bob jerked forward and hovered right next to me. He was terrified, yup, yes indeed. But hey, so was I.

"Good evening, gentlemen." Mr. Happy said. "You've managed to survive I see, Melvin. Mostly." He leaned forward and sniffed my face. A menacing chuckle filled the air.

"Wh-what are you doing here?" I squeaked.

"Where else would I be? Hmmm? You've piqued my curiosity, my boy. I've been watching for you, but you've flown beneath the radar. Very clever of you."

Flown beneath the radar? What?

"No," I said carefully. "I've been just living my life."

Mr. Happy laughed. "Living. Your. Life. Oh, that's a good one. By the way your blog is quite entertaining."

I gulped and Mr. Happy made a tsk-tsk sound. "Hiding behind words on a web. But you're hardly spider-like. Sucking on nothing but dreams and fantasy."

"I wasn't hiding."

"Well, you haven't been being a vampire in the true sense, now have you? No feeding yet." He waggled a finger in my face. "But somehow you've managed to survive. Very interesting indeed."

"You read my blog?" The wheels were turning in my head. "Let me guess, you're Anonymous. Right?"

Mr. Happy shook his head. "Now that's just insulting, Melvin. That poster is nothing but a hack."

"So you haven't seen Maddy?"

"Enough about her. And why would you care, eh? She abandoned you. Though to her credit I can see why. You've just been such a disappointment. But I suppose it's not all your fault."

"Do you know where she is?" I have no idea why I was pushing him like this. Perhaps I was finally suicidal, but at least I wasn't wriggling like a bug on the end of a stick like my ghost was at the moment; he was quite miserable as a matter of fact.

Pizza Bob was trying to disappear and it made me happy, in an evil way I guess, that he was suffering, unable to do anything while under Mr. Happy's power.

"Serves you right, BUDDY." I whispered to him.

"Ooh, such vitriol, Melvin," Mr. Happy crooned. "But I said enough about Maddy. You wouldn't want the details anyway; you haven't the stomach for it."

"Oh...." That didn't sound good. Nope. Not at all.

The demon snapped his fingers at Pizza Bob, and the ghost went rigid. "Why are you still here?"

Pizza Bob looked at me beseechingly, but I turned away.

"Speak!" Mr. Happy said ominously.

"I, I, don't know," Pizza Bob answered slowly.

"Wrong answer."

"I'm stuck."

"Wrong again. Third time's the charm," Mr. Happy said with a finger shake. "It's not a trick question, nor is it a difficult one."

"Uh," Pizza Bob sputtered. Mr. Happy shook his head in disgust and looked at me.

"Why he's just as gob smacked as you are, Melvin. You sure know how to pick them."

"You're very intimidating," I said, trying to sound brave.

"Am I? That's the nicest thing I've heard in ages. However, I'm still a bit cross with you."

I looked at my ghost who was struggling to get loose from Mr. Happy's weird mind hold thing, when he mouthed one word that sent a chill down my spine: Abby.

Crap. She was on her way here and I had no idea what Mr. Happy would do to her.

"Oh," I whispered again. "I'm sorry about that, the making you cross thing. I thought it was just a dream."

"Hmmm, not so much of an apology as an excuse, Melvin. So what about this ghost here? Aren't you curious why he's stayed with you?" The shadow flicked his finger and Pizza Bob fell to his knees. "Ready with your answer?"

Pizza Bob looked at me with guilt all over his face. He gritted his teeth and nodded.

"I'm waiting," Mr. Happy demanded.

"I was told to stay," said my ghost of the last two months.

"What?" I took a step towards him. "By whom?"

"Confession is good for the soul, my boy." Mr. Happy snapped his fingers and Pizza Bob slumped, freed from whatever had been holding him.

"Ask him." Pizza Bob pointed at the shadow.

"It's standard protocol. The first feed stays around to act as a guide, earn his freedom from the damning bite of a vampire." Mr. Happy chuckled. "If you would have been more hospitable and not so dense, I would have explained it, Melvin."

"But I didn't bite him," I said.

"Yes, funny that. He could have moved on at any time if he hadn't been so angry about the whole mess."

"What?" Pizza Bob roared.

"Oops, seems I played a little tricksie," the shadow said gleefully. "I'll give you this though, you've become quite the powerful spirit. An excellent experiment if I do say so myself. However, you didn't do the vampire much good."

"I tried."

"Not hard enough evidently. Feeding on monkeys? How insulting."

Pizza Bob frowned and then looked at me. "Sorry, dude."

I looked at Pizza Bob with more pity than anger. "You lied to me."

"I had to."

Mr. Happy said, "I never said you had to lie."

Pizza Bob glared at the shadow. "Well, you suggested what might happen to me if I told the truth. Something about a painful oblivion and endless torment if I gave away my mission."

"I may have embellished. You make me sound like a spymaster. That's delightful."

"You're evil," Pizza Bob said. "But Melvin isn't, and that just cheeses you, doesn't it?"

The shadow laughed. "Melvin is too stupid to be evil."

"Hey! I'm standing right here and can hear you!" I took a step towards him. "You've got some nerve playing with souls like that. Yeah, you're scary as hell, but you know what? I'm not afraid of you anymore." Okay, I lied. I was terrified with a high pucker factor in my nether regions. Pizza Bob shook his head no at me, and took a step back.

"Oh really?" Mr. Happy's voice dripped with sarcasm, and I swear the temperature dropped a few degrees around us.

"Really," I retorted, puffing out my chest to seem bigger. I hoped that scary clown head wasn't going to appear again. I'm sure I'd pee myself and go to the great beyond smelling like a diaper.

"It's time I put an end to your pitiful charade, Melvin. I knew you'd be a dreadful vampire, a waste of the Dark Gift. You should be afraid of me."

"Whatever, Mr. Happy. That's a stupid name, too. You're just like every bully I had chasing me my whole life, intimidating and full of hot air. I don't think you can hurt me, I think you're just a wannabe poser."

Oh, I was pushing it, but I was trying to work myself up. I was a vampire with super strength! Come on! I was also delusional as hell, and saw Pizza Bob shaking his head sadly at my bravado.

"And what you did to him is inexcusable." I pointed at Pizza Bob. Something changed in the ghost and he looked at me gratefully.

"Dude, you are so going to owe me," he said as the smell of ozone filled the air. Pizza Bob's body started glowing with crackling energy racing down his arms. "The things I do for you, ass hat. Give Emily a pat on the butt for me."

Mr. Happy started to reach for me when Pizza Bob yelled, "RUN!", which I did. Like my ass was on fire. Olympic quality.

Pizza Bob grabbed Mr. Happy in a bear hug, and there was an explosion of light that packed a wallop. I felt the concussion on my back as I cleared the parking lot. Luckily the street was one way and I knew Abby's limo would approach Morrison's from this direction. I guess the universe had decided to cut me a break because exactly as I hit the corner, Abby's Limo pulled up. I opened the door, jumped in, and started yelling for Giles to GO! GO! GO! Maybe it was the drama of the moment, but Giles just went, went, went, and we backed up quickly and peeled out onto the main road like a stunt car. Abby was too shocked to say anything until we were on the freeway.

"What the hell is going on?"

"Bad things, Abby. Scary things." I winced as I thought about Pizza Bob. Maybe he was okay. Yeah, I owed him. But what could top a Viking funeral? I started laughing and couldn't stop.

Hysteria is actually a good thing in my book. That little brain hiccup gives reality a chance to chill for a while, until it's safe for a reboot. Unfortunately, my reboot came in the form of a slap.

"Melvin! Snap out of it!" And then Abby slapped me again.

"Would you like me to give it a go?" Giles asked eagerly.

I growled at him. "Thanks, Giles. How's the nose?"

The chauffeur hunched down behind the wheel and drove faster.

"Melvin, I'm sorry I hit you. I saw that in a movie, but it actually works." I just nodded at Abby. "Are you okay?"

"No, Abby. I'm not. So far from not."

"Oh my god, Melvin. What's happened? Did you do something to Mrs. Ruttle?"

I laughed, and then let out a weary sigh. "No, nothing like that, but I hope she's okay. I have to tell you some things."

I told her about the troll, goblins, and Maddy's potential demise in some horrible way that made me nauseous just thinking about it. She hadn't been that bad I suppose. I would have dumped me too.

Wrong time for a pity party, Melvin.

I took a deep breath and told Abby about Mr. Happy, and finally about Pizza Bob; Abby's face crumpled in horror.

"I didn't like him one bit, but that ghost saved you from whatever that shadow thing is. Do you think he's dead?"

"Of course he's dead, Abby. Pizza Bob is a ghost."

"Don't be obtuse, Melvin. I meant do you think he's been destroyed? What about Mr. Happy, which is a creepy name by the way."

"I have no idea. If Pizza Bob is okay he'll show up. If he doesn't then, well, I still won't know. As far as Mr. Happy...I have no way of knowing.

"But if he's still around," I said while I took Abby's hand, "then you are in a lot of danger. I need to leave so you won't be more exposed than you already are."

"Where can I drop you?" Giles asked. I could feel the waves of hatred coming off of him. And I didn't care that he knew my secrets now; he'd probably already figured it out. He was a jerk but hardly a moron.

"That's enough, Giles," Abby snapped.

"Yes, ma'am."

Abby scowled at his back and then turned towards me. She had that determined look on her face when she knows she's going to get what she wants, no matter what. "Melvin, you are coming home and that's that. It's close to sunrise."

"Abby--"

"Enough!" she shouted. "That's enough. I'm tired, you're tired, so we'll go home and sleep on this. There'll be a solution tomorrow. I know it."

She was right. I was too exhausted to be self-righteous. I leaned back into the seat and let the sound of the limo tires on freeway lull me a bit. Pizza Bob had taken care of Mr. Happy, I hoped with a little touch of guilt thrown in for good measure. Giles was staring at me in the rearview mirror, his gaze locked like a laser, but I was too tired to fence with the jerk. A little tinge of worry snaked through me when I caught him smirking at me, though.

Abby patted my arm. "Melvin, Giles was good enough to bring you a snack. He thought you might be peckish after your time away." She handed me a carton of pig livers.

I looked back at Giles and his eyes were now locked on the road. Why was he being nice? Playing the toady for Abby's benefit? But I was hungry, damn it.

"Hmmm, that's unique." I stared at the carton for a moment.

"Oh just eat the damned things, Melvin." Abby took a big gulp of her cocktail and stared out the window.

I opened the lid and the aroma was just too tempting. I ate the whole batch in two gulps, much to my chagrin, and then reclined, feeling euphoric for some reason. I couldn't fathom why. I'd been attacked by my ghost, saved by my ghost who, I realized, was actually a friend that I would miss, encountered the ever-so-delightful Mr. Happy....

Why was I feeling so good? And maybe a little dizzy? Stress?

I licked my lips and ran my tongue over my teeth, dislodging a few chunks of masticated pig liver. There was a strange aftertaste, but Abby was always mixing some health thing into my diet.

Giles was full out smiling as my eyelids drooped.

Uh-oh.

CHAPTER 11

SERIOUSLY? SERIOUSLY.

I woke up in pitch-black darkness. That was odd; I usually left just a crack open in the velvet drapery so a peek of sunlight would grace my room. It was the little touches of normalcy that kept me grounded, I reasoned. I was an early riser, a vampire version of a morning person, and unless I'd slept through the whole day and into the night there should be some light around me. I didn't really remember coming home, but obviously Abby had put me to bed. It was close to dawn by the time my adventure had come to an end.

Poor Pizza Bob, I thought with a shudder. I reached for my face to scrub the sleep potatoes from my eyes, and panicked when I found my arms duct taped to my body. Lots and lots of duct tape. Oh boy. I sat up, or should say tried to sit up, but only ended up smacking my face against something solid. Okay, this was bad. Understatement much? I struggled against the tape, but apparently most of a roll had been used to bind me. Not even my super strength could budge it. Chalk one up for the inventor of duct tape; it's good stuff!

"I think he's awake, sir." Giles' voice. That smarmy little prick! What had he done now?

"Yes, I heard the thump, Giles. Are you sure he's secured?" a deep rumbling and unknown voice said just outside my box.

Yes, I was in a box; probably a coffin by the feel of the satin padding underneath me. Factor ten on the creepy scale. In a coffin and wrapped in duct tape.

"Yes, sir. He's wrapped up nice and tight!"

"Um, hello?" I called out. "I think there's been some kind of misunderstanding here." That sounded reasonable, like something I should say under the circumstances. The lid opened a crack and I was bathed in burning light. I had to blink from the glare.

Now when I say burning light, I mean BURNING light. It was like liquid fire on my retinas. I had wacky little green afterimages dancing behind my eyelids.

"Ow!" I yelped.

The lid flew open and the full effect of the light was torture on the rest of my face. A person stepped in front of the glow, obscuring the source briefly. "Now, are you going to be good or must I take more severe measures?" It was the deep voice again.

"Yup, I'm good," I whispered meekly.

More severe measures? Yikes.

"I think there's been some kind of mistake here."

"No mistake, Mr. Morton. No mistake at all." The man crossed his arms, my vision was clearing -- hooray for me -- and I finally saw my captor: Mr. Brokerman.

Oh crap. I recognized him from the various photographs spread throughout the mansion, and I must say he looked much scarier in person. Taller than I expected, less hair, though and more muscle than fat, Abby's husband looked like he was in great shape for a fifty-five year old torture king. Wonderful.

We were in the wine cellar; why did the bad things have to happen down here? It must be a basement thing. Giles was standing next to Mr. Brokerman, his arms crossed and a smug grin plastered on his face. But no Abby.

Oh, this was bad.

I cleared my throat. "Hello, sir, um, Mr. Brokerman. It's nice to finally meet you. Abby's told me all about you." Oh God, I was babbling like an idiot. Mr. Brokerman arched an eyebrow.

"Abby? No, it's Mrs. Brokerman to you. I'm afraid the feeling is not mutual, Mr. Morton. I was rather disturbed when Giles contacted me in Dubai."

I squinted at the chauffeur. Yup, I officially truly hated the bastard now.

"Disturbed?" I squeaked. I cleared my throat and tried to sound a little manlier, less squeaky, less me. "I'm sorry to hear that. Is there a reason for your disturbance?"

I was flexing and stretching, trying to break the hold of the tape, and I felt a little heart flutter from the exertion but not much give in the bindings. Stupid heart! Stupid mostly dead existence!

"Well aren't you the cocky fellow. Setting up in my house with my wife, wearing my suits while I'm away. And to top it off smelling up my home with your undead stink!"

That one hit the mark and I blushed a deep purple as my odor wafted up to my nose. Way to kick a guy when he's down. Or duct taped in a coffin. Wow.

"It's not like that, Mr. Brokerman. I've been ill and Abby, um, Mrs. Brokerman ran into me and was helping me to get better. I don't know what Giles told you, but he's lying."

"Really? Sick? Vampirism is a sickness now? Is that my suit?"

"Okay, yeah...but no, but yeah," I was waffling of course. "It's not your suit, but Abby said the others were old ones that I could use. This is my suit."

"Your suit? Bought with my money, you repugnant little toad. And her name is Priscilla." Mr. Brokerman stepped aside and I was bathed in the light again. It was a sun lamp. Damn! Overcast sunlight I could handle but a tanning lamp was just too strong!

"So is Giles also lying about you being a vampire?" he asked.

I writhed and groaned, sounding like a baby seal being clubbed as my skin started to smoke a bit. So much for sounding manly.

"Okay, yes...yes...I'm a vampire, mostly. Kind of. Ugh. Stop with the pain making and the light already." Apparently when I'm under duress I channel Jerry Lewis. Decidedly unattractive for a man my size.

"And is Giles lying about you and my wife?" Mr. Brokerman roared.

"Yes, most definitely." I felt the duct tape give a little on my left arm. I think the heat was breaking down the glue, or perhaps the sweat and juices of my slowly immolating body were to blame. Either way I was going with it.

Mr. Brokerman stepped in front of the light again and I sobbed in relief. I doubted I could take much more; my eyes were getting a green afterimage tinty-thing going again.

"I've found applied pressure actually works during interrogations." Mr. Brokerman leaned over and inspected the smoldering patches on my cheeks. I'm sure I was lovely -- smeared makeup, acne scars, Eua de BBQ Vamp.

He curled his lip and stood up. "Perhaps a little more encouragement for the truth."

As he stepped aside I was bathed in the light again. Who was this freak? Applied pressure during interrogations? Huh? Was he going to water board me with holy water next?

"Stop, please! This is insane! Why are you doing this? I'm not a bad guy, really, I swear!" Damn! Was I pathetic or what? Note to self: You'll crack under torture.

Was this guy for real? Obviously. Here I was, duct tapped in a coffin and being blasted with a sun lamp. How could Abby marry a monster like this?

Well, she fancies you in a way, doesn't she?

Brokerman prodded me with a finger and then wiped his hand on Giles' sleeve. "I ask you again, is Giles now lying about you and my wife?"

"Yes. He. Is. Lying." I blinked my eyes to try and get some moisture back into my crisping orbs. "Abby is my friend...my only friend. That is all. I have no designs on your wife!"

Wow, I actually managed that with a straight face. So much for truth through torture.

Brokerman stepped in front of the light and crossed his arms. "Giles is a loyal servant. I trust him, and maybe you're just saying what I want to hear so the pain stops. This is just the first level, Mr. Morton. I have a lot of questions for you, and you will be forthcoming. I guarantee it."

"You seem awfully comfortable with the pain-making, Mr. Brokerman. I have to admit I'm a bit nervous right now. Guaranteed. But this is all just some misunderstanding."

"I do take pride in my work. The government keeps me quite busy, thus the long stints away from home. But Mrs. Brokerman is my wife, my property. No man, or thing," he curled his lip at me, "can take that away from me. Giles keeps watch while I'm away, and I'm quite disturbed at what's been going on."

"He's lying." I scowled at Giles, and the man just winked at me. "Abby is my friend. No designs whatsoever."

"Perhaps not now, but I believe in time you'd try and turn my Priss into an abomination like you are."

"Nope. Never happen. I wouldn't wish this on anyone."

"I've seen the way he looks at her, sir," Giles piped in eagerly. "And I hate to tell you this but she looks at him the same way."

Really? How awesome was that? My glee was short lived though.

"Oh I'll deal with her shortly." The venom in Brokerman's voice made me very afraid for Abby. This guy was on par with Mr. Happy in the terror department.

"Don't you hurt her." The iciness of my voice made him step back. I caught a bit of sun lamp, but the pain was insignificant over my anger. "If you've hurt even one hair on Abby's head I'll make you suffer, you psychopath."

"You're in no position for threats. And for a supposed vampire you're rather pathetic." He sneered, and then produced my fake fangs from his jacket pocket. "Really, I must say this is beyond parody. No fangs, and not at all what I would have expected."

"Oh, I can be dangerous enough without the fangs! I'm warning you!" I was starting to channel something dark, the beast within, ramping up from the Cowardly Lion shtick to hide my embarrassment. At least that's what I was trying to do. Brokerman was unfazed.

He said, "When I'm done with you there are some interested parties who would love to take a peek at what makes you tick, so I'll have to leave them some sort of scrap to analyze." Brokerman smiled coldly.

Oh! That sounded bad. But by now I was far too angry to be really scared. I'm sure once I got out of this I'd have a proper, good old fashioned attack of the heebie-jeebies; the whole nine yards: shaking, stomach upset, perhaps a good vomit or two. But for now it was hero time. I fixed Mr. Brokerman with the scariest face I could muster. He just laughed at me. That did it.

"You have no idea what I am." I flexed and the duct tape ripped on my left arm. Adrenaline is adrenaline, even if you're undead. I moved faster than I've ever moved before and tore the tape away from my right arm. I jumped out of the coffin and backhanded Giles before he could even react. He went sprawling unconscious into the corner, his nose now smashed beyond repair. Hooray! Mr. Brokerman whipped out a crucifix and brandished it at me. Was he serious? I started laughing.

"You have to have faith for that to work on me, Mr. Brokerman." I couldn't help the Fright Nite homage as I grabbed the cross and snapped it in half.

"Is that the best you've got?" I was laughing maniacally, hopefully scaring the absolute bejesus out of the man.

Be the bad ass, Melvin!

Mr. Brokerman was a quick thinker though, and grabbed the sun lamp. He shoved it towards me and burned my arm. Now that just made me angrier.

I knocked the lamp out of his hand and stomped on the bulb. The look of sheer terror on the man's face was like an energy drink. My overbite extended as I grabbed him and slammed him against the wall, holding the man up by his throat so that his feet dangled uselessly. I shook him like a rag doll.

"What." I thumped his head against the wall. "Goes." Thump. "Through." Thump, thump. "That head," thump, thump, thump, "of yours?" I was shouting and caught up in my rage. I didn't notice that he'd gone limp. Oh crap. Just what I needed...another ghost haunting my ass. I let go of him, and Mr. Brokerman crumpled to the floor. I heard his heartbeat, strong and steady, so I'd just concussed the psycho.

Fair enough.

I looked over my shoulder and saw Giles, and smiled to myself. That nose was really a goner this time, just a fountain of blood and ruined cartilage.

Blood. I was dizzy from the scent of it, all that glorious blood just waiting for me to crouch down and take. The thought didn't even repulse me that much. I wondered if I could bite him without killing him? As long as he didn't have any of my blood he'd be fine. Ha! Like I cared.

If you do that there's no going back!

My overbite throbbed and I was getting a bit dizzy...stupid conscience!

To bite or not to bite, hmmm. I sighed and backed up, bumping into the coffin and thus back to reality.

No. My first foray into human blood wouldn't be an asshole like Giles. He'd probably taste bad anyway. I looked around and found a roll of duct tape. Perfect.

I bundled he and Mr. Brokerman face-to-face in the coffin, their hands taped to each other's butts in a touching, hallmark cuddle, and then punched a hole in the bottom of the silk-lined death box so they wouldn't suffocate.

I may be a vampire but I'm not a cold-blooded vampire. Well, actually I am technically cold blooded. Ah, never mind. I'm not like Brokerman. I eyed my handy work with a smile, wishing that Pizza Bob were around to appreciate it. I slammed the lid closed, and went to find Abby.

⚔

I started up the stairs slowly; I felt awful. I had a funky taste in my mouth, my skin was cracked and weeping, and I was hungry. So very hungry. Just the thought of all that blood pooled around Giles made my gums tingle; it also sent a spike of nausea rumbling through my stomach.

Don't go there!

Besides the obvious burns on the outside, my eyes were ruined; I could barely see. I could be the poster boy for what not to do in tanning beds. Safety first, folks, and remember: goggles are your friends. I paused at the landing and rubbed at my eyelids; it was like I was looking through mauve-tinted gauze, and hoped this wouldn't be permanent. Weren't vampires supposed to heal rapidly? Hollywood thought so, and since I'd never really been hurt this badly before I wanted to go with the movie lore. I was scared, but I was more terrified for Abby.

I closed my eyes and listened for her heart beat -- it was there, faint and weak, but there. I tried to locate her scent but couldn't smell anything but burned hair (eew!), my burned hair! But at least Abby was still alive.

The house was quiet and dark as I emerged from the wine cellar like some black and white movie monster. It lives!

The staff was gone, probably sent away by the crazed Mr. Brokerman so he could get his ya-yas torturing me in the basement. My hands started to shake as I thought about how it all could have ended.

Badly, that's how. Crispy and badly.

Snap out of it, Melvin! You can have your melt down later.

"Abby?" I called out. I jumped as I heard a thumping noise above me, and then rushed through the house and up the stairs. I found Abby in one of the far guest rooms, tied to a chair with a wad of silk stuffed in her mouth as a gag. She was sagged forward against her bindings, stomping on the floor, and she looked like she'd been drugged.

"Are you okay? Did he hurt you?" I crouched down next to her.

Abby's eyes went wide in terror when she saw me, and she flinched away when I snapped the ropes. I backed up slowly as she pulled the wad of silk out of mouth and coughed.

"Is that you, Melvin?" She tried to stand but wobbled back into the chair. "I'm, I'm fine." She ran a hand through her hair and then squinted at me.

"Oh yech, you're so gross! I hardly recognize you," she whispered. "Dear god, what did he do to you? Your poor face, your poor eyes, those sweet adoring eyes! What is that smell?" Abby wrinkled up her nose.

I reached up and touched my face gingerly, feeling crackling skin and something slimy. "Gah! Is it bad? I'm barbecued!"

"Oh, Melvin...I'm so sorry. I had no idea he was back yet; he came home a few days early. I thought we had more time. Giles must have drugged you in the limo. You were out cold when we got back to the mansion and Daniel was waiting for me."

"Daniel?" I was still poking at my face. "Oh, Mr. Psycho in the basement. He's charming, Abby. Quite the catch."

"Did you kill him?" She worried at her lip as she dabbed at the burns on my face with the silk scarf.

"Would you be upset?"

"At this point? No, not really."

I took her hand. "No, I didn't kill him. I'm not a monster, Abby."

"You look like one." She half smiled at me to ease the harshness out of her voice. "What the hell did he do to you?"

"Duct tape and a sun lamp. He's certainly creative with the pain making. Who exactly does he work for anyway?"

"He jokes and says he works in securities, you know to make people think he's a banker. He's a private security contractor; that's all I know and all I care to know. He has his money and I have mine."

"He's a psychopath."

"Yes, well, he's my psychopath, though."

And you're mine, Abby. You're mine.

"Why did you marry him?"

"I loved him once. We shared a common...." She put a finger to her lip, lost in thought.

"Scariness?" I offered with a headshake. I had finally come to the realization that there was just something not right in her head. But I loved her. Oh well.

Abby smirked at me. "Sure, Melvin. I suppose. Thanks for saving me. Who knows what he would have done to me when he got through with you."

"Let's not dwell on it. What are we going to do now, Abby?" I was starting to feel dizzier and a lot sick. "I left he and the good little butt monkey, Giles, in the wine cellar."

I sank to my knees. Was the room spinning? I heard birds chirping outside the window; dawn was close. I caught a hazy glimpse of myself in the mirror and gasped. Holy crap! No wonder she freaked out when she saw me -- I was a total freak show.

"Melvin, you need blood. You're badly injured!" She pulled my hand away from the place where I kept poking at my cheek. "Stop messing with it or you'll make it worse. Just bite me on the wrist and take a little blood. It's the least I could do."

"Don't be ridiculous, Abby! That's disgusting." But I think what actually came out was, ungh, ungh, bleh...ungh.

"Whoa, Melvin? Are you okay?" Abby tried to lay me down on the floor, but she was still weak from the drugs in her system. "Melvin! Answer me!"

"I think I've got sun stroke." I know that's what I said. Ever the comedian! I laughed feebly and then passed out.

Boy, some hero I turned out to be. A half-assed bad ass.

I was shivering. I never shiver because I don't have any body heat to begin with, but there I was shivering and miserable. There were mumbling voices next to me; I could barely make out the shadows of people in the dimly lit room. Did I mention that I was miserable? I tried to lift my arm and had a burst of panic when I realized it was strapped to the table. I was on a table.

Here we go again! I started flailing madly until a hand pressed down on my chest.

"Melvin! Calm down! You'll tear out the IV!" Abby loomed over me and I stopped struggling.

"IV?" I licked my lips and immediately started shivering again. "Where am I?"

"You're safe, Melvin. Trust me."

I looked down and saw a thin tube attached to the IV needle in my arm. There was a steady stream of blood inching down the line in glorious little bursts. What was even better is that I could see that tube. It was a little fuzzy but my vision was coming back. Yeah for Hollywood!

Abby spoke to someone over her shoulder. "Can we get a sedative please?"

She stepped away from the table and I saw a lab in the background. A faint hooting and clamor in another room, like cage bars rattling, drifted over me. Did I smell monkeys?

"No, I'll be good! I wanna stay up!" I started channeling that inner five year old, and Abby smiled indulgently.

"No, Melvin. You need to recuperate. I'll take care of you."

"Where the hell am I?" I asked feebly as a technician, a smiling red haired woman in a white lab coat, injected my IV with something that made me feel warm and woozy all at once.

"You're among friends, Mr. Morton. Now get some rest." The technician patted me on the arm, and then checked the blood line.

"Okay," I mumbled as I looked around the room. I turned my head and saw another table next to me with an arm poking out from beneath a blanket. Oh crap. There was an IV in that arm. That male arm. Oh double crap. That male arm with a male hand with a wedding band...and an IV line connected to my IV line.

"Oh, Abby...no--" but I passed out with a little bead of drool in the corner of my mouth.

Stellar.

The drugs made me dream. I saw Pizza Bob standing in the corner grinning at me, then he was next to the table giving me his trademark thumbs-up.

"Buddy, pal...what happened?" My tongue felt all squishy and weird in my mouth, but the words sounded right.

"Dude, you are so baked right now! I'm jealous!" Pizza Bob inspected my IV. "Finally going for the good stuff. I'm proud of you."

"What. Happened. To--to Mr. Happy--"

"Smoted, my friend. He kicked my butt good, though."

"Are you really here? I don't dream so you must be here."

"Nope, you're dreaming, dude." The ghost shimmered. "Actually it's more of a drug induced hallucination. Coolness and woohoo, yeah? It's the only way I could pop in. Mr. Happy kicked my butt good into the nothingness. Deep doo-doo. I'm working on getting back, though."

"Okay. Thanks for saving me."

"It's my job, ass hat."

"No...."

"That's what friends are for, Melvin. Hang in there, and figure out how you're gonna top the Viking funeral!" Pizza Bob shimmered and then fizzled away in a Hollywood-type special effects overkill that made the room seem all wobbly and rubbery, so I closed my eyes.

I slipped back into a stupor again and drifted in and out of consciousness for I don't know how long. Hours, days, months?

I finally woke up feeling much better, better than better actually. I woke up feeling great. I was still on the table but the IV was gone. I sat up and looked around, but the other table was gone; no sign of the illustrious Mr. Psycho Brokerman anywhere. That might be bad.

Oh, Abby. What did you do now?

I inspected my hands and then touched my face; the skin felt leathery and hard in places, probably a knot of scar tissue, but at least I was alive. And my hands didn't look as blue. Huh. Imagine that. I got off the table and stretched. I felt amazing. I was even wearing new clothes and had a momentary panic attack at who had seen me naked. Ugh. Oh well. It didn't matter; what's done is done, right? I went back to feeling great.

"You're awake."

I turned around and Abby was standing there with a radiant smile and a horrible black eye. My mood instantly darkened.

"What happened to you?" I went rushing over to her in a panic. She touched her cheek lightly, and then sighed.

"Daniel was less than pleased with the outcome of his interrogation."

I must have been too drugged to notice her bruises before. "I'll kill him." I started for the door, but Abby grabbed my arm.

"Whoa there, hero. Melvin, don't worry about it. I can take care of myself." Abby grinned wickedly at me. "How are you feeling?"

"Abby, what did you do? Is he--"

"Dead?" she finished for me with an arched eyebrow. "Well, that depends on how you look at it. How do you feel?"

I felt a little woozy. "That was him on the table, wasn't it."

"Would that upset you?" She hooked arms with me and led me to a couch.

"Did he give you that black eye?" I asked as we sat down.

"Yes, yes he did."

"Then I guess not." I was lying of course, but at the same time I was glad that psycho was out of the picture. "Tell me what happened."

"After you passed out I had to do some quick thinking. I went down to the wine cellar to see Daniel and Giles, and found them in the coffin. Nice touch by the way." She gave me a high five.

"I thought so."

"Anyway, he was awake and raving like a lunatic. Giles had thrown up all over him...I didn't kill Giles."

"Okay, that sounds ominous." I shifted on the couch and the cushion made a little farting noise. I was mortified, but Abby was preoccupied with the memory of the wine cellar and thankfully didn't hear it.

"Yes, well, um, Giles' broken nose and ensuing vomit episode sort of made him suffocate. You had him nestled in quite close, and he is, was, a bit shorter than Daniel. It was funny as hell what you did, and any other time I would have given anything to have a camera." She giggled, and it sent a little chill down my spine. "I tell you that Daniel didn't appreciate being duct taped to a dead man. Especially with that death grip he had on his ass!" She burst out laughing, and then sniffed self-consciously.

I looked around wildly, expecting to see Giles standing there, his ghost left behind to torment me because again I had accidentally killed someone. But there was just Abby and me. Whew.

"Melvin? What are you doing?"

"Ghost check."

"Oh, I didn't think of that...is anyone here?" Abby started to stand up, but I grabbed her hand.

"Nope. No sign of him." But then again Pizza Bob had waited a day before he showed up. "Um, how long have I been out?" I asked, trying to sound casual.

"Five days, why?"

Okay. Dodged that spectral bullet. "No reason. So what happened with psycho?"

"Well, I explained the situation to Daniel, that you were my friend and that I was very upset about what he had done to you. I informed him that I wanted a divorce and that I was going to press charges for him drugging me and holding me against my will."

"Okay...."

"You know what that bastard did?"

"Yeah, he duct taped me in a coffin and burned me with a sun lamp." I shrugged. "I was there."

Abby laughed and rolled her eyes at me. "No, smart ass. This is my princess moment. Daniel laughed at me. He just laughed at me. And not a nice laugh, either.

"He said he had friends in high places, and that I had better watch my step." Abby pursed her lips. "He said I was just a spoiled little socialite and that I wouldn't do anything to upset the status quo; that the scandal would undo me."

"Well, it would be a little awkward explaining the whole thing to the police--"

"I don't give a crap about the police. I don't even care about a scandal. But I won't be laughed at, not by anyone."

"So how did you get the black eye?" I had a vision of Abby letting Daniel out of the coffin, him beating her, and then I drew a blank.

"I leaned over to spit in his face, and he head butted me." Abby gave me a little embarrassed smile. "I should have seen it coming. Remember that bully in fifth grade? Recess all over again."

I was horrified. "That was a long time ago...we were just kids! Your husband head butted you? Still taped to Giles? I knew he was deranged, but I never thought he might actually really, truly hurt you. I'm so sorry...that must have been awful!" I started to put an arm around her and hesitated. "I should have been there."

"Yeah, it was pretty gruesome. He just came unhinged; talk about bringing your work home with you. Anyway, I was dazed for a moment, and then I slammed the lid closed and made some calls. You were too injured, and Daniel needed to be dealt with. Not to mention Giles' body. I know bad people, too." She winked at me. "Daniel isn't the only one who's connected."

"You sound like Tony Soprano." I smiled. "Psycho had no idea who he was messing with. That's my girl." My little psycho.

I looked around. "So, where are we?"

"The primate research center."

"Okay, there are bad people at the research center? Um, do they know about me?"

"No, the bad people are on call when I need them. Gerri, the woman who helped me get you taken care of is the head researcher here. She didn't ask any questions when I called her, and she will happily forget any of this ever happened. A few years ago I helped her out with a nasty ex-boyfriend problem. He was a real nut case."

"Should I ask what happened with that?" I was discovering it was a good idea to stay on Abby's good side.

"Let's just say he took a little trip. She's good people and was more than happy to help me with all of this. Trust me."

"Fair enough. I have to ask this one, though. Where is your husband?"

Abby smiled coldly. "Gone."

"And Giles?"

"Definitely gone."

This time I didn't hesitate. I put my arm around her. "And how are you doing?"

"You know, I'm surprisingly good. Better than good. I told you things would work out. I'm sorry all these bad things have happened to you, Melvin. I truly am."

"Abby, you've nothing to be sorry for." Well, except for possibly feeding me her hubby dearest. "So...what was in the IV?" I closed my eyes and braced myself for the answer.

"How do you feel?"

"I feel good." I hated to admit it, but I felt damned good.

"Then don't ask. Let's just say I think I solved your squeamish problem. Biting will not be an issue from now on. But I'd keep the fangs I gave you for a touch of theater."

I laughed, and Abby leaned in against me. "Do you think I'm a bad person?" she asked.

A little unstable, a touch of crazy, a lot scary, potentially psychopathic, but a bad person? Not so much if I weighed it all with a vampiric sense of right and wrong -- well, an evil vampire's sense of right and wrong. To me she was just a person I loved with every fiber of my being!

"No, Abby. You're perfect. But the less I know the happier I'll be for a while. Ignorance is bliss."

"A squeamish vampire, isn't that one for the books! You've always been a good person, Melvin."

"But won't there be questions about him and Giles?" Daniel's disappearance wouldn't be another Pizza Bob; people, the authorities, would ask questions. The last thing I wanted was for Abby's life to be destroyed because of me.

"Oh, I'm sure there will be," said Abby rather flippantly. "But the fiery car crash near Mt. Hood -- oh how Daniel loved his mountain view up close -- due to an intoxicated chauffeur, well, I'm sure they'll let the devastated widow deal with the loss accordingly."

"Oh, you're good. You actually did this already?" I couldn't believe my friend was so devious and frighteningly evil. Actually I could, and it scared me just a little bit.

"Yes, Melvin. It's all taken care of. My 'bad' people found a nice remote logging road, secluded enough that the bodies won't be found for a few more days yet. I'll file a missing person's report in a few days. That will give me time to practice my sad face."

"What about your black eye?" I winced because it looked pretty bad. "How are you going to explain that?"

"You could put some of your blood on it and heal it right up." Abby blinked her eyelashes at me.

"Been reading Ann Rice?" I asked with a laugh.

"Maybe. And also Charlaine Harris...I like those Sookie Stackhouse novels. She certainly knows a lot about vampires, Melvin. Maybe it would work?"

"No...I don't think so. That's all make-believe, and besides, I wouldn't want to risk any contamination."

"From me?" Abby arched an eyebrow. "The worst you'd get is some fashion sense."

"No, don't be silly. I meant from me. I wouldn't want you to catch the blue, stinky undead thing." I tried not to look embarrassed. "I'm not that much of a vampire. It took just one drop of Maddy's blood to ruin my life, and I think what I got was tainted anyhow. I couldn't bear it if something happened to you, Abby. I -- I..." I wanted to say, "Love you," but that would be a stupid, stupid thing to say. Abby had a crooked grin on her face.

"You, you what, Morton?" she asked coyly.

"I would never forgive myself."

"Oh. Hmmm. Melvin, being a vampire doesn't seem that bad."

"It's awful. Don't kid yourself." Except for the cool superpowers thing, but that hardly balanced out the whole undead creature of the night that craved blood thing. Bleh. "You really want that for yourself?"

"Well, I've already technically killed someone so I don't see what the big deal is. You never know what the future holds, right?" That sent a little shiver down my spine. "I'd make an awesome vampire."

Probably. I laughed a little. I had to. Otherwise I might cry.

"That's a weird thing to be proud of, my friend. Killing is a serious thing."

"Oh, whatever. He had it coming." She sighed, and touched her bruise. "Makeup is a girl's best friend. No one will see the black eye." Abby pouted for a moment. "I would make a great vampire."

"You're a very scary person, Abby."

"Why thank you. You will be too someday."

I shuddered. No, I just don't have that in me.

"So how bad is my face now?" I probed at the leathery patch with a grimace.

"Well," she hesitated, "actually it seemed to help. I know you're self conscious about your scars, which is just silly by the way. You know what I really look like under all this plastic surgery."

"I always thought you were beautiful."

"You had low standards. But back to you: the burned flesh healed up nicely. There are some shiny patches on your cheeks, but I think they'll fade in time." She looked up at me.

"You look good, Morton," said Abby, my best friend in the whole world.

"I--I, well, um, thanks. Let's hope it holds." Wow. She said I looked good.

Don't read anything into it. You're still blue, you still stink, and she's Abby... way out of your league, idiot. I sighed and decided to ignore that inner voice for once. Nothing could ruin this moment.

"Guess what?" I asked.

"What?"

"I'm not hungry anymore. Happy?"

"For now. Glad to help."

"You're a good friend, Abby. The best." I rested my chin on the top of her head, and then sniffed her hair.

"Did you just sniff my hair?"

"No...maybe...yes." My heart started up for a few beats and I blushed.

"I just heard your heart, Melvin. That's so cool. And hey," she sat up and looked at me, "you don't smell so much. A few more transfusions and you might be on track. A delightfully evil vampire, just like I promised." She leaned against my shoulder again. "I'm sorry we missed Halloween. It would have been a blast!"

True! The one night I could have just been myself, whoever that is. Oh well.

Abby said, "I'm tired, and there's so much left to do...but it's just you and me now, us against the world."

"Just rest, Abby."

I said a silent prayer to the universe: *Please, please, please, just let me have this without throwing me a curve ball. I deserve it. I know I'm happy and that's against your rules, but could you just cut me some slack...and I know I won't become evil. I promise. Just let me be happy for a little while.*

I shouldn't have drawn attention to myself. The universe hates me. Yes, yes indeed it does.

CHAPTER 12

IT'S ALL PART OF MY ROCK AND ROLL FANTASY

MASTERSOFTHENITE
Blogline ∞ November 8, 2014 ∞ MOOD: Blue, NOT!

Hello everyone! Sorry I haven't posted lately...things have been totally messed up and then great. I'm waiting for it to be messed up again. I have some sad news. Pizza Bob has left the building. I know I hated him for a while, but he and I became friends towards the end. He saved my life. Well, more to the point my undeath. To Mr. Happy I say this: SUCK IT!

I hope you're miserable wherever you are.

And Pizza Bob --I hope you're in the happy land of porn sites, lucky desperate housewife pizza deliveries, and clean Hawaiian shirts. Your Viking funeral should entitle you to a buffet table in Valhalla!

My other, and only, friend has been incredible. Which is bad because I'm good. I know that doesn't make sense...cryptic is my middle name now.

This blog kept me grounded for so long, and I'd like to thank those few, those happy few who were kind to me here. But having this blog has become dangerous for me. There are so many stories I'd like to share, but that's just not possible. Too many things have happened and there's no way to retell it without the damning details.

I will share this: I've graduated to human blood. While I'd like to take credit for the act, actually...no I wouldn't...I have become initiated. Sort of. Kind of. But it did make a difference for me. I don't stink that much anymore, and I'm not as blue.

That's all I can say. I so want to tell someone outside of all of this about what's happened. Maybe I'll change my mind down the road and post my full adventure here in the ether, but for now I'm just content to start living. Life is too short, and undeath may be too long, but I'm ready to give it a whirl. I still live in this mansion, and have a new appreciation for the finer things in life.

Well, here's one tidbit for the faithful readers -- trolls, goblins, demons, voodoo...it's all real. I met a troll. A weird, homeless, shopping cart-pushing troll. Yup. He told me about the goblins, and while I haven't seen any yet I believe that wacky little bagman. This town is filled with all kinds of stuff. Your D&D manuals can now serve as a guidebook for the world, for the things that hide in dark places and in shopping malls. But sometimes the monsters are just good old fashioned humans. No hit points or hot dice rolls will save you.

I got a dose of that dark side recently. To be all poetic-like: I looked in the mirror and the monster was not me. My advice is stick to the fiction of the Dark Gift. Those sparkly vampires are a nice distraction from the real world I live in. I'm no Edward, I'm no Lestat, I'm closer to Angel (but wish I could be Spike -- ha-ha), but I'm not a monster.

Wow. This post is so serious and mind-numbingly preachy. But hey, maybe I'm finally growing up. How After School Special is that, huh?

Important safety tip: wear your goggles in a tanning bed. Trust me. Your eyes will thank you.

Oh, and voodoo priestesses spit. A lot.

And ghosts can kick your ass if they get mad enough.

I also found out that Maddy might be gone. But if anyone spots her please let me know. There is unfinished business. I'll check in here occasionally.

Until next time, well, enjoy the sunshine, hug someone you love, be adventurous and leave that basement! Get a life, folks. I mean that in the nicest way possible.

-- Melvin

REPLY TO POSTER ∞ BLOCK USER ∞ REPORT POST

⅄

Life back at the mansion fell into a comfortable routine immediately. Too comfortable. I was too happy.

Abby filed a missing persons report, and then sat back and waited for someone to find her husband's body. The staff was none the wiser.

Everything happened quickly after that. I kept a low profile when the police showed up about the accident. Abby was quite the actress. I was impressed. I stayed out of the way when groups of friends came by to offer their sympathy or to help with the funeral arrangements. Abby played the grieving widow perfectly; draped in black, always with a tissue in hand. The staff had been giving me sideways looks, but that was par for the course. Abby and I spent a lot of time together; it was wonderful. Damn this giddiness! Strangely enough, Vernonia had kept her distance. But then again I hadn't checked on her either after the incident outside Morrison's. I hoped she hadn't had to deal with a ticked off Mr. Happy. Hopefully Pizza Bob had hurt him, or destroyed him, or banished him. I'd never know unless the demon showed up again.

I'd have to give Vernonia a call, though. Eventually.

Then this afternoon two detectives came back for an interview. They were an odd pairing, one short and heavy set, one tall and gangly; rather like Laurel and Hardy. I saw their reflection in the hallway mirror as I peeked down from the upstairs landing. I stood transfixed and eavesdropping, praying this wasn't where everything unraveled.

⅄

"Ma'am, we just have some follow up questions."

"Is there a development? I thought it was an accident." Abby looked concerned as she led them into the front parlor.

"Yes, it appears to have been an accident, but we just have some questions, just notes to close the file," said Laurel.

"I'll help you in any way I can. The stress of all this is almost more than I can bear, detectives. I can't believe he's gone!" She sat down delicately.

"We're sorry to take more of your time. One thing has bothered us. Why was your husband near Mt. Hood in the middle of the woods? Hadn't he already been away for four months? You're quite the catch, Mrs. Brokerman. It seems like he'd want to be with you." Detective Hardy smiled thinly.

The detectives were being thorough.

"Oh, thank you for that," Abby said with a blush. "I always missed Daniel so much when he traveled, but he'd been in Dubai...all that sand." She sniffled and wiped away a tear. "He loved the majesty of that mountain, missed it so when he was away. He was such a dear, sweet, gentle man! I would have been with him, but I had meetings to attend and he said he wouldn't be long, just a week away up at our mountain home so that he could get adjusted to the jet lag, find his center." Abby let out a theatrical little sob.

"Would you like a glass of water?" the other detective, Mr. Laurel, asked.

Good cop, bad cop. Ha! I'm sorry, Ollie.

I had to keep from giggling as I listened to the exchange. Naughty me for eavesdropping with my super ears!

"No...no...I just have to accept this...loss." Abby let another tear streak down her cheek.

"Jet lag can be awful. Are you sure that's where he was headed, to the mountain house? He was found in a very remote area." Ollie checked his notes.

"That's what Daniel said."

"Is that why you waited so long to file a missing person's report?" Laurel tented his fingers on his lap.

Abby tore at the tissue she held with shaking fingers. "He never took his phone with him when he went to meditate. He was a very spiritual and centered man. When he didn't come home.... Well....

"I suppose this is my fault. Giles had been acting erratically lately." Abby looked at the detectives guiltily.

"How do you mean?" they both asked in unison.

"Well, Giles had a drinking problem. I was on the verge of firing him because of it, but my dear sweet Daniel wanted to talk to him, help him out if he could. Giles had always been so loyal to this family." Abby blew her nose daintily.

"I understand. Unfortunately due to the severity of the fire in the vehicle, the chauffeur's body was too badly damaged to get a tox screen for alcohol. There really wasn't much left." Detective Laurel saw Abby wince. "Wow, I'm sorry about that. I'm sure he didn't suffer. But it makes sense...him being drunk and crashing like that."

Abby nodded slowly. "I'm trying to find some compassion in my heart for Giles. He killed my husband, but it was an accident. I should have pushed for the man to get into rehab."

"Did he appear drunk the night he left with Mr. Brokerman?"

Abby shook her head. "No, but sometimes he and Daniel would have cognac in the back of the limo. They were very close." She let that hang in the air.

Ollie arched an eyebrow and looked at his partner. The other man just waved him off with a let's not go there, okay? gesture. Abby watched this all with a slight grin, which disappeared when the detective looked up.

"Did Mr. Brokerman have any enemies? Anyone who had threatened him recently?"

Abby shook her head. "Not that I know of. He is, was a very good businessman, very well respected in his field. He tried not to bring his home work with him." Abby dabbed at her eyes.

Upstairs I rolled my eyes. *Um, Abby...he did bring his work home with him!*

"It's unclear what your husband did for a living," Ollie stated.

"He was in securities. Government subcontracting," Abby said quietly. "It was a very stressful job."

"Right, so that explains his need for some quiet time."

"He was a very complicated man." Abby dabbed at her eyes with the tissue. I snorted upstairs, a little too loudly, and I heard Abby's heartbeat elevate.

"You've had a guest staying here recently?" Laurel looked at Abby over the top of his notebook.

My heart started up, and I had a nervous rush of adrenaline. Uh-oh. Here's where everything unraveled. But Abby was ready with a cover story; she was quick on her mental feet!

"Yes, and old friend from grade school that I recently ran into." Abby stared at the floor. "I'm afraid he's dying. He's terminally ill and, well, I just felt it was the right thing to do to take him in and give him some compassion before he goes."

"Wow, that's very kind of you." Ollie sounded stunned. "Did Mr. Brokerman object to it? Did they get along?"

"Daniel was away when my friend came here to stay with us. He was medicated when Daniel arrived and they didn't meet before Daniel left for the mountain. Daniel was very supportive, though. He has, had a charitable heart."

"My condolences regarding your friend. And our sympathies for the tragedy that has befallen your household." Detective Laurel oozed class.

Whatever. Just leave already!

"And what is your friend's name?" Ollie asked.

"Melvin." Abby had calmed down, and let her voice quaver for effect. "He's sedated right now."

"We won't bother him for now, but his last name please? For the report?" Ollie smiled.

"Morton."

Oh crap. They knew who I was now. I did a little memory jog about Pizza Bob and his disappearance, hoping and praying that I didn't leave a trail for them to follow. My blog might be my undoing.

"One more routine question," said the bad cop, Ollie. "That we have to ask, you understand. Were you and your husband having any problems?"

I had to cover my mouth to keep from snorting again.

Bad form, Melvin.

He was a psychopath who tortured people for a living. What more of a problem would that be? Oh, and he tried to kill me! Oh, and he was going to kill Abby. Problems...no problems.

Ah, good old gallows humor!

Abby blinked, and then looked at the detectives in shock. "Not that I know of. We are, were very happy."

"Okay, well...I think that answers our questions, Mrs. Brokerman. We're truly sorry for your loss."

Upstairs I shook my head in wonder. She'd pulled it off.

"Thank you, detectives." Abby stood up and wiped at her eyes. "I just don't know how I'll cope with this. I had Daniel's remains--" Abby let that statement catch in her throat, and then said in a quavering voice, "What was left after the fire --"

"Oh, Mrs. Brokerman, we're sorry that this has happened to you," both detectives interrupted quickly, feeling awkward and uncomfortable with the details.

But Abby seemed to ignore them and kept talking. "I had the rest of him cremated this morning...the wake is tomorrow. I feel so empty inside."

"Would you listen to that line of bull from such a pretty little mouth! She doesn't even miss me."

I jumped at the voice next to my ear. I spun around and came face-to-face with none other than Daniel Brokerman. I slammed my hand over my mouth again to quiet the girly squeal. The ghost just grinned at me.

"Hello, you little toad!"

"You've got to be frickin' kidding me!" I hissed.

"I'm going to get you!" He lunged at me, but passed right through and into the wall. He was new to this ghost thing. I heard the front door close and Abby's footsteps coming towards the stairs.

"Melvin? You can come down now." She was standing there at the bottom of the stairs, her hand resting on the newel post, a shaft of golden sunlight beaming down on her like a divine spotlight. "Was it just me or did those two remind you of Laurel and Hardy?" She laughed. "It took everything I had not to start laughing when they'd talk! I had to keep up the sad face. It was easy to cry because I was laughing so hard on the inside! I think we'll be fine now."

There was a chill in the air and waves of anger coming at me from all directions. This was bad. Way off the scale on the bad counter! Should I tell Abby? Uh-uh, no way.

Daniel appeared in front of me. "That little minx, she's tougher than I ever gave her credit for; sadistic, dark, and kind of sexy in her evilness. If only I'd known before now! But she's going to pay."

"What the hell are you doing here?" I was trying not to yell for fear of alarming Abby. Hell, I was alarmed enough for the both of us. I couldn't believe it. This was so unfair!

Thanks, Universe.

"Go away! You're dead. Move on." I made a shooing motion with my hands.

"No. I was told I have to stay here, but that doesn't mean I like it." The ghost clenched his fist. "I plan on making your life hell, vampire. That's the only way I'll like it."

Oh, that's just craptastic! Told to stay?

Mr. Happy was at it again. That meant Pizza Bob had failed.

"Congratulations. I'm your first blood." Daniel's face twisted into an angry sneer. "I'm going to make you suffer, make her suffer, you haven't known pain before this."

"You're supposed to help me," I whispered. "That's the rule."

"Help you? I don't think so. That shadow thing said I could do whatever I want to you now. He doesn't like you very much, but then again who would?"

"You don't want to mess with me." I gritted my teeth.

"I really think that went well," Abby said as she climbed the stairs. "Laurel and Hardy had no problems with me taking care of everything so quickly, and they seemed satisfied with my answers. Daniel's body was cremated this morning. His ashes will go to the mausoleum tomorrow for the wake. Swept up all nice and tidy, don't you think?" Abby was smiling radiantly.

Swell. Awesome. The body was gone and now he could go anywhere he wanted to. It was the nightmare of Pizza Bob without the witty repartee. There was no way in hell I'd become friends with this psychopath!

"You bitch." Daniel was floating right in front of Abby. "You bled me dry like some farm animal!"

"Go away!" I hissed at him, my face a mask of utter despair and frustration, but Abby stopped dead in her tracks.

"Uh-oh, I've seen that look before. Is it Pizza Bob?"

"Abby, maybe you should go back downstairs."

"No. Who is it? Is it Giles? If so I'll have his corpse salted and buried in a vat of holy water!"

"She's got balls! I'm going to love breaking her down!" the ghost shouted as he whirled around her.

"It's complicated, Abby!" I took her hand and pulled her back down the stairs. "This is bad...oh, so very bad. I should have known better...I should have seen it coming!"

Abby yanked her hand away. "No, Melvin! Who is it?" Her eyes were like saucers, and Daniel laughed next to me.

"Go on, tell her. I want to see her face when she realizes I'm back. I'll be with you forever, both of you!"

"But I didn't kill you," I whispered. Abby heard me and blanched.

"Oh. God. No...it can't be! Why?" She grabbed my arm.

"Abby, it's time to go! We need to go somewhere safe."

"There's nowhere safe from me. You can run but you can't hide!" Daniel mocked.

"I can try!" I was pulling Abby towards the front door when she yanked her hand away.

"I'm not going to be run out of my home, Melvin. Where is he? Where is Daniel?" She demanded, unable to see him. "And why is he haunting you? I'm the one who killed the bastard!"

Daniel roared and flew at her, passing through her body like an icy vapor. Abby doubled over and started shivering, looking blindly over her shoulder to see the ghost that had attacked her, but Daniel was gone for the moment having used up all of his energy. He was still in the learning phase, thankfully, but Daniel would get stronger; ghosts always did if they were determined. And he was definitely determined. And angry. A very bad combination.

"Is he gone?" she whispered.

"For now. He blew a fuse, but he'll be back. I don't know when, but he will be back and sincerely pissed off if he's following the pattern."

"I'm so sorry, Melvin!" She looked devastated. "He should be haunting me, not you! It's not fair!"

I took Abby's hand and pulled her to me in tight embrace so she couldn't see my expression. "It doesn't matter, Abby. He was my first human blood. The first one always comes back."

I wish I had remembered that tidbit from Mr. Happy's lecture in the mortuary parking lot. Oh man, I was so screwed. Royally.

"I'm sorry, Melvin." Abby started to cry. "I didn't think about that...I wish it was Pizza Bob again."

I laughed. I had to; it was either laugh or puke. "Me too, Abby. Me too."

Abby pulled away from me, pulled her hair to the side and exposed her neck. "Melvin, bite me."

"Wha? Whoa, whoa, whoa!" I grabbed her arms and gave her a little shake. "Where the hell did that come from?"

"I want the Dark Gift. With two of us strong, maybe we can fight this together."

"That's not going to happen, Abby. I won't do that."

She looked up at me with scorn, and then a look I couldn't decipher in her eyes. It sent a little chill down my spine. "I told you...I want this."

"I can't. I won't."

"I'm going to get what I want, Melvin. And you will help me."

"Abby, now is not the time to talk about this." Actually never sounded like a good time. "The crap is hitting the fan, and frankly even if I wanted to make you a vampire I don't think I could. I can barely help myself. I can't help you with this." I tried not to sound whiny. Or sad. Or me.

"Daniel and that Mr. Happy thing have got you freaked out--"

"You bet your ass!"

"Well, me too. But I still think I'd make a kick-ass vamp, just think about it."

"Bigger fish, Abby. Let's just stay focused on one scary thing at a time. We're in a situation here."

"Understatement much?" Abby rolled her eyes.

"We need to find someone who can help us."

As if on cue, the doorbell rang.

⅄

Abby grabbed my hand and pulled me towards the stairs. "I have no idea who that could be, and I'm in no mood for surprises. Let the maid get it!"

But I recognized that heartbeat, that scent.

"Abby, wait." I peeked around the corner as the maid answered the door. Yup. I was right. My stomach did a little flip-flop when I saw Marcella standing there.

"I need to speak with Miss Priss. Urgently." She brushed past the maid and headed right for us.

"Oh great, what's she want now?" Abby ran a hand through her hair, and pursed her lips.

"Abby! She looks pissed." I so did not want to tangle with voodoo right now. The recent tanning lamp owies and the trauma of meeting spectral Daniel were bad enough.

The maid tried to step in front of Marcella, but the determined woman just nudged her aside. "Miss Priss, I know you dere wit dat ting, but I need to speak with you. Now." She tapped her foot impatiently.

Abby stepped into the foyer and waved the maid away. "Thank you, Emily. I will handle it from here."

The maid squeaked, "Yes, ma'am," took one look at me, and bolted for the kitchen.

Abby squinted at the Haitian woman. "What do you want, Marcella?"

"You got big problems, Miss Priss. Big problems. One dat gonna be back right soon, too." She pointed at where I was hiding around the corner. "Come out from dere, Loogaroo. We need to talk."

"What do you need to see Melvin for? Why all the drama, Marcella?" Abby had her arms crossed and she still looked rattled from her encounter with Daniel. "What do you mean come back?" She squinted at the Haitian woman, and then looked nervously at the front door.

"He blew past me, such cold big hatred wrapped up dere." Marcella tsk-tsked at Abby.

"You're not going to spit or mace me with that powder again, are you?" I peeked around the corner and saw Marcella roll her eyes.

"Fine then. Don't hear what I have to say." She turned to leave, but hesitated. "I'm trying to do the right ting now." She looked at Abby who was pale and shaking. "De right ting for everyone."

Well that piqued my curiosity.

"Wait," I said as I hustled around the corner. "Is it an apology?"

Fat chance of that, but what could it hurt to plant the seed.

"Vampire, I still don't like you one bit, but tings have been made clearer to me." Marcella took a step towards me, and then looked at Abby. "Bad tings done happen around you, Miss Priss, I see dat."

"Well this is all well and good, Marcella, but it's been a long day and Melvin and I were just about to step out." Abby was looking around for Daniel again, and I was staring at Marcella. The Haitian woman was just shaking her head back and forth at the both of us like we were idiot children.

"You can't out run it, Miss Priss. Dat be a bad ting you do, and you bring down de Petro on your friend because of it."

"How do you do that?" I had a little involuntary shudder run through me. "Damn, you're scary!"

"What do you mean by this?" Abby grabbed Marcella's arm. "What is a Petro?"

"An angry spirit, a bad spirit. You know dat husband of yours was no good, dat for sure, an evil man, but de scales don't quite balance out." Marcella squinted at me and flared her nostrils in distaste. "You've fed. On him no less. There's no going back now for you; you just have no control of where your life takes you."

"Duh!" I snorted.

Abby let go of Marcella's arm and sagged against the doorframe. "We really can't out run him?"

"No."

"Abby," I said, "it's going to be fine. I'll leave and he'll have to come with me. You'll be okay."

But I won't! Take one for the team, Melvin! Daniel will have to come with me, but Abby will be safe. Alone.

"No!" Abby yelled. "Not an option, Melvin. We've come too far to lose now. Marcella, you said I had big problems. Is this what you came to talk about?"

"Let's go and sit down. The new spirit, dat Petro is on the list of problems headed your way."

"Great, that's just great." Abby clasped her hands in front of her nervously. "Tea? Anyone? It's what I do when I'm stressed. I become the perfect hostess."

"Abby--"

"And perhaps some cookies," she said cutting me off quickly. "I'll have some tea brought into the parlor." Abby left me standing there with Miss Voodoo USA 2014.

"She's cracking." Marcella said it matter-of-fact.

"No, she just really likes tea." I crossed my arms to cover up the lie. Abby was definitely cracking. Yessir indeedy. No need to mention the desire to become a vampire like me. That would send Marcella over the edge.

"So, Marcella...." I squinted at her. "No apology then?"

"Don't push it, Loogaroo."

"Can you please just call me Melvin? I'm not a monster. Really." I smiled at her. "And maybe not spit on me?"

Marcella let a ghost of a smile touch the corners of her mouth, and then she looked at me. "You're like a child."

Abby met us in the parlor and flopped down onto the couch next to me. She watched Marcella perch on the edge of the couch, and then rubbed a hand across her face; she looked exhausted.

"Does this mean you'll help us now?" She sounded exhausted, too. This was all my fault. Oh, and the Universe's too.

"I don't want to, but I can't not help either." Marcella took a pouch out of her pocket and I flinched. "Calm down, looga--Melvin. This will keep us protected while we talk. Dat husband come back soon all rested and angry." She poured a circle of red dust onto the floor around the couch where we sat.

"So what happens now?" I was curious what the powder was, and also a little afraid.

"If you're not evil then nothing." Marcella winked at me.

"Enough of your games, Marcella. Tell us what's going on and why you've decided to help us." That was Abby. Blunt.

Marcella faced me. "Your spirit man been comin' round and speakin' wit me. Told me many tings, he has."

"Psycho? Don't believe a word he says."

"No, de other one."

"Pizza Bob is okay?" I was elated. "I thought he was gone for good."

Did I have a dream about him? No, I don't dream! Do I?

"No," Marcella arched an eyebrow at me. "He just trapped and weak for a while. He been trying to get back to you. That boy won't give me no peace...waking me up at all hours ranting and begging for help."

"Are we talking about the same guy?" Pizza Bob begging? No way.

"Oh yeah, da very same. He told me all about you, Melvin."

"Where is he now?" I looked around but couldn't sense anything near me.

"He's here, but weak. So very weak. He done good against that shadow man, but he paid a heavy price."

"Dude! Pizza Bob! Are you here?" I never thought I'd be so happy to hear one of Pizza Bob's sarcastic remarks. Nothing happened. Maybe Marcella was wrong, but the memory of that hallucination was floating towards the surface of my brain.

"Are you sure he's back?"

"I already told you he was here. He says to tell you, 'Awesome job wit de duct tape and the butts,' and yes...he told me all about dat too."

"Yup, I thought he'd like that. Glad to know he saw it." I had a goofy grin on my face.

"It was pretty funny, Melvin. I still wish I had a camera." Abby high-fived me.

"Melvin, I'm happy that you didn't kill those men. You could have, but you didn't." Marcella turned an accusing eye at Abby.

Abby twisted a lock of hair around her finger and pouted. "Don't look at me like that. I only killed one. Call it a preemptive strike. He would have come for me next, and Melvin was injured. I did what I had to do."

A faint clink of crockery caught her attention, and Abby looked up at the maid, Emily, who was hovering in the doorway with the tea tray.

Abby shrugged and pointed at the coffee table. "Just set it down there."

The maid set the tray down and scuttled out of the room quickly. Abby cocked an eyebrow at me.

"Do you think she heard that?"

"Probably. Sorry," I offered with a weak smile. "I should have heard her coming."

"You're not a watch dog, Melvin."

"Well, I do have super hearing."

"Slacker."

"You think she'll lead a mutiny?"

"I'll just give her a raise. You know...hazard pay--"

Marcella held her hand up. "Enough. This is no time for your odd kinship."

Abby burst out laughing. "Marcella, have you seen what's been going on lately? If I don't laugh I'll snap. Odd kinship. I like that."

"There are bad tings headed this way. De shadow man, dat demon, he is after you both now. He'll surround you with pain and darkness."

"Yeah, I've seen that already." I let out a hearty snort. "Been there, done that, got the haunting to show for it." I kept looking around for Pizza Bob. "You see I made Mr. Happy cross. He doesn't like that."

Marcella stared at me for a moment. "Mr. Happy?"

"That's what he calls himself, the shadow man."

"He is pure evil. Kalfu, bad nasty Loa. Ti Malice, trickster. Nothing happy wit dat demon, no sir." Marcella hugged herself. "He came to me last night wit a warning. Stay away, he say, or he make the Guinee turn me away when my time come. Sick the Sousson-Pannan on me."

"Guinee?" Abby looked puzzled.

"Heaven, Miss Priss. The afterlife what come wit peace."

"That's awful. Can he do that?"

"I don't know. He's a very powerful Loa. Demon."

"Did he peel off his face and turn into a clown?" I asked.

"No." Marcella looked at me sideways. "He keep de moon and night as his face. Kalfu, see?"

"I don't know anything about what you're talking about. Although now that you mention it he doesn't have a face; just a swirly, motion-sick-making, dark spot filled with sarcasm. Sorry. But clowns are scary, okay? Okay." I picked at a stray piece of lint on my sleeve. "I don't like clowns."

"You're a very odd vampire." The Haitian woman clucked her tongue. "Kalfu, Sousson-Pannan be much worse wit all dose sores and pain den some clown."

All of her dems, dats, de's and wacky Haitian pronunciations were starting to all run together in my head. I ran a hand over my face and then tapped my ear. "Your accent is really hard to understand, Marcella."

"I'm upset, Melvin. I been here a long time but it just so easy to go back to Kreyol when I get rattled. I'm upset. Very upset."

"I'm getting that. Welcome to my world." I shrugged at her.

"So if Mr. Happy told you to stay away then why did you come here?" Abby took a sip of her tea. "Why get involved? You made yourself pretty clear last time you were here."

"Because of the first spirit, your Pizza Bob, Melvin. He came to me and told me tings...tings I din' wan' ta hear."

"You know, I think he came to me a few days ago when I was drugged," I said. "I hoped I was finally dreaming. When I turned, I stopped dreaming. See? So if Pizza Bob was there and I saw him that meant I was dreaming...or it was probably an hallucination from being, well, drugged." I wrinkled up my forehead at the memory.

"Drugged? You've had it hard, vampire. So many tings come at you so. But it makes sense dat spirit find you then. When your barriers are down he can slip through to you. It was him. He won't let me be, though."

"He grows on you." I smiled.

"Like a fungus. He was persistent until I finally agreed to listen."

"Yup." I smiled at her. "I have to be honest here, I'm nervous that you're being so nice about all this."

"Nice?" Abby interjected.

"Well, she's not spitting and cursing me," I said.

"If she would have helped before--"

"Things worked out fine, Abby. Marcella is here now and that's all that matters."

"I suppose," said Abby as she laid her head on the sofa arm.

"Melvin," Marcella bowed her head, "where I come from the Loogaroo very bad tings. Very bad magic indeed." She looked up at me. "I don't traffic wit de bad tings. But your ghost man told me your sad story, vampire. I know all about you now. He told me his story, how he was tricked into staying here in dis world as a slave by that shadow.

"I help you now because I don't abide rule breakers, deal breakers or liars." She took a small sip of tea. "I pity you, vampire."

"Hey!" Abby stood up. "Don't you dare feel sorry for Melvin. He doesn't need your pity!"

"Abby, it's okay--" I wanted her to stay in the circle, to be protected from whatever was coming. It *was* my fault.

Okay, so maybe Abby fed me her husband. That never would have happened if I hadn't been so pitiful in the first place. I have to admit I kind of did deserve pity. I was pathetic. No matter how much I tried to dress it up, live in a fantasy, pretend that I was finally worth something while living in someone else's home, wearing someone else's clothes, mooning after someone else's wife.

I was pathetic. I'd lived life as a loser; never reaching my potential and just accepting whatever I was handed with a shrug. Before I didn't have friends in life; I was a loner. I became a vampire and wallowed in self-pity. It took the actions of my long lost best friend from childhood, a dear friend but a stranger of fate to feed and clothe me, and I stood back and accepted it. Sure I hemmed and hawed, but in the end I let Abby do all the heavy lifting. Let's not even mention the actions of Pizza Bob, my other friend born out of circumstance.

Marcella was staring at me like she could read my mind. Awkward. She gave me a sad smile.

"Yes, yes he does, Miss Priss. He's an undead, no chance for life in dis here world, but not by his choice. He's tried to be good. But you've seen to damning his soul."

I winced. Oh man, Marcella. Why go there?

Abby's face crumpled. She looked at me wide-eyed and started crying. "I never meant for that to happen."

"Yes, you did." Marcella set her cup down. "Wipe away dose crocodile tears. I tried to warn you off dis path but you wouldn't listen. You be all caught up in the spell. I see into your heart and know what dark tings lie there.

"Your soul is blacker den dis here vampire's," Marcella said with reproach.

"I'm sorry. I'm a bad person." Abby sniffled, but she had stopped crying. In fact she had that look in her eye that sent chills down my spine. I just hoped Marcella wouldn't laugh at her.

"Now wait a minute. I think we're getting off track here." I was trying to be the diplomat. "What's done is done, Marcella. You said so yourself. But Abby is a good person. I admit she can be scary--"

"Hey!" Abby poked me in the arm, but I waved my hand to silence her.

"But in this world you have to be sometimes. Everything Abby did, she did because she was trying to help me. Stop blaming her."

"I'm the undead, remember? The dark creature of the night, the blood craver...." I clasped my hands together. "I'm the freak who's causing all the problems."

"You're not causing problems," Abby interjected.

"Yes, yes, he did." Marcella nodded at her. "Bâ'y cou bliyé, pôté mâc sonjé – The giver of the blow forgets, the carrier of the scar remembers."

"Ouch, Marcella." I hated that she was right.

"But you...oh my, you on a bad path, Miss Priss." Marcella shook her head sadly.

Abby was on a bad path, and wanting more. Boy did I have my hands full.

I leaned in close to Marcella and whispered, "What can I do to save her?"

"I don't know yet, but will you do whatever it takes?" she whispered back.

That sounded ominous, but I nodded.

Marcella took my hand. "Dat is why I am here, Melvin. I will help you." There was a little spark when she touched me, a good spark. And she didn't spit on me! Score one for the good guy!

"Can you help Pizza Bob? Can you protect my friends?" I whispered, amazed that Marcella could hear me. Maybe she was reading my mind after all.

"You love her, don't you?" Marcella mouthed silently.

With all of my heart, and more when it beats. I looked over at Abby and felt a blush coming on. She was staring at me, and trying to hear what Marcella and I were saying, and getting decidedly frustrated by the exclusion. So she might be evil. So what? Nobody's perfect. Yup, I was in love with her, warts and all.

"Please don't tell her. It would make things difficult."

Marcella squeezed my hand and nodded.

"Can you help them?"

"Help who, Melvin?" Abby was leaning in close to me. "Stop being so damned secretive."

"We'll do it together," Marcella said as she stood up and took Abby's hand. "We have work to do before that Petro comes back. He close, and extra angry. Dat husband of yours determined for bad tings today. Take me to your kitchen."

⋏

"Are we going to cook up some potions?" Abby was leaning against the marble counter top, watching Marcella go through the cupboards. The kitchen staff had been dismissed for the day, and they were all too happy to leave.

Abby laughed. "I used to watch that show "Charmed" all the time. They were always cooking up potions in the kitchen to kick some demon butt."

Marcella looked over her shoulder and grinned. "I loved dat show. Silly and not real at all, but a fun show none de less, Wi! Sekonsa!"

"You're just full of surprises, Marcella." I was pouring out the bag of red powder in a wide circle in the kitchen, surrounding our work area with care. "Hey, am I doing this right?"

"Is de powder coming out de bag and onto de floor?"

"Um, yes." I was carefully spilling out the contents in a thin line, a bit on the obsessive-compulsive side really.

"Then you doin' it right." Marcella laughed.

"What is this stuff?" I finished up with the circle, and then took a pinch of the powder between my fingers; it was grainy and smelled like clay. I felt no spark or tingle when I touched it at all.

Ha! I'm not evil. Woohoo.

"It's red brick dust. Keep evil from crossing over." Marcella had found a bag of rice, some onions, some garlic, and she was now searching for a pot under the counter.

"Is that all? Red brick dust?" Abby sounded incredulous.

"Yes." Marcella found the pot and headed for the stove.

"So what are you doing now? Potions?" I set the bag on the counter and frowned. I felt silly dumping brick dust on the floor. But what did I know about voodoo except what I'd seen in the movies: The Serpent and the Rainbow and that Bond flick.

Marcella turned and looked at me. "Vampire, I don't make potions, and I wouldn't even do that here because my altar is at home. Preparations and ceremonies take time, two days minimum. Gris-Gris bags take time."

I didn't even want to know what a gris-gris bag was.

"So what are you doing then?" Abby was starting to crumble from the stress of the last week; she had dark circles under her eyes, and her voice was shaky.

Marcella patted her on the shoulder. "We're hungry. Food brings strength and a clear head, Miss Priss. Sac vid pa campé - You can't work without food."

"Are you kidding me?" I put my face in my hands and laughed. "The ectoplasmic poo is going to hit the fan shortly, people! Daniel is regaining his strength as we speak, and then he'll back, pissed off and determined.

"You're making a power lunch?" I yelled.

Daniel was way overdue; he should have been back by now, not that I missed his company. But the longer he was away, the stronger he'd get.

"Melvin, Miss Priss is weak from what she been through. No bad ting gonna cross that reddening, ya done see to that. If that nasty petro come back I'll send him away again before he make trouble. I need time to think dis through." Marcella tsk-tsked me. "Everything gonna be right as rain."

"Really?" I said caustically. "You going to throw rice at him?"

"If that's what it takes, vampire. You just all kinds of grump right now." Marcella grinned at me. "Dat petro not as scary as Kalfu. I got the keep away mojo, mister. Ya don' worry."

"Well," Abby said quietly. "That does smell good. How are you doing, Melvin? Peckish?"

Marcella looked at me over her shoulder and glared. Whoa! What happened to the newfound trust?

"No, Abby. I'm fine," I snapped.

"Don't get that way. I was going to say there's some health shake in the fridge."

"A health shake or a health shake?" I was worried she'd saved some of Daniel for me, which, ugh, I would not drink at all. An IV I could deal with if I was drugged and goofy. The lip smacking, blood sucking out of a mug was right out.

"Miss Priss, I don't want none of the funny business goin' on 'round me." Marcella pursed her lips.

"How about monkey business?" Abby sassed.

My stomach rumbled, and I smiled as Marcella looked utterly confused. Monkey I could do.

"Actually that sounds good, Abby. Thanks."

I left her to explain to Marcella about the forays into primate blood step-ladders, and found the thermos in the fridge. Abby had thought of everything. However, I was dreading what she would do to get me an IV soon. I'd have to keep a close eye on any door-to-door salesmen from now on.

"Melvin," Marcella said next to me as the microwave dinged. "It's still hard for me to be around what you are."

"Whatever, Marcella." I took a big gulp of the brew and shivered with delight, even as my overbite extended. Well, that was embarrassing. "I don't like what I am either, and I'm not too crazy about all this voodoo stuff, but you don't see me biting your head off." That may have been a poor choice of words. Marcella put a hand to her throat and winced.

"Way to make me feel self-conscious." I put my hand over my mouth, took my cup, and went to stand next to Abby.

Before Marcella could respond I heard a car door slam outside. "We've got company."

"What?" Abby jumped and looked around the room for signs of Daniel.

"Someone's at the door," I said just before the doorbell chimed. "Stay inside the circle, Abby."

I couldn't believe it. Vernonia was here. The head housekeeper, Mrs. Walmen, let her in and made the woman wait in the parlor.

"It's Vernonia," I said with a smile.

"Melvin, she shouldn't see all this," Abby said with worry as she looked from Marcella to the circle of brick dust.

"I think she can handle it, Abby. Marcella, you're going to want to meet this lady. She might be able to help."

"Melvin, we don't need no more help. I think we be jus' fine with tings de way dey are."

"Maybe she's right, Melvin." Abby looked nervously at the Haitian.

"Too late," I said with a smile as Mrs. Walmen came up the hallway.

She started to enter the kitchen and stopped when she saw the brick dust on the floor. The woman shook her head briefly, and then crossed into the room looking bewildered, shell shocked, and just plain put out.

"Mrs. Brokerman," she said nervously. "Ms. Ruttle is here to pay her respects about Mr. Brokerman. Shall I show her into the kitchen?" There was an edge of sarcasm in the woman's voice.

"Certainly." Abby smiled like nothing was out of the ordinary.

"Of course." The head housekeeper took one last look at Marcella, at the brick dust, and then at me, and then backed out of the room. She didn't bother to lead Vernonia to us; I heard her give directions to the kitchen and then walk out the front door.

"Abby, Mrs. Walmen just quit." I wondered if it would be a cascade effect with the rest of the staff.

"Why do you say that?" Abby asked with a laugh. "Why wouldn't she want to work in this circus?"

Vernonia walked into the room, briefly looking down at the red circle with a curious frown. "Good afternoon, Mrs. Brokerman. I was sorry to hear of the loss of your husband. Oh, and the maid just asked me to tell you that she quit."

"See?" I smirked. "Hello, Vernonia."

"Hello, Melvin." Vernonia was keeping her distance. "I see you're doing well, looking fit and well *fed*," she said with an abrupt tone.

"Vernonia, it's not what you think." I held my hands up and sighed. Actually, it kind of was what she thought...I did eat Daniel. Not of my own free vampiricly, blood lusty will, but the proof is in the pudding, er, IV.

I ate Daniel. Yup.

Vernonia looked at Marcella. "Bonjour. Vous êtes la prêtresse de vaudou qui les aident maintenant?"

Marcella nodded. "Oui. Vous parlez avec les morts?"

Vernonia sighed. "Mais oui."

Marcella arched an eyebrow at me as she said to Vernonia, "Et vous savez qu'il est un vampire?"

My high school French was failing me, but I caught that last part: vampire.

"Mais il a été un bon vampire, la plupart du temps, jusqu'ici." Vernonia crossed her arms and stared at me.

I frowned. "Um, it's very rude to speak a language in front of company when no one else speaks that language."

"I speak French," Abby said.

Of course she does...it's Abby. I felt suddenly very dumb, rather trailer parkish actually.

"You talk to dead people?" Abby looked at Vernonia in shock. "And he's still a good vampire."

"Translate please." I twirled my finger in the air.

Abby smirked. "Vernonia asked Marcella if she was the voodoo priestess who was helping us, and Marcella asked if Vernonia talked to dead people, and then Marcella asked if Vernonia knew you were a vampire -- which you could have told me that she knew by the way!" Abby took a deep breath. "And Vernonia said you'd been a good vampire, mostly until now. There. Happy?"

"Yes," I answered meekly. "How did you both know about each other? No, wait," I said while holding up my hand. "I actually don't want to know. Just another episode of let's spook the vampire."

"A very odd, odd undead you are." Marcella just shook her head, and Vernonia shrugged.

"What happened to Mr. Brokerman?" Vernonia looked at Abby. "It certainly wasn't any car crash."

"He came home early and tortured Melvin in a coffin with a sun lamp."

Vernonia curled her lip. "That sounds rather drastic. But what happened to Mr. Brokerman?"

"I didn't kill him," I said a little too defensively. "I escaped from the coffin and then duct taped he and Giles together in the coffin. Um, Giles threw up and suffocated."

"Coffins are air tight, Melvin." Vernonia had a disappointed look on her face.

"He punched an air hole in the bottom, Vernonia. Giles had a broken nose, one which he earned by the way." Abby crossed her arms. "Melvin's not a monster."

Marcella was busily preparing bowls of herbed rice and set them down with spoons on the counter. She looked at me and shrugged. I shrugged back as Abby kept up my defense with Vernonia.

"Vernonia, Melvin was badly injured when he rescued me."

"Rescued you? Oh this is just getting more and more dire, my dear."

"Yes, rescued me. Daniel drugged me, tied me up, and let me know that I was going to suffer for having a vampire in the house. After he finished torturing poor Melvin in the basement of course."

"Hmmm, of course."

"You don't have to sound so sarcastic about it." Abby crossed her arms.

"But the question remains this: How did Melvin feed on Mr. Brokerman?" Vernonia arched an eyebrow, an accusatory eyebrow. If that eyebrow had a mouth it would be yelling. I smirked to myself at the absurdity of my thought train, but Vernonia thought the smirk was about eating Daniel.

"You think it's amusing?" she snapped.

"Uh, no." I quickly put both hands up. "It's not what you think." I wasn't going to admit to her that Abby was responsible. Better to let everyone think I was the only monster. Right?

"Oh for god's sakes," Abby yelled. "I did it. I fed Daniel to Melvin. I did it all. He had no say in it, he was drugged, I did it, I did it, I did it."

Marcella and Vernonia exchanged a look, and then they both looked at me with pity, which set Abby off.

"Stop looking at him like that." Abby came over and took my hand. "I wasn't planning on killing Daniel, just using him for an IV source to heal Melvin."

"That was clever," Vernonia offered with a nod. Marcella still looked a bit horrified.

"The more I thought about it, though," Abby said, "the easier it was just to drain him."

"Okay," I squeezed her hand, "You should probably stop with the talking now. They don't need to hear the rest." Marcella and Vernonia didn't need to know how scary Abby really was, but she was determined.

"No, they think you are some kind of slavering, drooling monster." To Vernonia she said, "Melvin needed it, so I took it. If anyone is to blame it's me."

"Right. Well, no sense dwelling on what's already been done. All's fair in love and war, and it saved you a nasty divorce." Vernonia patted Abby on the arm, and gave me a little thin-lipped smile. Boy could she roll with the punches. "I never said one thing about Melvin being a monster. Let's just focus on the positive, shall we?"

"You're all a bit mad, aren't you?" Marcella said as she finished setting out the meal.

Vernonia grabbed a bowl and took a bite of rice. "Oh, this is divine! Marcella, right?" She waved a spoon at the Haitian woman.

"Wi, and you are Vernonia." Marcella gave a happy little nod.

"Your French is exquisite. I'm sorry I don't speak Kreyol."

"Merci. Mon Tante insisted I learn French as well."

"So, where do you come in in all of this, Marcella?"

"We will see."

"I suppose so," said Vernonia with a raised eyebrow. "And now here I am."

"Yes you are," I said with a grin. Maybe things were looking up for old Mostly Dead Melvin. I had a posse now: a psycho, a Voodoo Queen, and a ghost talking old woman. Weren't we the Misfits of Doom!

Marcella was watching me with a concerned look on her face, and it felt like she was inside my head again, listening to my inane pep talk to myself. I just grinned at her.

"Melvin, one question before tings go any further." Marcella took a pinch of herbs from a pouch she had in her pocket and sprinkled some on Vernonia's rice and then on Abby's portion. "You always awake during de daylight hours?"

"I have vampire insomnia," I said with a smirk. "I wake up late afternoon."

"Hmmm, how you handle de sun?"

That was an odd thing to ask. "As long as it's good old fashioned overcast Portland, I'm great. I can handle light sun for a few hours. Why?"

"Just planning ahead. It's raining today," she said with a satisfied smile.

Marcella handed a bowl to Abby, then motioned for her to take a bite. "You need your strength." Marcella crossed her arms and leaned against the counter while Vernonia and Abby devoured the rice dish.

"Eat it all up, you two. Every bite now." Marcella turned and winked at me. To Vernonia she said, "I wasn't expecting you here. I'm sure you are very powerful in your own way but you showing up now is very inconvenient. I got to set everything right."

She pointed at the women and said, "Ou domi."

This sounded ominous. Just then there was a crash as both Vernonia and Abby dropped their bowls on the floor. The dishes exploded in a spray of expensive crockery, sending little shards of porcelain in all directions like herringboned shrapnel. I lunged towards Abby as she started to slump to the floor, but Marcella stepped in front of me.

"No. Melvin, she be fine."

I shoved Marcella out of the way and caught Abby before she hit the floor. Vernonia wasn't so lucky. She toppled sideways into the cooking island and then fell face first on the floor. That was going to leave a mark.

I snarled at Marcella, a quite terrifying and guttural sound that should have made any mortal wet their pants, but the woman only held up the herb pouch and shook her finger at me.

"Don't you snarl at me like dat, I said she be fine. You gotta have a bit of trust, but she can't come wit us, Melvin."

"What did you do to them?"

"I put 'em to sleep. Domi...sleep, understand?"

I looked at Poor Vernonia and hoped her nose was all right. I laid Abby down on the tiles gently and reached out to check Vernonia's pulse. I smelled blood and knew that her nose was probably ruined. I felt so badly for her that my overbite didn't even extend from the scent, in fact it just made me nauseous.

"You've got some nerve, lady. This is inexcusable." My anger was bubbling up again so I closed my eyes and took a breath. "You drugged them, didn't you?"

"M wi. Yes I did." Marcella looked smug.

"Why didn't you just do a spell or something?"

"What you think I did?"

I pinched the bridge of my nose between my fingers and sighed. "Drugged them?"

"Semantics. It all come out de same in de wash." Marcella stuffed the pouch back into her pocket and crossed her arms.

"You could have warned me."

"Would you have cooperated?"

"No." I glared at her, and then stood up with Abby cradled in my arms.

"And if I told them dat you an I gotta go dis alone, you tink Miss Priss and dat ghost seer gonna say okay and stay behind?"

I believed in safety in numbers, but Marcella had a point. No sense in dragging Abby further into all of this madness, and endangering Vernonia. Things were going to get very ugly with Mr. Happy.

But still, poor Vernonia didn't need to wipe out like that. "I'm going to put Abby where she'll be comfortable. And for the record, you suck." I glared at Marcella, and then nodded towards Vernonia. "Check her and make sure her nose isn't broken."

"If it is, den it is."

"Wrong answer. Can't you do some sort of spell?" I asked sarcastically.

"What you tink I am? Dr. Quinn Medicine Woman?" she snapped back.

It was like dealing with a feminine and more sarcastic Pizza Bob. I glared at Marcella. "You broke it, you bought it. Just make her comfortable, damn it."

"Ah, go on. She be fine, just a little bonk on her face. Could be worse if Kalfu show up, so quit wasting time."

"Don't boss me."

"Move yer ass, vampire."

I bit my tongue as I cradled Abby in my arms. Marcella made a shooing motion with her hands, and I was tempted to yell something snarky back.

"Keep Miss Priss inside the red dust," said Marcella as she propped up Vernonia against the oven.

"It's everywhere," I muttered as I started to step over the circle line. I hesitated, just in case Daniel was waiting to swoop in, but nothing happened. Abby snorted in my arms and cuddled in as I walked into the hallway towards the grand room.

"Abby, I'm so sorry for all of this," I whispered as I laid her down on the couch. She looked so peaceful, so beautiful. I tucked a stray hair behind her ear, and then gently kissed her on the forehead. A smile curved the corner of her mouth, making my heart start up briefly.

"You be safe, and know that I love you more than anything in this world or beyond. Hopefully Marcella and I will make things right." I took her hand. "I hope I get to see you again."

"You will," Marcella said beside me, making me jump. I didn't hear her come in. Must be a voodoo ninja thing.

"Damn it! Don't do that!" I snapped.

Marcella pushed me aside and leaned in with a pair of scissors. I grabbed her hand, a little harder than I meant to.

She yelped, "Ouch! You watch yerself!"

"What the hell are you doing now?"

Marcella massaged her wrist for second and then reached out and snipped off a piece of Abby's hair. She put it in a pouch, and I saw a lock of Vernonia's hair coiled inside as well.

"I make a gris-gris bag for dem, keep 'em safe while we gone."

"Sorry for your wrist," I mumbled. "You spooked me with the scissors."

"You got to learn to trust, Melvin."

"I'm working on it," I said as I brushed Abby's bangs off of her forehead, and traced a finger over her smiling lips.

My gods she's beautiful. Maybe I should stay...

"Go on wit you mushy face tings. We got work to do." Marcella took me by the arm and pulled me out of the room. I looked back over my shoulder at Abby, hoping, more than I was entitled to, that the smile on her face was for me.

CHAPTER 13

Black Cat Mambo

"**S**o what do we do now?" I stood on the front lawn while Marcella placed a line of brick dust in front of the door of the mansion. She wiped her hands on her pants and came down the steps quickly, taking my hand and again leading me away like a child.

"We got to get far away from dis place; take your scent away from here. Only way to keep Miss Priss safe for now."

"Marcella, how long will she be out?"

"A few hours, but we be long gone before den."

I looked over my shoulder to get one last look at my life with Abby. Just one more look. "Are we going to make it?"

"I hope so," Marcella said. "No, I know so. Be cocky, fill your heart with power. Dat be the way to win." But she sounded a little too nervous.

I felt the temperature drop and ozone tickled my nose. Uh-oh. Nothing like a pissed off ghost to get the juices flowing. The voodoo queen squeezed my hand as she picked up her pace towards her car.

"Marcella--"

"Hush now. Don't run, it just feeds his power."

Daniel bellowed in rage behind me, and it took everything I had not to bolt for the car.

"I mean it, don't you run now. Like an energy bar fear is." She gave me a stern look.

"Running away?" Daniel shrieked. "You coward! You can try and run, but I'll find you. I'll get you after I take care of my wife."

"Don't acknowledge him, just keep walking," said Marcella as she dug for her keys in her pocket. "Don't worry none for Miss Priss. She be safe."

"This is bad." I was the master of understatement.

Marcella got the door open of her car and shoved me inside. "Trust me. That spirit no can get in."

"Priscilla! I'm going to get you, you bitch!" Daniel went flying at the mansion in a blur, hit the line of brick dust at the doorway, and exploded in a shower of blue sparks.

"Whoa!" I shouted. "Is he dead?"

"No."

"That would be too easy." I leaned my head on the dash and groaned.

"He can't get in dere, but he gonna come for you next. We got to be ready." Marcella sped down the street, taking the corner on two wheels.

"Where are we going?"

"Trust me."

"I hate it when you say that."

Marcella just ignored me and kept driving. And driving. And driving.... I finally realized that we were just doing loops of the city.

"What are we doing?" I asked. We'd been driving around until the sunset, and the cold November night air was making the streets foggy. The car smelled of fear, sweat, and good old ripe Melvin.

"I'm mixing up our trail," Marcella responded dully.

"Daniel doesn't need a trail, missy. He keys in on me."

Marcella's shoulders stiffened. Uh-oh.

"But you already knew that," I said with an eye roll and a dramatic little headshake for good measure.

"Yes," she said quietly.

"You don't really have a plan, do you?"

"Sort of...I just need time to get it right in my head. My people won't be ready for a while yet."

"Your people?"

"Mambo Armynel."

"What?"

"My priestess, Mambo Armynel, Fami mwen -- my family."

"I thought you were a Voodoo Queen?"

Marcella laughed. "No! Why you tink dat?"

"I just assumed--"

"You assumed wrong. I never said I was a queen. She's very powerful, my Mambo."

"Is she a dancer, too?" I asked with a smirk.

"What?"

"Never mind." I guess my witty repartee needed some work without Pizza Bob as the straight man.

"You're odd." Marcella gave a wave of her hand.

"So you keep telling me."

Pizza Bob would have gotten the joke. Maybe he was in the car, laughing his ass off at the moment. "Is Pizza Bob here now?"

"What? Maybe, maybe no. If he is he bein' quiet for once."

"These mumbos--"

"Mambo," she snapped.

"Whatever, can they help with him? Wouldn't it be better to get Pizza Bob back before we do anything?"

"I told you, they be ready later. Timing got to be right, days of preparation, and then got to wait until midnight for the calling of Papa Legba. He da one gonna bring back your Pizza Bob."

"Is he Mambo's wife?"

"No, he much beloved and be de keeper of de crossroads. Very powerful Loa." Marcella was starting to get annoyed, but so what?

"Okay, but why can't we just go there and wait with your family?" It seemed like a reasonable request, I didn't sound whiny, and frankly I was tired of being in the car.

Marcella chewed her lip, and looked at me sideways. "They don't want no trafficking wit a Loogaroo." She shrugged. "Sorry. But I tink I can change dey mind before dey try and kill you."

"Oh, this is not good. Not good at all."

"No, it be fine. Dey will see you not a bad ting at all. I'm sure Mama Erzulie make the path easy."

"Mambo's Mama?"

Marcella sighed. "You could say that."

"Right. Another Loa. I wish I knew more about all this."

"Me, too. But I will tell you as we go. We'll make it right."

I hoped Marcella wasn't too naive. The last thing I wanted was to be in a room filled with people who wanted me dead. I'd had enough of that already from Daniel; toss two angry Loas into the mix and I'd get the trifecta. Good times. Marcella was driving the 405, passing under one of the overpasses, and I thought of Bertram, the troll.

"I have an idea," I said. "Get off at the next exit."

"If we stop moving, that spirit gonna show up again," Marcella said as she took the Everett street exit. "What you tink about dat?"

I leaned back and grinned. If she hated vampires I wondered how she'd feel about trolls? Time to shake up her world a little bit!

"I think I may know someone who might be able to give us a hand."

She arched an eyebrow, and pulled the car over. "Am I going to like it?"

"Probably not," I answered with a grin. "Have I got one for you, Voodoo Queen."

"I'm not a queen," she snapped at me, rather haughtily with a touch of imperiousness. I smiled.

"You certainly act like one sometimes, your highness. But wait till you hear this...." I told her about Bertram, about the goblins, and then sat back waiting for the freak out. Much to my disappointment, my Voodoo Queen just shrugged.

"Why you tink he help you?"

"You aren't even surprised are you?" I just shook my head. "Not even a little bit?"

"Why would I be? Dere all kinds of tings in dis here world. You tink you so special?"

Ouch. "No." I sank down in my seat a little bit. "He seemed nice."

"Nice? Oh I don't tink so." She tsk-tsked me. "Bèl dan pa di zami – Just because one smiles at you doesn't mean they're your friend."

Actually, Bertram wasn't nice, but he didn't eat me. And he gave me money to use the phone. A nice, grandfatherly troll. Okay, maybe not so much. But I never said he was my friend! And his smile was a little scary. Okay, a lot scary.

"Bertram could see Pizza Bob. Maybe he can help you get him back." I sounded a little petulant.

"Anyone wit a lick of otherness goin' to see tings. It de way it is. He no be able to help us. Mambo Armynel sort us out. You see." She rolled down her window and leaned out for some fresh air. After a moment, an eternity of me being mortified about my own odor, she turned and looked at me. "But dem goblins, hoo, dey might know someting 'bout Kalfu."

"Oh no, no. Bertram said to avoid them."

"Exactly." She smiled wickedly. "What you know about dem?"

"Just what's on World of Warcraft."

Marcella wrinkled up her forehead at me. "A video game?"

"I don't play. If I did, I would never have left my apartment, met Maddy, been bitten... I guess there's something to be said for being an addict." I snorted.

"That's just sad."

"Have you been paying attention to anything since you met me?" I smirked at her. "I'm the poster boy for losers."

"Get over you self. Dis no time for a pity party, Mr. Vampire. But dem goblins, well, I know dey nasty little tings. All short and hairy, greedy, sneaky but powerful."

"I don't think we should mess with them."

"Bah. Maybe we should go find this Bertram. He'll take us to the goblins, and we go from there." Marcella's Kreyol accent had faded. Uh-oh.

"On second thought, let's just keep driving." I wanted no part of dealing with goblins. In the dark. In the fog. Or ever. I'd rather face the Mambo.

"You just a baby." She opened her car door and got out. "Come on, big baby. Let's find dat troll and make some trouble."

I just shook my head.

Yeah, this was going to end badly.

✦

"We got about ten hours before de sun rises," Marcella said as she opened the trunk of the car and got out a rain jacket and a flashlight.

"I doubt we will find Bertram," I said as I crossed my arms.

"Oh, we find him. You just use your power."

"My power?"

"Yes, Melvin. Just concentrate. You be able to find other beings from de outside...listen for they hum." She held up a jacket for me. I wanted it, not because I was cold, I just didn't want to get my suit wet.

Hey! It's expensive! Italian silk.

"A troll that hums? Like show tunes or something?" I snickered.

"L'en Medi! You don' know nothing, do you!"

"Well, don't get mad. I told you, I made Mr. Happy cross and he didn't give me a manual or anything." I jerked the jacket out of her hands. "Sheesh."

"Just close your eyes and focus."

"You aren't going to do anything to me while my eyes are closed, are you?"

"Trust me." Marcella grinned. I hated it when she did that.

"What if Daniel comes back?"

Marcella shook a pouch of brick dust at me. "We be fine. Just concentrate."

I sighed, and then closed my eyes. "I feel stupid."

"Just hush and concentrate."

"This is some Obiwon Kenobi snipe hunt, isn't it?" I said after a few seconds as I cracked open an eyelid.

"It no goin' work if you keep yapping!"

"Let's just start moving, okay?"

"Fine, but we try again soon." Marcella looked around. "You say he live under de freeway?"

I just nodded and started heading towards the overpass. The fog gave the streets an echoic desolation that made my skin crawl. It reminded me of the night I ascended six months ago. Or descended, depending on how I looked at it. I could still hear the whispering in that mist, see the shadowy figures crawling towards me as I lay dying on my bed. I still didn't know who or what those things were. I looked around nervously at the darkness, letting my mind creep back into that scary place.

Stop it!

I was my own worst enemy when it came to mind games and things that go bump in the night. On the street, sounds carried easily, and I jumped at every grind of gears or other car noises around me. I felt Marcella's annoyance coming at me in waves, and I tried to cover my little squeals and squeaks with manly sounding coughs. She wasn't buying it.

"I can't believe you such a scaredy. You a creature of de night, Melvin. Embrace it."

"That's what everyone keeps telling me. I'm just not built for this," I said miserably.

"Looking back don't know why I was fearing you at all," she said with a snicker.

"That's doing wonders for my confidence, Marcella."

I just kept walking and ignored her chuckle. Glad you're amused at my expense. Who was I kidding? Everyone was amused at my expense. It's what I did best. I was the Richard Lewis of the undead. Poor pitiful me, ha-ha. Actually, I guess I could be pretty amusing, just not when I meant to. I'd have to work on that...if I survived what was coming. I shivered and looked around.

Enough with the morbid already.

There weren't many people out, except the occasional homeless person shuffling towards shelter someplace. I wondered if they were trolls, too.

Just stop it!

After a few more blocks of wandering, Marcella tapped me on the shoulder. "Here's a good place to try it again."

We were actually close to my old apartment building. How did she know? I pursed my lips at her, and she just shrugged at me in return.

"Go on now, close your eyes and concentrate," she said.

"Can't you just do it? You've got the mojo."

She stared at me, holding my gaze until I flinched and looked away. Damn, she could be intimidating.

After another moment of me staring at my own feet she said, "You have de power, time to learn to use it."

"I'm not that good of a vampire. You know that."

"I'm learning dat you a lazy vampire...go on...listen for a hum."

I looked around at the dark, empty street, feeling far too exposed for my own comfort, and finally closed my eyes. I listened to the night.

I heard a faint heart beat, and then flared my nostrils; a rat. Strike one. I took a deep breath and tried to relax, tried to get my vampire on. My hearing and senses were on overdrive, and I thought just for a moment that I felt something out there listening to me; but then my stomach made a squishy blurp noise that ruined the moment. I opened my eyes and saw Marcella holding her nose. I smiled apologetically.

"What the hell are you doing, son?"

I jumped, and spun around to come face-to-face with none other than the very person I was looking for. Bertram. The troll. The real source of the odor Marcella was reacting to. Ha!

"Holy crap, you just scared the bejesus out of me!" I shouted.

"Hey, newbie. What a nice thing to say." Bertram grinned at me.

Remember, just because he smiles doesn't mean he's your friend!

"Good evening, Bertram. I was actually looking for you." I took a little step back so I wasn't standing within his arm reach.

"You found me. Who's the chicky babe? She ain't your maker...don't smell right. Your squeeze, your nibble?" he asked, pointing at Marcella. She had the pouch of powder in her hand, and looked ready to either fight or flee. I hoped she wasn't going to flee; that would be awkward.

"This is Marcella. She's, um, well, she's--"

"I'm Vodouisant." Marcella finished.

"Voodoo, eh?" Bertram arched an eyebrow. "You run with the weirdest folks, kid."

He leaned in and sniffed me. "I see you've fed finally. Good for you." The troll took a big gulp out of a bottle wrapped in a brown paper bag. "What happened to your buddy? He's all fuzzy and unhappy."

I looked around me quickly. "He's here?" Poor Pizza Bob -- unseen and unheard, and probably coming up with the best one-liners.

"Of course he's here...standing right next to you. Kinda faded and dismal looking. She do that?"

"No, it's a long story." I felt like time was running out for my ghost. Tic-tock.

"Well, I won't even pretend that I care, so...got any change?" The troll held out his hand.

"Um, not on me." I shifted from foot to foot nervously.

"Right, the pauper in a silk suit. Whatever, newbie." He started pushing his cart away.

"Wait!" Marcella stepped in front of him.

"Heh, this should be good," he cackled.

"We seek de goblins," she said.

"Good for you." He maneuvered around her.

"Melvin, talk to him." Marcella gave me a little push.

I really, really was starting to be done with this adventure. But then I thought of Abby passed out on her couch, poor Vernonia and her ruined nose, Daniel who might show up any second, of Pizza Bob floating in the ether somewhere and unable to move on....

"Bertram," I called out. "Please wait." I jogged and caught up with him.

"Whaddayawantnow?" he slurred.

"We are looking for the goblins. Marcella thinks they can help us with the shadow thing, Mr. Happy."

The troll stopped is cart abruptly. "Who?"

"Mr. Happy. A shadow demon thing."

"Oh," he said with a smirk. "That ass hat still running around? I haven't dealt with that little busy body in years."

"You know him?" I don't know why I was so surprised.

"Squeaky little piss ant with an English accent?"

"Yup."

Bertram chuckled. "What did you do to him?"

"I didn't do anything. Well, except make him cross."

"So what?"

"He's scary."

"So am I," Bertram replied.

"Yes," I offered quickly. "Yes you are indeed. But he says he's in charge of vampires, and he's screwing with me royally right now."

"Hmmm, he must have got a promotion. Whatever. Not my problem. And I'd keep away from those goblins. They'd just eat you up," he said with a nasty leer. I gulped. Audibly. It just made the troll grin wider.

I heard Marcella come up behind me, and I hoped that she wasn't going to do something stupid.

"Mr. Troll, sir," she said quietly.

"The name's Bertram. I like your manners, missy. Wanna sip?" He offered her the bag, and to my surprise Marcella accepted the bottle and took a long pull before handing it back. Inside I gagged a little; who knew the last time Bertram had seen a toothbrush. Bleh.

"Bertram, we seek de goblins. I know dey been causing you some trouble... nasty tings dey are...but dey got some power I can use right now."

Bertram took off his hat and picked at the inside of his ear. He looked at me sideways and said, "You sure about this, newbie?"

"Not really," I whined.

He stared at Marcella, all the while digging in his ear, his finger imbedded up to the knuckle, and finally said, "I don't work for free."

Marcella nodded. "Everyting got it's price, wi, I accept dat. Si travày té bon bagày, moun rich t'à pran'l lontan – If work were a good thing, the rich would've grabbed it a long time ago."

Bertram turned and grinned at me. Uh-oh.

"Marcella--"

"Hush now, Melvin." To the troll she said, "We work someting out."

"I'm hungry." Bertram finally pulled out a glob of earwax and popped it into his mouth. "Really hungry." He again leered at me as his stomach growled.

Double uh-oh. Between the goblin threat and Bertram's unnerving stare, I was starting to feel very low on the food chain.

"Well," Marcella prompted. "What you want?" She crossed her arms.

"You still use goats in rituals?" he asked, and I let out the nervous breath I was holding.

"Wi."

"I want one, wait...no make that two."

"Live or dead?" she asked.

"Live." The troll grinned wickedly.

Marcella spit in her hand and held it out for him to shake. "Done."

Bertram shook her hand and then pulled her close, sniffing her face and hair. "I got your scent now, so if you go back on your word I'll find you."

I was expecting her to whip out that nasty powder she doused me with when we first met, and I winced. But, of course, Marcella surprised me yet again.

"My word is my bond, troll. You get your goats."

Where in the hell were we going to get two goats? That was the least of my worries as I listened to Bertram tell Marcella where we would find the goblins, and what their price would be.

"Seriously?" I yelped.

"Oh yeah," Bertram said with a wink. "Have fun with that, newbie. Give 'em hell."

⅄

"Are you kidding me?" I whined as we got back in the car. "Marcella, I'm so not doing that."

"Suck it up, Melvin. You want to get your life back?" Marcella revved the engine.

"You know I do."

Goblins weren't what you would expect. They hid in plain sight, and they were all female; except for the King. King Chuck. Yes, that was his name. The goblins also ran most of the local strip clubs. Gah! To think I had seen a goblin in a G-string and never knew it. I felt exceptionally dirty, poke out my mind's eye dirty. Bleh.

But what the goblins wanted was just too much. They demanded a tribute in exchange for any services in the magical department. You see where this is going? King Chuck had a daughter that was in need of a good time. Yeah. I said it. I was expected to fight her, then woo her if I survived, then god only knows what else. There was also a serious chance that I might get eaten as part of the deal, too.

I most certainly wasn't going let that happen. Again with the bleh!

Marcella interrupted my train of thought just as it was screaming off the tracks. "It's close to dawn so we gotta get someplace safe for you sleep time." Marcella started driving again. "I'm sure dat Petro gonna be here soon."

In all of the misery of the impending Goblin encounter I'd completely forgotten about Daniel. And of course, just thinking about him let the universe hone in on my signal.

Of course.

I felt a little tingle on my skin as the temperature dropped in the car.

"Oh, come on!" I yelled as Daniel materialized in the back seat.

Marcella slammed on the brakes, and whipped out the pouch of brick dust.

"Wait!" he yelled. "I just want to talk."

"All you gonna say is lies, petro," Marcella growled.

"Why are you helping him? He's a coward. Dumped Priscilla and he'll dump you too. You want some of what I'm dishing out?" he taunted.

"What are you waiting for?" I yelled at Marcella. "Zap him!"

She opened the pouch and flung a spray of powder into the car. But the ghost dematerialized an instant before it hit where he had been sitting. There was no wonderful explosion of blue sparks so I knew things were going to get bad real quick-like. The ghost reappeared on the hood of the car.

"I'm on to you, bitch." Daniel wagged his finger at us. "Bouzin!"

Marcella gripped the steering wheel tightly in anger. I don't know what that word, Bouzin, meant, but it was the wrong thing to say.

"Ou santi tankou swe ki sot nan pwel yon leza!" Marcella shouted at him. It was obviously something very rude, because Daniel's eyes bugged in his head. Marcella sneered at him.

"He speaks Haitian?" I asked.

"Obviously," she snapped. To Daniel she yelled, "Salopri," while making a rude gesture with her hand.

"I thought we weren't supposed to encourage him," I snapped.

"Bah." She turned on the windshield wipers, and that scattered his form briefly. But he came back quickly and started pounding on the windshield.

"Do something besides piss him off!" I was leaning as far back in my seat as I could without actually jumping into the back of the car.

"He no can get in here from de powder I dump. He stuck out dere! Ha!" Marcella started the car and pulled forward. As we picked up speed Daniel faded away.

I looked over at Marcella in awe. "What did you say to him?"

"He called me a bitch, I don't like dat one bit, so I tell him he smell like de sweat off a lizard's pubic hair."

I burst out laughing. "That's nasty, Marcella!"

"I know." She grinned as she pulled onto the 405. "But now we got a problem."

"What?"

"We stuck in dis here car for a while." She wrinkled her nose. "No offense, Melvin, but you ripe, man!"

"Your nose will burn out, and then you won't even notice," I said glumly. "The sun will be up soon." I yawned and stretched. "Find a mall with an underground garage."

"Dat's a good idea. Finally you using dat brain for someting."

"I have my moments, Marcella." I smiled weakly. "Daniel is after me, mostly, so you should be safe to go inside and get some breakfast; no sense both of us suffering."

"He just all mouth when it comes to me. No power, just insults."

"Then you aren't stuck in the car. Go get a Cinnabon or something." I realized I was getting hungry. That would be awkward. But I needed to eat. "Um, Marcella--"

"Uh-oh. I don't like dat look on you face."

"I'm real sorry, but I'm getting hungry. I can't help it."

"Don't look at me."

I rolled my eyes. "I'm just saying I'll need a snack soon."

The sun was coming up, making the gray morning look less intimidating, rather rosy and happy actually. I leaned back in my seat and closed my eyes as we rolled over the bridge into North East Portland. I was exhausted.

Marcella nudged me awake, and I saw we were in the Lloyd Center garage.

"I'm going inside. Don't get out of de car and you be safe from dat Petro."

"Yup," I muttered as my eyelids drooped.

"What you want to eat?"

"Pig livers."

"How about a Cinnabon for now?"

"With O Positive frosting," I joked as I slipped into my undead coma. I didn't even hear Marcella leave.

⚔

The smell of ozone and a tapping noise woke me. I cracked open an eyelid and saw Daniel sitting cross-legged on the hood of the car. How long had I been out? He reached out and knocked on the glass again. I ignored him and picked a sleep crusty out of the corner of my eye as I stretched and brushed up against something. I jumped, and took a quick peek at Daniel to make sure he was still on the hood.

Yup, still there, and now laughing at me. Damn. I casually looked over and saw a small paper grocery bag sitting in the driver's seat with a note taped to it. Daniel watched me with a sick grin as I pulled the paper loose and held the note up in front of my face. It was from Marcella. She probably couldn't wake me up, I reasoned. I hoped.

She probably dumped your sorry, blue butt.

I took a deep breath and read the note:

Change of plans. I've got to make the gris-gris bags, meet up with Mambo Armynel, try and plead our case. Can't do that with the petro tagging along. Also going to set up the meeting with Chuck. Take the car and meet me tomorrow night. Flamingo Hotel on NE Interstate -- the key will be at the front desk,

just ask for my room. Don't do something stupid before then. And don't wreck
my car! -- Marcella

I groaned. What the hell was I supposed to do in the mean time? And have
a little faith, Marcella. What stupid thing could I do trapped in a car? I was frustrated that I was expected to just sit back, yet again, and let someone else take
care of me. I knew Marcella was working to bring Pizza Bob back, and get me
some semblance of peace, but it was Abby all over again in my mind. But then
again I didn't know my ass from my hat when it came to dealing with ghosts and
goblins. I'd done such stellar work on my own in the vampire department so
far! I wished that I had maybe paid a little more attention in my youth to those
RPG's; Maybe memorized a Monster Manual or two like a good little shut-in
nerd. Oh well, add that to the list, blah, blah, blah.

Daniel started knocking again, I ignored him, he knocked some more. If
this was his tactic -- drive Melvin crazy with persistent tapping -- he'd be sorely
disappointed. I'd survived all of Pizza Bob's petty torments; this would be a walk
in the park. My stomach rumbled, reminding me that I was running on empty,
so I peeked inside the bag. There were three cartons of pig livers waiting for me.
And a donut. But not just any donut.... A Voodoo Donut doughnut. The Voodoo
Queen had a sense of humor like no other!

I wonder if she got a discount at their shop? I chuckled to myself, ignored
Daniel's knocking, and pulled out the cartons.

"Marcella, you rock!" I devoured the unrefrigerated livers quickly.

Can I get food poisoning? I wondered as I tipped back the last carton and let
the juices run down the back of my throat. At this point anything was possible;
simply another way for the Universe to screw with me. Although I truly doubted
it. That would make me the epitome of pathetic.

Daniel watched me eat, a look of sick fascination on his face, as I slurped and
drained the last of the blood from the carton. I locked eyes with him as I popped
the whole doughnut into my mouth, delighting in the burst of sugary sweet jelly
filling. I opened my mouth and let the jelly roll onto my chin in little globs, like
mock blood, while I crossed my eyes and stuck out my tongue at the ghost on the

hood. It had the desired effect, and riled him up wonderfully. I don't know why I felt so giddy. He did want to hurt me after all.

"Hey!" Daniel shouted. "You can't stay in there forever! Step outside and do that!"

I flipped him the bird and scooted over into the driver's seat. I had a momentary panic attack that they keys weren't in the ignition, but then quickly found them in the bottom of the grocery bag along with another pouch of brick dust.

Thanks, Marcella!

Where to now?

I looked at my watch -- only 3:30 in the afternoon and a little under two hours until sunset. I started the car, noted a half tank of gas, and decided I felt like doing something stupid after all. Stupid is as stupid does, but at least it's something. I flicked on the windshield wipers, sent Daniel scattering, and pulled out of the garage with a smile on my face.

CHAPTER 14

Run Forrest, RUN!

I kept looking in my rear view mirror as I drove because Daniel was sitting on the trunk of the car. There were no rear windshield wipers, nothing to scatter him with. I had to hand it to him for being clever, though; he was learning. But it was unnerving to have him behind my back while I drove, especially since he was blocking my view of traffic. Not to mention the ick factor of having a spectral psycho staring at the back of my head.

I pulled into a parking space behind Powell's Books in downtown Portland, and took a deep breath as I went over the plan in my head. It should work. Daniel perked up when I shut off the car.

"I'm going to tear a hole in your head and crawl down your neck, and then I'm going to rip out that undead heart of yours from the inside," he taunted.

Wow. That was graphic. He must have been very good at his job before. I shuddered, remembering that look of sadistic glee on his face when he was frying me with the sun lamp in Abby's basement. My hands were shaking as I opened the pouch of brick dust, and then poured a small mound into my palm.

"I hope this works," I whispered.

Daniel was standing next to the driver's side window, watching me with a look of pure hatred on his pale, drawn face. The blood loss before his death made his already intimidating scowl look that much scarier up close. My bravado from the mall parking lot had faded. Definitely.

Don't let him get to you!

I looked at my reflection in disgust; smeared makeup and rather peaked blue skin again. Back to good old me. I rubbed the brick dust into my hair and my face, my hands, everywhere I might be exposed to Daniel's ghostly wrath. I examined the state of my nice suit, all wrinkled and decidedly smelly, and with a wistful sigh dumped another handful all over my jacket and pants. Now I looked like a homeless person! Oh well, while I might be safe from the ghost, I most likely was going to get booted from Powell's.

One thing at a time.

"I'm going to get you," Daniel sing-songed at me.

I really hoped this was going to work. Before I could talk myself out of it, I opened the car door and jumped out.

Immediately Daniel flew at me, and then bounced off in a shower of blue sparks that tingled when they hit my skin.

"Son of a bitch!" he shouted as he fizzled out of existence.

I flopped back against the car, and then slumped down into a crouch. I felt like I was going to vomit I was so scared. But at least it had worked; I didn't know how much time I had before he came back, or if the powder would keep working, but at least I was still in one piece. And I hadn't peed my pants either. Bonus!

I closed my eyes and tried to sense Pizza Bob. Was he here now? Or was he with Marcella? I concentrated, trying to calm myself and think happy thoughts, but I was just too freaked out. I was on my own now. I stood up on shaking legs and made my way into the massive bookstore where I headed straight to the occult section.

Thankfully this corner was secluded and vacant; no one to ogle the blue, filthy weirdo. I felt like I was running the gauntlet as I wove through crowds of hipsters, tourists, and literary elitists to get upstairs. At least the staff didn't eyeball me too much. I grabbed a bunch of books on voodoo, hauntings, myths and legends, and then sat down in the corner against the wall. I smiled, remembering how I would have to roust all the manga and Goth kids at the mall when they would do this same thing in the stores. Now that the shoe was on the other foot I felt a little bad about being such a hard guy before. However, I doubted all those little wannabes had my problems. And boy did I have problems.

I poured a thin line of brick dust in a half circle touching the edges of the wall, hoping that would help keep Daniel at bay if he came back all charged up again. I wondered if security would come and roust me, too. Ha! It would be ironic.

I stared at the pile of books and chose one about voodoo. I had no idea how cool and interesting, and complicated this religion is. African slaves melded their gods and beliefs with catholic saints and rituals so they could still practice a faith system in secret. Most of the stuff people, people like me, thought they knew about voodoo was just as wrong as all the hoopla about vampires. Hollywood focused on only a minor segment of voodoo, the creepy black magic rituals, zombies, but it was a religion of balance and justice, and life.

Papa Legba is like St. Peter; he controlled the crossroads of the afterlife. He is also the guardian of the poto mitan--the center post--a post in the center of a peristyle regarded as a doorway for spirits. Marcella seemed to think Papa Legba could, and would, bring Pizza Bob back from wherever he'd been sent by Mr. Happy. The Loa seemed like a nice guy, a good guy, so I truly hoped he would help us. I'd have to be on my best behavior, though. Definitely. No sarcasm! Hopefully he'd smite Mr. Happy, too.

Speaking of Mr. Happy, I also read about Kalfu; I understood why Marcella would think that's who Mr. Happy is. Bad news, that Kalfu. Brrrr. In the book, Kalfu was described as Legba's opposite. He is also a keeper of the crossroads, but only the off center points, the entry points for bad things. He controls the evil forces in the spirit world that allowed in bad luck, misfortune, injustice, and destruction. Papa Legba is good. Kalfu is bad. Very, very bad. And apparently powerful, too. My stomach did a little uncomfortable roll when I remembered how I'd taunted him in Morrison's parking lot. Talk about poking the bear with a short stick!

Kalfu controls the evil forces of the night. While the book didn't go into detail, I supposed that vampires were part of that group, and I was a vampire; mostly. But I wasn't a bad guy. Well, not yet, and hoping everyday that I wouldn't become evil, and maybe that's why Mr. Happy hated me so much.

Perhaps he was just an impostor. Possibly. A poser who was riding on Kalfu's coat tails. A smarmy little English poser. Regardless, I was less than eager to meet him again, but I knew I was going to sooner or later.

I then read about Loogaroos. Haitians referred to them as werewolves, but they seemed more like vampires in the description because they sucked blood. Disgusting! They take off their skin at night and float around as a ball of light, sucking up blood from unsuspecting victims. Then they return to their body at dawn, all bloated and slimy.

Loogaroo are ruled by a Loa called Marinette-Bwa-Chech -- literally Marinette of the dry arms. Lovely. She is a she-demon of the nastiest degree, and again a hint that Mr. Happy is a poser claiming title to a job he didn't really have. But I wasn't Haitian and I didn't fit the description of a Loogaroo at all. Not even remotely.

Here's the really insulting part: Loogaroo were supposed to be female. That's why Marcella called me he-she when we met. Wow.

I was grossed out and doubly insulted by Marcella's name calling. But I also understood why she hated what I was supposed to be. She seemed to be okay with me now. I obviously wasn't a Loogaroo.

Just a good old vampire. Kind of. Yay for me.

After two hours of reading, I stretched. There was so much to absorb, and there's no way I could become an expert on any voodoo rituals before I met with Mambo Armynel, but at least I had some more information. Hopefully I wouldn't appear the idiot. Well, more so than I already was.

I cracked open the book on myths and read about goblins. They didn't seem to fit Bertram's description at all, nothing Tolkien or Rowling in his account. In fact I had no idea what would be waiting for me. I gave up on that book and switched to hauntings. Yet again I found nothing that would be of any help in getting Pizza Bob back on my own, or giving him peace; at least anything I didn't know already. I definitely needed Marcella's help.

"Pizza Bob," I said quietly, "if you are here with me I want you to know how much I appreciate what you did. I still think you're a jerk sometimes, but...well, I'm glad you're my friend."

The air got just a fraction colder around me, and I smiled. I hoped it was him. It made me miss my life, miss Abby. I needed to see if she was okay. Maybe I could call her....

I stood up and started to brush off my pants. I froze and looked around in a panic, realizing how stupid I was being, and I was terrified that Daniel was going to swoop in and attack me.

Don't wipe off the brick dust, dumb ass!

I was running on fumes, with exhaustion, terror, and hunger making me slop along on autopilot. I smelled patchouli oil, and looked up to see a young girl with long red dread locks and dressed like a hippie staring at me as she pulled a book on ancient religions from the shelf down the aisle. She looked down at the brick dust on the floor, smirked, and then pulled out a book on Wicca.

"Rough day?" she asked without looking at me.

"You could say that."

"It will get better. Bright blessings upon you, troubled soul." She put the book under her arm, and smiled.

"Um, thanks. Right back at you."

She started towards me. "Do you need some help?"

Ha! Of course I do.

"No, I'm good." I just wanted her to leave. Even though she was beautiful and I had no idea why she would even speak to a freak like me; she had to go.

She dug into her pocket and took out a five-dollar bill, which she held out to me. "Get yourself some coffee, it might help. There's a shelter of kind brothers under the Burnside Bridge. They can put you up for the night if you need it."

I was stunned at her kindness. But this was Portland after all.

She cocked her head to the side, and then reached out and took my hand, sending a warm little shiver all the way up into my shoulder. Whoa.

"You look like you just need a break. The universe doesn't hate you," she said with a sly grin as she slipped the money into my palm. She let go, and the sensation flooded through my body. Double whoa. I was too shocked to move. She turned away and was half way down the aisle when I finally got my feet back under me.

"Wait! What?"

"Hang in there." She didn't even look back.

"Who are you?" I stepped over the half circle and caught up with her.

"I'm just me."

Okay. I'd had enough of cryptic encounters and the whole shebang of oddness that seemed to creep up on me at every turn.

"Why did you say that?" I stepped in front of her.

"Because I am. Just me." She smiled and stepped around me.

"No." I followed her into the stairwell. "The other thing...about the universe."

"Why do you think I said it?" she asked coyly.

"Are you screwing with me?" I crossed my arms, and then uncrossed them. She was starting to make me nervous.

"Nope." She smiled and showed a row of perfectly white, normal teeth. "Go see the Kind Brothers. They'll fix you right up." She patted me on the shoulder and then hopped down the stairs two at a time.

"Who are you?" I called after her.

"One of the good guys," she called out as she turned the corner and disappeared out of sight.

There were good guys? Who in the hell were the Kind Brothers? In Oregon that was reefer code. She did look like a hippie, but that crack about the universe.... Should I wander under the Burnside Bridge? Would it be just another invitation for chaos? Damn. The Universe's messenger didn't look like anything but a hippie kid, but then again I didn't look like a vampire.

Whatever.

I headed back towards my pile of books, and paused when a book on vampires in a shelf caught my eye: Sanguinacious Servitude -- a blood craver's guide to the universe.

Oh, that looked pretentious and intriguing. I pulled the book out and a small flyer slipped free and floated to the floor. Someone had stuffed this card in this particular book, hoping a vampire groupie would find it. Betting it was a religious thing slamming vampires and ready for a laugh, I picked it up and read it. Oh boy. Not what I was expecting...not at all.

Are you alone? Desperate? Hungry? Seeking more of your kind?

Join us! Vampire League of Roses

Nightly at CLUB SANG -- 3rd and Ash
sunset to sunrise
$5 cover

Club Sang? Why had I never heard of this place before? A vampire club in Portland? I felt very stupid all of a sudden. All of my whining and searching the last six months and there had been a group here the whole time? Maybe it was just a place for all the posers to hang out, play vampire, drink red drinks and pretend it was blood. But maybe not. I fit their target audience to a tee. Forget the Kind Brothers, I needed to hit this club and take a look around for myself. And the Universe had even given me the five-dollar cover charge! Bonus!

As I started to leave, I had a guilty twinge about the mess I'd left behind in the corner. I went back, picked up the books and put them back on the shelf, and realized that I might need that brick dust again. I crouched down, opened up the pouch, and was ready to scoop up the half circle with the vampire flyer, when I noticed something written in the powder on the floor.

Scrawled in childlike letters, ***be the bad ass!*** emboldened me.

Pizza Bob! He was still with me after all. I felt better knowing that I wasn't headed to the club all by myself. Even if I couldn't see my ghost, just knowing he was there made me happy. I gathered up the dust, closed the pouch, and headed out into the night, finally confident that things were going my way.

⅄

Daniel was waiting for me at the car. He looked angry. Very, very angry. And smug. I stopped and clutched the pouch in my hand.

"Don't worry, freak. I'm not going to touch you," he said with a sneer.

I just stood there looking at him, afraid to move. He was up to something.

I said, "Go away or I'll dust you again."

He laughed at me, a nasty laugh as he put his hands up in mock surrender. Oh, he was definitely up to something all right.

"Can't touch you with that stuff all over you." He floated away from the car and smirked at me.

"I've got plenty so stay back." I was proud of myself for not whimpering out loud. Maybe Daniel had learned his lesson. Yeah, right. I took a cautious step forward and he stayed still. With all the vampire speed I could muster I blurred past him, unlocked the car and jumped in. The ghost was still standing there just watching me as I tried to start the car.

It wouldn't start. The engine wouldn't even turn over. In fact the dash lights were out; everything was dead. Uh-oh, this wasn't good. I groaned as I put my forehead against the steering wheel, and knocked my face against the horn a few times without even the satisfaction of a honk to rouse me from the creeping dread filling me up inside. I finally looked up and saw Daniel staring at me with his arms crossed and an evil smile on that dead, smug face of his.

"Okay, don't panic," I mumbled as I popped the latch for the hood. "It's just a loose connection. I can fix this."

I opened the pouch, just in case Daniel tried something, and got out of the car. He stayed put, just floating and leering. I opened the hood and stared in shock at where the engine used to be. Now there were just jagged twists of ruined metal, stray wires, and a pile of shredded belts. How did he do that?

"You son of a bitch," I shouted. I whirled around and saw the ghost standing right in front of me. I jumped and flung a spray of dust at him, but he was quick. He disappeared and then rematerialized on the other side of the car, laughing.

"Missed." And then he disappeared again.

In my terror I had flung almost all of the dust at him. Damn it! I had to be more careful from now on. "Screw you, psycho. I've got plenty more where that came from," I lied.

Marcella was going to kill me. I had, after all, wrecked her car. Sort of. I closed the hood, looked around, and saw a pay phone, a graffiti-covered antique, just down the street and that hopefully still worked.

I wondered if Abby was still safe?

Daniel was getting very powerful, and I feared for her more than ever now.

I dialed her number, and listened to the endless ringing on the other end. *Please be okay!*

"Hello, Brokerman residence," answered Emily the maid.

"Emily, this is Melvin." Silence greeted me. "Don't hang up! I need to talk to Ab--," I caught myself, "Priscilla."

"Please hold," the maid said curtly. Which I did; time and silence stretched out until I was certain that Emily had actually hung up on me. I was just getting ready to hang up and redial when I heard her; my reason for living.

"Melvin." One word. One very uptight, curt word from Abby.

"Abby." I couldn't help the quaver in my voice. But I had to sound strong. "Are you safe?"

"Where are you?"

"I can't tell you, but I'm okay. Are you safe?" I asked again urgently.

"Melvin, why did you leave?" She sounded so hurt. "When are you coming back?"

"I don't know, Abby. Please be careful. Daniel is very powerful right now. Stay inside the brick dust."

"I'm fine, Melvin. You shouldn't have left, but I'm going to help you." Her tone was cold and detached. A sick feeling filled me; I'd lost her. I was now a project, a task. Damn.

"No, Abby. Stay there where it's safe. I'm fine...really. I had to leave to protect you." She had to realize that, she had to.

"Was that Vernonia's blood in the kitchen?" Abby asked. "How could you do that to her?"

"It was, and I didn't hurt her." I winced. "Is she still there?"

"No. She left...before I woke up. At least I think she did. I haven't heard from her, and why would I after what happened!"

"If you talk to her, let her know that I'm sorry." Poor Vernonia.

"Somehow I doubt that, Melvin." Ouch. "Is Marcella with you?" Abby demanded. "I found a box on my front steps with a gross little bag in it from her."

The gris-gris bag! Hooray! I hoped Vernonia had hers, too. I realized Abby was waiting for me to answer.

I said, "Not right now--"

"That cow! How dare she knock me out like that!" Abby snapped.

"Don't blame her. She is just trying to keep us all safe in her own way. She made you a gris-gris bag to protect you. I think you need to wear it. Don't be angry with her, please."

"Oh, I'll have a discussion with her. You can bet on it."

I knew that would be a very bad idea and I didn't want to be in the middle when those two met again! Angry Abby was a storm I didn't want Marcella to weather.

"I can't believe you chose her."

I was stunned. "Abby, I didn't choose her, I chose to keep you safe. Really. Please just calm down." Big old tough Melvin was ready to cry. Wow.

"Whatever, Melvin. After everything I've done for you."

"Abby, I can't stay on the line much longer. I just wanted you to know I'm okay...to hear your voice...I-I--"

She cut me off. "Daniel's wake was this morning. Some of his associates came."

The phone started making a strange hissing noise.

"What did they want?" I asked, fearing Daniel had told them about me. That's just what I'd need -- a crack team of torture commandos hunting me down, too. The phone again started hissing, and I got a nervous feeling in my stomach. I thought I heard a voice say, "BITCH!" but it was faint, also not Abby's voice. Uh-oh.

"They came to pay their respects," she said. "I don't think Daniel told anyone about us... he wanted to have his fun first."

"Just be careful, Abby." I looked around at the darkened street, feeling exposed and vulnerable again. I hoped Daniel had kept his mouth shut. Oh, I really hoped so.

Abby said, "I may have found some people who can--" The line started filling with static.

"Abby! Abby!" I yelled frantically, banging the phone against the platform.

She kept talking through the static on my end like she couldn't hear it. "They...know....vampi....looking...I'm going to..." It was all coming through in bits and bursts.

"Abby!" I yelled.

A blaring screech filled the earpiece and, in absolute agony, I dropped the phone; Daniel was laughing behind me. I spun around, ripping the phone from the wire as I did so to brandish as a weapon. What I was going to do with it I had no idea, but that's me: idiot on autopilot. Daniel shook his finger at me, and then the phone box exploded in flames, the phone in my hand following suit. I jumped back, threw the phone at him which just passed through his ghostly form, but I wasn't badly burned; freaked out at his growing power, but thankfully my hand was already healing. My ear, however, felt like it had been rammed with an ice pick.

"Stay away from Abby," I growled, as I stuck my finger in my ear and wiggled it around. I think it diminished the effect of my growl because the ghost just smirked at me.

"Are you crying? Did my little vixen break your heart?" he taunted. Damn it.

"No. Just shut up!" I yelled in frustration.

"No tears for the freak; she hates you, she sees what you are...a rotting bag of meat." Daniel laughed. "How could you think she even likes you? You're just a hobby, a distraction, a slight indiscretion. I'll enjoy her punishment!"

"I'm warning you, stay away from her!" I tried to ignore his attempt at psychological warfare, but the ghost's words did indeed hit me where it counted. Boy, he must have been really good at his job before.

"My fight is with you now," he said. "I'll take care of her when you are gone. She's my reward." Daniel bowed dramatically, and then disappeared again with puff of ozone and something sulfuric that burned my nose. I wrinkled my nose at the odor banquet surrounding me: melted plastic, singed vampire, Melvin rot, and fear. My fear. My vampire eyesight could still make out Daniel's shimmer from where he'd disappeared. Spooky.

Creepy theatrics aside, Abby was safe for now. I knew that the ghost wanted me dead and that as long as I was alive she was safe. So, I had better not die any time soon.

I had to keep moving; the glow of the burning phone box was undoubtedly going to draw the police so I started walking towards downtown. What else could I do? Club Sang wasn't far and I was determined to check it out. Wouldn't it just be great if I found Maddy there? She'd have to help me. This was all her fault anyway. I smiled slightly at my resemblance to Pizza Bob in the blame game. I really missed him.

Daniel appeared ahead of me on the sidewalk, his form shimmering in the darkness as he floated backwards with his arms crossed.

"Go away," I said.

"Hmmm, pretty good trick you've got going with that powder. I have to hand it you, it was clever thinking to cover yourself in it. Pretty quick thinking indeed," he said.

"Shut up," I hissed.

"Sure. But here's the thing, freak. It's going to rub off and then I'm going to get you." He started floating around me in circles, just out of range of my dust flinging abilities. "Oh my. I do think it's going to rain soon."

I looked up, and sure enough the clouds were hanging low and heavy in the night sky. Crap. That would be bad.

"Looks like someone's going to get wet. I'll be waiting!" Daniel said as he disappeared again.

"Why? Why? Why?" I moaned as fat little rain droplets started pelting me. I just could not catch a break! I broke out in a run and skidded to a halt twenty blocks later in front of a dingy looking club, fronted by a towering doorman. He was dressed in black leather, and had a variety of piercings sprouting from his face like rusted acne. There were two horns poking out from his forehead, and I gulped audibly.

"Is this Club Sang?" I asked, trying to scoot under the awning and out of the rain.

The doorman, who was menacing in his six-foot-four frame, placed a hand on my chest and pushed me back. "Who wants to know?"

I rolled my eyes and pulled the flyer out of my pocket. "I found this, here I am. Is this Club Sang or not?" The man grinned at me. He had fangs. Whoa. But he smelled human, so it was all costume and theater. "Come on, I'm getting soaked."

"Are you a cop?"

"No."

"Are you with the health department?"

"No." I was now completely soaked, the brick dust clumping in wads in my hair and on my clothing. Daniel would be here any minute. "Just let me in!"

"This is an exclusive club. What are you?"

"Seriously?"

"We don't accept lookie-loos, tourists, or zombies," he said with a sneer.

Okay, that was it. I'd had it. I grabbed him by the throat and lifted him off the ground. "I am not a zombie! I've had a very bad day, a very bad ascension, I'm being chased by a ghost who wants me dead, I'm hungry, and I'm a frickin' vampire!"

He held out his hand and said in a calm voice, "Five dollars." He wasn't even scared. Maybe that was good sign, and maybe this was a real vampire club after all. Or maybe he was just amused at my outburst; he was a big guy.

I dropped him and handed him the money. He stamped my hand, and said, "Enjoy your evening, Melvin."

I looked at him in shock. "How did you know my name?" I asked, suddenly very afraid.

"Come on, save that shtick for inside," he said with an eye roll. "Personally, I think this trend is going to fade quickly, but whatever gets your rocks off I guess." He crossed his arms and nodded towards the door.

I looked around for Daniel, all clear, and then went inside.

CHAPTER 15

WHAT_THE_EFF???.COM

The music was a dull throb of bass that made the heavy velvet curtain blocking the entrance to the club sway gently back and forth. I was standing in a dark hallway, nervous anticipation about what lay inside making my hands sweat. I closed my eyes and opened up my senses, sniffing the air trying to smell out any otherness. I smelled perfume, incense, clove smoke, but that was it. I heard many heartbeats, all living, but I just didn't get the sense that there were other creatures of the night inside waiting for me. But what did I know? I hadn't mastered that gift with Marcella, and I didn't really think I could now. I took another sniff and smelled fresh blood. Intriguing. It made my gums tingle. I wiped my palm on my pant leg, and stepped through the curtain.

The club was bigger than it looked, quite cavernous and deep. There was a hallway that led to another room, and another hallway that led to yet another room on the side. There was a big sign posted on the wall to my left: Enter at your own risk. Be respectful and remember, NO MEANS NO.

I wrinkled my nose and thought about just leaving, but Daniel was waiting for me, it was raining, and part of me was just morbidly curious. Maybe this trip wouldn't be a bust; maybe there were some real vampires back there. Maybe they knew Maddy. Maybe seemed to be my mantra now.

I had to get some new material.

A waitress came up to me, looked me over, and then tapped her foot impatiently. "What'll it be?"

"I'm good for now." I put my hands in my pockets and smiled sheepishly.

She sighed and nodded towards the back of the club. "Psys are in the mid room, Sangs are in back."

Psys? Sangs? Oh, right, psychic vampires and blood drinkers. My fascination, when I was alive, was with real vampires, not the world of vampire wannabes. I could tell you anything you wanted to know about Vlad, Lestat, or Angel, but the folks who actually lived in the subculture were a mystery, save what I had read on the Masters of the Nite website. Disturbed folks. Certainly.

I kept my head down and strolled towards the Sang Room; it was illuminated by both black light and candlelight. There were candles everywhere hanging from sconces in the ceiling, in cups on tables, in little nooks in the walls; very gothic. Everything was painted black, and the walls had glowing streaks and spots fluoresced by the black light to look like blood spray patterns. Bleh. That was cheery, in a cemetery undead kind of way I supposed.

I wandered towards the back and settled in against the wall to people watch. The club goers were definitely posers. Yes indeed. Men and women decked out in varying degrees of leather and bondage gear, flowing silk gowns open to expose breasts and bellies, lounging in over-stuffed chairs and couches. I cringed at the amount of body piercings peeking out at me. I was horrified when I saw a woman run a razor blade over her forearm and a man bend down and put his mouth over the open wound.

"Oh, that's gross," I mumbled through my extending overbite as I took a step back to turn around and get the hell out of this place.

I headed into the Psy room, and just rolled my eyes at the pale, sleepy, funky looking crowd of posers sprawled in their chairs. Psychic vampires? Really? This was just sad. I strolled into the front room ready to just leave and take my chances in the rain when I bumped into a girl -- a pale girl in a slinky see through robe. I tried not to stare, but couldn't help it.

"Hey, are you trying for Melvin?" she asked me.

"What?" Why did people know my name tonight?

She crinkled up her eyebrows then shrugged. "Yeah, you should get a security guard uniform. The suit doesn't work too well, but your dye job is pretty good."

"What the hell are you talking about?" Things were getting weird again in Melvin Land.

"Well, Melvin over there," she pointed across the room, "is rocking a real security uniform, and Melvin over there --"

"What the hell?" I saw a man dressed up like me, talking to a group of people. He held up a glass of something red and mock toasted me. "What the hell is going on? I'm Melvin!"

How had I not noticed them before? One of me was enough for the world. I suppose I should have been flattered, but just seeing a room full of Melvin wannabes made me sick to my stomach.

"Yeah, yeah...whatever," the girl said with another shrug. "I don't think you are going to win the contest tonight."

I stumbled back and found a chair, plopping down heavily. "Contest?" I asked.

"You new here or something?" She sat down at the table next to me. "We did Twilight last week, and next week will be Vampire Diaries. But tonight is Mostly Dead Melvin night." She twirled a lock of dark black dyed hair around her fingertip. "It's a popular blog, obviously you read it."

"Um, yeah...sometimes," I squeaked. This was unreal. But hey, I was finally one of the popular people, yet it just made me mad, and sad, and flustered.

"What's with all that dirt?" she asked.

"It's brick dust," I mumbled.

"What for?" She was determined to talk to me and I kept staring at the table, trying to be polite and not ogle her ogle bits.

"Keeps ghosts away."

"Really? That's not in the blog." She crossed her arms, and thankfully also covered the ogle bits.

"I don't put everything in there. I'm actually a complicated person, not just what I write in a blog. Sheesh."

"Yeah, whatever. Well, nice try with your persona, but I think Roger," she pointed at another guy standing by the bar, "will take home the prize."

I stared at Roger in disbelief. He was me. Mostly. It was like looking in a creepy mirror. The girl waved to him and he headed over to our table.

"Hey, Demoana," he said brightly but with a lisp.

"Hey yourself. Looking good tonight." She uncrossed her arms and leaned back. "Did you hear about Eddy?"

"I got your tweet." Roger winced.

Demoana visibly shivered. "Oh, yeah. It was awful. Why would someone do that to him?"

Roger shrugged. "Some psycho. They found him drained...and his head was missing. That's just so messed up."

My ears perked up. Drained? "Who's Eddy?" I asked the girl, ignoring the Melvin standing within arm's reach.

"He probably would have won tonight. He does the best Melvin," she said. "Sorry, Roger." She winked.

My stomach did an uncomfortable little roll; a Melvin impersonator was dead. Drained. His head missing. Uh-oh. Coincidence, or was someone hunting me, and poor Eddy got snagged instead.

Roger shrugged. "No worries, D. He was good but we all know I'm better!"

I made a little snorting sound, but Roger ignored me, focusing all of his supposed concern at Demoana.

He said, "I hope they find whoever did that to him." Roger was openly leering at Demoana's chest, and he didn't sound too sad about Eddy at all. Hmmmm.

I asked Demoana, "Where did they find the guy's body?"

"In Forest Park, which was weird because he never really went anywhere except work. There's no way he'd be out hiking unless he was Larping." She giggled. "They actually found two more bodies with him, all dressed in Melvin personas, too." Her eyes glittered. "I have a friend who works in records at the cop shop. She told me about it."

Uh-oh. Someone was killing Melvins. That was bad. Was it Daniel's crew?

"When was this?" I asked quietly.

"Yesterday. It's not in the news yet. The cops think a serial killer might be out...in fact there might be some PO-PO here tonight under cover." She smiled at me sweetly.

Roger stared at me for a second. "Who's the new guy?"

"I'm Melvin," I answered gruffly.

He laughed. "Not tonight. I'm doing him tonight. Nice dye job though. What'd you use?" He leaned in and stared at my cheek. "I've been going with RIT clothing dye."

I stared back. He had in a retainer, his glasses were taped on one side, and he was wearing a night security uniform. It was unreal. And he was indeed blue, but he didn't smell bad. Damn it.

"It's my little secret," I snapped.

"Jeez, don't get all bitchy. Good luck tonight." He backed away. "Catch ya later, D?"

"I hope so," she purred back. Bleh.

"I'm Melvin. Me. Not you," I said petulantly to Roger's back.

"Wow, that was mean," Demoana said. "Melvin isn't mean."

"You don't know anything about me."

"Are you a cop?"

"No. I'm a vampire."

"As if," she sassed back. "You're a dick."

Demoana got up and left the table.

Unreal! I saw a group of women clustered together and looking identical in the same kind of outfit; obviously costumed in plain jeans and sweatshirts. One of them came up to me and smiled.

"Hi, Melvin," she said through a fanged giggle. "Do you have a partner for the contest? I could be your Maddy."

"Are you kidding me?" I shouted.

"N-no...." she stammered.

"You don't look a thing like her," I said with a sneer. Why was I being so mean?

"Hey! I look good, better than you! What's your problem?"

"This!" I said, pointing at the other Melvins. "All of you making fun of my life. None of you know anything about vampires! You're just pathetic."

"Go to hell, and your costume sucks!" She stormed off and rejoined her friends. People were starting to stare at me. In fact Roger was fixated on me. It sent a little nervous flutter through my chest. What was his deal?

"You seem to be making friends left and right," Daniel said next to me.

"Gah!" I squealed as I jumped up, and started waving my arms around in a frenzy to disperse him. People stared, some clapped, but I was too terrified to be embarrassed.

Someone yelled, "Go get him, Pizza Bob," which made the crowd start cheering. I fled the club, howling like a mad man.

⚓

At least it's not raining.

I had no idea where to go or what to do as I ran down the middle of the road The Club Sang was a bad idea, shined a spot light on all my bad traits and self pity, and I was more depressed than ever. Plus I had Daniel hot on my tail. And someone was killing Melvins in town. The hits just kept on coming.

Someone said, "Hey there, lost soul!"

I skidded to a halt and saw the girl from Powell's Books leaning against a food cart, eating a falafel.

"Whachya doin'?" she asked.

I looked over my shoulder for Daniel, and then stared at her wide-eyed.

What am I doing?

"Running," I said.

"How's that working out for you so far?" she asked through a mouth full of food.

"Um, well...." I smelled ozone and knew Daniel's arrival was imminent. Oh boy. "Hey, uh, I gotta go."

"What's the rush?" She wiped her face with a napkin, balled up the falafel wrapper, and then dropped it in a bag hanging at her hip. She smiled at me, and arched an eyebrow.

The smell of ozone was now mixing with sulfur, and I felt a tingle in the air. The ghost was close. The girl peered around my shoulder, then looked at me curiously.

"Expecting someone?"

"Um, you, um," I mumbled. "It's complicated...uh...." I was a stammering idiot. "Look, I gotta go," I said just as Daniel flamed into existence right next to me. I let out one of my trademark girly Melvin squeals as the ghost reached out to grab me, but the girl just pointed at him.

"You, go away," she said.

And he did. Bam. Just like that.

"Whoa," I whispered.

"You haven't been to see the Kind Brothers yet," she admonished. "And I gave you that money for some coffee, not bar hopping, lad."

"Who are you?" I was completely, totally, mind-numbingly shell shocked.

"I told you. You aren't very quick, are you?" she asked with a chuckle.

"You said JUST ME."

"No," she shook her head, "I said Teas Maith, but you heard just me."

"Yeah...Just Me."

She sighed. "Let's spell it out: T-E-A-S M-A-I-T-H. Pronounce it like Jyoss May," she lowered her voice and emulated a stoner surfer accent, "and not Just Me. 'Kay, Bruh?" She laughed.

"That's a weird name."

She shrugged. "It's a brilliant name. It suits me and my Irish sensibilities."

I crouched down, dizzy and overwhelmed. "I need a minute."

"Sounds fair." She sat down on the sidewalk next to me.

"How did you do that? Is he gone for good?" I finally asked.

"Not exactly," she said with a smirk.

"Of course not. He's never gone." I sighed heavily.

"He's changing, becoming. He's more than a ghost now."

"Oh, that's just great! So what are you?"

"Hey, you remember playing tag when you were a kid? You were safe if you reached base?" She twirled a dread lock around her finger, and grinned at me. "I'm like base, I guess. A time out. A reprieve. A breather --"

"I get the picture," I interrupted. "But why? What are you?"

She smiled. "A better question is what am I not?"

I stood up. "You know, I appreciate the help and all, but I've pretty much had it with cryptic quips and beautiful women who want to help me, and basically the universe gunning for me. So, if you don't mind could you just please give me a straight answer?"

She stood up, took my hand, and started leading me down the sidewalk. "Sure, why not."

She'd said she was one of the good guys when I had first met her, she seemed powerful enough to banish Daniel, and I felt safe with her. Well, safer than with Daniel or Mr. Happy! Teas Maith didn't look scary, or give off an aura of danger, but for all I knew she was really a hideous monster in disguise and just screwing with me; that was more plausible than the universe actually giving a damn. But still....

What the hell. Why not? I just let my mind go blank and followed her. Okay, Universe. You've got my attention.

We walked in silence for a few blocks, her smiling at passers-by who stared at me in disgust, and then Teas Maith led me to a concrete bench next to one of the big water fountains in the park blocks.

"Here's the deal, Melvin. You caught a bad break. You were never a bad guy, and now you are always trying to do the right thing. That counts. It really does." She patted me on the shoulder.

"Thanks." I was waiting for the other shoe to drop. "So what are you? My guardian angel or something?"

Teas Maith laughed. "Of course not. That's silly. You're a vampire."

"Of course." I felt stupid all of a sudden.

"Now, don't be that way. There's a balance to everything, at least there's supposed to be. You've never had it easy, but never really had it hard until now."

"That's the understatement of the year," I said glumly. "So, again, why are you helping me? And why now? Why couldn't you have shown up the night I met Maddy?"

"Oh, Melvin, Melvin, Melvin. You have to walk your own path and make your own choices. You knew something was off with Maddy when you met her; your fascination with mhealladh dorcha ar an oíche --"

"What?"

Teas Maith giggled. "Sorry. Your fascination with the dark lure of the night--" She wrinkled up her nose. "It sounds better in the Irish, don't you think?"

"You're really Irish? You don't have an accent."

"I'm old school, Melvin. But I've been here a very, very long time," she answered with a wink.

"Of course you have." I took a deep breath and started rambling. "So what are you? A god? An angel? A witch? Nothing would surprise me at this point. What is it with all the exotic women and me lately?

I rubbed my face and then let out a long, tortured sigh. "I've lived thirty years in almost total social isolation and within the span of six months I've met more wacky beings than I ever thought possible."

Teas Maith just sat looking at me with a crooked grin tugging at the corners of her mouth.

"Yes," I said. "I know I'm pathetic."

"I find you charming, Melvin."

"Gee, thanks."

"Are you done?" she asked.

"For now."

"Right. As I was saying, your fascination with all the dark things in the night set you on a collision course with fate. One thing led to another, and now here you are all flusterpated."

Flusterpated. I liked that word. I looked at Teas Maith, and it was like a little hole was opening up in my heart, even as it started beating briefly.

"I didn't think it was all real you know," I whispered. "It was just a fantasy, a wish. I just wanted to be something else instead of me." Wow. The truth hurts.

"Lessons learned, sweetie." She put her arm around me. "This whole thing was a cock up from the start. And then," she hooked her fingers in the air like quote marks, "your Mr. Happy stepped in and made it worse."

"Yeah!" I nodded. "He's not very nice at all."

"He's not supposed to be."

I smirked. "Then he's very good at his job."

"Well, that's what got our attention." She stood up and stretched. "As I said, there's supposed to be a balance to things, and he's meddling a little too much."

I stood up, too. "What are you? The balance police or something?"

Teas Maith laughed. "I like you, you're funny, Melvin." She started walking away. Was I supposed to follow her?

She called over her shoulder, "Come on," so I trotted after her like a lost puppy.

"By meddling do you mean the con he pulled on Pizza Bob?" I asked.

"Among other things. Your guide, the first blood which was given and not taken of your own free will, is too powerful."

I shuddered. "Daniel. He's very scary."

"Yes, he is. And he'll get scarier."

"You know I didn't kill him, right?"

Teas Maith said, "Yes, Melvin. I know everything."

I smirked. "What's the meaning of life?"

"If I told you then I'd have to kill you," she said deadpan.

"Okay," I said slowly. Was she kidding?

"You need to lighten up, my boy." She elbowed me playfully as we walked. "It's 42."

I smiled. Anyone who could quote Douglas Adams was A-Okay in my book.

"We're all fellow travelers in one way or another," she said with a smile.

"So what happens now?" I asked. "Am I one of the good guys?"

"Not exactly. You're a vampire, and that's usually not so on with the nice guy role. But you weren't given proper instructions, your transformation was completely bungled, and your soul is still mostly human and pure. So far." She stopped in front of an espresso cart and ordered two vanilla lattes.

"You're an anomaly, Melvin," she said, handing me one of the drinks. "Nothing like a little vanilla'd caffeine to chase the ick away, eh?"

"I guess." I knew I wasn't evil. That was something at least.

We sat down on the sidewalk next to a bike rack, and let the world pass us by as we people watched under the glow of a street lamp. Teas Maith pulled a bag of breadcrumbs out of her pocket and began tossing bits to some crows that were starting to gather around us, mumbling in Irish and laughing when the crows cawed back. It seemed like they were having a conversation. They probably were. Probably talking about me.

"So, Just Me, am I saying that right now?"

"No, but close enough."

More crows flew down and crowded around us, unafraid and a little too familiar for my comfort. There was quite the flock now, a full murder of crows. A murder. Ugh, morbid much? I wondered just how powerful Teas Maith was, what she was. I wished that I knew more about Irish mythology; I'd have to brush up on it if I survived all of this. I looked at the woman and a wave of calm washed over me, like possibly everything might be okay. But I was a sucker and the universe knew it.

"Are you going to help me?" I took a little sip of the coffee, despite my dislike of vanilla; the months of air fresheners had pretty much ruined the scent of vanilla and even strawberry for me. When the warm coffee hit my stomach it rumbled loudly, reminding me I was over due for a snack.

"Drink your coffee, Melvin. It will help. Trust me."

I took another tentative sip, and suddenly it tasted divine; like the health shakes Abby had made for me. I smiled and then gulped the rest of the cup down. Hooray, awkward feeding issues averted.

Teas Maith smiled. "All I can do is give you this little break, give you a snack without actually letting you snack on someone." She toasted my empty cup.

"Thank you, I was getting peckish and panicked. I didn't want to freak you out."

"Sweetie, you can't freak me out. Trust me. I've seen it all."

"Should I ask?"

"No, suffice it to say my world is beyond your security clearance." She giggled again. "I'm here to let you get your head together before the next wave of boo-boo lip hits you and rocks your world." Teas Maith downed her drink in one gulp, and then winked at me. My heart fluttered in my chest, yes indeed it did.

I liked this lady. I loved the way she spoke, her funny phrases; I loved how gentle she was. If I wasn't careful I might even start to like her as much as I loved Abby, who probably hated me now. I sighed wistfully. Teas Maith giggled and patted my knee.

"You're a sweet kid, but I'm old enough to be your great, great, great, and so on grandmother, boyo."

I blushed. And with the blush came a wave of my odor. Damn. Of course she could read my mind; all the powerful women around me, except for Abby I hoped, could read my mind. I was a stupid open book! I stood up quickly, just desperate to run away and hide. The crows launched into the air around me, flapping and cawing madly.

Teas Maith stood up, and the crows circled around her a few times before flying off into the night. She just stood there smiling sweetly at me until I couldn't take the silence anymore.

I cleared my throat. "Thanks for your help. I appreciate it. I hate to ask, but what do I do?"

"Well, you're on the right track. The old gods will sort you out, but there will be a price, a choice, a sacrifice."

"That sounds ominous."

"A word of advice, Melvin. Follow your heart. And don't lose hope. The Goblin King will try and trick you with riddles and obfuscation, and the Loas will probably scare the muffins outta ya. Be brave when you face the dark guardian of the doorway."

"Oh boy."

She smiled. "He's the one you really have to worry about."

"Is that Mr. Happy?" I shuddered. "Is he Kalfu or just a poser?"

"He is what he is, just like I am what I am."

"You sound like Popeye," I said with a little snort.

Teas Maith laughed. "I consider myself to be more like Jiminy Cricket, with a little Wonder Woman mixed in."

"But I'll never be a real boy...." I sounded wistful and rather pathetic.

"You've got lots of people who care about you, you've made strong connections in your undeath...more than when you were alive. That means something. Cherish it. You aren't alone."

"Is Pizza Bob here now?" I looked around me.

"Not here, he can't be with me in my space. He's weak but he's out there doing what he does. He's been a good friend to you."

"Can you bring him back?"

Teas Maith sighed. "Nope. I can't interfere with that path."

"Okay. Right. I knew that."

"One thing I need to say. The Vodouisant woman may be in over her head. She means well, but you should be a little more take charge."

"Marcella?" I frowned. She seemed pretty sure of herself so far. "How do you mean?"

"She's dabbling with forces outside her craft. That's all I can say."

"But I don't know anything about voodoo, except what I just read at Powell's. And she seemed certain that if I just showed up her family would try and kill me."

Teas Maith rolled her eyes. "Think on what I said...maybe you should be looking for other sources of power you will need instead of just her for the immediate game plan. It's a choice thing, toots. I'm trying to paint a picture between the lines." She patted my cheek.

I winced when I realized what she meant. The goblins. Bleh. But it was Marcella's idea in the first place! I so wasn't ready to deal with that yet. But was it the choice or a choice. Man, what I wouldn't give for a straight answer just once in my life. Teas Maith cleared her throat to get my attention.

"I shouldn't really tell you this, but, what the hell. In for a penny, in for a pound right?" She looked up at the sky and gave a little thumbs-up to whoever (or whatever) was in charge. She took a deep breath and said ominously, "The woman you love loves you back, in her own way. But she's dangerous, Melvin."

I sighed and shook my head. Yes, Abby was definitely a live wire, but she loved me! Yes! I truly hoped I'd get to see her again.

"Yes, Melvin," Teas Maith said a bit sadly as she read my mind yet again. "But focus in on what I said, you're skipping over the dangerous part. You will see her again, but things will have changed."

"What do you mean?" I got that nervous flutter in my stomach. "She was trying to tell me something, but Daniel wouldn't let me hear it."

"You'll find out. I can't interfere any more. You'll have your happy family together again, but it's going to cost you dearly."

"How?" I hated all of this mysterious wait and see mumbo-jumbo. It was frustrating.

"You'll find out. Remember, everyone walks their own path accordingly. Speaking of which, it's time for you to go." She hugged me, gave me a little peck on the cheek, and then turned to leave. "You've got a free pass from your ghost demon thing for a bit. Make the best of it! Good luck."

"Wait!" I cried. "Will I see you again?

She stopped and looked over her shoulder. "Sure, why not? If things balance out okay. Time's all relative from here, but get moving, Melvin."

"Where?"

"Duh. Go find the Goblin King."

"Crap," I moaned as I watched the merry messenger skip down the street and disappear around a corner. I realized I still didn't know exactly what she was or where I would find the Goblin King.

Damn it!

CHAPTER 16

MOSTLY DEAD MAN WALKING

I went through my own little morbid checklist in my mind. Hungry? Nope. Magic latte consumed. Check. Tired? Nope. Magic latte to the rescue yet again. Check. Terrified? Demons, torture commandos and or serial killer creepos possibly after me, a date with Loas, an angry and dangerous Abby? That would be a yes. Check. Check. Check. Big old check!

Even though I had a free pass from Daniel, I had no idea when it expired or when he'd be back to finish what he had started. I knew that when he finally did arrive the ghost would be extra pissed off, and probably even more powerful. Wonderful.

I also had no idea where to start looking for the goblins, or any heart felt inclination to do so. But, those were my marching orders from Teas Maith so I headed towards the strip club district in downtown, hoping to hit pay dirt on the first try and not have to travel out to Eighty-Second Avenue, Portland's unofficial red light district. It was only midnight, so I had a few hours yet before the clubs all closed. I also didn't have any cash on me for a cover charge, but I'd wing it; charm my way in.

Yeah, right, I thought as I caught my reflection in a shop window. Just maybe I'd get lucky and the first place I hit would be goblin central. Probably not.

Come on Universe...just one more little break, okay?

I started at a club called Peepers, fingers crossed and ever hopeful, but of course it was a resounding no. I then made my way down the block to Long Johns, HotGirlz, and finally Peek-a-Boo(b), which made me chuckle at their clever use of parentheses. I couldn't get past the doorman at any of the places, and when asked no one knew "Chuck". How does one ask if a Goblin King owns the club anyway? I saw a variety of nasty looking folks, some potential goblin girls, but my hinky meter never really went off. I was terrible at the 'otherness' sensing, and was ready to just make the trek to prostitute alley in southeast, when I stopped in front of The Hideaway. It was a smaller club with tinted windows and pulsing neon signs above the door. The place had the slick grimy feel of a booze cave, but there was also an undercurrent of something off. Something not quite right.

Bingo.

I opened the door, stepped into a hallway leading to another doorway, and was blocked by a midget -- little person? Dwarf? I had no idea what the politically correct term was anymore -- sitting on a stool. I couldn't tell if it was male or female! There were breasts that sagged low in a vintage Iron Maiden tee-shirt, but there was also a beard and a variety of moles and warts on its bulbous face; less than attractive on the whole. I just stood there blinking. I had a fear of midgets, I know...I'm a bad person, but they creeped me out almost as much as clowns. But if anyone looked like a goblin, this thing sure did. And if it was a goblin then it had to be female, unless this was Chuck, the Goblin King. But that would be too easy.

"Ten dollars," it said gruffly, holding out a finely manicured hand for the money.

"Um, hi," I squeaked. "I, uh, I'm looking for someone."

"We all are, sweetie. Ten dollars gets you all the looking you want." It cackled, and rubbed its fingers together.

I looked over the thing's head, trying to peek into the club through scratches in the tinted glass door, when I felt a hard whack on my leg. Startled, I jumped back and saw that the thing on the stool had smacked me with a wooden walking stick.

"No, no, no. No pay, no peek!" It chided.

"Wow," I snapped. "You've got quite the swing, don't you!" I reached down and massaged a lump forming above my kneecap. It didn't hurt that much, enough that I winced from the burning sensation, but any regular guy would have been rolling on the floor in agony by now.

"It's an ash stick, vampy," the thing said through a row of blackened, Chiclet-looking teeth.

My heart started up, painfully thudding in my chest as a fear-tinged rush blasted through me. Ash wood was deadly for vampires. Every source cited that fact, and from the lingering and slight burning pain I realized that it might be true; more than holy water at least.

"Any more funny business and I'll ram it into your heart." It held out its hand again for money. "Ten dollars."

"You know I'm a vampire?" I asked quietly, afraid to make any sudden moves.

"We don't discriminate here. You wanna look at some bobblies then your money's as good as the next guy's." It squinted its eyes at me. "Just don't get fresh with the girls. We can get you a meal, but it'll cost a pretty penny."

"Right, okay then." I took another little step back. "You're a goblin?"

The thing just looked at me. "What do you think?"

"Yes?" I took another step back.

"Yes." It smirked at me. "You know, you're kinda cute. I'm off at two if you want to grab a drink or something."

I shook my head no a little too quickly. "Oh, no, thanks, but I'm just here to find someone." I gulped. "Are you...are you Chuck?"

"Do I look like his Regal Majesty? No, sweetie. I'm all woman. My name's Bonsel," she said with a gross tongue waggle.

I gagged inside. "So, is he here?"

"Nope." She adjusted something under her shirt; I think it was her left breast, but it was pointed to the side. Bonsel kept fiddling with it until I coughed politely.

"Will he be here?" I asked, ignoring her attempt at a seductive eye wiggle that looked more like a facial tic.

"Nope."

"Can you tell me where he is?" I couldn't take much more of this.

"Well, you didn't say the magic word."

I tried not to look confused. Magic word? Bertram didn't say anything about a magic word!

"Magic word...um..." I cleared my throat of the nervous squeak and said, "Abracadabra?"

"That's cute. I meant please." Bonsel winked at me.

I decided to bluff my way in. "Look, I'm on a schedule here, and I just need to speak to the guy." I arched an eyebrow and added, "Please?"

"What do you want to see our most revered and exalted King for?"

"That's personal." I crossed my arms and tried to look intimidating while keeping my eye on that walking stick.

"Well look at you all big and studly," Bonsel said with a smirk. "He's a busy man with a full calendar. He doesn't have time for vampire drama."

"No drama," I assured.

"He's a popular quest lately. Everybody's looking for him." Bonsel tapped a nail against her teeth.

"A Voodoo Queen been here?" I asked, aware that I was potentially stepping on Marcella's toes.

"Who are you exactly?" Bonsel hopped down off of her stool, and then leaned in and sniffed me.

"I'm," I gulped, "I'm Melvin."

Bonsel's eyes widened, and then she grinned at me. Not a nice grin either. Uh-oh.

"Wait here, sweetums. I'll be right back," she said as she pulled a cell phone from her pocket and hobbled down the hallway towards the other door into the club. I focused in and heard her make a call to someone who answered the phone with one word, "Barbaro's."

Club Barbaro, a combo biker bar and strip club, was out on Eighty-Second Avenue. I heard Bonsel ask for the Regent, whoever that was, in an excited voice.

She said, "I claim the bounty. He's here."

That couldn't be good. A bounty? On me? I knew Mr. Happy was behind it, he had to be. I just hoped that Marcella was safe.

I turned and ran for the front door just as two larger little people, muscular looking little people, more goblins in fact, followed by Bonsel came into the hallway.

"Get him," she shouted as my hand made contact with the door's push bar. I almost made it!

The goblin on the left dove for me, and grabbed me around the waist, dragging me down to the floor in a jumble of arms and legs. The residual brick dust on my clothing had no effect on the creature whatsoever. Damn! The thing had me pinned, and was mashing my face into the sticky carpet while the other goblin grabbed my legs. They were terrifyingly strong, but I was stronger. I kicked out with my foot and sent the goblin sprawling against the wall with a satisfying thud that shook the hallway, and then flipped over onto my back. The one that had me around the waist was now pinned underneath me and struggling for air. Bonsel came running at me, her ash walking stick raised over her head like a club, and then slammed it down, point first into my stomach.

"Ooof," I yelled as the spike went through me, through the goblin beneath me, and pinned me to the floor. It was excruciating, even more painful than the sun lamp had been! I couldn't believe I was still alive through all of that pain.

I couldn't move. A sickly sweet smell filled the air as my blood bubbled and oozed out of the wound and started pooling around me.

The goblin underneath me gurgled and quit struggling.

"Now look what you made me do! I killed Wiggin because of you!" Bonsel shrieked.

She had her hand resting on the stick, and it started glowing, which sent a burning sensation through my limbs. I felt like I was on fire yet paralyzed and still unable to move. My vision started getting all swimmy and I knew I was going to die. I couldn't believe this was the end; killed by a warty little goblin with a bad boob job.

She said, "Gurbin, get up!" to the goblin sprawled against the wall, but the thing didn't move. Bonsel nudged the body with her foot, and Gurbin's head lolled grossly to one side. I'd broken its neck! Good for me. I didn't even feel guilty.

Bonsel screamed and ground the stick further into my abdomen. "The bounty was dead or alive, you bastard. So dead it is! As slow and painful as I can make it!"

"Abby, I'm sorry," I mumbled, my heart breaking that I wouldn't be able to protect her from Daniel, that I would never get to tell her that I loved her. I decided to be brave and meet my death with my eyes wide open, and held Bonsel's gaze as she twisted, with a feral look on her face, the wood deeper into my gut. I was eerily calm as I lay dying. There was nothing more I could do now, and I tried to fill my heart with all of my unspoken love, hoping Abby would at least sense it in the aether.

Would I crumble into a pile of ash?

Would I melt?

I hoped the pain would stop soon.

The air cooled around me and I saw a shimmering haze rise up behind Bonsel. Maybe this was the light that would meet me and whisk me away to nothingness. The haze started to take shape, a faint outline of a person, and I smiled because it looked like Pizza Bob. Maybe he'd catch a ride on the Passing On Express.

"Dude," I said with a slight grin.

Suddenly Bonsel went rigid, her eyes bugging in her head, and she started making a choked, gurgling noise. She let go of the stick, which stopped glowing instantly, and she fell backwards with a dull thud. It looked like she'd had a stroke.

Karma's a bitch, ain't it, toots!

I laughed and coughed up a fountain of blood that splashed all over my face; it was ice cold and tasted like rotten meat. I gagged from the odor, embarrassed even in death by my own stink. I was too weak to move, to pull out the stick, and I was probably only seconds away from death anyway; but hey, I hadn't peed my pants and the pain had stopped. Silver lining.

Bonsel's foot twitched, and then her arms began jerking. She sat up, blinked a few times, and then croaked a word at me.

"Dude."

No. It couldn't be. I watched the goblin try and stand up, but her coordination was off; nothing but rubbery and jerky movements from her limbs. She finally gave up and crawled towards me.

She said in a jumble of mushy sounding words, "It's gross in here, dude. No room to maneuver."

"Pizza Bob?" I whispered in disbelief. "Is that you?"

Bonsel's head nodded yes as she yanked the wood sticking out of my stomach; it came free with a gross little slurping noise. I groaned and went limp again.

"The things I do for you, ass hat," she slurred, still trying to get her mouth to work right.

With the wood removed I could move, but I was weak, too weak from the blood loss. "I can't believe it. You saved me," I whispered.

"It's what I do, buddy." Pizza Bob's voice came out of Bonsel's mouth. He was definitely in control now, but it was creepy seeing a ghost wearing a goblin. He chewed his lip, and frowned at me. "But you're hurt bad, man. Can you stand? We need to get moving."

"I don't think so. I think I'm done for," I said. "You get to Marcella...she can still help you...protect Abby." I closed my eyes trying to be noble in my last moments.

Pizza Bob grabbed my arms and pulled me up into a sitting position. "Stop being so melodramatic. You're not dying."

I cracked open an eyelid and stared at him. I was weak, it was hard to concentrate, but I actually didn't feel like I was dying anymore. Maybe he was right. But I had a huge hole in my abdomen that was still oozing blood; it hadn't started healing up yet. I reached down and stuck a finger in the hole tentatively, and then pulled my hand away and saw my fingers slick with black blood.

"Ugh, that's gross," I said as I gagged, and flopped onto my back again.

"Don't mess with it!" Pizza Bob snapped. "You'll make it worse!" He reached into his pocket and pulled out a wicked looking switchblade. He flicked it open, made a long, jagged cut on his wrist, and then pushed the wound towards my mouth before I could stop him.

I don't know why but I latched on and began sucking, maybe it was a self-preservation instinct, but I did it. I was drinking blood! I'd finally done it! Then my inner revulsion kicked in; it was goblin blood!

I tried to pull away but Pizza Bob pushed the wound against my mouth tightly and held my chin with his other hand. He had goblin strength now. The blood was hot and bitter, and it burned as it flowed down my throat.

It was amazing. Euphoric. Satiating. When it hit my stomach the wound began hurting; stabby little pokes and pinches that made me whimper in both pain and delight.

After a minute Pizza Bob pulled his hand away forcefully and sat back on his butt. "Don't kill the goblin, we still need her." He ripped a piece of his tee shirt off in a strip, and bound the wound tightly.

I was dizzy and tingling. Blood was rushing in my ears as I sat up and looked down in awe at the healing wound on my stomach. *Awesome*, I thought as I probed the puckered flesh, still a bit shocky from the trauma.

Sensations flooded though my body, my vampire senses on over drive. I heard Bonsel's heart beating rapidly in her chest, pumping all of that glorious, delicious blood.

Oh, god! What did I just do!

I felt my guts twist and I put my hand over my mouth to keep from puking. I'd just drunk blood, and enjoyed it. I looked at Pizza Bob with a mixed expression of horror, delight, revulsion, and scrunched up puke face.

"Don't puss out on me here and gack, Melvin. Be the bad ass. Suck it up!"

I looked at Pizza Bob in Bonsel's body and burst out laughing. I admit it sounded a little hysterical.

"You okay?" he asked.

I gave him a thumbs-up, and then belched; blow out averted. Wow, I did feel great. There must be something magical about goblin blood, of course there would be, and my gums tingled just thinking about it. But I had in fact drunk Bonsel's blood while she was possessed by a ghost; did that make a difference?

"How in the hell did you manage to take over her body?" I asked as I stood up.

"Vernonia told me how to do it." Pizza Bob reached up, grabbed my arm with his creepy little goblin fingers, and started pulling me out the front door.

"But I thought you were all zapped and stuff." I sounded stoned, slurring my words a bit.

"It's complicated. I had help."

"Okay. That's cool," I said, a little repulsed by his touch yet still feeling giddy from the blood. And weird. Really, really weird.

My thoughts were racing wildly in my head, but I needed to focus. He had help. Vernonia is okay. And still helping -- she must not be that mad at me! I had so many questions!

"But--"

"Move it! I'll tell you everything," Pizza Bob snapped at me. "But we need to get out of here. The others inside are gonna catch us if we don't get moving."

"Yeah, sure...whatever," I said with a chuckle as we ran out the front door and into the night. Pizza Bob was moving pretty fast on Bonsel's stubby legs, and I started laughing again as we ran hand-in-hand around the corner to a parking lot.

"You're looking good, Pizza Bob!"

He turned and grimaced at me. "It's a tight fit, and this goblin's brain is all lumpy and gross."

"So's the outside."

"Yeah, well you ever run barefoot through a yard and then stepped on a slug?" he asked. "That's what it feels like on the inside." He shuddered.

"Thanks for the visual. Bleh."

"Look in a mirror recently? You're no prize, Melvin." But he said it with a smile. A gross goblin, blackened, Chiclet-like toothed smile.

"Touché," I said with a shudder.

"The only plus to me being in here is I can feel again. I can smell, and you reek to high heaven, dude." He laughed. "I'm hungry, I'm horny, and I'm kind of happy about it!"

I smiled. I was glad that he was able to feel alive again, but the thought of him doing something about the horny part, especially in Bonsel's body, made me gag a little.

Okay, a lot. "But you look like an extra from a Leprechaun movie."

"Yeah...I'm not too psyched about having lady parts in this body. I always thought that would be so cool!" Of course he did. "This chick is seriously twisted in the libido department, in every department." He reached into a pocket and pulled out some car keys. "She's got some sick things going on in here, man." He shuddered as he tapped his forehead.

"It's hard to even look at you while you're talking to me," I said with a snort, my midget fear nudging me a bit as he stopped in front of a large black SUV -- a Hummer.

I watched him unlock the passenger door. "What are we doing?"

"This goblin has a sweet ride, we're gonna take it." Pizza Bob gave me a fist bump.

"How did you know this was hers?"

"Meat soup," he said, poking himself in the forehead again. "All kinds of info in here."

"Right."

"Plus, take a look." He jumped -- apparently goblins were like pogo sticks on stubby legs -- up into the giant truck.

I climbed in and saw that the driver's side was decked out for a small person -- the steering wheel had levers for the gas pedal and brakes, and that the seat was elevated and customized for Bonsel's goblin stature. There was no way I'd be able to drive it comfortably. I just shook my head as Pizza Bob stroked the steering wheel lovingly.

"Sweet, sweet ride, though. I always wanted a Hummer; just not from a goblin," Pizza Bob said with a snort.

A Hummer? Of course a strip club working goblin henchwoman would own a Hummer. Funny on so many levels.

Pizza Bob nodded and said, "Ironic, yeah?" as he started the engine. He made a face and started fiddling with the make shift wrap on his wrist. "This stings, man."

"Maybe you got some of my blood in the wound," I said nervously. That would be bad; a possessed goblin vampire.

"Oh, man, I didn't even think of that. You think she'll turn?"

"Who knows," I said miserably. "How long can you stay in her body?"

"I don't know." Pizza Bob unwrapped his wrist and stared at the cut. It looked painful.

It looks delicious.

I jumped. Where the hell did that come from?

"Oh, crap," I whispered to myself and realized Pizza Bob was saying something.

"...I've got some crazy stuff to tell you," was all I heard as blood started rushing through my ears; the beginning of one of my trademark panic attacks.

After everything I'd been through in the last two days I doubted very much anything Pizza Bob had to say would seem crazy. I was getting too used to all the ups and downs the universe decided to throw at me, including my brush with death. A shiver ran through me when I thought about it, about how I'd been saved. I licked my lips, remembering the bitter taste of goblin blood, and my overbite started to extend.

Whoa! Don't go there.

I was staring at the drips of blood on Pizza Bob's/Bonsel's wrist, fixated on the way the light reflected in the ruby beads.

"Melvin...what are you doing?" Pizza Bob cradled his wrist protectively.

"I--I can't stop thinking about the blood."

"Dude, you are creeping me out by looking at me like a Happy Meal."

"I'm sorry," I whispered, lisped actually because of my extending overbite. "There's something powerful in that blood."

"We need to get out of here, man. You need to get yourself under control and not attack me. Seriously. We need this goblin for now. I don't know if I have enough juice to possess somebody else before we get to Vernonia."

Vernonia!

"Or," Pizza Bob snapped, "before this goblin turns into a vampire. I don't think I could hang on through the transition."

Oh crap.

"You're right. I'm sorry. Do you feel different?"

"Nope. Still grossly goblinish. I think gobs are okay with vampire bites. At least Bonsel isn't screaming about it, so who knows?"

"You can hear her?" I was grossed out beyond belief. I didn't realize that the goblin would still be awake inside her mind and I felt a little sorry for her. Just a little.

"Don't worry about her. She was gonna kill you, was killing you! Remember? Jeez, man! Be the bad ass."

"Okay," I said half-heartedly. "Is Vernonia okay?"

"Not really, well, yeah she is, but I'll fill you in on the go. We've got some rescuing to do."

"That doesn't sound good," I pinched the bridge of my nose between my finger tips and squeezed. Please don't let it have something to do with Mr. Happy.

"Let's get moving. Are you cool?" he asked as he bound the wound again with a fresh strip of tee shirt. He tossed the old blood soaked wrap into the back of the car and I followed its arc with a longing look. Maybe I could snag it when we got wherever we were going.

Seriously? Melvin, you're losing it. That's disgusting.

I rubbed my face with my palms and said, "I'm good. We're good. But we better hurry because the body you are in doesn't have long."

Because I might attack you and drain you and not be able to stop myself! I started shaking, and clutched at the armrest to steady myself, willing my overbite to retract.

"Then we better get some curly fries. Stat." Pizza Bob grinned at me. "Can't be a hero without some curly fries."

I started laughing, my own sickening thirst for blood forgotten. "I've missed you."

"Need a tissue, princess?"

"Jerk." But I still felt better.

As we drove out of the lot I saw a herd of goblins (a mob, a crew, a gaggle?) come rushing out of the club. Pizza Bob slammed on the brakes.

"Dude," he said to me as he rolled down the window. "Lean back in the seat with your head lolling. Make it look good."

I grinned. "The Wookie maneuver, I like it."

"What? Oh, yeah...whatever, nerd." He rolled his eyes and then leaned his head out the window.

"I'm taking him to the Regent," he yelled to the advancing crew. "I claim the bounty." One of the goblins scampered up the driver's side door and leaned in the window.

"What happened to Gurbin and Wiggin?" it demanded.

"He killed them before I could ash him," Pizza Bob said in Bonsel's voice. "But I got him good. He's done for, and the bounty is mine."

I felt the goblin's gaze boring into me, and I stayed still even though all I wanted to do was leap out and tear open its throat, drink my fill, and then go throw up in a corner because I was a monster.

The goblin said, "Gurbin was my mate. I claim life price."

"Wiggin was Gurbin's mate," Pizza Bob said, banking on Bonsel's memory to bluff his way through. "Your claim has no merit, Scarpa." The goblin narrowed its eyes, but Pizza Bob didn't flinch.

"We were in a triad...I claim life price for both."

Pizza Bob scowled and then spit in his hand. He held it out to the other goblin and said, "Done."

Scarpa climbed down and started to open the rear door.

"No. I claim the bounty alone!" Pizza Bob pushed the automatic door lock and grinned smugly.

"I want to be sure I get my life price," Scarpa said with another eye squint.

Part of me wanted Pizza Bob to just let the thing in. I was now obsessed with having another taste of goblin, but I was also desperately afraid of my craving. What was happening to me?

"You'll have your price, I said. Now piss off." Pizza Bob revved the engine and pulled away from the growing goblin mob, and also ran over Scarpa's foot in the process.

I watched her reflection in the side mirror, hopping up and down, her foot a bloody mess. *Blood!* I flared my nostrils, and could smell it, taunting me, calling me back as we sped down the street. I moaned, but Pizza Bob was too amped up to notice.

"I don't think they are on to me. I pulled it off, dude!" Pizza Bob honked the horn as we rounded a corner.

I felt strange, still all tingly and jittery as I sat up in the seat, and put a shaking hand to my mouth. My hand was almost a normal color underneath the crusted bloodstains from my own wound. I pulled down the visor and stared at myself in amazement in the tiny square of mirror. I looked normal, no more blue tint. I pulled up my shirt and inspected the wound site, but it was gone; all healed. Goblin blood was amazing. Was this why Marcella wanted to see the Goblin King? Did she know? Did Teas Maith know this would happen?

"I'm real again," I whispered.

"Good for you, Pinocchio," Pizza Bob said. "Glad to help."

I glanced at him and did a double take. He had a faint glow around him. Was this the otherness? Could I finally see it? Marcella would be pleased that I'd mastered the power. As we drove the streets I started sensing other creatures in the night; it was like I had magic sonar in my brain. I just couldn't tell what the creatures were yet. More trolls? Goblins? Vampires? Probably not vampires...I was alone in this city for some reason. But I shivered as I sensed the other beings out there; could they sense me? Boy, did I feel weird right now!

It had to be the goblin blood coursing through me. I hoped this is what Teas Maith wanted me to do, but who knew? She just said find the Goblin King. By my drinking blood from the source, again out of happenstance like Daniel's IV donation and not a direct bite of my own doing, had I turned the corner towards being evil? I didn't feel particularly evil. My craving frightened me, but when I thought about biting a human I still retched a bit.

That's a good sign. Right?

Goblins didn't set off my no-no button, but they were still living creatures, though. Maybe I could eat evil things and be okay. That seemed a little too Anne Rice for my comfort.

I flexed my fingers, and smiled at the normal tint. I wondered how long it would last?

Pizza Bob pulled into a fast food drive through. "You want anything?"

"Nope. I'm good." I thought wistfully of the bloody bandage hiding in the back of the car somewhere, blushed self-consciously, and sank down in my seat. Pizza Bob got a burger and a large basket of his precious curly fries.

"Do we have time for this?" I asked, aware that Vernonia needed rescuing somewhere.

"Dude, you will not deny me the joy of finally getting a last meal. I have been pining for fries since the night I died. Seriously." Pizza Bob pulled out onto the road, and started shoveling food into his large mouth, actually unhinging his jaw to cram food in as he drove. It was fascinating and revolting at the same time.

"You got to eat," he said. "So I get to eat. Vernonia was fine when I left her. She's being held by the Goblin Regent."

"At Barbaro's?" I asked.

Pizza Bob arched an eyebrow. "She was. How'd you know that?"

"I overheard Bonsel's phone call to him. Did you know there's a bounty on me?"

"To her. The Regent's a she. But, oh yeah. That ass hat demon worked a deal with the goblins to screw with you. He pointed them at Vernonia since he promised Abby to Daniel."

"But Abby's safe as long as I'm alive."

Pizza Bob said, "Exactly."

I watched the road and realized we weren't headed towards the club. "Where are we going?"

"According to my lovely host here," he tapped his temple, "the goblins are all meeting at a party at the reservoir. They are taking her there."

"What about Marcella?" I asked.

"Whole other bag of issues there, but the demon won't go near her or sic the goblins on her. She's in some trouble with her family; they are less than amused by all of this. I saw Marcella trying to get a hold of Chuck, but that was before Ass Hat really got involved. While Marcella was talking to the Regent, I overheard some of the goblins talking."

"Seems King Chuck has a coup going on and doesn't know it yet." Pizza Bob laughed. "Bonsel is involved. All her scheming is right in the front of her brain."

"You said Vernonia told you how to take over a body?"

"Yup. She's a clever old biddy. It was pretty easy after she walked me through it."

"I didn't think Vernonia had that kind of power." I knew she could see and hear ghosts, but boosting Pizza Bob's power for possession?

"No. It wasn't her. It's complicated. Just suddenly I was there with you, you were staked, and I was jumping into the goblin."

"That was convenient."

"I guess," he said, being a bit evasive. "Maybe it was Vernonia. Who knows?"

"Hmmm, well, glad you're back." I decided to let it go for now. I was alive. "How long do you have?"

"Me, too. And I don't know."

"I mean you aren't going to lose control and crash the car and stick me with that creepy little goblin again? Because that would suck on so many levels."

"It's fine. When I was with Vernonia," Pizza Bob said, shifting the conversation away from him. "I tried to warn her that the goblins were coming for her, but she already knew. She said she'd be fine, that I had other things I needed to take care of. I figured you'd be getting into trouble soon, probably doing something stupid like looking for goblins."

I smiled and thought of Marcella's warning not to do anything stupid. Ha! She was going to be less than happy with me when I saw her later. "Yup, you know me well, Pizza Bob. Stupid is as stupid does."

"You're the king of stupid, Melvin. But I mean that in the nicest way possible. It's a kind of stupid that people find endearing. Especially Vernonia."

I missed Vernonia. "So...how's her nose? Is she mad?"

"Naw, she knows it wasn't you. She's a tough old bird."

We pulled up in front of a big house in the hills of Northwest Portland and stopped the car. Pizza Bob pushed a button on the visor, and a big bay door rolled open at the front of a spacious garage. He pulled in and parked the Hummer.

"Bonsel's digs?" I asked in awe.

"Oh yeah. She lives well."

"I guess so, but shouldn't we be going to get Vernonia now?"

"Dude, you need to clean up, change your clothes, and we need to form a plan."

"Your goblin suit is like three feet tall. Change my clothes? Into what?"

"She's living with a biker. There's stuff that will fit you." Pizza Bob snorted. "This is gonna be good."

"Is he home?"

"Nope. The housemate is out."

"You're being cagey. I don't like it when you get this way."

"This is gonna be so good," Pizza Bob said with a laugh.

I had a very bad feeling about this.

⚤

I felt great after the shower. I admit it was a good idea; I was a stinky, gooey, bloody mess, and now reveled in the feeling of my clean, mostly unblue skin. But I was less than happy when I saw what my outfit choices were.

Bonsel's biker roomie was a cyclist. Not a biker. A female cyclist. Ha-ha, Pizza Bob. Good one. I had my choice of spandex pants galore. Out of all of the garish, bright colors available, I finally chose a pair of black leggings with some team logo scrawled across the ass, a black tee shirt that was long enough to hang down over my manly bits scrunched up and wedged into the material, and I stood in front of the mirror in misery. These pants were the least offensive of the pile, but still an ego killer. They definitely made me look fat. Hell, I was fat. But now the whole world could see every bulge and ripple.

But at least my skin wasn't blue anymore. I inspected the state of my destroyed silk suit, the last vestiges of my pretend life with Abby, and finally just crumpled it up and tossed it in a garbage bag. My shoes were destroyed as well from all of the running I'd been doing, so with a disgusted sigh, I tossed those in, too. If everything worked out I'd be able to reclaim my fancy wardrobe when I was home with Abby again.

The housemate had black running shoes in my size and, as I laced them up tightly, I thought she must be an amazon. The shoes completed my man-in-black costume.

Whatever. I sighed wistfully, and steeled myself for the journey ahead. I had hope. That might be dangerous.

I found Pizza Bob in the kitchen, raiding the refrigerator with glee. If the goblin body was in transition to become undead, the ghost didn't have much

254

time left, but so far there were no symptoms beyond the sting and itch in the knife cut on the creature's wrist and the ravenous hunger. Maybe goblins really were immune to vampire blood? Who knew? Maybe they were always hungry, too.

Pizza Bob kicked the refrigerator door closed with his foot, his arms piled high with packages of lunch meat and cheese, and smiled at me through a mouth full of something gloppy.

"You hungry?" He slurred.

"No. I'm good for now." I pulled out a chair and sat down at the large breakfast island set low for a goblin's small stature. This house had everything; Bonsel definitely lived in style. The cycling pants pinched me uncomfortably in my nether region, so I sat in a sprawl on the tiny chair, glaring at Pizza Bob as he made a sandwich.

He produced a plate from a cabinet and set the sandwich down with a flourish. He turned and grinned at me, taking in my spandex pants with an amused eyebrow wiggle.

"Oh, this one's priceless," he said with a snort. "Just like old times, huh?"

I refused to rise to the bait. "These clothes are too big for a goblin. Bonsel has a human roommate?"

"Yup. She's just full of surprises."

"Does the human know what Bonsel is?"

"Oh, yeah. I told you the goblin was into some kinky stuff. Bonsel is sucking the life force out of the human, kind of like a vampire I guess. But in return the woman gets power boosts. She's some sort of competitive athlete, and goblin mojo doesn't show up on drug screens." He laughed.

"On second thought, if it doesn't involve my problems, I don't care. Tell me what's going on with my world."

"You've gotten so serious," he said as he sat down beside me. "It's the same old, same old. Bad guys, monsters, mayhem."

"Any pitchforks yet?"

"Naw, but plenty of folks that want to kill you."

"It's getting old." I crossed my legs, got pinched in the crotch, and uncrossed them again with a scowl.

"I like your ninja costume," Pizza Bob said with a snicker.

That did it. I stood up and grabbed him. "I'm feeling very weird right now! I'm stressed, I'm in drag in women's pants, and I've had a crappy past few days!" I gave him a little shake and he just hung there, smirking at me. "I've missed you, but I'm also remembering how you made my life hell!" I shouted.

Wow. I even shocked myself. My gums started tingling and I knew that my overbite was just itching to extend.

"It's the goblin blood, dude," Pizza Bob said as he pried my hands loose from his collar. "Got you all amped up. We can use that." He sat down and took another bite of his sandwich like nothing had happened.

"I'm sorry," I mumbled, finally sitting down again with an embarrassed sigh.

"No worries." He kept eating. "I'm doing good, not that you've asked at all."

Ouch. "I'm sorry. Again. Was it bad where you were?"

Pizza Bob shrugged. "Not really. It wasn't really anywhere and that was the scary part. After I blasted Mr. Happy, which only worked a little by the way --"

"I figured that when Daniel showed up," I said. "But I am thankful. I felt bad that you got nuked."

"Yeah, well, it was freaky. It was like I was drugged or something, and not in the good way. Everything was fuzzy and shadowy, I couldn't think straight. But I could see you, just couldn't talk to you."

"So," I wrinkled up my forehead, "what all do you know about what's happened? I know what Marcella said you said, and I think I felt you a couple of times."

"I saw the whole deal with Daniel go down at the mansion, and yes, it was a Hallmark moment at Powell's." He fluttered his eyelashes. "I just seemed to float between lots of places. I'd start thinking I heard my name being called and then I'd be with Marcella or Abby or Vernonia or back with you. But no one was even thinking about me, except you. Thanks for that; I think it's what kept me here."

"So when I was drugged you really came to see me." I nodded.

"Yup, your barriers were down and I could get to you, just like Marcella said. I had to check in, make sure you were okay after the frying you got. You should have just killed both of them yourself."

"I couldn't kill Giles, and I wouldn't kill Daniel. You know I can't kill people. I just can't."

"You are gonna have to start living sometime, Melvin. It's what you're supposed to do." Pizza Bob winked at me. "Abby and I can only do so much."

"I don't want to talk about it." I tapped my fingers on the counter top. *Start living? I am mostly dead; it's what I do now.*

"Go on with your story."

"Melvin, you're going have to face this soon. I'm just sayin'--"

I cut him off. "How did Marcella hear you?"

"Okay, message received." Pizza Bob sighed in annoyance. "It was weird, dude. I was just floating there all freaked out and fading away when I thought I heard a woman say 'go to Marcella', and I felt this weird zappy, itchy feeling all over my body and my head cleared. It was warm. And kind of freaky. Did I mention how freaky it was?"

"A woman? Did you see the woman who helped me?" I asked, certain that it was Teas Maith that had helped Pizza Bob. Was she the one who gave him enough power to possess Bonsel, too? That didn't seem her style because of the whole non-interference thing she had going.

Pizza Bob shook his head. "No. I lost you at Powell's for a bit, everything got dizzy for me, and then the same thing happened when you were running from that vampire club, which was Hi-frickin-Larious, dude!" He elbowed me.

"A room full of me!" I had to laugh. "But tell me about Marcella."

"I showed up, and just like that she could hear me. She tried to ignore me, but I wore her down. Once I got Marcella set to help you, I got yanked to Vernonia."

"Have you seen Mr. Happy again?"

"Nope. But I can feel him sometimes."

I shuddered. "Have you had any run-ins with Daniel?"

"No. I'm below his radar for some reason. But he's getting very powerful; I think Mr. Happy is doing another experiment."

"Yeah, that's what Teas Maith told me."

"Just me? You talking to yourself a lot these days?"

"No, and yes sometimes, but no! That's her name."

"Is that the girl you mentioned?" Pizza Bob stretched and then belched loudly as he patted his stomach.

"She's an Emissary of the Universe, whatever that means. She told me things are out of balance and that's why she helped me with Daniel and sent him away so I could catch a break. I don't know how long that will last, though."

"Well, he's not here now so let's get a plan together."

"I have questions first." I wanted to know how he had gotten so powerful.

"Dude. I've told you everything I know." Pizza Bob shrugged, but I sensed that evasiveness again.

"You'd tell me if it was Mr. Happy helping you. Wouldn't you?"

"Trust me, dude. That demon scares the crap out of me."

I squinted my eyes and stared at him. Another evasive answer. I wanted to trust Pizza Bob, I really did especially after he had saved me yet again, but I had a feeling things weren't quite what they seemed.

"How's your hold on Bonsel?" I asked.

"So far so good. She's inside screaming her head off, but I can ignore that."

"I'm supposed to meet Marcella tomorrow night...oops I mean tonight," I said, realizing it was three in the morning, "at the Flamingo Hotel."

"That dump? Why?"

"I don't know. She probably wanted someplace neutral to regroup so Daniel wouldn't freak out her Mambo."

"Whatever. That's a no-tell-motel so she got that one right. Getting to her shouldn't be an issue. We'll be done rescuing Vernonia quickly, if all goes well, so we can meet up with Marcella and start with the demon smiting."

Pizza Bob seemed to be in denial about his problem. He was stuck in limbo, except for when he was in the goblin's body, and didn't realize the whole point of going to see the voodoo family was for him. There wasn't much of a plan for Mr. Happy yet, not yet, but I'm sure that Marcella would come up with something.

I said, "Hopefully she'll have her family on board by then and we can do the ritual to get you back, get rid of Mr. Happy for good, and be all happy again."

"I'm actually okay with the goblin body for now," Pizza Bob said with a smirk. "If I go back to being just a ghost I'll miss the whole touchy, feely, eatie thing I've got going."

I frowned at him. "Hey, um I realize I was going to get killed by her, that's she's a goblin and all, but she's a living thing. You can't keep that body forever."

"Says who?" he said with a gross pout of that goblin mouth.

"Seriously? It's just not okay. Besides the whole possession thing--"

"Possession is nine tenths of the law," he replied smartly.

"Whatever, smart ass, think about it. You're in a goblin body; a funky little disgusting goblin body that is uglier than should be possible. Is that how you want to live?"

"At least it's living. I feel fine," he said with a little grimace. He looked down at his body, poked at one of his lopsided breasts, and then shrugged. "But I see your point."

"Good." Staring at Bonsel's face was starting to make me queasy. If Pizza Bob stuck around inside her for the next fifty years I'd probably go insane.

"Maybe I can take over somebody else when this is over," he said hopefully.

Uh-oh.

"That's kind of a bad thing to do, buddy. You don't want to go down that path. Right now we are on the good side."

"For now," he added.

I winced, but he was right. I was supposed to go all evil soon according to the vampire handbook, which I didn't even own! But why burst his bubble for now? Pizza Bob was happy. Let him have it for a bit even if it was stuffed into a three-foot tall, smelly goblin.

"We'll see," I said indulgently.

"Righteous, dude."

We were wasting time. I could feel the Universe rolling into position for another grand Melvin screw, regardless of Teas Maith's intervention.

I sighed and asked, "Why do the goblins have Vernonia?"

"Bait." Pizza Bob stood up and pulled the Hummer keys out of his pocket.

"Good plan. They knew I'd come." I stood up, suddenly ready for action; a little mayhem, a little blood letting. This new me was kind of scary.

Pizza Bob looked at a clock on the wall over the stove and shrugged. "The party should be totally rolling by now. Four in the morning is their favorite time; something about circadian rhythms of the night, whatever that means. I say we just show up and wing it." He grinned at me. "I can bluff my way in with Bonsel's body here, and when the time's right you just go all bad ass!"

"Sounds good to me." It did. It really, really did.

Silly me. When would I learn?

CHAPTER 17

I Love It When A Plan Comes Together

We climbed into the Hummer feeling braver than we should have. Pizza Bob was ensconced in a feisty little goblin body, and I was suped up and delusional on goblin blood. Sure we could take on an army of goblins all by ourselves, rescue Vernonia, battle Daniel, and smite Mr. Happy. All in a night's work, right? Right.

"This truck--"

"Hummer," Pizza Bob corrected.

"Hummer...makes me feel all commando, kinda like the A-Team."

"I call Hannibal!"

"Hey!" I pouted. "I get to be Hannibal."

"Nope." Pizza Bob had a big grin on his face, but it looked more like a weird grimace on Bonsel's features.

"Well then I'm Mr. T." I smiled to myself. The way I was feeling right now I did indeed pity the fool who messed with me!

I felt powerful. Giddy. I was happy. It was easy to slip back into the familiar rhythm of banter with Pizza Bob, the inanity of our collective pop culture repertoire, even as we headed towards a possibly gruesome and painful death at the hands of an angry mob of goblins waiting to get paid a bounty placed by a psychotic demon. Wow.

Pizza Bob glanced at me and started laughing. "Nope. You're more like Murdoch. A big old bag of crazy, blue-tinted Murdoch!"

"That's not nice. I'm not that blue anymore, so there. And I think you're more like Murdoch." I crossed my arms and leaned back in the seat. Even I knew I couldn't pull off Face, but Murdoch? Well, everyone always forgot about Face. "Whatever," I pouted again.

"Whatever, princess. Reality check. No one ever dies in the A-Team."

"Classic A-Team no, but new Neeson A-Team yes."

"Yeah, whatever, Melvin. Tonight we're ganking some goblins for sure. This is real life, not some TV show."

I burst out laughing, then sobered quickly. Real life. My life was anything but real; more of a reality show parody for losers. Suddenly I felt childish for everything that had happened to me before. Every little foible or cluster of hurt feelings, every struggle to just live day-to-day and pay my bills, eat, survive, not get evicted from my desperate squalor in Loserville, was a grease spot on my current resume. I had changed. I had evolved. I had become. What? I didn't know, I was a work in progress. Yes, people were going to die tonight. Hopefully not me, or Pizza Bob, or Vernonia, but anything could happen. I'd learned that the hard way over the last six months.

"What, no come back?" Pizza Bob asked, breaking the silence.

"Nope. It just hit me what we're doing." I flared my nostrils and the scent of that soiled bandage tickled my nose. Yup, I still wanted it. I shifted uncomfortably in my seat and the spandex bunched at my crotch painfully, wedging in deep in my butt crack.

"Be the bad ass."

"We both know how that usually pans out," I said as I worked the spandex free and sat sideways in my seat. Pizza Bob snorted and then went quiet, focused on the road ahead.

My brain was on overload because of the torrent of info rushing at me from the darkness. The night was teeming with supernaturals and, as we wound our way up the darkened road towards Washington Park and the city's two open-water reservoirs, my nerves hummed with anticipation. And fear. I had no idea what was about to happen tonight or how far my newfound blood lust would take me.

"Why are they partying at the water tanks?" I asked.

"The goblins run a betting pool. They do bad things up here to the water supply, then take bets on how long it will be before Portlanders get sick from it."

"No way." I shook my head. "What kinds of bad things?"

Pizza Bob said, "Well, you know the water boil alerts that go out sometimes for Ecoli and stuff?"

"Yeah...."

"The goblins take turns peeing, pooping, and throwing dead things into the reservoir. They swim in it, they come up with some crazy stuff to do, and then sit back and watch."

"That's disgusting." I had a wave of nausea roll over me in sympathy for all the Portlanders who drank the city water. Our water is famous for quality, the Bull Run Watershed is supposed to be pristine, but the reservoirs are outdated with large open-air containment systems built in the 1890's. There was a push after 9/11 to make them more secure because of terrorist threats, but of course there was no money in the budget, and the laid back Northwest attitude kept things status quo. And who would guess all the recent problems were indeed domestic terror? Goblin Al Qaeda.

"I know. Major gack factor," Pizza Bob said with a foul smelling belch. "And the sewer spillage into the river issues after rain? It's actually the goblins who control the dump system. After being inside Bonsel's head I know too much to ever trust our city government again. The goblins have the city council in their pockets, dude. Crazy."

Ah, the dark underbelly of Portland. If only people here really knew what went bump in the night. I had to laugh. Keep Portland Weird.

Pizza Bob looked over at me. "My Viking funeral...well, let's just say you indeed sent me up shit creek."

I started laughing harder. "But it was epic."

"Totally worth it, dude."

We pulled up into a dimly lit parking lot at the base of a trail up to the reservoirs, and, with a wistful sigh, Pizza Bob shut off the engine. "Whatever happens now, I'm good with it. It's been fun, Melvin."

"Don't talk like that. We're going to go in, get Vernonia, get out." I tried to sound brave, but I was just as freaked out as my friend.

So much for the new me. My palms were sweaty as I opened the door and hopped out onto the pavement. The pulse of the goblins' power was coming at me in waves from the park ahead, and I wiped my hands on the nonabsorbent spandex over and over again. Pizza Bob came up next to me with the ash walking stick in his hand. I didn't see him pick it up before at the club, and winced nervously.

"Be careful with that thing," I whined, instantly embarrassed that I was in Cowardly Lion mode again. Pizza Bob grinned at me.

"I just need it for show, dude. Man up. I'm not gonna whack you with it." He tapped it on the ground and it started glowing. I was both scared and impressed that Pizza Bob had so much control over Bonsel's goblin magic.

"I can feel its power," I said quietly.

But here's the wild thing: it had no negative effect on me now. It must be the goblin blood, I thought smugly. "I'm not getting all woozy...."

"That's good. Okay, walk in front of me...shuffle a bit like you are in a trance."

We practiced walking in circles until I had the zombie shuffle down pat. "This is going to work. I know it," I said just as a group of goblins pulled up in a mini van and parked next to the Hummer.

"Yo, Bonsel," one of them said as it got out of the car. "Heard about Gurbin and Wiggin. Is this the leech that killed them?"

Pizza Bob stepped in front of me. "Yes it is. I'm taking him to the Regent."

"Is that wise? The King is in attendance tonight." The goblin walked up and stared at me. I did my best to keep my face slack; I even let a little drool run down my chin. "I heard this was an outsource, not regal business, and our King might not like it."

Pizza Bob growled, a nasty guttural sound that made the hairs on my neck stand up. He pushed the goblin back from me.

"Are you in or out, Hildegarde? Tonight's the night things change." Pizza Bob sounded very scary, and I flinched. He seemed a little too into this coup.

Uh-oh. I hoped Bonsel wasn't regaining control over her body; that would be bad. We had other priorities, and I wanted no part of goblin politics. Actually, all I wanted some more of their blood. Just thinking about it my overbite started extending. Awkward. I wanted to save Vernonia too, of course, but a little snack on the side sounded too tempting.

"Now just one minute--" Hildegarde started to yell back at Bonsel/Pizza Bob when she noticed my overbite and took a step back. "Um, is this thing going to wake up?"

Pizza Bob jabbed me with the walking stick, and I went rigid and let out a little moan; it was all for show, though. The ash had no effect on me anymore, but did Pizza Bob really know that? The other goblins scuttled back and let out little oohs and ahs of glee at my supposed torture.

"I've got him tamed," Pizza Bob said with a snarl. "You get up to the crowd and wait for my signal," he said to the group. They bowed and then scuttled off up the trail. When they were gone I spun around and glared down at Bonsel's face.

"Really?" I asked. "Did you really just poke me with that thing?" I was ready to pounce on the goblin if Pizza Bob was no longer in control.

"Dude, I knew it wouldn't hurt you. Stop being such a pussy." Pizza Bob winked at me and started walking towards the trail. "I had to make it look good. We can use all the in fighting to make this work. You'll see."

I just stood there with a shocked look on my face. "Buddy, you're freaking me out a bit. Are you sure you're still in control? And how were you so sure that stick wouldn't put me down for the count?"

"Because you've ingested goblin blood. It's like an antidote, dude. Besides, I knew it wouldn't be that bad even if you did get a jolt. Suck it up, princess." He motioned for me to follow and then pushed me ahead of him on the trail.

"So you gambled. I'm not happy right now."

"It worked. Stop talking and start shuffling."

I glared at him and then started my zombie walk up the trail in silence, but I was fuming inside.

"Go ahead and stay mad. It will keep you all amped up for the fight. You embrace that blood lust, Melvin. Think about all that yummy goblin blood just waiting," he whispered.

"Your pep talks are getting creepier and creepier," I hissed back as we rounded a corner and came into a clearing filled with hundreds of goblins. They were gathered around a large concrete and stone water reservoir illuminated by floodlights. The whole thing had a crazed, manic feel like a rave.

"Show time," Pizza Bob said as he nudged me forward with the stick.

I kept my face slack as I shuffled forward, but I took in everything, plotting my escape route if necessary. I spotted Vernonia seated next to a particularly ugly little goblin wearing a gaudy crown covered in red velvet, gold, and sparkling jewels that looked fake, but were possibly real.

King Chuck. Oh boy. The Goblin King was lounging in a heavy canvas camp chair and, sitting down, he was two feet tall but weighed over two hundred pounds. He had a long, brightly dyed orange beard, and a bald head that looked lumpy and warty underneath that ridiculous crown. Chuck wore leather pants, a silk shirt open to the belly button with tufts of gray-green hair poking out, and a faded members only jacket with a fur ruff sewn on to the collar. He looked ridiculous; not regal at all, but maybe he was sporting goblin chic for all I knew.

Vernonia didn't look scared, nor was she tied up or restrained in any way that I could see. Curious. She was just chatting away with the King like they were old friends. I did see that she had a weird pouch dangling from a black chord around her neck. That had to be Marcella's gris-gris bag. That made me feel better.

There was a larger goblin wearing a maroon velour tracksuit, hovering near Vernonia. That might be the Regent because of the officious way it kept ordering other goblins around. It looked up, saw Bonsel's face, and paled a bit. The goblin quickly started coming towards us.

"It looks pissed," I whispered so only Pizza Bob could hear.

"That's Melinda, the Regent, and I was counting on it!" he whispered back.

"I told you to take him to Barbaro's!" The Regent said when she got in front of us. She looked over her shoulder at the King, who was still chatting amiably with Vernonia. Off to the side I heard a splash, and then a cheer. Ugh. The goblins had thrown something into the water supply. They were all shouting dates and amounts of money for their bets. Gross.

"Good tidings, Regent Melinda," Pizza Bob purred, ignoring the chaos around him. "Change of plans."

"Our deal cannot involve his majesty! You know that!"

"Then why did you bring the woman?" Pizza Bob asked with a smirk.

"She can be useful in other ways. I made the decision. Take this leech back to Barbaro's. Now." Melinda poked Pizza Bob in the chest. He just smiled. Uh-oh.

"Regent!" a deep voice bellowed. "Come forward!"

Melinda flinched and then bowed her head. "You've don   fight

tered to Pizza Bob as she turned and headed back towards   form

shoulders hunched.

"Okay," Pizza Bob said to me quietly. "We won't have r   wher

up the act until we get in front of Vernonia, then pounce on   scen

him out quickly. He's got a lot of mojo, and I'll take out the   and

time."   be. P

"What? Oh, that's not a good plan," I said a little too lou   ento

gone silent and they were all staring at us now.

"It's a great plan! Get moving!" He prodded me with th   Rege

I stumbled forward to within ten feet of the King and his   the g

was going to end badly.   cloth

There was a commotion off to the side and I saw a group

a hog-tied body over their heads, cutting their way through   ward

the King as well. I was trying to stay in zombie character, but

double take when I saw whom they had.   said,

It was me.

Actually it was that creep from Club Sang, Roger, wh

me for the contest. He was unconscious and gagged, but   favor

Ironic.   I

"Oh crap," I said with a snort as they stopped next to u   I was

goblin Scarpa from the club parking lot, and from her lim

had crunched her foot with the Hummer. She squinted her   snee

grinned wickedly at Pizza Bob.

"I claim the bounty," she shrieked.

Pizza Bob smacked her in the head with his walking   migh

down instantly; deader than a doornail.   I

What the hell? I was stunned that he did that, but that's

to do; gank some goblins. I just didn't expect it so quickly.

struggled to keep Roger aloft, and then fell down with him

tangled heap of arms and legs.

Pizza Bob shouted, "Plan B!", and dove for Vernonia. The   is un

in the park went insane at Bonsel's supposed signal for the

ng with each other, some trying to grab me or grab Bonsel's body, some
d a protective ring around the King. It was loud, and crazy, and violent!
ernonia hit Bonsel in the face with a cup and then quickly hugged her
Pizza Bob let her know what was going on. I just stood there, frozen. The
of goblin blood in the air was making me dizzy, making my overbite throb
xtend, but I couldn't move. How humiliating! Some hero I'd turned out to
an B? What was I supposed to do? I took a tentative step towards the royal
cage. Eat the King? Sounded good.

ing Chuck got out of his chair, pointed a jewel encrusted staff at the
t, who was coming up next to me with a nasty looking sword, and blasted
blin into a foul smelling puddle of green slime that splashed my face and
s when she exploded.

Gross!" I shouted, wiping Regent goo from my lips. The King turned to-
me, and I froze.

Silence!" he roared, and the melee in the park stopped instantly. "You," he
ointing the staff at me. "Come forward and explain this insult."

He's just along for the ride," Pizza Bob said as he stepped in front of me.

Bonsel," the King said with a note of affection in his voice, "What has my
e daughter done now?"

ooked over at Pizza Bob in shock. He was in the King's daughter? The one
supposed to fight and then woo and then whatever? I burst out laughing.

Immmm, Bonsel's not in right now," Pizza Bob said with a nasty looking
"But I can take a message if you like."

Who are you?"

'm his guide," Pizza Bob said pointing to me. "But I like this body and
just keep it."

groaned. "I knew it. You're freaking out."

shut up, Melvin." Pizza Bob crossed his arms defiantly.

s my daughter still alive?" Chuck demanded.

Yes. She's still in here, for now, despite the fact she tried to kill my charge."

he King leaned in and sniffed me. "The leech has fed on my daughter. That
cceptable. Are you two bonded?"

Eeew," I shouted. "No!"

"It was a little gay," Pizza Bob said with a smirk as he toyed with the bandage on his wrist.

"Don't start that again." I shifted from one foot to the other. "You've just got issues."

"You liked it," Pizza Bob said with a snort.

"Enough," The King commanded. "This is highly unacceptable indeed."

The King scratched his nose, then beckoned for Vernonia to come forward. As she passed me she patted my arm and said, "Hello, dear boy."

"Hi," I squeaked back as she approached the King. Wait! If she went back to the King we'd have to start all of the fighting again. I jumped forward and took her hand, but she shrugged me off with a smile.

"It's fine, Melvin. None of this is what you think."

What did I think?

She stood next to Chuck, bent down and began whispering in his ear. Whoa. I looked at Pizza Bob and he shrugged.

"Buddy, you've got some explaining to do," I whispered to him. "Why didn't you say you were the King's daughter?"

He shrugged. "Didn't seem important. Besides, how cool would it be if I were King?"

Oh crap. Pizza Bob was definitely losing it.

"You don't have as much control as you said you do." I shook my head. Either that or he was melding with Bonsel's personality.

"I'm fine," he barked. "Things are going to work out. I think."

"You're delusional, man. You can't be the Goblin King."

"I'd run a peeler bar empire. It would be sweet." Pizza Bob gave me one of his trademark thumbs-up.

I snorted and looked down at the other Melvin, hog tied and trussed up like a roast. "Serves you right, poser," I said with another snort.

The King and Vernonia ended their whispering and he eyed me greedily as he walked forward. "Are you aiding and abetting this coup?"

I swallowed nervously. "I don't care about goblin politics. I was originally going to come to you and ask for help. But then your daughter," I rolled my eyes, "attacked me. There's a bounty on my head now. That's not cool."

"I knew nothing of the bounty," he said. "My Regent was power hungry, but she could not be King." He spit on the puddle of Regent goo and smiled. "Wrong equipment, Tootsie Pop."

"Right. Well, um, so this is all a big misunderstanding then. I don't think I need your help now, so, if you don't mind we'll be on our merry way," I said, holding out my hand to Vernonia.

"No. I now know about the bounty, so you are staying here." He pointed his staff at me, and again I froze.

"Chuck," Vernonia said sweetly as she put a hand on the staff and pushed it down. "Now that would be unfortunate if you went and did something like that. Melvin is a friend of mine."

He scowled at her. "Vernonia, I told you to call me your highness in public."

What the hell? My mouth was hanging open in shock.

"Oh, whatever. Your Highness, just let Melvin go." She rolled her eyes. "Melvin, close your mouth, dear. You'll draw flies," said Vernonia, the ghost talking, goblin whisperer.

"Do I want to know how close you two are?" I asked, not really wanting an answer.

"We're old friends. I do makeup for some of his girls at the clubs. He's quite charming in his own way."

"Of course." I looked down at Pizza Bob, who standing there like a kid caught with his hand in a cookie jar. "Can this night get any weirder?"

This rescue was turning out to be rather tame, but I was relieved. I talked a good game, the goblin blood made me feel invincible, but I just wasn't a monster at heart. The weird stuff I could handle; it's what always happened with me. The weirder, the more Melvin.

"Most likely," Vernonia said with a melancholy smile. "Okay, Chuck, you are going to let Melvin go. Pizza Bob will stay in Bonsel's body until he's done doing what he needs to do, you will ignore the shadow demon, and all will be well."

"I can't do that, Vernonia. That leech killed two goblins tonight. And Bonsel was behind the coup. She has blood on her hands." King chuck glared at me. "I have to stand firm before my subjects or I lose my street cred."

Pizza Bob looked down at Roger, then at me, and grinned evilly. "Here's an idea. Give the crowd that guy."

"He's not a vampire," I said.

"Well, neither are you, really," the King retorted.

"Hey, that's not nice." I crossed my arms and pouted.

Vernonia tapped me on the shoulder then pointed at three shimmering figures hovering near the edge of the crowd. I focused in and saw they were ghosts; beheaded ghosts that looked like me.

"What the hell?" I said again.

"Your Melvin clone killed those three."

"Oh, wow, it's the guys from Forest Park. Bummer." I waved, but they didn't wave back. Okay, so they weren't friendly ghosts.

Vernonia looked down at Roger with pity and a little anger for good measure. "That man is unstable and wants to be you. Why not give him his wish?" she said. She looked at Chuck and winked. "It could work. Let the crowd have him, but keep the shadow demon out of the mix. He'd know right off that wasn't really Melvin."

"Um, I'm not comfortable with letting the goblins kill that guy." I looked down at Roger, who was regaining consciousness. His eyes were wide and glassy, and I smelled the fear radiating off of him in waves.

"He's a serial killer, Melvin. Not a nice man at all," Vernonia said. "It's a fair trade. Those three he killed," she pointed at the ghosts hovering over the reservoir, "said he made them suffer. They said he was tracking you after you left the club. He planned on killing you in a terrible way."

I shuddered. What a nut job! But if he was killing Melvins then that meant the commandos might not be on to me; Abby would be safe. I just had to deal with Daniel, and of course Mr. Happy now. Once I thought it through, the decision was an easy one.

Maybe a little too easy.

"Sucks to be you," I said to Roger.

Absurdly I wondered if the girl from Club Sang, Demoana, would mourn him with ghoulish delight on Twitter. Roger started squirming in his bindings, but he wasn't going anywhere. I had a moment of pity and almost changed my mind, but he started saying something through his gag. I crouched down and pulled off the duct tape sealing his mouth closed.

"You freak!" he snarled. "I'm Melvin! Me! Me! Let me go and I'll give you the dark gift; you can be my apprentice." He looked around at the goblins and yelled, "Fear me! I am Melvin!"

Some of the crowd started chanting, "Life price, life price, death to the leech!" and I shuddered. Roger was toast. Delusional toast.

I leaned in and whispered for only him to hear, "I hate to break it to you, but this is for real. I'm Melvin, not you. You slaughtered three human beings for your fantasy, and now you're going to pay the price. I'm sure it's going to be painful and scary, too. You should have stuck with your own life."

He screamed and I stuck the duct tape over his mouth again. I didn't want to see what the goblins had in store for him; it was going to be gross. Maybe he'd end up in the reservoir. Was this a bad thing I was doing? Well, only time would tell. I was definitely starting my slide over to the dark side.

"He is so going to regret that costume," Pizza Bob said. "But at least you're still safe." He playfully punched me in the arm.

"For now," I said miserably. I was starting to feel guilty about Roger again, and terrified that Daniel was going to show up any minute. And Mr. Happy was still gunning for me. I wondered who would go for the bounty now?

"Stupid bounty," I muttered.

The King stroked his beard, and then squinted at his possessed daughter. "What was the bounty?"

Pizza Bob shrugged. "Mr. Happy was going to help us take you out then install the Regent as King, and me, I mean Bonsel, as the Regent, and pay out $10,000 in pocket money."

I frowned. Where would a demon get $10,000? And why was it so cheap a bounty? Only ten K for me? As a vampire I should have fetched at least a cool million.

Yeah, right.

You're whining because your death price was cheap? It was a bounty, dumb ass. Who cares how much it was. And you're no prize to begin with!

I was making faces as I argued with myself, and didn't realize everyone was staring at me. Of course they were. King Chuck coughed into his hand and I looked up.

"Hi," I said, falling back on my usual autopilot shtick.

The King just stared at me curiously for a second, then said to Pizza Bob, "Bonsel, I'm both proud and disturbed at your larceny. Daddy still loves you."

Pizza Bob smirked. "She knows. I would have made a kick ass King, though."

"Wrong equipment, Tootsie Pop." the King adjusted his crown. "The demon wants the leech for what reason?"

"Leech?" I shouted. I blushed when I noticed the group staring at me. "Why does everyone keep calling me a leech? That sucks!"

"Yes, they do. Get it? Ha-ha. Goblins don't like vampires very much," Pizza Bob said.

"Whatever." I crossed my arms. "King Chuck, the demon is named Mr. Happy, at least that's what he calls himself. I'm surprised you don't know him. Everyone seems to know him."

"Does he have an annoying English accent?" Chuck asked.

"That's the one."

"We've met," he said but didn't elaborate.

"Yeah, whatever," I said sarcastically. "I pissed him off, made him cross, at the beginning when I first turned into a vampire, and he's been after me since then."

"Why?" He arched a fuzzy eyebrow. "You're not much of a vampire."

"I'm working on it," I mumbled.

"By feeding on my daughter. Highly unacceptable." The King took a step back, and put his chin in the palm of his hand. "Ten thousand dollars is a nice little token for that transgression."

"Don't be greedy, dear," Vernonia said. "That's chump change and hardly worth your notice."

I blushed. I was right! It was a cheap out. *Damn you, Mr. Happy.*

"You're right, Vee." Chuck smiled at me.

Vee? Oh, Vernonia...please don't have gone there!

Chuck waved his hand in front of his nose like he smelled something horrid. "Hardly a decent bounty. Besides, I can't stand shadow demons. They are vile little things."

I had to hold back a laugh when he said that. Hello pot, meet kettle, I thought to myself.

Pizza Bob clasped his hands together. "So it's settled then. We give the masses a nice scapegoat for Gurbin and Wiggin, Melvin walks, on to the next adventure."

"Not quite," the King said. "I want my daughter back, possession free, I want $10,000 for the blood transgression," he stared at me, "and I want a promise that you won't hunt goblins in the future. Our blood is unique and important; much too valuable to be wasted on a leech. Besides it's poison to you. Drink too much and you'll explode like a cherry bomb."

I took a deep breath and was ready to shout, but Vernonia shook her head at me, and Pizza Bob grabbed my arm.

"Don't call me a leech," I muttered as Pizza Bob shushed me.

"Melvin, Abby has the Ten K." Pizza Bob turned to Chuck. He said, "I need this body for a bit longer, and that's the way it is. You can't force me out, but Bonsel is in here and miserable. Call it her punishment for the coup, and you get something out of all of this, too. Deal?"

"Would I really explode?" I asked, but Vernonia and Pizza Bob ignored me. All I wanted was one more sip, just one more little taste. Teas Maith had warned me the Goblin King would try and trick me.

The King smiled, not a nice smile either. "No, that is not all I want. I want the names of the traitors."

"Oh, no problemo." Pizza Bob started pointing out goblins in the crowd and naming names. They tried to run, but a group of goblin guards rounded them up and made them kneel in front of Chuck.

Hildegarde, the goblin from the parking lot, began sobbing and groveled at Pizza Bob's feet. "Bonsel, please tell him I wasn't one of them, that I tried to stop you."

"No dice, honey," Pizza Bob said with a shrug. "I told you that tonight things changed."

"Leech, what help were you going to ask me for?" the King demanded.

I fumed at the name calling, the bad grammar, and then thought about Marcella, about her quest, and shrugged.

"My name is Melvin, not Leech...okay? To be perfectly honest I didn't know what to ask for. My friend Marcella, well, this was her idea. She thought you might have something that would smite Mr. Happy."

"Hmmmm," Chuck said with a sinister grin. "Marcella the Vodouisant. My Regent informed me that I was going to meet with her later today."

"Well, now you don't have to," I said quickly. "I think we're good. We'll just be on our way now. Have fun with your water gross out thing, and, um, have a nice day."

"I can help you," the king said coyly.

Uh-oh. I didn't like the look in his eye. "No thanks. I'm good."

"Melvin, listen to his offer," Pizza Bob said.

"Um, no. I think we should go." I was getting a hinky feeling in the pit of my stomach; either Daniel or Mr. Happy was going to show up, or this was the thing that Teas Maith had warned me about.

The King pointed at me. "You've felt the power in our blood, no? Because of that you are marked. But one sip is not enough, Leech. Not for what's coming."

"You said I'd explode!" I gulped audibly.

"Perhaps you will, perhaps it's just a metaphor."

A metaphor? Great, mind games. Just what I need to add to my stress.

"Pizza Bob, let's go." I tried to turn and walk away, but Vernonia blocked my path.

"He's right, Melvin. Mr. Happy is more powerful than you realize. If you want things to get better you need to take the next step. Look at yourself. The goblin blood has helped. You know it."

"But," I squeaked. "You told me to stay a dear boy as long as I could."

"Power is dear, my boy. You need to make a choice." She patted my arm and stepped back. "You are a vampire after all."

I looked at Chuck, at Pizza Bob, at the crowd of goblins inching their way closer to me, and I moaned. The smell of blood was making me dizzy again. Of course I wanted it. But I'd never be the same if I took it. But if I didn't everyone I loved would be destroyed.

Teas Maith! Please come and save me!

I squeezed my eyes shut and hoped that she would come. I wasn't a monster. I didn't want to be a monster. The wind kicked up, carrying the scent of fear and blood and impending death, and I shuddered. I was on my own; no one was coming to save me. I opened my eyes, and my heart skipped for a beat.

Be the bad ass, Melvin. It's time.

"What do I have to do?" My voice was barely a whisper, and I had my hand up in front of my mouth to hide that stupid overbite.

King Chuck smiled. Another not-so-nice smile. "Kill them, remove my little patch of discord, take their blood as you will, and our transaction is completed."

He thumped his staff on the ground and it began glowing. "Blood is power, power is death, life from death! Gringorim andahl bibamus." The goblins on the ground began glowing, marked as my snack now and ready for slaughter.

"Oh, wait a minute...I can't...um...." I started backing up. My blood lust disappeared. Faced with the opportunity now, I couldn't take it. It wasn't supposed to be like this; we were just coming to rescue Vernonia. On the drive over, the impending violence had had a cartoon feel, not real, just bravado as we talked about killing goblins. I wasn't ready for this. No, not at all.

Pizza Bob gave me a push towards the goblin, and I ended up stumbling and falling down. I looked Hildegarde in the eye, and she blinked a few times, terrified of what was coming.

"I can't do this!" I tried to stand up, but my legs felt like rubber.

Pizza Bob nudged me with his foot. "Oh seriously, princess? Do I have to do everything for you?" He whipped out his switchblade. "Don't be such a wuss. Here!" He bent down and slashed open Hildegarde's throat in one quick, deliberate motion.

I looked at him in horror. I couldn't believe he'd done it as I grabbed at the wound, trying desperately to staunch the flow of blood.

"Go on," he said. "No one is stopping you. Be the bad ass."

I was numb. I was horrified. I was sad. The people around me were the monsters. I stared down at Hildegarde's face as she lay there dying in my arms, fountains of glorious blood pumping out into my hands...just inches away, so easy for me to take. The power from the king's staff made the blood glow a deep burgundy. It was hypnotic.

"I can't believe you just did that," I moaned, heartbroken that Pizza Bob had gone so utterly and completely bad. This was a nightmare. Things had spun out of control.

"We do what we have to," he said as he started killing the other goblins, one by one. He seemed like he was enjoying it, too. I looked up and saw Chuck staring at me coldly, a hint of malice in his sneer.

Nothing is ever free, you idiot. There will be a price for this! said a little voice inside of me. I blinked back tears.

Vernonia was just standing there and she had tears in her eyes, too. She held my gaze, mouthed 'Good bye, dear boy', and then looked away. Everything had changed now.

I'm still me, the good guy, Mostly Dead Melvin, the loser.

But the scent of the goblin blood was making me dizzy; I was starting to lose control.

I was also hungry.

"I'm so sorry," I whispered through my overbite, ignoring the little voice in my head. "Please forgive me."

CHAPTER 18

A Low Down Dirty Shame

I awoke in the hummer, strapped into the passenger seat with warm light on my face. The sun was low in the late afternoon cloudy sky; how long had I been unconscious? I had a coppery taste in my mouth and looked down at my clothes covered in dead Regent goo, and stiff with dried blood. Goblin blood. The horror of what I had done, what had happened, came crashing over me and I began to shake. Suddenly I was nauseous.

Pizza Bob was whistling as he drove, a happy sounding tune that turned my stomach even more, and I groaned.

"You're awake. That's good." Pizza Bob reached over and patted my shoulder. I shrugged off his hand and fumbled with the window control. I needed air. I smelled like blood and suffering.

I smelled like a monster.

I gulped at the cool air, but it wasn't enough. "Pull over, I'm going to be sick!"

I got the door open and tumbled out into the gutter as the car rolled to a stop in front of a vacant, weedy lot in a run down industrial neighborhood. I got on my hands and knees and threw up thick black gobs, foul smelling bile... goblin blood, and then I started crying; loud, pitiful sobs that wracked my body. I sat up against the curb and raised my face to let the misty rain wash it clean.

But I'd never be clean again. I spit between my feet and winced at the pool of black saliva.

Pizza Bob got out of the Hummer and stood in front of me, watching me sob. I didn't care anymore. I felt destroyed.

"Melvin," he said quietly.

"Just shut up." I wiped my nose on my sleeve and closed my eyes against the bright light around me. Even though it was overcast and raining, the sunlight hurt my eyes; as it should. I was a vampire now.

I looked up at the sky and spread my arms for the universe. "I'm tired. I'm so very tired and I can't do this anymore. I just want my old life back. I'd do a better job of it this time, I promise!"

"Stop talking that way. I'm sorry this is so hard, but you had to take the next step, Melvin." Pizza Bob shifted from foot to foot. "That which doesn't kill you--"

"Just makes you wish you were dead," I finished for him. "I don't want to do this anymore. Go away."

"Melvin, way too much with the morbid. It's gonna be okay. You did what you had to do. Abby is counting on you to make it, dude."

Abby...my dear, psychotic Abby. There was no way that I could face her now, although she might actually be pleased at my new predatory nature. That thought made me even sadder. But I was dangerous, maybe even too dangerous for her. I needed to go on alone now.

I wiped the tears from my face as my soul grew cold and hard. "I said shut up. I'm a monster. You're a monster. I don't want to hear anything you have to say."

"Listen to me," Pizza Bob said angrily. "You did what you had to do."

I stood up and glared down at him. "Who are you? Whatever happened to you when you got blasted, well, you came back hard and dark and evil. You were my friend once--"

"I'm still your friend!" he said back quietly.

"But what you did to those goblins, I can't even get my head around it! You enjoyed it!"

"If I wouldn't have killed them--"

"Shut up!" I roared. "Don't you dare say you did that for me. Don't you dare!" I stepped up onto the sidewalk. "I thought you were my friend."

"I am your friend, dude," he said sadly.

"You're a monster."

But so am I.

I took another step back on the sidewalk. I was ready to move on.

"Melvin, I am your friend, the same old me." Pizza Bob bowed his head. "I just did what I had to do, man. I'm your guide, it's my job."

I just shook my head. "No, you aren't. I never drank your blood...I didn't kill you! Daniel is my guide. He was my first blood! He's the one who's supposed to be psychotic. Not you."

"I thought we were past that," Pizza Bob snapped back.

"No! I can't trust you now."

"Come on, you're being a diva." Pizza Bob started to walk forward to grab my arm, but I jumped back and growled, a feral sound from deep inside; from the monster within.

"What's one more dead goblin to me?" I hissed. "I could drink you dry in seconds and not even look back."

"That's the goblin blood talking, Melvin. That's not who you really are."

"Of course it is, dumb ass!" I shoved him back, and growled again. "Just go away. I'm done." The air started getting colder around me and I smelled ozone with a touch of sulfur.

"That's just perfect," I muttered, as I braced for whomever was going to show up. My money was on Daniel. Teas Maith had revoked my free pass, and why not? I'd started down that dark path and there was no going back. I was done with all the running. If it was time for me to die, well, so be it. I was just too tired to keep going. Abby would be fine without me. Marcella would keep her protected; maybe. None of that mattered much anymore.

"Dude, we need to go. Now!" Pizza Bob shouted. I flipped him the bird, and braced myself for what was coming.

There was a bright flash of light behind me, and Pizza Bob's eyes bugged in his head as he turned and ran for the Hummer. Part of me was disappointed that he ran, but I'd told him to go; he was different now. Not my Pizza Bob at all. I took a deep breath and turned around.

I was face-to-face with Mr. Happy. I had been expecting Daniel.

"Crap," I muttered.

"Hello, Melvin," Mr. Happy said as he grabbed me. His touch was icy cold like a knife stab all the way to my bones. Through the pain I realized that I wasn't that scared, though. Not anymore. I was too empty to be scared.

"Look," I said, "if you are here to kill me then just do it and get it over with."

Mr. Happy laughed at me. "Kill you? Why would I do that? You've finally started taking the dark gift seriously. It will be so much more fun now, taunting and torturing. More sport."

I stared into the swirling void that was his face in shock.

"Where's your little piss boy? Daniel?" I asked without even a quaver in my voice.

"Oh, he'll be along soon enough. No matter what you do or who you get to help you now, I'll always be one step ahead." Mr. Happy had an edge to his voice that sounded like a bluff. Teas Maith and her intervention had obviously been unexpected.

"I'm just full of surprises, dick head." I sneered.

He said, "You've done quite the turn around, taken in so much power. I'm impressed."

"Screw you."

"Oh, this is delicious," Mr. Happy purred. "Finally some point and counterpoint. I've so enjoyed your machinations of late. Your little cadre and their attempts to save you."

Anger bubbled up from someplace deep inside of me. Suddenly I wanted to live. I pried Mr. Happy's hands off my shoulders and growled.

"Hey, Ass Hat, now look what you've gone and done. You've made me cross." I shoved him back from me and squared my stance, ready to fight and amazed at my strength now. My soul was weary, my heart was broken, but I'd be damned if I was going to let the demon take me without a fight. "I'm going to destroy you."

The goblin blood coursing through my veins made me reckless with new power. But I remembered Hildegarde's face, her eyes so empty and pleading as she lay dying in my arms. All of the other dead goblins' faces rose up in my mind, and I felt my soul crack in shame and self-pity. There was still a little non-monster left inside after all.

Mr. Happy laughed at me again. "I don't think so, my boy. But I look forward to the attempt when the time comes. I love what you have planned."

I sensed movement behind me, and swung around in time to see Pizza Bob come running at Mr. Happy, the glowing ash walking stick held high like a club. He yelled, "Get away from my friend!"

Damn it. Pizza Bob was going to get himself killed. I couldn't let that happen. As a last act of my humanity, and a nod to what he had meant to me, I stepped in front of Pizza Bob and shoved him back. His small goblin body went flying and slammed into the Hummer, where he crumpled in a heap, dazed but still alive

Mr. Happy started clapping, and then pointed a finger at Pizza Bob. He said, "Well aren't you the tenacious spirit! I'm impressed with your cleverness, your cunning. Possession? Good job indeed."

Pizza Bob just lay there staring at me in silence while Mr. Happy laughed.

"Melvin, I will enjoy killing him. Watching him fade into nothingness. The upcoming battle will be epic between you and I, and I look forward to it," the demon said.

So he knew what we were planning with the Loas. Oh well, so much for the element of surprise. It would either work or it wouldn't. I was growing numb again, my humanity slipping further and further away because of the goblin blood coursing through me, but I knew I had to see this through to the end.

I sighed and turned to face him. "Look, if you aren't going to kill me now then I'm just going to go. I'm too tired to deal with this right now."

Anticlimactic, I know, but it's all I had left in my arsenal. I turned my back on the shadow demon and walked to the Hummer, ignoring Pizza Bob on the way. I opened the passenger side door and climbed in. Mr. Happy floated there for a minute, just watching me, and then disappeared in a blinding flash of light as I leaned back into the seat and closed my eyes.

Pizza Bob climbed into the Hummer, started the car, and headed towards Marcella and the motel in unhappy silence.

⋏

"So, it's the silent treatment now?" Pizza Bob asked as I unlocked the motel room door with a passkey from the front desk. "Seriously? You have to talk to me sometime!"

I ignored him. I wasn't ready to have a conversation yet...not at all. I walked in to the room and saw Marcella standing there, pouch in hand, and she smiled when she saw me.

"Melvin! You made it!" She put down the pouch and then snatched it up quickly when Pizza Bob followed me in. "Kiyès sa? Who's dat wit you? A goblin? No...dat be someting more! Oh, Melvin! What you do now?" She clicked her tongue and put the pouch down on the table.

I just shrugged and headed for the king sized bed, where I flopped down and put my arm over my eyes.

"What's dat all over you? Blood? On Mal Bagay! Bad ting!" She rubbed at her arms like she had goose bumps. "I told you don't do nothin' stupid!" She slapped my leg, but I stayed silent.

"Hey, Marcella! Miss me?" Pizza Bob crowed, eager for attention after being ignored for so long.

Marcella shook her head and sighed. "Pizza Bob! Look at you riding a goblin like some high walking Loa! Is dis why dat Goblin King no wanna see me? What you two been up to?" Marcella sat down on the bed next to me. "Hey, Melvin, answer me."

"He's not talking." Pizza Bob sat down next to her. "He's pouting."

I gave him the bird with my free hand, and he sighed.

With a shrug he said, "Well, that's something at least.

Marcella said, "Somebody better explain what's happened."

"It's a long complicated story," Pizza Bob answered.

I sat up and scowled at him. "Just tell her. I'm going to go take a shower."

"Hooray," Pizza Bob sniped. "He speaks."

I went back to ignoring him.

Marcella jumped up. "Where's my car?"

I winced. I'd forgotten all about it. "It wasn't my fault."

"Mwen oto? My Car? Non! Kisa ki rive m'oto? What happened to my car?"

"Daniel." I shrugged. "Sorry," I said flatly, not really that sorry at all actually.

I walked into the bathroom and shut the door in her face. I heard her ranting at Pizza Bob, him trying to calm her down, and then hushed voices as he told her what had happened so far. I turned on the shower and started to undress, but even the thought of doing it took too much energy. Instead I stepped into the stream of hot water fully clothed. The water pooled in dark puddles around my feet, and I numbly watched the bloody water streak towards the drain. I thought about having another cry, a good old-fashioned Melvin pity party, but I pushed the thought away. I was done with all of that now and couldn't muster up enough emotion even if I wanted to. I had changed. Not necessarily for the better, either. I flexed my fingers and saw pink flesh; the blue was gone, and my mind felt sharp and clear. I turned off the water, pulled back the shower curtain and just stood there, staring at the foggy mirror. What would I see? I didn't want to know.

Pizza Bob knocked on the door. "Melvin? I can get you some fresh clothes."

I looked down at my soaked pants and tee shirt, wiggled my toes in my wet shoes and just sighed. I climbed out of the shower and opened the bathroom door. "I'm fine." I brushed past him and sat down in a chair next to the bed.

"Dude! Did you shower fully dressed? That's nuts."

"It doesn't matter. These clothes are fine." I just stared at him.

Marcella held out a big paper bag for me. "I thought you might be hungry so I picked these up for you."

I flared my nostrils and smelled pig livers. They smelled disgusting to me now. "I'm not hungry."

"Melvin, I can feel dat power humming through you, but stay focused, man. Don't let it change you."

"It's too late for that, Marcella. Let's just get this ceremony thing done so I can be on my way."

"I told you, he's in shock," Pizza Bob said as he sat down on the bed.

"I'm not in shock, asshole. I'm just done with all of this."

"Thanks for saving me back there," he mumbled. "I just didn't want Mr. Happy--"

"Shut up. We're even now." I heard the drips and drops of water from my clothing hitting the floor beneath me, my hearing was on overdrive, and wondered if it would stain the carpet with blood.

Who cares.

"You can't stay mad at me forever, dude." Pizza Bob picked at the coverlet on the bed.

Marcella stepped between us. "Okay, Melvin...dat's enough."

"Things have changed," I said. "Let's just get all of our cards on the table, shall we?"

"I told you, Marcella. He's buggin'" Pizza Bob said.

"I'm not anything. I was told I'd have to make a choice and a sacrifice to see all this through." I held Pizza Bob's gaze until he looked down. "And that's what I did."

"I think it was a mistake," he whispered, but I heard him loud and clear.

"What's done is done. Live with it."

Marcella paced back and forth between the bed and the chair. "Melvin, you humming wit power now. I can feel it, taste it in de air. It will be enough to draw down the Loas." She nodded, ignoring the tension in the room. "Mambo Armynel agreed to help us, and she's been preparing the ceremony."

"Then what are we waiting for?" I asked as I stood up.

Marcella stopped pacing and looked up at me, a worried frown creasing her forehead into heavy lines. She looked like she'd aged since I saw her last.

"What's wrong?" I sat back down, annoyed at the drama.

"You were right. Tings have changed. Your heart is filled wit so much pain and darkness now. I'm worried for you. The Loas can be unforgiving if you come wit anger. Papa Legba won't be amenable wit you dis way."

"Oh come on! I did what you wanted. I got the goblin mojo, but I think you knew I'd change. You both did." Damned if you do, damned if you don't. I leaned back in the chair. "The only reason I was going to the stupid ceremony was to get Pizza Bob back."

At the mention of his name, Pizza Bob hopped off the bed. "Really?"

"Yeah, dumb ass. I was trying to get you some closure. I actually missed you, felt bad that you were in limbo. I thought you could either regain your ghost whatever, or move on and be free if I did this.

"But you went ahead and took the next step by yourself. I don't see the point of the ceremony now, really. Why bother? You are eager to just stay in that goblin and set up shop."

"No," he sniped back. "That was just a little hiccup. I got body greedy." He sat back down on the bed with a defeated sigh.

Marcella snapped her fingers. "He can't stay in dat dere body, Melvin. You friend using up all his power to just to stay rooted in. And we can take out Kalfu and dat petro at de same time tonight; make everyting right again."

I sneered at Pizza Bob. "Frankly, I just don't care anymore."

"Yes you do," Marcella snapped. "If not, den why you come here?"

"I don't know. It's like a switch flipped in my brain. I feel hollow. The longer the goblin blood is in my system, the more I feel distant from all of this. Like an observer." I laughed, not a nice laugh either. "It doesn't even hurt anymore that he killed those goblins to be perfectly honest."

"I miss the old Melvin," Pizza Bob said sadly. "He was funny, and bumbling and naive. All of this is my fault."

"Yeah, pretty much." I crossed my arms, and saw Pizza Bob wince like he'd been slapped.

But then Marcella actually slapped me. "What de hell is wrong wit you?"

I looked at her in shock, and she slapped me again. "You feel dat?"

I nodded slowly. Wow. I didn't see that coming. I looked over and saw Pizza Bob's mouth was hanging open in surprise.

"You need some more?" She raised her hand, and I actually flinched. "De Melvin I know, de one we all fighting for is still inside you, man. Don't you dare let youself get swallowed up in darkness! You hear me?" She slapped me once more, this time in frustration, and my heart gave a little stutter in my chest.

My face flushed in embarrassment, and I bowed my head. What the hell had I been thinking? I'd let my pity party in over drive consume me. Goblin blood was indeed poison, and Chuck had been right; sort of. I didn't explode; I imploded when I took in all of that power.

"Wow." I blinked a few times as my mind cleared the hold of the poison blood.

Pizza Bob snickered and said, "Yeah, wow."

Marcella swung around to Pizza Bob, and he ducked. "Whoa! Don't slap me! I'm good," he yelped. Marcella scowled at him.

The dam completely broke inside me, and just like that I was back to being me. I started laughing. I laughed so hard that I began to cry, and again I didn't care who saw me.

Marcella patted me on the back and said, "Dat's good, Melvin. Let it out. Woch nan dlo pa conné doulê woch nan soléy – The rock in the water doesn't know the pain of the rock in the sun."

That started me laughing again. "Marcella, you say the weirdest yet kindest things to me." I squeezed her hand.

"Tout al byan," she said. "It's all good, my friend."

Pizza Bob came hobbling up to me. "Are we good? Should we hug this out?"

"It's hard to feel warm and fuzzy with that face staring back at me." I smiled at him. "Dude, you're a psychotic goblin."

"Not for long," he replied with a smile. "Look at the bright side, Melvin. So you went a little dark side for a bit, but you aren't blue anymore."

"Yeah, but how long will it last?"

"Long enough," he said with a wink.

"Are you two done wit all the bromance tings? Can we focus on the real fight now?" Marcella asked with an impatient foot tap.

Where did she come up with this stuff? I smiled, but then real life tapped me on the shoulder and I took a deep breath. No more wallowing. No more pity party. I was among friends again. Friends who were counting on me.

"Marcella, the demon knows what we are planning. Is this ceremony going to work?" I arched an eyebrow. "Will we take out Mr. Happy and Daniel?"

"He don't know everyting. Trust me," she said with a smile.

I loved it when she said that.

I grinned and said, "Tell me what I have to do."

Pizza Bob paced back and forth between the bed where Marcella was napping, and the chair where I was sitting in the dark. We'd been ordered to rest, to get ourselves prepared for the ornate voodoo ceremony at midnight, and had been just hanging in the motel room in limbo for the last three hours. But I couldn't relax. There were so many steps, so many instructions that Marcella had given me, making me repeat what I had learned over and over again until she was satisfied that I knew my role perfectly. I was keyed up and obsessed with the details. The ceremony was complicated, but Marcella was an excellent tutor and very patient. She was confident that even Pizza Bob would do fine, his goblin possession rather like a tribute to the Loas, or so she hoped. Nothing was a certainty. Marcella tried to seem confident and calm, but I could hear her heart racing, smell the fear coming off of her like sweet smelling nectar. Yes, I was still feeling the dark pull of the goblin blood, but I was fighting to stay me. I was afraid bad things were going to happen later. I was sure of it. I had a deep, nagging sense of doom that someone was going to die. I wished that I could say goodbye to Abby, just in case things didn't work out.

Every few minutes Pizza Bob would flick open the heavy curtain and peek out into the parking lot, mumbling under his breath while he scratched at a mole on his chin. I couldn't take it anymore.

"What in the hell are you so keyed up about?" I reached around him and snapped the curtain closed.

"Peace talks in Uzbekistan. What the hell do you think?"

"No. Something more has you wired. I've been around you long enough to know when you are hiding something." I opened the motel room door and pulled Pizza Bob outside so we wouldn't wake up Marcella from her power nap. She snorted in her sleep and rolled over as I pulled the door closed behind me.

"Marcella said to stay inside," Pizza Bob whined.

What was going on with him? I pulled Pizza Bob over to some stairs illuminated by a faded yellow bulb, and sat him down forcefully. His goblin pallor looked worse in the dull glow.

"Spill it." I crossed my arms.

"I'm losing my hold on the goblin."

Uh-oh. But I could tell that wasn't the only thing wrong. "How much time do we have? We don't really need you to be in that body for the ceremony.

Marcella explained everything, we just need to get your ghosty mojo into the circle and let Papa Legba do the rest."

"Yeah, well, um, about that...." Pizza Bob started to stand, but I pushed him back down.

"You need to tell me who helped you get enough power to take over that goblin body in the first place."

"Dude, I am so screwed." Pizza Bob put his face in his hands.

"What did you do?" I sat down beside him. "It is Mr. Happy, isn't it." I was trying not to be mad.

"No!" He frowned at me through splayed fingers. "Not exactly."

"Just tell me so that I can deal with it," I said, sounding remarkably calmer than I felt.

"You remember your ascension? That mist with all those writhing forms that crawled all over you?" he asked.

I shuddered and nodded yes.

"When I was in limbo, I was part of that mist. I'd get away for a bit and then it would come find me and drag me back into the fold again."

I groaned. "What did you do?"

"I started talking to the others. They ignored me at first, but then this one thing -- I don't exactly know what it was -- started answering me. It said it could help me, for a price."

"Thing? What kind of thing, you idiot! You've got to be more specific."

Pizza Bob shrugged. "It was a little like Mr. Happy...you know...all shadowy and spooky, but I was desperate!"

I stood up and started pacing. "What kind of deal did you make?" I finally asked.

"Don't be mad."

"Too late."

"It seemed like a good idea at the time--"

I crouched down in front of him and hissed, "Quit making excuses! What exactly am I in for here?"

"Geez, thanks for the concern," he mumbled.

I shook my head and sat down next to him. "Sorry. Just tell me already."

Pizza Bob stared down at his knobby knees poking out of a mini skirt, and then sighed heavily. "It hitched a ride. I'm not the only one in here," he said, tapping his forehead.

That explained a lot. The goblin killing spree made sense to me now, at least I hoped that hadn't been my friend enjoying it. "So it's evil then? Okay, but you have control right now?"

"Mostly," Pizza Bob muttered. "It wants control, it needs to get away before the things in the mist come for us. But if I let go then I'll fade away."

"Then we better wake up Marcella and get to the Mambo." I stood up. "Why didn't you tell me all of this sooner?"

"I don't know. I got caught up. I could feel things again. I just wanted to hold on to this for as long as I could."

"You're a dumb ass," I said with a snort. "You've got a mini Mr. Happy time bomb ticking inside of you. Something should have been said."

Pizza Bob stood up. "It's gonna get ugly at the voodoo to-do. The thing in here with me was never human I think; its thoughts are all dark and twisted, and I lost control a few times. What's extra creepy is that it/we can feel the mist coming for us again; and with that mist might come Mr. Happy."

"That's why I lost it earlier; I thought he was coming for me. I'm sorry I ran off," he said.

"You came back. That counts." I patted him awkwardly on the shoulder.

"The thing, whatever, it wants to stand up to Mr. Happy, but only to show how evil it is. It wants me gone."

"Great. Does Marcella know about any of this?"

"I didn't say anything, but you know how she is. She keeps looking at me funny."

"Come on. You need to tell her."

"You think she'll be mad?"

"You should have come clean." I opened the motel room door and saw Marcella sitting up waiting for us. She just squinted her eyes at Pizza Bob, and I knew she knew.

"Do you think she's going to slap me?" he whispered.

"Probably." I pushed him inside. "You just fill her in. I have something I need to do." Marcella cocked her head to the side and then made a shooing motion at me.

Pizza Bob grabbed my hand. "Don't leave me alone with her! And you aren't supposed to go anywhere. It's too dangerous."

"It'll be fine." I sighed and closed the door.

I turned around and stared at the darkened parking lot, my senses open and scanning for trouble, but I was alone; the only creature of the night around for miles. I wondered why Daniel had stayed away for so long, not that I was eager to see him yet, but it made me nervous about how powerful he would be when we finally did meet again. Had he been tormenting Abby in my stead?

Abby. Just thinking about her made the doomy feeling flood through me again. But I wouldn't call her. No, I couldn't be brave enough on the phone if I heard her voice. She'd know I was scared. And I couldn't bear it if she was cold and distant. That would destroy me.

I saw a light on in the motel office so I headed in that direction. There was a computer. And Internet. Access to the real world....

That would have to do for my swan song.

⚔

MASTERSOFTHENITE
Blogline ∞ November 18, 2014 ∞ MOOD: RESIGNED

This post will act as my last will and testament. How's that for drama? I don't own anything but my story, and some of you here on the web have even taken that as your own. You know who you are...I visited you in your club...saw the clones and posers that pranced and preened while pretending to be me. But I ask you all this: Why on earth would anyone want to be me? My life is nothing but one big, bad luck buffet. The only bright spot is the one person I have loved since before I actually knew what love was. Corny, eh? Yes. I love her. Despite her flaws, her darkness, her black heart that hopefully beats for the both of us, I love her. But I've brought suffering to her doorstep, and danger.

I've changed since I first started posting here. I've grown up. Funny how it took a pathetic undeath to make me miss my life, miss what could have been. But if I hadn't become this sham vampire then I never would have found her again. Ironic? Definitely. But I may have lost her forever....

I have changed. I had my first blood, not of my own free will, but it happened. And he is psychotic and intent on destroying me. But then I took more blood...I drank from a living being and it broke me. You people have no idea what hides in the darkness...what creatures masquerade as human among you. I have seen things that would make you run screaming. Please heed my warning and stop your fascination with the dark lure of the night. It's not a game. It's not fun. It is pain and death and unhappiness. Things are out of balance because of me.

I'm going to try and fix it tonight. I'm going to save Pizza Bob, I'm going to destroy Mr. Happy, I'm going to send my psychotic haunter straight to hell (if there is a hell), and then I'm going home if I can. If she'll have me. I will tell her how much I love her.

There will be Loas in the air tonight. And magic. And suffering. Those of you who have been kind to me here...well, I thank you. Heed my warning and move on with your life. Enjoy the sunshine. Embrace life. Cherish your friendships.

I learned the universe does not hate me. I hope I see you again, Teas Maith. Thank you.

Regrets? I have many. In fact too many to list here. I never found Maddy...I'm not even angry with her anymore for this curse. I've had quite the run this last six months. The things I've seen...the people and creatures I've met (and killed...and eaten!).

If I die tonight, hopefully my life will have had some meaning. I'm not evil. I almost was...but I was saved from myself by the love of two friends...two dear friends that I may die for tonight. I hope that I don't die, and pray I am not damned if I do. But if it's a choice between my life and theirs...I'd gladly die to save them.

I will leave you with some words my friend would say:

Bèl entêman pa di paradi – A beautiful funeral doesn't guarantee heaven.

Let's hope I don't have to find out.

-Melvin

REPLY TO POSTER ∞ BLOCK USER ∞ REPORT POST

CHAPTER 19

POMP AND CIRCUMSTANCE AND POSSESSION

I opened the motel room door expecting chaos, but instead found Pizza Bob and Marcella sitting quietly on the bed, waiting for me.

"Did you find some peace?" she asked me.

"I think so."

Pizza Bob rolled his eyes. "You blogged, didn't you?"

"Maybe." I sat down in the chair and shrugged. "It was rather maudlin and gothic and perfectly sappy. I said my goodbyes. It was for Abby."

"That's morbid, dude. Let's hope she doesn't read it and freak out. You're such a tender princess sometimes," Pizza Bob said with a snort. Marcella elbowed him, and he smiled at me.

"So, Marcella...we all good?" I asked.

She nodded. "I didn't slap Pizza Bob, though I should for good measure for bein' such a dumb ass!"

Pizza Bob said, "She didn't yell, didn't even look too surprised by the revelation of a stow away in this goblin's body."

"We'll deal wit dat ting when de time comes. Mal bagay." Marcella shook her head in disapproval, gathered up her stuff and told us to get moving. "It's time."

"Oh boy." My legs felt like rubber. It was time. Damn it.

"We're all in this together, dude. Ride the adrenaline wave and it will be righteous!" Pizza Bob hobbled out the motel room door without looking back.

"I can do this," I whispered.

When we got to the Hummer I opened the back hatch and searched for that soiled bandage.

"What are you doing back there?" Pizza Bob asked as he fired up the vehicle.

I had the strip of blood soaked cloth pressed up against my nose, fighting the temptation to pop it into my mouth and suck on it with my overbite for one last burst of goblin-laced blood mojo despite the side effects. I looked up and saw Marcella staring at me with her lips pursed and a concerned expression on her face that spoke more than anything she could say out loud.

I stuffed the cloth into my sleeve quickly. "I'm good," I called out to Pizza Bob while keeping eye contact with Marcella. "Just checking on something."

"Melvin," she whispered. "Stay focused."

"I said I'm good, Marcella. Don't worry." I climbed into the back passenger seat and let her ride shotgun up front. Instead of driving away towards battle, we sat idling in the parking lot.

"Guys...." Pizza Bob turned around and looked at me. "I just want to say good luck."

"Dis night is the end of tings. When dawn comes," Marcella said as she adjusted her dress under the seat belt strap, "it's a new beginning. We don't need luck, we got right on our side."

"I like the sound of that." I tried to smile, but I was a jumble of nervous energy.

"Just stay focused." She nodded, and gave Pizza Bob directions to Mambo Armynel's home. "Fill up your hearts wit happy tings, be brave, feel love, feel power."

I closed my eyes and pictured Abby's smiling face, and tried to fill my heart with all of the love I'd had bottled up inside for the last twenty years. I needed to be brave for her no matter what. I needed to be brave for all of us. Then I had a sudden and overwhelming image of Marcella dying; it was so vivid and clear that I gasped. She turned in the seat and looked at me.

"It's all going to be fine, Melvin."

I just stared at her, my heart skipping a few beats in my chest painfully. That was new. I realized it was profound sorrow causing the ache.

"Are we friends?" I asked her.

"Nou se zanmi, we are friends." She nodded.

"What a love fest, eh?" Pizza Bob chimed in, but he could sense the mood in the car and let Marcella and I have our talk as he drove the quiet streets.

I stared out the window at the lights of this beautiful city that I loved so much, and took a calming breath. Bad things were going to happen...bad, bad things. I felt Marcella's gaze and finally looked at her.

I said, "I want to thank you for all of this, Marcella. You taught me so much. You've helped me stay me. Maybe we should rethink this thing tonight...I have a bad feeling about it."

"Melvin, M'ap viv, mwen la, tout bagay an fòm." She reached back and patted my hand without a translation, but I didn't need one. The vampire power inside me had taken hold and I could understand her now: I'm living, I'm fine, everything is fine.

But I knew better; she wouldn't be fine.

"Marcella, I think something bad is going to happen to you. I can't let it happen. I couldn't live with myself."

"Melvin, I will be safe. We are in good hands with my family. Nèg di san fè, bon Dié fè san di – People say without doing, God does without saying. Remember dat."

I smiled sadly. "Pòté'w bien!" I said. Take care.

Marcella reached back and squeezed my hand. "Your accent needs work, my friend. We'll practice when dis here ting is all done."

Pizza Bob stopped the car in front of a large treed lot in the boonies of southwest Portland, and killed the engine. "All right, guys. Touchy-feely time is over. We're here."

I felt the pulses of power emanating from this place. There was a small stone house recessed deep in the trees, and I smelled fresh water...a natural spring bubbled and flowed behind the house. I flared my nostrils and took in the scent of wood smoke, incense, roasting meat and blood. Lots of blood. It made my gums tingle in anticipation, but I forced myself to be calm like Marcella had instructed. My sensitive ears picked up the sound of chanting, singing, and rhythmic drumming that resonated deep in my bones. Marcella started swaying in her seat, and I knew she was already being drawn into the pull of the ceremony.

Flickering lights started weaving between the trees, and a procession of torch bearing women clad in white made their way towards our car. These were the Hounsi, the servers of the ceremony.

"Whoa," Pizza Bob whispered. "I saw this in a movie once!"

I shushed him as the Hounsi opened the car doors and pulled us out one-by-one into the cold night air, separating us by encircling with six women each. Marcella began twirling and swaying, hugging and kissing the other women around her with manic joy.

"I'm freaking out!" Pizza Bob moaned.

"Stay calm. It's all going to be okay," I said as a woman put her hands on my cheeks and stared into my eyes. Her touch sent electric zings through my flesh. I hope it's going to be okay!

"Loogaroo, kisa ou vle? - what do you want?" she asked.

"Eske ou ka ede nou, souple? - Can you help us please?" I kept eye contact and willed myself to be calm. The woman had something inside of her, another presence that scared the absolute holy hell out of me: Marinette-Bwa-Chech, the actual Loa for Loogaroo. I felt her power washing over me, but I was determined to be brave.

"Kisa ki rive ou? - What happened to you?" Her voice modulated lower, sending a chill down my spine.

"Kalfu," I responded, and the possessed woman grinned wickedly and then spit between my feet as she pushed me back and turned away.

I looked over my shoulder and saw Pizza Bob shaking uncontrollably, his head lolled back like he was unconscious while two women on either side held him up. It looked bad, and I hoped that whatever was inside Bonsel's body with him hadn't taken control. Maybe this is what was supposed to happen. Marcella danced in front of him briefly and then swayed towards me.

"Move on, move on," she said in a high-pitched voice, and I knew she was in the midst of a Loa possession.

Another Hounsi took my hand and I let myself be led down a path that wound through the trees, past the small house, and into a circular clearing centered with a bare limbed tree that had been carved into a pole; the poto mitan. The pure water spring bubbled out of a stone fountain that fed a small pond in front of the pole, and more people here, the serviteurs (practitioners), danced and swayed in the glow of a bonfire off to the side. It was beautiful. I tasted the power in the air, and felt dizzy from the sensory overload.

Tables were set with plates of roasted meat, candles, rum, and figurines representing different Loas. There were circles drawn in cornmeal all over the ground, some intersecting at a pen filled with goats, pigs, and chickens. I knew the animals were for the blood sacrifices, but the beasts seemed calm, at peace with their fate. I wondered if some of the goats were for Bertram the troll?

An old woman dressed in a bright white dress that intensely contrasted her black skin started towards me, hobbling along on a cane in a slow, languid style. Her face was a map of wrinkles, but her eyes were piercing, aglow with an inner light that sent shivers through my body. The woman opened a pouch and poured some powder into her hand as she approached me. Uh-oh.

She said, "Loogaroo...Mwen rélé Armynel." So this was the Mambo. She looked the part, definitely, with a side of scary. Marcella joined her and nodded at me. It was time for me to make my plea.

"I'm Melvin. I ask for your help. I seek Papa Legba. I seek the Loas." I tried to keep my voice calm, but I knew the Mambo could feel the fear coming off of me. I stood frozen as she held up her palm and then blew a handful of the mixture into my face.

"Yo t'a rémé jwé, they want to play, let it begin," she said as the dust enveloped me.

It was as if someone threw a blanket over my head. My vision tunneled, all of my strength disappeared and I crumpled to the ground as the serviteurs started making a strange undulating cry. Mambo Armynel crouched down and stared at me, but she looked like she was covered in shimmering dust -- the air around me had a kaleidoscope effect. My body began tingling, an uncomfortable itch that started at the soles of my feet and sped up towards my scalp. Marcella hadn't said anything about this happening, no warning at all, and suddenly I was terrified that her family had changed their minds; that they were just going to kill me. I tried to move, but I was paralyzed. The dust was making me see things; there were flashes of color that twirled and whipped around the crowd. Faces formed in the air around me, some terrifying, some gentle, and I sensed these were the

Loa eager to take form in the serviteurs' bodies. The drumming intensified as the serviteurs, led by Armynel, began to sing the songs for Legba and Ghede.

A man danced up in front of me and started convulsing, falling to the ground as his eyes rolled in their sockets. As he lay there, a terrible popping noise came from his leg sockets, and I watched in horror as his leg twisted and rotated into a crooked bow. Another serviteur bent down and helped him to stand, then produced a small corncob pipe, which the man began to puff eagerly. Mambo Armynel bowed to the now crippled man and the people all started chanting, "Papa Legba!" and crowding around him, touching his hands reverently. Someone handed him a crutch, and Papa Legba started doing a hobble dance around me as I lay there still paralyzed and completely terrified. Finally he bent at the waist and pointed at me.

"Hey, you dere, get on up," he said in heavily accented English, and my body sprang to life like I was a marionette. "What you want from dis here life, half man? Eh?"

I gulped and stared into Papa Legba's eyes. "I want my friends to be okay," I whispered. "Please, Papa. Souple."

Papa Legba threw back his head and laughed. "Dat's all? You got de soul of a giver inside you wit all dat darkness...don' want no ting fer yaself, no more power? No more life, blood drinker?" He snatched the soiled bandage from inside my sleeve and waved it in my face. I was ashamed.

"No," I said forcefully. "I just want my friends to be okay. I've brought a demon down on them...can you help me?" I stood there, my body suspended by Legba's will, unable to move on my own.

"Oooh, de crossroads been closed to you, Loogaroo. Ghede goin' sort you out now." He laughed and went hobbling away towards Pizza Bob as the drumming and chanting intensified around us. Papa Legba reached out and pushed his hand into the goblin's chest, then pulled out something that glowed dull amber. The Loa-possessed man clapped his hands together on the glow, Bonsel shrieked pitifully and slumped forward, and then Pizza Bob was shimmering next to her with a terrified look on his face. Papa Legba had Pizza Bob by the hand, anchoring him in the world, and was standing over the goblin. He reached out with his free hand and plunged it into Bonsel's chest again; I saw something dark and shadowy inside the body trying to escape from Legba's grasp.

"Be brave!" I yelled to Pizza Bob, but he couldn't hear me over the din. The serviteurs were howling and chanting, whirling around me in a frenzy. Some started convulsing, and they'd fall and stand up again possessed by Loas. It was terrifying to watch, and I saw the shimmer and glow of each new presence. The Loas were angry. This was all my fault! I'd lost track of Marcella, and knew that she was in terrible danger from all of this.

I watched a man get possessed next to Pizza Bob. The man stood up and put on a pair of sunglasses with one lens poked out. Another serviteur handed him a top hat and a long black coat, an undertaker's jacket. I recognized him immediately as Papa Ghede, Baron Samedi...the Loa of death. He grinned at me and then embraced Papa Legba. Now that he was here I knew things were going to get even scarier.

Mambo Armynel appeared before me with a large knife in one of her tiny hands, and a stone bowl in the other. That couldn't be good. But I was ready to die if it meant that Pizza Bob would be saved and all of this would stop before Marcella got hurt.

"None of this is Marcella's fault!" I yelled. "Don't be mad at her, don't be mad at Pizza Bob...just help them. Protect them after you kill me!" I meant every word. Armynel just shook her head.

"We gonna summon that dark one now, make him pay the price for his greed," she said as she reached out and sliced my arm. Thick, black blood, vampire essence mixed with goblin mojo, oozed from the cut and Armynel caught the drips in the bowl. She dumped them on the ground and then spit in the mixture.

The air grew colder around me and smelled of ozone and sulfur. Instantly the drumming stopped and the ceremony went silent. I blinked a few times through the haze of smoke and magic dust, and saw Mr. Happy and Daniel striding through the crowd towards me. I still couldn't move. Oh, this was bad. Very, very bad! Daniel grinned and came flying at me. I hate to admit it, but I closed my eyes and flinched.

I heard a scream and then a thud, and opened my eyes to see that Marcella had stepped in front of me and taken the brunt of Daniel's blow.

"No!" I yelled as Marcella started convulsing. The serviteurs remained silent, just watching as Daniel possessed Marcella.

Mr. Happy started clapping gleefully, like he usually did when something amused him. He was so predictable in his arrogance, and I hated him more than I ever had before. He definitely had to die. Oh yes. Painfully, if possible.

"Stop him!" I pleaded with Armynel, but she held her hand up for me to be quiet. I watched in silent horror Marcella stand up, now under the control of the ghost inside of her. Daniel ran his hands over her body, crudely massaging her breasts, as he lewdly poked his tongue out at me.

"Marcella, listen to me!" I cried. "Fight him, you're stronger than him."

But Marcella was gone. Daniel started pulling out her hair while the Mambo just stood there passively watching it happen. Why wasn't Papa Legba helping us? How had Daniel Possessed Marcella if she already had a Loa inside of her? Where was Ghede?

"Melvin," Mr. Happy cooed as he reached up and patted my cheek. "This is lovely. I love all the pomp and circumstance and possession for my arrival."

"You son of a bitch. Your fight is with me, damn it. Get your little piss boy out of my friend!"

"Why would I do that? It hurts you so!" He cackled as Daniel took a knife and started jabbing it into Marcella's arm. Blood poured from the wounds, and I knew it was only a matter of time before he killed her out right.

Mr. Happy turned to the crowd. "Where is my tribute?" he demanded, but no one moved.

"Do you know who I am?" he crowed.

Someone touched my shoulder and I looked back to see Ghede grinning at me. "Listen to me, Loogaroo. You want to fight this thing what come here?" he whispered. I nodded. "Time to let yourself go." He put his hand on my back and I felt a sharp stab.

The world tilted sideways as an ice-cold presence slipped into my body. My blood felt like it was boiling inside of me from all of that power, and I had a moment of resistance when the thing identified itself. Holy crap. This was unexpected. I knew Mr. Happy was a big faker!

Kalfu, the real shadow demon stretched inside of me and took over.

"Demon," I roared with Kalfu's voice. "Did you not think I would come and kill you for your insolence?"

Mr. Happy swung around and cowered. "You!" He took a step back. "You can't be inside that thing!"

"He is mine, impostor. You are not the lord of the crossroads." Kalfu reached out with my hands and grabbed Mr. Happy, pulling his body into a tight embrace. The demon struggled, but I was far too strong, and delighted that Mr. Happy was indeed going to die now. My overbite extended and I ripped out his neck without any hesitation. Ice cold, bitter blood flowed down my throat as I drank the shadow demon dry, screaming in agony inside my own mind as his essence roared through my body. The goblin blood tempered the pain, and I realized now why it had been so crucial to have all of that goblin blood inside me; it's the only thing that would make me strong enough to survive this fight, to survive Kalfu's possession.

Mr. Happy shriveled in my arms, and then dissolved into slimy wads of black goo that pooled at my feet. I wiped my mouth on my sleeve, spit on the puddle, and then turned towards Daniel with a savage smile on my face, reveling in the power.

That was easy! I gloated, now totally ready to dispatch Daniel.

"Petro, you've grown strong by your master's hand, overstepped what was given, but he is dead. You serve me now." I balked inside, wanting to see Kalfu destroy Daniel. There was no way he could keep on living!

"No. I serve no one." Daniel's voice coming out of Marcella's mouth made me sick. But as long as he kept talking, he'd just keep pissing off Kalfu.

Keep it up, asshole.

Unfortunately, Kalfu didn't seem too bothered; in fact he seemed a bit amused.

"Leave the Hounsi and face your punishment!" Kalfu roared.

But Daniel just grinned at me. "I'm not done yet," he said as he slammed the knife into Marcella's chest all the way to the hilt.

"See you around, Melvin." Daniel exploded out of Marcella's body like a shot and disappeared; Kalfu let him go.

That wasn't a good sign.

I tried to rush to Marcella's side, but Kalfu still had control over my body. Papa Legba let go of Pizza Bob and he was instantly at Marcella's side, but no one else spoke or moved to help her.

Pizza Bob said, "Melvin, if they speak then Kalfu can stay. You need to make him go now!"

Um, hello, I said in my mind. *Um, thanks, I think we are done here. I knew Mr. Happy was a big faker and I appreciate you letting me kill him and all, but can you go now so I can save my friend?*

"I demand my tribute," Kalfu said out loud. Mambo Armynel led a pig out of the pen, then sliced its throat. She caught the blood in another stone bowl, which she carried over to me in silence. Kalfu took the bowl, gulped down the offering, and then sat down.

"Melvin," he said. "I have been watching you. You and I will meet again. Our journey is not over."

And just like that he let go of his hold and left my body. Wow, despite the pucker factor it was kind of cool. I'd just killed Mr. Happy. Hooray for me, but Kalfu's warning rushed through my mind. Oh, that was going to stick with me. I sagged forward as the drumming started up again around me. I got up and staggered over to Marcella, who was near death from all of the blood loss, and of course the knife sticking out of her chest. She blinked a few times and looked up at me with glowing eyes.

"Melvin, you are a true and kind friend to this Hounsi."

I saw another spirit inside of her. "Ki moun ki la?" I asked. Who is there?

Marcella smiled. "Mama Ezrulie. But you knew dat, dear boy. She knew dis was gonna happen, asked me to give her strength. Now it's time for you to do your part. Give her your blood."

I sat back on my butt. "Oh, no. I won't damn her to this undeath."

"Rip your flesh like a ripe mango, and let dem juices flow over her wounds, Loogaroo. Loogaroo with a pure spirit. Share your ti-bon-ange wit her and she live again."

I winced at her descriptive grossness, but nodded in understanding. In voo-doo they believed that the soul had two parts: the ti-bon-ange which was part of the soul of an individual -- the changeless impersonal cosmic consciousness that could be reused upon death, and the second part was the gro-ban-ange which was the personal soul that animated the human body. Marcella could have my ti-bon-ange, my gro-ban-ange, whatever she needed if it meant she'd live.

I bit into my wrist, reopening Armynel's healed slice, and dripped my blood over Marcella's wounds. I kept repeating the process, willing my soul into her until I was dizzy and weak from my own blood loss.

"What about Pizza Bob?" I whispered.

"Oh, he gonna be fine just de way he is for now. No gonna move on yet." Mama Ezrulie smiled up at me, and then patted my cheek. "I'm gonna go now, let dis here girl have her time, but I see you again soon, cherie."

"Thank you," I said with a smile as I tipped over in the dirt. I had no idea if I would live or die, or whether I still had a soul left to keep me grounded. I flexed my fingers in front of my face and had to laugh. They were blue...I was blue again. Of course I was. Oh well. Mr. Happy was gone, Daniel was still out there yet I doubted he'd come for me any time soon, but Pizza Bob and Marcella were safe.

All good things in my book. I was at peace and finally happy. I thought of Abby and just hoped she knew that I had loved her. Daniel might be a problem later, but that was for later; everything would work out.

Pizza Bob was next to me, holding my hand and Marcella's hand together. "We did it. Hooray for the good guys!"

"I don't feel so good," I mumbled.

"Don't puss out on us, Melvin. You're going to be fine, dude. After everything tonight, you deserve it!"

Marcella sat up and looked at me. "I'd take you home but you broke my car," she frowned at me and then looked down at the knife sticking out of her dress. "Dis here was one of my favorite frocks! Salpouri!"

I laughed. I'd just saved her life, I was maybe dying myself, and all she could think about was her car and the dress.

"We still have the Hummer," Pizza Bob said eagerly, then paled. "Oh, crapa-roni. I forgot about Bonsel...."

We looked over and saw the goblin's body laying there, a wide, blackened hole in her chest where the shadow thing had burst free in the chaos around us. No one had noticed that it had happened.

I groaned. "Uh-oh. That's going to be a problem on so many levels."

"Another mess to clean up. I swear you two gonna drive me to de crazy place wit all you petro nonsense!" Marcella stood up, pulled the knife out of her chest, and frowned. "Bah!"

Pizza Bob said. "Marcella, you are awesomely hard core. If I was still alive I'd be all over you."

"Go on wit you mushy face tings," she said as she waved him off.

He grinned then suddenly sobered when he remembered Bonsel's body. "I feel kind of bad for her. She was a creepy little thing, but she helped me out. Oh well, I hope Abby doesn't mind writing a big life price check for Chuck's daughter."

I felt bad for the goblin, too; another casualty of my ascension. I'm sure there would be more.

Pizza Bob winked at me. "But we get to keep the car now."

Marcella sighed. "I can't drive dat ting. It's all tiny and wired for a goblin. How am I supposed to mash myself up in dat seat. Bah."

I laughed. I had to. I just had to. The more things changed, the more they stayed the same. Yes, Mr. Happy was gone, but mini Mr. Happy was free. So was Daniel. And now the goblins were going to be after me, too. Damn it. But just maybe the Universe was finally done with me.

I cringed even thinking that. I knew better.

"Can we go home now?" I asked as my stomach rumbled. I was hungry again. Double damn it.

"That was cool how you got possessed, dude. Total bad ass! Did you see that, Marcella? Did you see me all brave, too? I can't wait to get back home. Abby won't believe any of this...this voodoo stuff is actually wicked awesome...."

I lay back and listened to Pizza Bob ramble on, finally content for the first time in a long time. I was going home.

Roll credits....

EPILOGUE:

After Getting Out of the Well, Zorro Aka Stinky Saved the Day

"**M**elvin, dude, there's something you have to see in the drawing room."

I sat up in bed and saw Pizza Bob practically bouncing from foot to foot, grinning at me like a fool from the doorway.

"Is it going to make me laugh or cry?" I rubbed a sleep potato from my eye; I was unconscious when we got home, didn't recall being put to bed, and I wasn't ready for any surprises. I'd said my goodbyes to Marcella, and that's the last thing I remembered. I was still exhausted, and hadn't even had time to see Abby yet or regale her with my heroics. Or even apologize for everything.

But there was time. I was home and all was good in the universe. I just wanted my happy place. I felt normal again; well, more like the original Mostly Dead Melvin version. When I bled myself dry for Marcella I lost some of my mojo. But that was okay; things were going to be fine now. I was in my happy place after all.

Silly, silly me for thinking I was done with being the universe's piss boy.

"Well?" I prompted.

"Probably both."

"Seriously, it's been a hard few days and I don't need cryptic right now."

"Trust me. We have visitors, and well, you just have to see it to believe it."

I sniffed and there was a unique scent in the air; a little dusty, a little moth bally, and a little suntan lotiony?

What? I smelled coconut oil.

The ghost grinned and pointed downstairs. "Just come see."

▲

I stopped dead in the doorway to the grand sitting room and just stared at the surprise.

"I am Vincente." The vampire unfolded himself from the chair and stood up, towering over me with a languid grin, actually more of a smirk, on his face.

"Okay," I said through pursed lips.

Who the hell was this freak? Okay, so he was a vampire. Another vampire! But he looked like an asshole. Great. I finally encountered more of "my" kind and he had to be type that I would automatically hate. I crossed my arms and took in his outfit: leather pants, a flowing silk shirt that was open to the waist, long black hair tied back with a piece of leather, and the requisite pale skin. But the best part of his get-up was the six-inch gold sun medallion hanging on a heavy chain between his pecs. It took everything I had not to burst out laughing when I realized his attire was so Anne Rice wannabe. And what was with the Italian accent? Of course he was one of those lucky vampires who was handsome to begin with. Life had not been unkind, and his undeath seemed to be going splendidly. At least from where I was standing.

"Okay?" He arched an eyebrow at me. "You must be The Melvin."

"Nope, just Melvin. The "the" is silent at the beginning." Pizza Bob snickered behind me, and Vincente squinted his eyes.

"Hmmm. Amusing, no?" He waved his hand and the other vampires in the room stood up, they were all dressed in various replications of his outfit, and they all wore the sun medallion.

"So, Vincente, and mini Vincentes, what can I do for you?" I impatiently tapped my foot on the floor, and again the vampire arched an eyebrow at me.

"You have been searching for more of our kind, no? Here we are. We have followed your postings and are intrigued by your unique situation. You offer up more questions, you are an enigma? How you say, a riddle, no? Not human. Not Vampire. But chosen and marked, yes."

"I guess." It was like listening to Yoda in Fabio's body -- disconcerting to say the least. "Who are you again?" I looked around at the group and felt more than a little defensive suddenly.

"I am Vincente. I am the sanctioned leader of this collective."

"Collective?"

"We are--" another of the vamps, I guess the second in command, started to say but Vincente glared.

The vampire held up his hands and mouthed, "Sorry, boss."

"We are," Vincente said with a slight scowl, "Piangente della stella di giorno, the Mourners of the Day Star."

This was met by a chorus of, "Repentant and ever lamenting its loss," by the other vampires while they held up their medallions.

Creepy. But at least the tanning lotion smell made sense now; it was the vampire version of the way the smell of chocolate chip cookies makes a girl who just broke up with her boyfriend feel better. Or something like that. I was glad Pizza Bob couldn't hear my thoughts. I would never hear the end of my Seventeen Magazine moment.

I studied the other vampires and noticed something very odd. Some had ghosts floating next to them, and some didn't. Vincente didn't have one. What did that mean? I saw he was stealing glances at Pizza Bob then back at me, then back at the ghost again.

"Okay, why are you here?" I was suddenly very uncomfortable.

"You can walk in daylight, no?" He looked like he was salivating. Definitely creepy.

"Well, I'm no Blade, ha-ha," I gave him a thumbs-up, "but I do all right."

"Blade?" The vampire looked confused, and Pizza Bob just burst out laughing. Vincente's minion leaned in and whispered in his ear, then looked at me apologetically.

The lead vampire nodded and gave me that stupidly repetitive arched eyebrow of his.

"Funny, no?" Vincente leaned forward and sniffed, wrinkling his nose slightly. He turned to the other vampire and asked, "Che cosa è quell'odore?"

I'd lost my language auto-translate super power during the voodoo ceremony, so I didn't speak Italian, but odore was probably odor.

"That would be me," I said defiantly.

"Ah, yes."

"How did you get in here?" I was suddenly very concerned that they were in the house. "Who let you in?"

"La padrona de la casa," Vincente answered with a smirk.

"English please."

"Your woman."

I looked at Pizza Bob quickly, a cold feeling starting up in the pit of my stomach. He shrugged.

"Find her," I said to Pizza Bob, and he shimmered out of sight quickly.

"Why?" I looked at the group of vampires slowly, eyeing each one until they looked away, and then settled my most intimidating gaze on their inglorious leader. He seemed unruffled.

"Because I asked her to. She has been very accommodating, no?" Vincente licked his lips, and I was now extremely concerned. "We've had many conversations while you were away, an understanding between us. She is quite striking."

"What does that mean?" I took a step towards him.

"L'anima del immortal."

That sounded ominous. "And that would be?"

Oh, Abby. What have you done now?

He shook his head in annoyance and said, "The Blood of the Immortal."

There was a collective sigh from the other vamps.

"Fabio--"

"Vincente," he corrected.

"Whatever. I don't think I like you very much."

"That wounds me." His tone was less than sincere. "But, no matter. We are here to see the reality of what you are...to study you, exchange thoughts on our evolution to mastery."

"Whoa." I put my hand on his chest and pushed him back.

"No, no. No one touches me," he squealed, without an accent, and it caught me off guard. Faker! I knew it!

His minion shook his head in embarrassment, and then stepped forward aggressively; Vincente fanned himself and then went back into character like nothing had happened.

"Let us begin again," faker said with an exaggerated accent.

Pizza Bob appeared next to me, looking less than happy. "Dude, um, we have a situation."

"Your ghost is distracting us...tell him to go away." Vincente made a shooing motion with his hand.

I held up a finger, take a guess which one, and said, "Hush."

I glared at him, dreading what was coming.

Abby, Abby, Abby. I hope you haven't done something I'll regret.

The Blood of the Immortals....

"The woman was very determined, very persuasive." Vincente ran a finger over his chest, smiling crudely at a private memory. It made my skin crawl. He shrugged and said, "She was very sad that you were gone. I did my best to comfort her in your absence."

"I will kill you if you have hurt her."

He just smiled at me.

To Pizza Bob I asked, "Is she okay?"

"You want the good news or the bad?"

"Is there good news?" Please don't let her be dead.

"Well, if I put a spin on it...." But Pizza Bob didn't have a chance to tell me.

"Hello, Melvin."

I turned around slowly and saw her.... My Abby looking beautiful, happy, and decidedly undead. Floating next to her in ghostly form was the maid, Emily; she was less than happy.

"Surprise!" Abby smiled and ran a tongue over her fangs.

"No!" I wailed.

"Yes," the vampires all chorused behind Vincente as Abby stepped forward and took his hand.

"I did it so that I could help find you," Abby said with a grin.

No, you did it because you wanted to.

I felt my heart flutter, and then stop beating. I think for good. I think the last part of me died forever as I stared at Abby in horror.

"At least she looks good," Pizza Bob offered. "And she snacked on Emily just for me!"

"So you're the jerk who's been freaking me out," the newly dead maid said in disgust. "This is so totally unfair."

"Oh, be quiet. You could have been hit by a bus tomorrow," Abby snapped at her. "This, at least, is more exciting."

"Nice to finally meet you, Pizza Bob." Abby nodded at him and then reached for me. I flinched.

"Oh, Abby...you shouldn't have done this."

"Be happy for me. We are going to have so much fun together!"

"Now, Melvin," Vincente interrupted. "No hard feelings, eh? So I am her maker. She is not blue." He snickered.

Before I could stop and think about it, I hauled off and punched Fabio Yoda right in the face. My goblin mojo was all gone but I still packed quite the punch. Vincente crumpled, then I was rushed by the other vampires who grabbed my arms and pinned me to the floor.

Uh-oh. I had a bad feeling about this. Pizza Bob was trying to get to me, but all of the other ghosts in the room swarmed him and he shimmered out of existence. Damn it! I hoped he was okay; he had to be! Abby was just standing there watching it all happen with a passive look on her face.

Vincente stood up, adjusted his shirt and flipped his ponytail back over his shoulder. He held out his hand for Abby and she stepped forward gracefully without looking down at me. Wow, that hurt. After everything I had been through!

"Melvin," Vincente said with a patronizing tone to his fake accent. "That is something you should have not done. Now we must do things the hard way."

The hard way? Aw, crap.

"Is this ever going to end?" I muttered. "Fabio, I've just dealt with a whole bunch of scarier folks than you, so, if you don't mind I'd like to skip your verbal foreplay and get to the punch line."

"You are much more pathetic than I imagined. This was too easy. I am sad." He mock-wiped a tear from his eye. What a dick!

"Abby, could you maybe call off thug muscles there? I think we need a do over."

"Melvin, darling," said Abby without much emotion. "You should have let me know you were okay. I read that blog post and my heart just broke."

"Abby, honey, you're scaring me here." I struggled, but the vampires definitely had me pinned. "It's the blood talking...trust me, I've been there. You need to focus and remember who you are."

Abby, why did you have to go and die!

"I'm going to help you, Melvin. You're going to be a delightfully evil vampire when I'm through with you."

"Oh, no, no.... Not again! I just got home!"

"I have a surprise for you," she said. There was a commotion behind her, and two of the vampires carried in a squirming, human-shaped bundle wrapped in a blanket, which they dropped on the floor next to me.

Not another magazine salesman!

Abby leaned down and unwrapped the blanket from around my morbid present to display a woman who was, of course, bound with duct tape.

I flinched when I recognized her. Uh-oh.

Staring angrily back at me was none other than my maker, Maddy.

Oh, this was going to end badly

The End (Mostly....)

𐤷

ACKNOWLEDGEMENTS

Writing a novel is not an easy thing to do; it's rather like navigating a maze, tilting at windmills, and/or exorcising inner demons. Sounds rather dramatic, doesn't it!

I am very lucky in that I had a wonderful support network and safety net while I toiled away at the whim of my muse.

Derek, my sweet, thank you for letting me be me, and thank you for making sure that I ate real food when I was on epic writing binges. Your support means the world to me! My girls, Solas and Luna, thank you for being so patient (mostly) while I tried to write. I'm grateful that my family acknowledges and accepts my particular brand of Loon!

Gisele, my most excellent mother-in-law, thank you for everything during the initial writing of this book! And a special thank you for the French lessons!

Michael, my brother, wonder twin powers activate!

Steve Barber: You wonderful Haggis, you! Without your nudge, Melvin would still be a short story! Thank you for believing in my favorite blue weirdo.

Carole, your heart and strength inspire me. I adore you, Tatertot.

Trish, you know just what to say right when I need to hear it. You rock! Your writer-fu is strong and Melvin is better because of your tireless edit suggestions.

Terri, you are such a rock star! Thank you!

Ari, thanks for being patient while I finished Melvin. Our project is next on the agenda! Pyrates!

A huge thank you and shout out to Absolute Write, an invaluable resource for writers! A hearty huzzah to my Mod companions and to the members who make the site so incredible!

Larry, I miss you.

And finally – Thank you to all the friends and beta readers who helped shape Melvin's story along the way. Thank you, thank you, THANK YOU!

I have taken certain geographic liberties with Portland. I know that the industrial area of NW Portland is above Sauvie Island and not down river as used in this novel.

Terry Currier brought the Keep Portland Weird slogan to Portland in 2003. Thank you, Mr. Currier, for our unofficial motto.

And finally, no actual Loas were harmed in the writing of this novel.

ᛉ

About the Author

Foinah Jameson lives in Portland, Oregon, the delightfully weird center of the Pacific Northwest, and spends her days with a fabulous husband, two Norse Gods disguised as her daughters, and a menagerie of used animals. At night, Foinah sneaks out to her office on the back deck under an umbrella where she writes feverishly on a battered Mac laptop, typing away madly until the sun rises. Dark, comic, creepy tales come to life as she sips cold coffee and chain-smokes aromatic cigars in the crisp night air.

She is the author of Marker of Faith -- a supernatural thriller, Weeku -- a soon-to-be-released graphic novel featuring the amazing artwork of Michael O'Manion, and five short story collections. Her short stories and novels run the gamut of the supernatural to poignant vignettes of everyday life.

In a previous life Foinah was a musician, a publican, a fortune-teller, a chef, a burgeoning astrophysicist, and an artist rep.

Now a domestic goddess and a mother by day/writer by night, Foinah enjoys her alter ego as the smoking monkey who gets to use a laptop.

"Writing is so much cheaper than therapy! And you can drink while you do it."

For more information and updates visit www.foinahjameson.com

Look for Book II in the Mostly Dead Melvin series –
Late For Dead Dinner
Fall 2015

www.ingramcontent.com/pod-product-compliance
Lightning Source LLC
Chambersburg PA
CBHW071242170626
46809CB00001B/49